S0-AXC-310

Also by Brooke Johnson

The Brass Giant
The Mechanical Theater at Chroniker City (novella)

THE GUILD CONSPIRACY

Also by Brooke Johnson

The Brass Giant
The Mechanical Theater: A Chroniker City Novella

THE GUILD CONSPIRACY

A Chroniker City Story

BROOKE JOHNSON

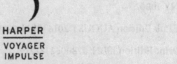

HARPER

VOYAGER
IMPULSE

An Imprint of HarperCollinsPublishers

This is a work of fiction. Names, characters, places, and incidents are products of the author's imagination or are used fictitiously and are not to be construed as real. Any resemblance to actual events, locales, organizations, or persons, living or dead, is entirely coincidental.

THE GUILD CONSPIRACY. Copyright © 2016 by Brooke Johnson. All rights reserved under International and Pan-American Copyright Conventions. By payment of the required fees, you have been granted the nonexclusive, nontransferable right to access and read the text of this e-book on screen. No part of this text may be reproduced, transmitted, downloaded, decompiled, reverse-engineered, or stored in or introduced into any information storage and retrieval system, in any form or by any means, whether electronic or mechanical, now known or hereafter invented, without the express written permission of HarperCollins e-books. For information, address HarperCollins Publishers, 195 Broadway, New York, NY 10007.

EPub Edition AUGUST 2016 ISBN: 9780062387202

Print Edition ISBN: 9780062387219

10 9 8 7 6 5 4 3 2 1

To all the girls who were told they couldn't.
To the girls who tried and failed.
To the girls who keep fighting anyway.

MAP OF CHRONIKER CITY

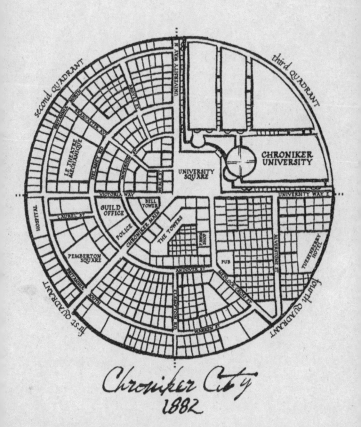

Chroniker City
1882

It is our aim that, in partnership with the Guild, the University becomes a central edifice of technological learning and progress, advancing the world into a new age through the fostering and education of the next generation of engineers. This has long been my dream, and it is by the accomplishment of my granddaughter, Adelaide, and the hard work of many businessmen and engineers that today, we open our doors to all who share this dream.
Aedificium futurum.
Together, we will build the future.

— LORD GUMARICH CHRONIKER, 1861

CHAPTER 1

Petra paced outside the Guild council chambers, wringing her hands as she counted each minute of the deliberation. Her dream of becoming a Guild engineer was in reach, so close she could almost feel it. Should the council choose to accept her application, a certified position within the Guild would give her the protection she so desperately needed. But if the council chose to reject her again . . .

She was running out of options.

The door to the council chambers creaked open, and the clerk stepped into the hall. "They are ready for you, Miss Wade."

She stopped her pacing and straightened. Five times, she had stood before these doors, waiting to hear the council's decision, hoping for their approval. Five times, she had failed.

This time would be different. It had to be.

Swallowing hard against the knot in her throat, she raised her chin and followed the clerk into the council chambers—hopefully for the last time.

The council members' bench stood at one end of the room, a stately half-circle of dark wood, and behind it, all fifteen gears of the Guild seal ticked in an elaborate clockwork dance.

To the side of the council bench stood a party of military officers, redcoats sent to the Guild by Her Imperial Majesty to oversee the progression of technology for the war effort. Three of them stood watch today, and Petra eyed them as she entered, their red uniforms a blaze of color in the dark chambers. The superior officer, a broad man with a thick, graying mustache and severe brow, had attended all of her proposals so far, his expression growing more dissatisfied with each rejected attempt.

Today, he was accompanied by two junior officers, and as she entered the room, the soldier to his right glanced up. For a brief moment, their eyes met, locked together in silent judgement. He looked to be about her age, maybe older, freckled and lean, with a noticeable lack of contempt or suspicion in his shrewd gaze. A refreshing change. The rest of the soldiers had perfected expressing their distaste of her with a sneer. But not him.

She turned her attention back to the council and approached the bench. She could feel the weight of the council's gaze upon her, but none more so than the dark copper eyes of Julian Goss. Sitting to the right of the vice-chancellor, he glowered at her from his high seat, his features lit in sharp relief by the harsh light of the dark hall. Every line in his face was taut, his jaw clenched tight, bristling with impatience at her continued disobedience, her determined rebellion.

She stood tall under his scrutiny.

Let him be angry. Let him see she would not bend.

Finally, Vice-Chancellor Lyndon sat forward in his chair, the wood and leather creaking beneath the strain of his weight. For a quiet moment, he regarded her over the rims of his round glasses, his expression unreadable. Then he drew in a deep breath and cleared his throat, directing his gaze to the collected council members. "On the subject of Miss Wade's proposal to the Guild . . ." he began, his voice slow and gravelly, "the council has come to a decision."

Petra crossed her fingers in the folds of her skirt. If the council voted to accept her application, she would be free of Julian's demands, free of his threats, free to pursue her own interests as a Guild engineer.

But if not . . .

For six months, she had stalled, rebelling against Julian's requests for a war machine. For six months, she had refused to comply, to cooperate, doing whatever she could to delay the war Julian was so determined to start, but it had all come to nothing. Project after project rejected, followed by threats upon threats, and she had persisted. But now she was out of ideas, out of time. She had exhausted all of her resources, and if she failed now . . . she had nothing left to fight with.

"After much consideration," the vice-chancellor continued, "the Guild council regrets to inform Miss Wade that her proposal has been rejected by a majority vote. I am sorry," he said more gently, shutting her application folder. "Your application is denied."

Petra clenched her jaw, a flood of anger and disappointment warring in her chest. She refused to accept defeat, not after all the work she had done to get here, not when so much hinged on this decision.

She would not fail, not now.

"Did you even read the proposal?" she demanded, her voice breaking. "This project would vastly improve the city's existing energy output." She marched forward and snatched her notes from the bench, turning to the first page of schematics. "If we implemented these designs, the efficiency of the city's subcity engines would increase threefold with the barest minimum of adjustments. The math is here in my notes," she said, striking the back of her hand against the pages. "I've done the research and the calculations and—"

"The decision is made, Miss Wade," said Mr. Goss, rising from his chair. "Our aims for the Guild have a particular focus," he said, gesturing to the military officers to the side of the council bench. "It is not prudent for the council to accept projects that do not benefit our contract with Her Imperial Majesty's Royal Forces. By bringing forth this *civic* proposal, you have wasted our time."

Petra held Julian's glare, speaking her next words through gritted teeth. "I was under the impression that a student may bring forth *any* proposal of merit to the city, University, or Guild. Rejecting my project outright because of some misguided war—"

"The contract for your studentship stipulates that you agree to provide war technology for the Royal Forces, with priority to any other potential projects. By neglecting your duty—"

"Duty?" she countered. "My duty is to the Guild and the University, *not* the Royal Forces. I refuse to let my studentship be dictated—"

"Your duty is to the *Empire*, Miss Wade," said Julian. "And the Empire requires war technology."

She started to respond, but Lyndon cut her off.

"It is not a matter of your project not meeting Guild standards, or a question of your commitment to the Guild and University, Petra," he said gently, directing her attention away from Julian. "While I understand your hesitation to apply your talents to developing war technology, Mr. Goss is correct: we are not currently accepting civic projects for consideration. All government funding for Guild projects has been diverted to technological advancements for the Royal Forces. All students requesting entry into the Guild have been informed of this—including you."

"But—"

The vice-chancellor raised his hand with a glare of warning. "We will retain your application and your proposal for optimizing the city's power efficiency until a later date, when an imminent conflict with France and the anti-imperialists is no longer a concern.

Then, if you decide to reapply, we will review your proposal and reconsider your application to the Guild." There was a snort of suppressed laughter from one of the other councilors, but Lyndon ignored him. "That is all we can do at this time."

"That's it?"

"I'm afraid so," he said. "You are dismissed."

Petra clenched her hands into fists and whirled away from Lyndon and the rest of the council with a growl, the hair at the nape of her neck bristling as she stalked from the chambers and into the hallway. The clerk shut the heavy doors behind her, leaving her in cold, empty silence.

She exhaled sharply, forcing all of her anger out in a single breath. She should have expected rejection. But she had dared to hope that maybe—just maybe—this time would be different. But the Guild's obsession was with war machines, not more efficient power distribution.

As much as she had hoped to defy Julian Goss a moment longer, weasel her way into the Guild under his nose and earn herself the protection of an official position, she feared his patience was wearing thin.

With the pressures of the Royal Forces at Julian's back, it was only a matter of time before she no longer had the ability to defy him. She knew the consequences of her actions. All she had ever hoped to do was delay the war long enough for Lyndon or Emmerich to find a way to stop it, but they had yet to come up with a plan, and she was running out of time.

Behind her, the council chamber doors opened again, and she turned to see Julian stride into the hall. He reminded her so much of Emmerich—dark hair, thick eyebrows, sharp jaw—but when she looked at him, all she could think of was everything she had lost, everything *he* had taken from her.

Emmerich was gone, working in Paris at the newly founded Continental Edison Company, unable to send a letter or telegram without his father intercepting it. Any words they exchanged were monitored, censored, questioned. By removing Emmerich, Julian had taken away the one person who had ever truly understood her, the one person she could trust. And here she remained, a slave to Julian's schemes, unable to expose his plans for the Guild, unable to stop his plans for war. She was nothing but a pawn, a game piece in his plot to create a new world.

"What do you want?" she spat.

Mr. Goss arched an eyebrow. "You would do well to show a little respect, Miss Wade," he said, his usual honeyed voice carrying a hint of impatience. He gestured down the hall, away from the council chamber. "A quick word, if you please."

She didn't move. "I know what you're going to say. You're asking me to start a war."

"No," he said, forcibly taking her arm and leading her away from the council chambers. She tried to resist, but his fingers tightened like a vice. "I am *asking* you to keep your word. We had an agreement."

He stopped at the end of the hall, far from the council chambers, and glared at her, his grip still tight on her arm. "I grow tired of this game of yours. This war will happen, and it will go far better for you if you cooperate."

Petra raised her chin. "I will not."

"You will," he said, lowering his voice to a whisper. "I have been patient with you, Miss Wade. I have allowed you to study here, to inconvenience the council with your banal proposals and Guild applications. I have even allowed you to continue communications with my son . . . but my generosity is now at an end."

He released her arm and gathered to his full height. "Understand me, Miss Wade. If your next project is not in line with our agreement, not only will I revoke your studentship and prevent further association with my son, I will repeal the council's pardon of your crimes and deliver you to the Royal Forces as a traitor and a spy. You will be conscripted into the military as a prisoner of war, forced to build my war machines—or else hang for your crimes."

She swallowed, her mouth dry. "You can't."

"I can, and I will." Footsteps sounded down the hall, and Julian leaned close. "You *will* build a war machine for me. By choice or by force, I will have what I want. Make no mistake."

One of the redcoats from the council meeting rounded the corner and spotted them. "Pardon the interruption, Minister," he said crisply, "but you are needed back in the council chambers."

Julian glared at the junior officer. "Very well. Inform them that I will return shortly."

But the soldier made no motion to leave. "The vice-chancellor is expecting you now, sir."

"Well, as you can see, I am presently occupied," he said sharply. "The vice-chancellor can wait. I have important matters to discuss with Miss Wade, and I require a measure of privacy. Now go."

The soldier hesitated, his gaze lingering a moment on Petra. "Of course, sir," he said with a stiff bow. Then he strode away.

Julian waited until the officer was well out of ear-shot before turning back to Petra. "I leave the decision to you, Miss Wade," he said. "You know the conse-quences should you refuse my request. However, if you cooperate, I give you my word that I will not ques-tion your studentship, I will continue to allow your relations with my son, and I will even offer you my recommendation for Guild placement. Help me, and I will help you. Do you understand?"

Petra glared at him. "Yes, sir," she hissed.

"Good," he said, his charismatic smile brightening his face with the same easy handsomeness as his son. "Then I expect your next proposal will be most satis-factory. Good day, Miss Wade." With that, he turned on his heel and left.

His footsteps faded into silence, and Petra pressed against the wall with a shaky sigh, hands trembling. Damn him! Damn the Guild for giving him such power over her. He could do it. He could take away her freedoms and hand her over to the Royal Forces with a single order. He would, if given the chance.

If she defied him again, he would end her.

Slow footsteps approached, and Petra started, but it was only the Royal Forces officer again, the same soldier who had caught her eye in the council chambers.

"Are you all right?" he asked, his voice kinder than she expected.

"I'm fine," she said automatically.

He looked less like a stoic, bland-faced soldier now, no longer wearing his military cap. His hair was short, shaved at the sides with a shock of golden-brown waves at the top, his narrow jawline roughened by the beginnings of a scruffy beard. His eyes were an almost colorless blue, like a slate gray sky.

"Are you sure?" he asked. "The minister seemed angry with you."

A bitter laugh escaped her throat, Julian's threats still fresh in her mind.

Forced conscription.

That was her punishment for her disobedience if she defied Julian again. She had delayed and resisted as long as she could, had pushed his patience to the brink, and now her choice was made for her—choose to build his war machine or lose everything she had left.

"For what it's worth, I thought your project had merit," he said. "Assuming you could achieve what you proposed."

"Of course I could," she snapped. She peered down

the hall toward the council chambers. "Not that it matters to them."

"Why not?"

"Why do you think? They want a war machine. Anything less isn't worth their time."

"Then why don't you build one? A war machine, I mean."

She glanced sharply at the soldier.

"That's what they want from you, isn't it?" he went on. "Why the minister is so angry with you, why the council keeps rejecting your projects. I overheard them talking. You've applied to the Guild five times in the last six months, but none of your proposals were for war technology. Why not? If you built what they wanted, they'd accept you into the Guild, wouldn't they?"

"Probably."

"Then why don't you?"

"Because becoming a Guild engineer isn't worth *that*," she said. "If I earn my certification, I want it to be on my own terms, not theirs."

Not that she had a choice. Julian had made that very clear.

"Could you, though?" he asked, a hesitancy to his voice. "If you wanted to? Could you build a war machine?"

She dropped her gaze to the floor, thinking of the automaton she and Emmerich had built together the previous summer, how brilliant it had been when Emmerich powered it up for the first time, all its gears exposed, whirring and ticking with musical synchronicity. It had been a terrible, wonderful thing to behold, a beautiful monstrosity . . . capable of so much destruction.

Yes, she could build a war machine. She already had.

But she never wanted to build another like it, not for the rest of her life.

Petra turned away from the soldier and checked her pocket watch—less than a half-hour until her next lecture. "I should be going," she said, returning the pocket watch to the waist of her skirt. "I have to get to class."

The soldier stepped forward. "Wait, I—I didn't meant to offend. If I have, I apologize. Forgive my curiosity. It wasn't my intent."

"Don't bother yourself," she said, waving him away. "I'm used to it."

"I didn't introduce myself before," he said, laying a hand on his chest and executing a formal bow. "Braith Cartwright, Officer Cadet of Her Imperial Majesty's Royal Forces, at your service."

She eyed him warily and then offered her hand. "Petra."

The faint twitch of a smile lifted the corner of his mouth, and he took her hand—not delicately, as he might have taken a lady's, but deliberately, like an equal. He gave it a firm shake. "A pleasure to make your acquaintance, Petra," he said. Then his smile broadened, a handsome change to his reserved demeanor. "You can call me Braith."

Petra spent her combustion-enginery lecture mulling over Julian's threats, barely listening as Professor Calligaris droned on about piston chambers and increasing cubic capacity to improve engine efficiency.

How soon would Julian expect her to comply with his demands? How much longer could she resist him? She didn't want to give in, but what choice did she have? Julian's ultimatum was clear. Cooperate, or face judgement for her crimes—that was her choice. Dead, she was of no use to anyone, but to agree? To build what he wanted? No, she needed to find another way to divert his plans, act against the war without openly declaring herself against him.

There had to be a way to beat him, even now.

She pulled out her mother's pocket watch, watching the slow movement of the minute hand as it ticked across the gilded face.

Emmerich would know what to do.

The last time they spoke, he told her to wait, but for what? For how long? She had delayed and resisted for six months, and neither of them were any closer to stopping this war.

It had been months since they had spoken, months since she had heard his voice—nothing but a handful of sparse telegrams, a single handwritten letter, and one telephone call at the end of September, her only word of him since he arrived in Paris.

Either he was too busy to return her letters, or Julian, despite promises of allowing them to maintain contact, was scheming to keep them apart. She didn't want to consider the third option—that he didn't *want* to talk to her.

She hated it. The silence. The lack of communication. The not knowing.

Above all, she missed him, and she hated him for it.

She hated him for his cowardice, for agreeing to his father's demands, for leaving. He had given in, letting his father control his life because it was easier than standing up for himself, because he thought it would keep her safe.

Safe. Petra scoffed. She was anything but safe.

All Emmerich's sacrifice had bought her was loneliness.

With a sharp crack, Professor Calligaris slammed his wooden pointer down on her desk, and she jumped an inch out of her chair, suddenly aware of the classroom full of students. She clenched her jaw, anger bubbling up her throat as she blinked away the sting of tears.

"Pay attention, Miss Wade," drawled the professor. "Your knowledge of advanced machinery is already lacking. It wouldn't do for you to fall further behind."

Petra's cheeks flamed, but she said nothing, gritting her teeth with as much force as she could muster. If her marks were low, it wasn't for lack of knowledge. Her talents were wasted in a classroom, all those hours spent on lectures and diagrams and pointless essays. Give her a screwdriver, and she'd engineer circles around any other student here. Not that Calligaris would ever allow her to prove it. The workshops remained off-limits to her, by order of the Guild council. She had Julian to thank for that.

Calligaris smirked and returned to the front of the classroom to resume his lecture, but the bell rang before he could continue.

"Don't forget," he called out to the shuffle of departing students, "your essays on the evolution of commercial engines are due on Monday. I expect a minimum of five pages."

There was a collective groan among the other students as they gathered their things to leave. Chairs and desks scraped as the others left the lecture hall, starting up idle conversations as they headed toward the door. Petra quietly scooped up her unused pencils and shoved her unopened textbook and blank notepaper into her bag, waiting until most of the students had gone ahead before standing up from her desk, not keen on giving anyone an excuse to pester her.

But as she stood, two boys brushed past, knocking her into the nearest desk as they hurried by. She stumbled backward and tried to catch herself, losing her grip on her bag. It flopped open at her feet, its contents spilling everywhere. Pencils rolled across the floor, her notes scattered, and textbooks tumbled down the stairs, the cloth-bound covers fluttering open before landing page-side down with a loud flump.

The boys laughed as they retreated through the door.

Petra fumed. Just once, she'd like to leave class in

peace—without insults, without any teasing, without having to recover her things because some stuck-up bastard decided they had a right to upend the contents of her bag. Running her fingers through her already disheveled hair, she set to collecting her things from the floor for what felt like the thousandth time since she first started classes at the University.

As she reached for the last of her things, she heard the sound of footsteps coming down the stairs behind her. She tensed, expecting it to be another student who had made it their solemn vow to make her life a living hell, but when she turned around, she relaxed, recognizing her friend Rupert, with his sandy-blond hair and easy smile. He came down the stairs at a leisurely stride, hands in his pockets. He grinned and crouched beside her at the bottom landing, picking up her last textbook.

"Selby again?" he asked, handing her the copy of *Advanced Rotary Mechanics*.

"Not this time," she said, tucking the book into her bag. "Selby usually likes to insult me first." She stood and massaged her brow, already exhausted despite the day being only half-over.

"Don't let it get to you," he said, nudging her arm. "They'll grow bored of you eventually."

She laughed dryly. "Yes, of course they will. Maybe when I'm no longer a student here, maybe *then* they'll leave me alone."

"When you prove to them you belong here, they will."

"And how am I supposed to do that?" she asked. "I've been here six months, Rupert. Six *months*, and they *still* treat me like this. Nothing I do is going to change that."

Rupert shrugged, a sly smile on his face. "You never know." He took the bag of books and papers from her hands and draped the strap over his chest. "So, how did your Guild proposal go?" he asked, leading the way up the stairs to the exit.

She groaned. "About as well as the last one. Worse, in fact."

"Have you thought of another idea to pitch?"

Petra shook her head, a hollow pit opening in her chest at the thought of what her next project would likely be. "Not yet."

He nudged her arm. "Don't worry. I'm sure you'll think of something. You always do."

They stopped at the classroom door. Students milled about the hallway, a shifting stream of engineers heading to their next classes. Petra still had another hour of lecture left before she finished for the day. Maybe by then she would come up with a plan for how to delay Julian's war.

Rupert leaned against the doorframe, his hands in his pockets. "Listen . . . if you think you might be up for it, there's a thing tonight, after hours. Might cheer you up, help you get your mind off this whole Guild business."

"I doubt there's anything that could do that right now."

"That's only because you don't know what it is," he said with a grin.

She looked at him expectantly. "Well?"

He slid her bag over his head and handed it to her. "Meet me at the University side entrance after hours— ten o'clock," he said, keeping his voice low. "There's a sort of . . . meeting going on in the recreation hall between some of the students. You'll want to be there."

Petra narrowed her eyes. "What sort of meeting?"

Rupert grinned. "You'll see." He checked the time on the wall clock next to the door. "I have to head to my next class, but I'll see you tonight?" he said, starting down the hall. "Ten o'clock. At the side door. And wear trousers," he added. "Don't want anyone recognizing you."

"Trousers?"

"Trust me," he said, walking backward against the stream of oncoming students. "So, you'll come?" he asked, more persuasion than question.

She suppressed a laugh. "All right," she finally agreed. "I'll be there. Now get to class. You'll be late."

He grinned. "Ten o'clock. Don't forget."

CHAPTER 2

Night hung over the streets of Chroniker City as Petra crept through the fourth quadrant, the chill of winter still lingering on the air. Adjusting the collar of her coat against the wind, she turned up Medlock Cross and passed the pub, the late-night sounds of drinking and gambling filtering through the open door.

Ahead, she saw the familiar sign of Stricket & Monfore, a light on somewhere inside. She missed it—even now, as a student at the University and on her way to becoming a Guild engineer. She missed the late nights working in the back room, Mr. Stricket teaching her the intricacies of clockwork. What she wouldn't give to return to the shop every evening and work with him again, but between her classwork and her failed efforts to join the Guild, she didn't have time. She paused at the display of repaired mechanisms in the window, wondering if it wouldn't have been better had she never met Emmerich that fateful day. If not for him, she never would have created that blasted clockwork automaton and gotten herself into this mess.

But Julian would have managed his war one way or another. His plans went far deeper than Petra's involvement; forcing Emmerich to present his prototype to the Guild, twisting it into a war machine—that had all come before she ever stepped foot in Emmerich's workshop. What else had he contrived in his madness? She shivered at the thought. He wanted to burn this world with his war and rebuild a new one from the ashes: an age of science with the Guild at its core, but at what cost?

At least this way, she had a chance to stop him.

She moved on from the pawn shop and continued to the University. The street was empty apart from the occasional late-night worker heading to or from the boilers, and she was grateful her brother no longer worked that shift. He'd moved on to a better life, with a girl he loved and a job that paid him his worth, better than anything he could have hoped to earn working the boilers from sunup to sundown. An ache filled her chest as she realized how long it had been since she had last talked to him—since she had talked to *anyone* outside of the Guild. Solomon, Emmerich, Mr. Stricket . . . She had lost so much because of Julian and his stupid war.

Petra reached the University square and crept toward the student entrance, hiding in the shadow of a nearby steam duct. Tucking her hair into the brim of her hat, she glanced down at her pocket watch, grazing her fingertips over the intricate C that decorated the case—just a few minutes before ten. She peeked out from her hiding place and searched the empty square, but no sign of Rupert.

With a sigh, she pressed her back against the warm metal of the exposed ductwork and waited, listening to the rush of steam hissing through the pipes. The machines of the subcity rattled and whirred beneath the stone street, synchronized gears and linkages ticking a rhythm of mechanical perfection beneath her feet. She inhaled a deep breath, catching the scent of coal and gasoline amidst the humid air billowing through the grates. It smelled of home.

A few minutes later, the lock above the student entrance unlatched, the gears knocking and grating as ratchets shifted the deadbolts—added security after the Luddite attacks and the supposed anti-imperialist infiltration the previous summer. The door creaked inward, and Rupert's blond head peered out, his face lit by the flickering gas lamps at the bottom of the stairs.

"Petra?" he called, his voice barely above a whisper. "You out here?"

She slipped out from behind the steam duct and met him atop the stairs. Rupert opened the door wider, letting her into the narrow hall that sat adjacent to the lobby, before closing the door behind her. He removed his student key from the lock, and heavy gears ratcheted the deadbolts back into place, locking the door with a resounding clunk.

Petra leaned against the smooth brass-plated wall

and breathed in the familiar air of the University, the lingering scents of grease and metal polish putting her at ease. The usual bustle of engineers, students, and professors was absent from the dark, empty lobby, the echo of distant machinery lurking in the shadows like haunting ghosts. Her skin tingled with excitement. It had been months since she'd been here after dark—when Emmerich was still here and her only worry was keeping their automaton project secret. It seemed an eternity ago now.

Rupert touched her shoulder. "Come on," he whispered, ushering her forward. "Or we'll miss it."

He took her to the lift and used his student key to propel them up to the eighth floor, the whirring belts and pulleys singing as they ascended. The lift slowed to an abrupt stop, and the lights above the gates spilled across the hall, startlingly bright in the quiet darkness of the University.

"So what's this meeting about?" she asked Rupert.

"You'll see."

Their brisk footsteps echoed off the hard floor as Rupert led her down the hall toward the student lounges and recreation room.

As they approached, a muffled cacophony met Petra's ears—shouts and curses, cheers, a clash of metal on metal, the clear sound of a combustion engine igniting. Petra's heartbeat quickened, and she pressed her ear to the door, feeling the vibrating hum of a purring engine in the room beyond, the sigh of exhaust, the smell of burnt fuel reaching her nose.

Rupert nudged her aside and keyed into the room, the clash of metal rising to a deafening thunder as he opened the door.

Inside, the billiard table, chess tables, chairs, and sofas had been pushed to the walls, the usual carpets and rugs thrown over the furniture. A spotlight illuminated a few dozen students near the center of the room, surrounding a hulk of moving brass, its shiny surface flashing in the glow of the electric light. The crunch of crumpling metal and subsequent jeers echoed off the walls, and the metal beast reeled out of Petra's sight.

Leaving Rupert behind, she elbowed her way through the crowd of students and stumbled headlong into the center of the ring. A quick hand caught her by the collar and yanked her back into the crowd just as a metal arm swiped through the air, inches from her nose.

Petra stumbled into the student next to her, gaping in delighted disbelief at the scene before her. Two imposing metal figures stood in the center of the ring—a squat trapezoidal machine and a grotesque humanoid—dripping oil and smelling of exhaust. Jagged trenches tore through the outer shell of the larger machine, exposing a mesh of combustion enginery and electrical wiring inside, while the smaller, wheeled contraption had a stump of shredded linkages and twisted gears where its second arm should have been, its stout body half-crushed and front wheels bent.

The bipedal machine lunged, much to the crowd's

delight, and there was a terrible, teeth-grinding crunch as the metal shells crumpled and warped on impact. The biped hammered its fist into the squat trapezoid, the blocky machine's outer shell buckling under the assault. Yet the smaller contraption held its ground, wheels spinning forward as it pressed against the hulking mass of metal, its remaining arm buried halfway into the biped's central system, pulling wires and tubes from its body like rubber intestines, oil and hydraulic fluid spilling onto the floor.

With a sputtering whine, the combustion engine rumbled to a halt, the spin of gears slowing to a groan as the mechanical biped powered down. The heavily damaged trapezoid pushed the biped away, and the mutation of combustion enginery and electricity toppled over with a resounding crash.

Silence followed.

And then the room erupted in cheers.

From the far side of the ring, a young man stepped forward and waved the crowd into silence. Petra recognized him by his long, narrow face and shrewd eyes—Vice-Chancellor Lyndon's son, Yancy. Though with his bright blond hair and dashing smile, he carried none of the somber gravitas of his father.

Yancy spread his hands wide. "Gentlemen! I believe we have our winner!"

He gestured to one side of the ring, and the winning engineer stepped forward. Black hair and blue eyes, a cocky grin on his smug face: John *bloody* Selby. Petra scowled, her admiration dissipating in an instant.

Since her first day at the University, Selby had made it his vow to make her studentship as miserable as possible, mocking her for everything from her gender to her station, insulting her intelligence at every turn. Insufferable prat.

The fact that he was a decent engineer—a *good* one, actually—only made her hate him more.

"As winner," continued Yancy, "Selby gets the twenty-pound pot and bragging rights until next tournament."

Selby swept into a low bow, tucking a metal control box behind his back. Petra noted the thick cord of coated wire trailing from the brass case, snaking across the oil-slicked floor to the back of the trapezoidal machine. So that was how he controlled it.

She suppressed a smirk. Rudimentary technology.

If she could get her hands on the right tools, she could make use of Emmerich's wireless control apparatus to operate such a machine. She was familiar enough with the science now to do it herself, but there would be certain challenges involved applying it for this kind of use, she wagered.

Rupert squeezed in beside her. "What do you think?"

"It's brilliant," she said, her voice nearly lost amidst the cheers and shouts around them. "How long has this been going on?"

"Started about midterm, last semester. You know about the failed automaton project, right? Some of the boys who work in the armory found the remains of it and got the idea to start a mechanical fight ring."

Petra pressed her mouth shut and nodded. So they had kept it then, the ruined prototype that Emmerich had so expertly smashed through the floor of his workshop—now collecting dust in the armory. The failed automaton project. That was what the rest of them called it, not knowing she had helped design and build it, not knowing what her involvement had cost her.

She recalled the events that led to its "failure" with vivid clarity. None of them knew what had really happened that day, not even Rupert. There were whispers, of course, and rumors, but the anti-imperialist plot, the lies of her treason, the conspiracy to start a war, her involvement with Emmerich and the automaton . . . all pardoned and forgotten, erased from all records thanks to Vice-Chancellor Lyndon.

"Where do they get the parts?" she asked.

"Discards and surplus from the workshops," said Rupert. "Some of the richer blokes buy parts offshore and have them shipped in. Most of it is scrap, though."

In the center of the ring, Yancy quieted the crowd with a wave of his hand and then cleared his throat. "That concludes the inaugural competition of our mech fights." Another boy brought forward an end table and handed Yancy a pad of paper and a pencil. "If you wish to participate in the next tournament," he said, waving the paper over his head, "sign up by the first bell tomorrow and have your mech ready for the first round sometime next month, date to be decided. If you're new to the fights, make sure you get the rules from me or John before you build your machine. Entry fee is a pound note—or equivalent—the sum of all entries to be rewarded to our next winner."

He dropped the paper and pencil onto the table, and a handful of students stepped forward to enter. Petra watched as they scribbled their names, one after the other, knowing she could outmaneuver every single one of them with a machine of her own.

For six long months, she'd been stuck in boring classrooms, listening to dry lectures and permitted to do nothing more than scribble designs on paper and write academic essays. She missed the feel of a screwdriver in her hand, the smell of grease under her fingernails, the late nights of working with her hands deep inside a machine.

She *yearned* for it.

Rupert nudged her with his elbow. "Go on. Sign up."

Petra considered it, absently twisting the stem of her pocket watch between her thumb and forefinger. She could enter, write her name down and fight in the next tournament, finally have the chance to *build* something again. Yet . . . she knew they wouldn't let her. Selby, Yancy, all the rest of them, they'd only laugh at her, mock her for thinking she could compete with them, for thinking she was their equal.

She stared at the sign-up sheet, the determination to prove herself burning in her chest.

To hell with them.

She'd win the damn tournament and show them just how good an engineer she really was. She belonged here, building machines alongside the best of them. She'd win, and then they'd see.

She released the breath she'd been holding and stepped forward, heart beating faster. Leaning over the table, she took the pencil into her hand and pressed the point of graphite to the paper, quickly scribbling her name at the bottom of the list of entrants before she second-guessed herself.

As she penned the last letter of her name, the slip of paper whipped out from under her hand, leaving a long line of graphite trailing down the page.

"This has to be a joke."

Gritting her teeth, she raised her gaze to the boy standing across the table. "Something wrong, Selby?" she asked, propping a hand on her hip. Rupert was at her side in an instant.

Selby's gaze swept over her disguise—her brother's old trousers and loose shirt, hair tucked into her hat. He wrinkled his nose. "Yance," he called. "Come see who's signed up for the next tournament."

Lyndon's son wandered over, and Selby passed the paper to him.

Yancy scanned the list of names, finally reaching the bottom. "Petra . . . *Wade?*" There was a disapproving murmur among the students as Yancy glanced up from the paper, a deep frown on his face as he recognized her through her disguise. "You can't be serious."

"And why not?" she asked. Her face burned, heat rising up her cheeks, but she refused to back down. "I'm a student. I can pay the entry fee. Let me fight."

Selby scoffed. "The very idea."

A titter of laughter rolled through the crowd of students.

"What would be the point?" he went on. "You'll just lose."

"Isn't that for my mech to decide?"

"You can't possibly think you might *win*?"

"I know it," she said, stepping closer. Her heart beat faster, filling her with an empowering defiance she had kept quiet for too long. She jabbed a finger into his chest, meeting his cold gaze with one of her own. "I'll win your little tournament, and when I beat *your* miserable contraption into scrap, you'll see who the better engineer is."

Selby glared daggers at her, roughly pushing her hand away. "You have no idea what you're up against, *Miss Wade*," he spat. "This is *our* domain, not yours. Go back to your stitchery and whatever else it is you women do."

Petra inhaled a slow, measured breath, her teeth clenched hard. "Is it because you're afraid to face me, Selby?" she asked, keeping her voice level. She could see the tension in his face, flushed with contempt. Provoke him enough and he would let her fight. He had too much pride to back down from a direct challenge. "Afraid to lose to a girl? Is that it?"

He scowled, grinding his teeth. "As if I'd be afraid of *you*," he hissed. "Fine. Enter the tournament if you must. But you'll get no special treatment. No handicaps for being a girl. You fight by *our* rules, win or lose."

"I wouldn't have it otherwise." She offered her hand. "Deal?"

Selby glowered at her open palm.

"John . . ." said Yancy, glancing between them. "She *can't* fight; she's not one of us. She's—"

"No," said Selby. "She *isn't*. And when she loses, it will only prove we were right about her. She doesn't belong here. It's time she recognizes that."

Yancy eyed his friend a moment longer, the conviction in Selby's expression unyielding. "All right, then." With a resigned shake of his head, he turned toward Petra and regarded her warily, his frown so like his father's. "Entry is a pound note, date of first fight to be decided. Have your mech ready in time and you're in." He slowly stuck out his hand. "Welcome to the tournament, Miss Wade."

The fighters and spectators disbanded then, returning the room to its usual state. They replaced the rugs and positioned the furniture over the haphazard scorch marks and grease stains. Petra stood out of the way, a nervous laugh bubbling up her throat. She gripped the brass railing at the wide window overlooking the city, grinning to herself.

After so many months of playing the part of the meek, obedient girl, subdued by the Guild in exchange for her freedom, she finally felt herself again. And though the Guild still refused to acknowledge her, refused to give her access to the workshops, she now had the mech fights. It was a small thing, a small victory, but it was enough.

Rupert joined her at the window, hands in his pockets. He leaned his back against the railing and nudged her lightly. "Nicely done."

She laughed, her chest tight with the thrill of the last hour. "I can't believe I let you talk me into that."

"You needed less persuading than I thought."

"Is that why you brought me here?" she asked.

"Why else?"

She suppressed a smile and gazed out into the brilliant night sky. "You know me too well."

They stood in silence for a time.

"Do you think I can do it?" she asked. "Do you think I could win?"

He faced the window next to her, settling against the railing with his shoulder touching hers. She found comfort in that solid presence. "Of course I do," he said companionably. "Once you face them in the ring, no one will doubt what you can do anymore. You belong here, Petra. This is your chance to prove it."

"Supposing I can actually build a mech in time," she said, reality starting to sink in. "In case it escaped your notice, I don't have one, and with only a month to build one, I'd need—"

"But you do have one."

"What?"

"You do have a mech."

Petra frowned. "I do?"

Rupert nodded, a mischievous smile on his lips. "Come on," he said, pushing away from the railing. "I'll show you."

He led her to the lower levels of the University and keyed into the storage rooms near the Guild workshops. Each room was filled wall to wall with crates of tools and machine parts, the surplus stored in the wide hallway. Rupert dragged her to the end of the overcrowded corridor and slid open a panel in the back wall, revealing a cavernous dumbwaiter chute, at least six feet deep and equally wide.

"What's this?" she asked, peering down the dark shaft.

"Our ride."

Rupert grabbed a lever inside the open panel and pressed it forward. A whir of gear trains and pulley cords hummed behind the walls, and the dumbwaiter platform descended rapidly, the gear boxes clicking and grating as it came to a screeching halt.

"Found it my first semester," he explained. "Goes up to the sixth floor and down to the third level of the subcity. There's a network of them in the walls; it's how the engineers move equipment from floor to floor."

Petra leaned into the chute and peered up the long passageway, the walls lined with guiderails and cables. "I had no idea."

Rupert climbed expertly onto the platform and held out his hand to help her onto the lift. "There's a room at the bottom," he went on. "An old subcity office, looks like it's been abandoned. The door's blocked by some old machinery, cutting it off from the rest of the subcity, so no chance of any engineers stumbling in on you while you're working, and no one topside has reason to visit an empty office." Once she seated herself across from him, he grabbed the lever and pushed it downward. The drive motors hummed, and he grinned. "Perfect place to build a mech."

The lift sank into darkness, the inner walls of the chute rising up and away. Petra hugged her knees to her chest, nothing else to hold on to as the dumbwaiter descended. The heavy thrum of the subcity grew louder, enveloping her in its familiar pulse. Finally, the platform slowed with a piercing screech and jolted to a halt, throwing Petra into the wall. She cracked her head against the metal guiderails.

She winced, rubbing the sharp sting at her crown. "Ouch."

"Ah, sorry," said Rupert. "Should have warned you."

There was a crack and a snap, and the dumbwaiter panel swung outward, letting a flood of warm light into the chute. The room beyond was small, hardly ten feet square. Several stacks of crates lined the walls, and a small desk sat in the corner, covered in papers, pencils, and other drafting utensils.

Rupert hopped down from the lift and Petra followed, the room ripe with the smell of grease, burning coal, and hot metal. The thrum of the subcity pulsed like a heartbeat through the floor, engines roaring, the click of cranks and rhythmic thrust of pistons singing beyond the walls. Whispers of steam hissed musically through the network of pipes beyond the blocked doorway. The opening was stacked high with sections of tarnished machinery.

Rupert gestured to the room at large. "Well? Do you like it?"

She laid her hand on the desk, brushing her fingers over the bulky mechanical calculator and measuring tools, the smooth drafting paper, and the polished wood surface. An electric thrill tingled up her arm. "It's perfect."

He grinned. "Wait until you see this."

Moving to the stack of crates next to the door, he dragged the topmost box from the column and carefully lowered it to the floor. With a crack, the lid pried loose, and he rummaged through the crinkled paper packing. "Help me with this, will you? It's heavy."

Petra hurried to the other side of the crate and reached into the box. Her fingers met cool metal, a rounded joint roughly welded together by thick soldering lines. She positioned her hands around it, and then, on a count of three, she and Rupert hauled the ruined mass of machinery out of the crate and onto the floor.

Petra stepped back and peered at the damaged hulk of metal, absently wiping her hands on her trousers. Charred scraps of dented and twisted brass, bolts and welds torn apart, crumpled linkages and melted gear trains—the frame so brutally warped it was impossible to tell what it once looked like.

"Well?" said Rupert. "What do you think?"

She circled the blackened mass of machinery. "What is it?"

"My mech."

Petra arched an eyebrow. "What happened to it?"

"Darrow," he said darkly. "Did it in with a super-charged blowlamp affixed to his mech's arm. More like a flamethrower, if you ask me. Melted right through the shell and destroyed the transmission."

"That sort of thing is allowed?"

Rupert nodded. "Oh, yeah. The rules are rather straightforward: don't tell any of the professors or Guild engineers about the mech fights; no projectile weapons allowed; and mechs can only be constructed of copper, brass, or aluminum—no steel. Beyond that, last mech standing is the winner. Once you're in the ring, anything goes."

Petra blinked, staring at the misshapen machine at her feet.

"I know it doesn't look like much," he said quickly, "but I thought you could use it for base materials. It took a beating there at the end, but the plating can be hammered back into shape, the engine is still good as far as I can tell, and most of what's left can be reused or refitted." He wiped the sweat from his brow with his shirtsleeve and shuffled to the stack of crates again, pulling another down. "I have some loose parts too. Between what's left of the mech and all this here, you should have enough to build something battle worthy." He set the crate beside the charred machine with a thud. "And if there's anything else you need, we can probably get our hands on it. You'd be surprised what we can salvage from the workshops."

Petra lifted the lid of the crate of spare parts, filled with unfitted gears, dented cams, and flattened pipe. "Where did you get all of this?"

"I've been collecting scraps after workshop lessons and finding busted pieces thrown out from Guild projects; I even traded dorm duties for a few of the harder-to-find parts. I wanted to make sure you had what you needed when the time came." He paused. "Do you think you can build something out of it?"

She surveyed the boxes of parts and the twisted hunk of metal that was once his mech. "I think so," she said with a nod. "With the right tools, but . . ." She glanced up at him. "Why would you do this for me?"

Rupert shrugged. "I know how frustrated you've been, barred from the workshops. I thought you might like something to work on, something a bit more diverting than labeling diagrams or writing up technical summaries."

Petra smiled. "I don't expect you know many girls who would find this sort of thing diverting."

"Just the one."

She rose to her feet and rested her hands on her waist, eyeing the busted machine and crate of spare parts. After months of idleness, she finally had a machine to build—a *proper* machine—and it was *hers*. "Rupert, this is . . . This is *marvelous*." She glanced up at him, a sudden warmth welling behind in her eyes. "Thank you," she said thickly. "I don't deserve it."

"Yes, you do," he said, slipping his hands into his pockets. "Besides . . . I can't wait to see Selby's face when you beat him in the tournament. That alone will be worth it."

Petra laughed, her spirits briefly unburdened of the weight of the last six months. She bowed her head with a smile and bumped Rupert's shoulder. "Thanks," she said quietly, looking at the damaged mech in front of them. "For everything. I never would have survived this place without you."

He shrugged. "It's what friends are for."

CHAPTER 3

Petra stared at the nameplate on the office door, and the name of her enemy stared back: JULIAN H. GOSS, MINISTER TO THE VICE-CHANCELLOR.

She had thought long and hard on his threats, considering every possible avenue of choice ahead of her, and it came down to one simple thing: she had do whatever it took to stop this war, and if that meant conceding to his demands and appearing to cooperate with his plans, so be it. She wasn't giving up. Far from it. But as she stared at that name, it still felt like the worst decision of her life. The moment she walked through this door and offered to build his war machine, there would be no turning back. She would be his to command, his to control. But what choice did she have? It was either this or forced labor under the watchful eye of the Royal Forces. At least this way, she still had some freedom, some small chance of thwarting his plans.

Petra closed her eyes, her hands curled into fists. She could do this, she told herself. She had to. It was the only way.

She raised her hand to the door and knocked.

"Come in."

Before she could second-guess herself, she opened the door and went inside.

"Miss Wade," said Julian, with only a slight hint of surprise as he looked up from his desk. "To what do I owe the pleasure?"

She swallowed thickly, her chest constricting as the reality of her decision stared her in the face. "I came to discuss my next proposal to the council."

"I see," he said, leaning back in his chair. "Well, then . . . Please, have a seat." He gestured to the chair opposite his desk and waited until she obeyed before folding his hands in his lap. "What is it you would like to discuss?"

"The war machine," she said hesitantly. "I thought about what you said, and I—" Her voice wavered as she looked into his eyes, smoldering with a dark intensity that once again reminded her of Emmerich. "I would like to remain here, at the University, rather than . . . the alternative."

"I see." He rested his elbows on his desk and clasped his hands. "I must say I am pleased to hear it. The Guild needs engineers of your caliber."

"Yes, well, the thing is . . ." she continued. "I need time to come up with a design, to work out the necessary functions and corresponding mechanisms, and—"

"You have a week."

Petra blinked, the rest of her carefully rehearsed proposal evaporating in an instant. "A *week*? But—"

"You will present your war machine to the Guild council first thing Thursday morning," he said, dropping his gaze to a leather calendar book atop his desk. He grabbed a pen and scribbled a note at the bottom of the page. "Should we find the proposal satisfactory, a team will be assembled, the design finalized, and we will begin work on the project immediately. In exchange, you may remain here and continue your studies."

She gaped at him, struggling to find her voice. "You haven't even told me what you want me to build!"

"A war machine, Miss Wade," he said, glancing up from his desk with the patience of a viper. "You are to build a device for *war*."

"I understand that, *sir*," she said evenly. "But I need parameters, requisites." She scrambled to think, anything to give her more time. "For starters, I'll need to know the basic functions of the machine, and there are financial margins to consider, physical limitations, materials . . . not to mention more *time*. You can't expect me to design something like this in a week, not on my own."

Julian relaxed in his chair, regarding her with the ease of a practiced businessman. "A week is what you have," he said, a tone of finality to his voice. "Perhaps if you had complied with my request sooner, you would have more time to design the machine you already promised me. But here we are," he said, gesturing grandly between the two of them. "As for parameters, we require the design accommodate direct personal control by a soldier of the British Armed Forces. The remainder of the design specifics I leave to your discretion and to that of your engineering team."

"Direct control?" Her professional curiosity got the better of her. "Wouldn't it be more efficient to control it remotely, using Emmerich's wireless control apparatus?"

"Perhaps, but the wireless technology used in the automaton project has not been developed to the degree that the Royal Forces requires, and it has proved too costly for the Guild to produce on a large scale, which is why we are in need of an alternative."

She stared at him, realizing what he meant. "You built them, didn't you? The automatons." A hollow laugh escaped her lips. "You tried to build your army, but you failed."

A muscle twitched in his jaw. "The failure was not *mine*. The design was inferior, too flawed for our purposes, so the project was scrapped. The responsibility for its failure lies solely on its engineer."

"Its engineer? Your *son*, you mean?" She scoffed. "Emmerich could have revolutionized modern science with that design. Instead, you used him to create a weapon."

"My son knew what he was building the day he signed his contract. Make no mistake. He *knew*. And in choosing to break his agreement, he failed me. *You* will not." Julian leaned back in his chair and folded his hands in his lap. "You have your parameters now. I suggest you get started on your design. Your proposal is Thursday."

She held her ground. "What you're asking is impossible. There are too many variables to consider for a machine this complex, not least of all the secondary systems I'll need to implement, many of which I'll need assistance with. I don't know the first thing about weapons or manual control interfaces. I need time to—"

"You will have a team of engineers assigned to the project to make up for such shortcomings," said Julian, his voice sharp, final. "What we need from you is the overall design, the base mechanical construction. You have the most experience with designing mobile war machines and understand best how such a machine needs to function. Therefore this task falls to you."

"But—"

"You have until Thursday."

"And if I can't finish it in time?" she asked, her voice rising.

"You will. You are rather resourceful when you need to be."

Petra just stared at him.

"Now go," he said, waving her off. "We are done here."

She swallowed hard, the last of her arguments dissolving into silence as she rose from her chair and turned toward the door. Her mind whirled through a jumble of half-imagined designs, trying to think of what she might be able to cobble together in a week.

"One more thing," he said amiably, masking his words with the feigned politeness she so despised. "The arrangement I previously proposed still stands. Defy me, try to delay this project any further, and it will be the end of you."

She hesitated at the door, her throat suddenly dry. Slowly, she turned around and met his smoldering copper stare, her chin set, not daring to quail under his gaze. "Understood, sir."

"Good." He smiled pleasantly then, his casual handsomeness lighting a fire in her stomach. "Then I look forward to hearing of your progress. Do keep me updated, Miss Wade."

She nodded curtly. "Of course."

When he said nothing else, she took it as her signal to leave. She clenched her hands into fists. A week! How could he expect her to come up with a workable design in so little time? And if she failed . . .

She pushed through the door to the stairwell and leaned against the wall, kneading her brow. She'd have to come up with a design—and fast.

There was no time to panic.

Petra stood over the drafting table in her hidden subcity office, a dozen nonviable war machine schematics littering the desk and floor, the designs crude and uninspired. She stared at the crumpled paper in her hand, anger rippling down her arms. She didn't want to build this. She didn't know how.

Yet Julian had given her a week to deliver a completed design.

She didn't even know where to start.

Because of the war machine's requirements, any remnant of the automaton was useless. The new machine couldn't be powered with clockwork or controlled remotely, which meant she would need to increase the internal cavities of the machine to house the pilot and controls. And accounting for the added size and weight of an engine, the leg frames would need to be much larger in order to support the additional weight and maintain stability. While balancing the machine with automatic gyroscopic adjustments was ideal, the technology was still in its infancy. Yet relying on manual compensation risked human error. She focused on her notes, absently tapping her pencil against the desk. Perhaps the potential danger of tipping the machine could be reduced if she designed a regulating feedback system to inform the pilot to manually adjust the machine as needed, but that would require a complex system of weights, levers, gyroscopes, and wiring to manage.

And that still left the matter of her sabotage.

She'd be damned if she gave Julian the designs for a fully functional war machine—not without a backup plan.

With sufficient time, she might be able to do it—

the complete design, the sabotage, the subterfuge to hide her treason. In fact, she was certain she could. But to design all of that within a single week, to present a buildable design to the council by Thursday, was next to impossible.

But that was the deadline given to her.

She stared at the three sketches in front of her—a big, hulking beast with stout arms and widely spaced legs, a four-legged contraption with a swiveling control cabin, and a towering machine with jointed legs. There were too many possibilities, so many different ways she could build this war machine, and so many reasons she shouldn't.

She chewed on her lip. Rupert was bound to show up soon, and she'd have to put her war machine schematics away so that they could work on the mech. Part of her welcomed the distraction, but she also knew that if she didn't finish the concept for the war machine in time for her proposal next week, she wouldn't have the privilege of distractions.

Julian would see to that.

Focusing on the task at hand, she turned to the bipedal design again, trying to wrap her head around the idea of manual interior controls, but the thought of what such a machine could do in the hands of a soldier made her stomach churn. And the idea of a soldier inside such a devastating machine—a machine of her own making—made the war suddenly more personal, more real.

She didn't want to send men to war in her machines.

Yet here she was, and for what? Because she feared for her own life? For her freedom?

Was she really willing to put the lives of others before her own?

Was she really that much of a coward?

The belts in the dumbwaiter chute whirred to life and the platform rattled up into the darkness of the shaft. Resolved to finish the design concept later, Petra gathered her schematics and shoved the files into her bag. She needed to distract herself with something else for a while. The dumbwaiter descended a few moments later, clattering loudly down the tracks.

Rupert appeared at the bottom, stepping down from the platform into her office, a bag over his shoulder. "Brought my design sketches," he said, pulling a stack of drafting pages out of his bag—the original designs for the mech. He laid the pages on the desk. "I wasn't very meticulous with the measurements, but this is the basic layout."

"This will do fine," she said, sifting through the draft notes, the pencil marks thick and smudged. "I just needed to see how you put it together so I would know what adjustments to make as we made repairs."

"Do you know what you're going to build yet?"

"Vaguely," she said, pushing the war machine to the back of her mind as she glanced over the rough sketches of the mech's central power mechanism. "I took a general inventory of the parts last night, and I think I can salvage most of what's already there, though we'll need to take it apart and remove what's no longer usable."

Half the mech was a total ruin—plating, gears, and part of the frame melted and warped—but the rest seemed to be in working order, as best she could tell without firing up the engine.

The worst damage was to the right arm, the frame destroyed beyond recognition.

According to the schematics, Rupert had fitted the arm with a hidden blade, but the gear mechanism used to protract the knife was flawed—the gears would never rotate properly, not with the joint movement of the elbow.

"Rupert . . . these notes don't make sense. How did you make this work?"

He came to stand over her shoulder. "I didn't," he said, seeing what she meant. "I told you Darrow used his blowlamp to melt the transmission? Well, he never would have had the chance had I been able to activate the punch-blade. But it locked up midfight, and Darrow found his opening." He frowned at the schematics. "I'm not sure what I did wrong."

"It's the gear makeup," she explained. "The angle of the arm joint interferes with the rotation at this linkage here, and this one, knocking these two gears out of alignment. See?" She pointed to the fault. "Maybe if the arm were locked straight, it might have worked, but not with all of these rotational variables involved." She tapped the edge of the page with her finger, thinking. "No, a spring launch would have worked better, or a pneumatic device."

"This is why I leave the mechanical genius to you," he said with a laugh, rubbing his hand over the edge of his jaw. "There's a reason I'm in aviation."

"Too bad you can't build a flying mech."

"Not enough air clearance in the recreation hall."

Petra laughed and turned back to Rupert's notes. The rest of the mech's systems were mostly sound, with a few mistakes buried here and there. Nothing to cause the machine to malfunction outright, but enough to make it operate at suboptimal efficiency. She paused. That gave her an idea. A possible way to delay Julian's war. But the war machine would have to wait.

She looked over the designs more closely. With a few adjustments to the engine chambers and connecting gear trains, rerouting many of the linkage paths to provide optimal power distribution, she could easily bring it to full capacity. Calligaris's combustion-enginery lecture wasn't a *total* waste, after all.

She marked a few pages of draft notes for further study and then glanced up from the smudged sketches. "Did you bring the tools I asked for?"

Rupert nodded, dropping his bag on the table with a clatter of metal. Riffling through the main compartment, he dragged out a collection of welding supplies—a portable blowlamp, multiple spanners, two kinds of pliers, a pair of bolt cutters, several clamps, and a manual hand drill.

Petra brushed her fingers across the smooth handle of an adjustable spanner and picked it up, the solid metal weight familiar to her hand. It was like coming back to a place she had almost forgotten, reminding her of days spent turning bolts and fitting linkages in a brightly lit office, Emmerich at her side and not a care in the world beyond the grease under her nails and the touch of metal beneath her fingers. She had missed it.

"Let's get started."

They spent the next couple of hours deconstructing what was left of Rupert's mech, inspecting each piece of the machine for damage before sorting the parts into what could be reused and what couldn't. Petra kept a detailed inventory, recording the measurements and dimensions of each piece before moving on to what was in the crates. When they had finished with that, she surveyed the list of parts, flipping through Rupert's notes as she considered possible designs for the repaired mech. After watching the mech battle with Selby, she knew she needed a machine that was both fast and destructive, but also hardy enough to withstand a brutal amount of damage.

There were several options for construction depending on how she wanted to focus her mech's functions—speed over hardiness, brute strength instead of agility, or resilience in sacrifice of an aggressive offense. Ideally, the machine would accomplish all of those things, but with a limited number of parts and the short amount of time before the first fight, she had to pick her battles.

Of course, there was nothing in the rules that said she couldn't alter her machine between fights. That ought to keep the other engineers on their toes.

She drummed her fingers against her knee, chewing her lip as she considered the baseline construction of the new mech. Knowing Selby, he would make sure to pit her against the most difficult opponent first, get her out of the tournament as quickly as possible. Likely someone with a strong offense, a mech heavy on weapons, quick and dangerous.

She glanced at Rupert. "You said anything goes once we're in the ring, right? Everything but projectiles."

He nodded. "That's right."

"What have you seen so far?" she asked. "I know you said Darrow had a supercharged blowlamp, but what else am I up against?"

Rupert seemed to think about it for a minute. "Well . . . Darrow's sure to equip his mech with as many rules-legal weapons as he can squeeze into it, so I would expect a barrage of assault weapons from him. You saw Selby's mech—sturdy build, relied on precision attacks, getting behind his opponent's defenses and wrecking them from the inside. Fletcher—the engineer Selby beat in that last round—he relied on brute force, modeled his mech after the failed automaton project. It packed a hell of a punch. Beat all of his opponents to a pulp until Selby."

"What else?"

"Let's see . . . Lambert's had hacksaws for arms;

Salamanca tried some kind of protracted saber, but Greer damaged it when he rammed the thing. Most of the engineers went for sheer power over specialized weapons—though I don't expect many of them to use the same strategy again."

Petra chewed on the end of her pencil, thinking through defensive measures. Without knowing her opponents' weapon choices, her best strategy was to equip her mech to survive anything—double-plated, reinforced frame, inner workings well protected. It would be slow, and she would need to maximize the engine efficiency just to get the mech in motion, but her first priority was survivability. She'd worry about the rest later.

But that still left the matter of an offense.

The goal of the fights was to incapacitate the other mech as quickly as possible—disabling movement, gutting systems, or deactivating its power source. With a heavier machine, her strength was in her resilience, but she wasn't really winning if all she did was outlast her opponent.

She scowled at the dismantled mech, examining her half-sketched designs for potential weapons, anything to add to the mech without jeopardizing the integrity of its defenses. The mech had two bulky arms she could fit with weapons, something to sabotage her opponent's systems quickly and efficiently. A pneumatic fist, perhaps? She could overcome her mech's lack of speed with a pressure-charged punch. That could work; though she would need to calculate the recharge time between each punch. Perhaps one at the end of each arm?

She pulled her drafting paper into her lap and scribbled a few notes, writing down a few other ideas—electrified prongs, protractible saw-blades, Darrow's supercharged blowlamp. As much as she hated to take inspiration from her competition, she had no qualms against playing dirty, not when she had a score to settle with the other students.

Rupert leaned close and looked over her shoulder as she sketched. He let out a low whistle. "Selby is going to regret letting you fight."

Petra set the designs on the desk. "What do you think?" she asked, pointing to the list of potential weapons. "Could we put this together?"

"If anyone could, you can," he said with a grin.

"Then let's see what we can do."

By the end of the night, she had a rough draft sketched out for the new design—mostly true to Rupert's original design, with a few improvements and adjustments of her own. There were a few extra supplies she needed before she would be able to complete construction of some of the more complicated weaponry she had devised, but all things considered, she could build a workable, battle-ready mech in time for the first fight, hopefully one sturdy enough to survive first contact with the enemy. It would be difficult, but with Rupert's help, she was confident they could get it done.

Once Rupert left the office for the evening, Petra remained behind, returning her attention to the war machine. She pulled her chair up to the desk and grabbed a fresh stack of drafting paper, her mind whirring with ideas now that she had a plan. She had been approaching the war machine all wrong, trying to create the best possible machine for the job, when what she really needed to do was create a machine with the greatest potential for error and most likely to cause delays.

She had gotten the idea from the small errors riddled throughout Rupert's original mech design. If enough errors found their way into the war machine, she could delay the approval of the schematics and ultimately, the production of the prototype. By inserting simple malfunctions, so infinitesimally small that they could be considered honest mistakes, perhaps she might buy herself the time she needed to find a way to end Julian's schemes once and for all.

If she could get the faulty design past the Guild council.

That was her first hurdle, but if she could earn their approval—mistakes intact—once the production team began construction of the prototype, those small mistakes would lead to delays, necessitating parts reorders, reconstruction of faulty systems, further trials and tests to confirm the mistakes were corrected. She could delay the completion of the prototype almost indefinitely.

Without a war machine, Julian could not have his war.

She put pencil to paper and sketched out a new

design, adopting the four-legged construction with the swiveling control cabin. The more systems involved, the more parts needed, the more connective transmissions and gear arrays embroiled in the design, the higher the likelihood of error and number of delays. No automatic systems. All manual control. A combustion engine to power the beast, a combination of hydraulic and pneumatic power in the legs, mechanical input controls, electric gauges, and telegraphic readouts.

But she couldn't rely on her mistakes alone. Mistakes could be fixed. She needed a contingency plan, something to prevent the prototype from reaching completion, even after all the other mistakes had been found and corrected.

She drummed her fingers against the desk.

The sabotage would have to be expertly hidden, with no possible chance of anyone finding it before the Guild finished the prototype . . . something to cause the prototype to fail, but not until after the construction phase, lest her sabotage be discovered too soon. And she would have to find a way to integrate the sabotaging device into every system within the war machine, triggered only when the finished prototype was activated. Something that would lead to complete and utter failure. Movement, weapons, gauges— everything. But how?

She leaned back in her chair and tapped the end of her pencil against her bottom lip, staring at the sketches in front of her.

A jamming device.

Just as Rupert's mech had failed to launch the hidden blade from its arm, she could fashion a clockwork mechanism to sabotage the war machine from within. The right assemblage of gears and springs, designed to incapacitate the machine at the base level . . . it would require a staggeringly complex design in order to go unnoticed, but she was up to the task.

She had to stop this war. One way or another.

CHAPTER 4

The next week passed too quickly. Petra scrambled to finish her war machine design before her scheduled proposal, spending every moment of her spare time in her hidden office drafting the complicated schematics, her production notes vague and equations convoluted, with slight enough error that her intentional mistakes might go unnoticed—or so she hoped.

And then there was her sabotage.

After several nights of sketching out complex designs for disabling the prototype, she settled on a mechanism that tied into the regulator, a device that measured the synchronicity of the connected machineries and adjusted power distribution as needed. The mechanism could be disabled, if necessary, with the removal of a single axle plate and attached gear system, but to do so would render system inert. Intact, the device would trigger the sabotaging clockwork mechanism once all primary systems were activated, initiating a slow, systematic malfunction that would disable the entire machine within a matter of minutes. It was a complicated bit of clockwork design, a network of tension springs and ratchet wheels designed to activate only when all systems were operating in unison, but she was confident it would work.

Now the day of her proposal meeting, Petra stood once more before the council chamber doors, her designs clutched tightly to her chest. She exhaled a shaky breath, her nerves betraying her. If Julian suspected her treachery, if anyone discovered the sabotaging mechanism, she had no fallback plan, no genius excuse to escape Julian's threat.

Everything hinged on their ignorance of her true intent.

And if she failed, it would be the end of her.

"Miss Wade?" said a smooth voice. "They are ready for you."

Petra glanced up from her silent vigil, expecting to see the usual thin-lipped clerk waiting for her in the doorway. Instead, she spotted the bright red uniform of a Royal Forces officer, the same junior officer who had been at her last meeting. He regarded her expectantly, but she only nodded wordlessly in reply, her voice stuck somewhere in the pit of her throat.

He stepped aside and gestured through the door. "After you."

Swallowing thickly, she held the war machine schematics close to her chest and stared into the dark recesses of the council chambers, her heartbeat quickening. She could do this. Julian *needed* this war machine. All she had to do was convince the council to accept it, that it was the war machine they needed, and everything would be fine.

With a deep, steadying breath, she left her doubts behind and strode into the council chambers.

The men's conversation ceased when she entered, and she tried not to drown in the silence. All eyes fixed on her as she walked across the hard floor, her shoes clicking loudly with each slow step. Officer Cartwright led her to the center of the room and nodded politely in farewell before joining the other red uniforms to the side of the bench.

Vice-Chancellor Lyndon acknowledged her with a nod. "Miss Wade, if you would give your designs to the clerk, we will start the official proceedings."

The entire council was in attendance, glaring down at her from their high seats, and at least a half-dozen soldiers stood to the side of the bench. Ignoring the weight of their unrelenting gazes, she opened her folder of project notes and handed the necessary papers to the clerk, who distributed the designs to the council members and attending officers of rank. She waited as they flipped through her designs, watching their reactions change from habitual indifference to mild surprise. Some nodded appreciatively; others remained skeptical.

Lyndon peered intently over the designs, adjusting his glasses as he read her carefully worded notes, his face steadily declining into a mask of disappointment. One of the council engineers threw the pages down in disgust, and a tiny seed of shame rose up in Petra's throat, warming her cheeks. He was one of the only men on the council still staunchly against the war. If only she could tell him the truth, assure him that she would give almost anything to not be here right now presenting a war machine to the council. But she had run out of options. She had been offered no other choice.

Only Julian seemed unsurprised by the proposal, a satisfied smirk plastered on his face. The war machine he so desperately wanted was finally in his grasp. All he needed now was the council's endorsement, and he would be one step closer to securing his war.

"Miss Wade," said Lyndon, his gravelly voice low and quiet. "If you would please explain your project to the council."

Petra cleared her throat and stood a little straighter, determined to succeed where she had failed so many times before. She could do this, she reminded herself. This meeting was no different than her first five proposals to the Guild. She only had to convince them to accept the project and distract them from discovering her sabotage. No problem.

"Thank you, Vice-Chancellor," she said, her voice quaking slightly as she turned to the first page of her project proposal, her finished war machine design neatly sketched and labeled. She exhaled a trembling breath, trying not to think of what dire consequences awaited her should she fail.

Another deep breath. *Here goes nothing.*

"For the Guild's consideration, I wish to propose a design for a piece of technology compatible with the Guild's current contract with Her Imperial Majesty's Royal Forces. In preparation for the inevitable war against the rising anti-imperialists, the British Empire is in need of a machine capable of securing victory against our enemies." She swallowed the hard lump in her throat and continued with the rehearsed speech, fighting the urge to grit her teeth as she spoke. "I believe the quadruped is that machine, as I hope you will agree."

Ignoring the weighty silence pressing down on the room, Petra consulted her notes, flipping to the next page. "If you turn to the interior design on the second page of my proposal, you will see that the quadruped is operated from within an armored control cabin, protecting the soldier piloting the machine with a double layer of reinforced steel plating and hermetically fortified glass.

"I have named the machine 'quadruped' for the four supports that provide its primary mobility. These walking apparatuses will be able to travel over a wide variety of terrain, and the base of the machine will be equipped with gyroscopic sensors that can alert the quadruped's pilot to subtle gradient changes in the machine's immediate path so that the pilot can adjust his motion accordingly. The legs are equipped to handle the stress of both the full weight of the machine and its pilot, as well as the potential recoil force of any weapons that might be affixed to the device—within a set of conditional parameters.

"The control cabin itself can rotate two hundred and seventy degrees, providing a wide range of visibility for the pilot, as well as multidirectional aiming capabilities for whatever weapons might be mounted to the exterior of the control cabin. As you may have noted, I have not drawn any weapons into the design, but I have indicated the best possible locations for potential weapon placement, based on the structural integrity of the frame and multiple calculations for compensating against potential recoiling force."

She continued by explaining the various systems involved in the war machine's construction—the internal combustion engine and backup fuel reserves, the specialized chamber she proposed to prevent ignition of the gas tank from outside forces, detailed explanations of the hydraulic system, gyroscopic sensors, and proposed operational controls.

At the end of her proposal, Petra surveyed the council bench. "If anyone has questions, I would be happy to address any concerns."

Vice-Chancellor Lyndon cleared his throat and pushed his glasses further up his nose. "I think that will suffice, Miss Wade. Now, if you will wait outside, we will consider your proposal and come to a decision shortly."

Petra bowed respectfully to the council. "Thank you, Vice-Chancellor."

She turned and left the council chambers, her stomach twisting in knots as the heavy doors closed behind her. Immediately, she began pacing up and down the hall, wringing her hands as the council deliberated over her designs. If anyone found her mistakes or suspected her of sabotage, at best, Julian would have her locked up and shipped off to work under the thumb of the Royal Forces. At worst . . . she didn't want to think about that.

After a few fretful minutes, she neared the door again and slowed her pace, hearing the council's muffled voices on the other side. They were arguing now. She inched closer and pressed her ear to the wood. The door shifted at her touch, opening just enough that she could make out voices on the other side.

Mr. Fowler spoke heatedly. "I do not believe the girl can be trusted, no matter her skill. Lest you all forget, she was convicted of treason and espionage, among other things, only last summer."

"Those charges were dropped," said Vice-Chancellor Lyndon.

"Against the majority vote of the Guild council!" said Fowler, slamming his hand on the desk. "It is my vote that we reject this project and the girl's application, as well as revoke her studentship. She never should have been allowed one in the first place."

"Miss Wade's status as a student is not in question here."

"It should be," replied Mr. Fowler.

There was a murmur of agreement from the other council members.

Lyndon cleared his throat. "I should remind you, Mr. Fowler, the current vote concerns only the quadruped project, not any previous crime Miss Wade might have been falsely accused of."

"*Falsely?*" repeated Mr. Fowler. "That bloody machine broke two of my ribs, and then she had the gall to destroy it! Months of effort wasted. You were *there*, Lyndon! You—"

"That is enough." Julian's voice cut through the argument, and Fowler fell silent. "Give your vote on the project at hand and say nothing else of Miss Wade's previous misconducts. That is not why we are here."

There was a pause.

"Fine," said Fowler. "I vote to reject the project."

"Are you certain?" asked Julian, a hint of warning in his tone.

"She does not belong here," he hissed. "Mark my words, Julian. Your obsession with this girl is going to ruin you. A dozen engineers have brought forward suitable enough designs, with the potential for mass production. Why not use one of theirs instead?"

There was another long pause.

"It is a fair question," said one of the other councilors. "You have asked us to be patient, to withhold funding until Miss Wade provided us with a war machine, but six months have passed since you promised us a project from her. We could have built any number of other designs by now. Why must we use hers?"

"Because not one of our engineers has her skill. Not one of them can think their way around a machine like she does," he replied. "Regardless of her loyalties or inexperience, her innate talent cannot be ignored. Her design meets our every requirement. How many times have I delivered the Royal Forces' parameters to applying engineers, only to have them come back with a mediocre design unworthy of the Guild—or worse, tell me it isn't possible to create a war machine of that caliber? We are not in the business of 'suitable enough,' gentlemen. We are at the front lines of modern science. We should want *innovation*, not a rehash of decades-old technology. And we will never have progress if we don't push ourselves toward higher standards." He paused, a thick silence descending on the hall. "The Royal Forces has asked us for a war machine to end all wars, greater than anything that has come before. I believe that machine is sitting before you now."

A heavy silence followed his words.

"Even so, I stand by my vote," said Mr. Fowler. "Miss Wade is a traitor, and I will have no hand in her treachery. If you allow her to work on this project, the anti-imperialists will win."

"Your opinion has been noted," said Julian, his voice sharp. "Vice-Chancellor, I believe Mr. Fowler has had his say. Do continue with the deliberations. I believe it is Dr. Reid's vote next."

"Very well. Mr. Fowler's vote has been recorded," said Lyndon. "Dr. Reid?"

The engineer cleared his throat. "I have no reservations toward Miss Wade's acceptance into the Guild.

As I have said before, she would be a valuable asset for the Guild to acquire. I vote to accept."

"Duly noted," said Lyndon. "Now, Mr. Goss, if you would share your vote."

Petra held her breath and pressed closer to the door to hear the result, when she felt the wooden surface shift beneath her touch. She jumped back, but too late. The door swung open, revealing a familiar face in a scarlet uniform.

"Officer Cartwright," she said airily, her heartbeat thundering in her ears. She swallowed against the sudden tightness in her throat and tried to make out Julian's decision as he delivered his vote on the project. "I was just—"

"Eavesdropping?" Officer Cartwright carefully closed the door behind him, shutting the rest of Julian's words inside the council chambers. There was a slight tilt to his lips, the barest hint of a smile.

"And if I was?" she asked.

"I wouldn't worry," he said lightly, stepping away from the doors to stand against the wall. He fished a battered cigarette case from inside his coat. "The council is going to accept the project."

"What makes you say that?"

He shrugged, lifting a hand-rolled cigarette from its case. "The Guild needs this design of yours. My superiors have made that fact very clear to the council." He dragged a match across the inside of the case and quickly lit the end of his cigarette as the match flared, then took a long drag before continuing. "But I thought you said you didn't want to be a part of this war," he said, blowing a cloud of smoke into the air. "What changed?"

She pressed her lips together and glanced away. *Everything*, she wanted to say. Everything had changed.

The soldier raised the cigarette to his lips again, but hesitated. "I thought you wanted to join the Guild on your own terms."

"I did," she said bitterly.

"Yet here you are."

She wanted to laugh, but she felt too hollow. "Here I am."

He remained quiet for a moment, smoking his cigarette in silence. "Do you mind if I ask you something?" he asked, blowing another cloud of smoke across the hallway.

"What?"

"Why does the Guild council distrust you so much?" he asked. "They seem to think you're their enemy."

She scoffed. "Fancy that."

"Are you?" he asked.

"Am I what?"

"What they say."

She arched an eyebrow. "That depends on what's being said."

Footsteps approached the doors, and her throat tightened as she realized the council's deliberation must be over already. She glanced away from the soldier, her nerves twisting into a knot in her chest.

The door to the council chambers opened, and the clerk peered into the hall, his face betraying no hint of what the council had decided. "They're ready for you, Miss Wade."

She hesitated, eyeing the soldier as he took another drag off his cigarette. She wondered what he had been told about her, what he had heard, if he knew anything close to the truth. She knew what some of the council members said about her, like Fowler, how they considered her their enemy, undeserving of the Guild's consideration.

But they were wrong.

She was more deserving than anyone.

"No," she said finally, meeting his challenging gaze with one of her own. "I'm not anything like they say."

His expression seemed to soften then, and she thought she saw a hint of a smile as he took another puff of his cigarette, but she did not linger after that. She left the soldier in the hall and followed the clerk into the council chambers.

Lyndon stood as she entered, but the rest of the council members remained seated, a solemn, dead silence weighing on the room.

Petra stopped in the center of the chamber, standing tall and proud amidst their stern gazes, her chin held high. Whatever their decision, she had done as Julian asked. She had designed his war machine, cooperated with his plans, and submitted the design to the Guild. He could not punish her for the council's decision, not when she had done exactly as she was told.

Any engineer worth his degree could see that the war machine was viable—mistakes notwithstanding. That had to count for something.

Behind her, the doors to the council room opened, and Officer Cartwright slipped quietly back inside, rejoining the group of redcoats at the edge of the room. He met Petra's eye as he took up position among the other soldiers, offering a brief smile before assuming the statuesque posture of his fellows.

Vice-Chancellor Lyndon cleared his throat. "After due consideration, the council has deliberated on the quadruped project and come to a decision," he said slowly, his gaze sweeping the full perimeter of the hall before settling on Julian Goss. "As proposed, we have considered Miss Wade's application and have thus decided to *accept* the quadruped project for immediate commission."

Petra's eyes widened, a wash of relief sweeping through her. She could hardly believe it.

"However . . ." Lyndon continued, his gravelly voice suddenly heavy.

Her smile faltered.

"In light of Miss Wade's past misconducts and questions of her allegiance to the Guild and the Empire," he went on, "the council has deemed her unworthy of joining the Guild and therefore rejects her formal application for Guild placement."

"What? No . . ."

Petra turned toward Julian, sitting relaxed in his chair with a satisfied smile on his lips.

So this was his plan . . . He never intended to let her be a member of the Guild. All he ever wanted was his war machine. And now he had it.

"But you can't just *take* the quadruped," she said, turning back toward Lyndon. "You can't accept the project without also accepting my application. That's not how this works."

"The council's decision has been made," said Julian. "The Guild has accepted the quadruped for immediate development, and you are denied Guild membership. There will be no further discussion on the matter."

"But you can't do that!" she said, curling her fingers into fists. "The proposal is my application into the Guild. You can't accept one and not the other." She glared at Julian and approached the vice-chancellor. "Don't let him do this," she pleaded, gesturing toward Julian. "He can't just take my designs and refuse me the right to be on the project. I designed the quadruped. It's *mine*."

"It is the Guild's property now," said a sallow voice—one of Julian's toadies, Mr. Pelletier. "The council has the authority to accept or reject applications as we please, and we have decided that you are not fit to work as an engineer for the Guild."

"Not fit?"

"Given your . . . history."

Julian glared down at her from the lofty council bench. "The decision is final, Miss Wade."

"No, it isn't," she said, gritting her teeth. "If I can't be on the project, if you reject my application to join the Guild, then—then you can't have the quadruped. I withdraw the project from consideration."

"Petra," said Lyndon, suddenly sitting forward in his chair. "If you withdraw your project, then—"

"No," she said, silencing him with the darkest of glares she could muster. "I know my rights as a student. The Guild cannot develop the quadruped without my consent. Those are the legalities of Guild contracts, are they not?" She glared at the vice-chancellor, daring him to contradict her.

"She's right," said another man. "Her consent is required. We cannot commission a project without the designing engineer's explicit approval, student or otherwise. Should you choose to build the machine without such approval, you will be in violation of her rights as an engineer, as defined in the Guild bylaws. If Miss Wade wishes to withdraw the project, she may do so, and not one of us can do anything to stop her."

Petra glanced at Julian. There was at least one person in the room who could choose to punish her for withdrawing the project, but she prayed it wouldn't come to that.

She faced Lyndon again. "There is an alternative."

"And what is that?" asked Mr. Pelletier.

"Let me work on the project. Induct me into the Guild. If—"

"Absolutely not! If there is one thing we can all agree on, it is that you do not belong in the Guild." He shook his head and turned to the other council members. "Surely there is a way we might subvert the contract bylaws. Miss Wade may study here, but she is not a proper student. She is not, and never will be, equal to the engineers in our employ. She is a woman, and therefore the bylaws should not apply. The very idea that—"

"I am just as good an engineer as any of the other students," she said, her voice rising. "My designs prove that, and if I were a man, you wouldn't hesitate to accept my application. I may be a woman, but I am also an engineer, and I deserve the same consideration you would give any man."

"It is not only your sex—or even your skill—that is in question," said another man, "but your loyalties. You have been previously accused of anti-imperialist associations and were once party to the destruction of Guild property. Given such history, we cannot afford to risk—"

"Those accusations were proved false," said Lyndon, cutting across the arguing council members with his deep, gravelly voice. "Miss Wade is guilty of no crime here. Let that be a reminder to you all."

"A matter of opinion," countered the other councilor. "Not all of us were party to the evidence proving Miss Wade's innocence, Vice-Chancellor, and I, for one, find it highly negligent for the Guild to give her access to such a sensitive project in this delicate time—whether she designed it or not."

There was a murmur of agreement from many of the other council members, their arguments against her only growing more and more heated as both Lyndon and a few of the elder members came to her defense. They were nearly shouting over one another now.

Her attempt to negotiate was crumbling around her ears.

"I have a suggestion."

The voice came not from behind the council bench but beside it. Petra turned toward the soldiers standing at the edge of the council chambers. Officer Cartwright stood firmly in front of the rest of the men, his hands clasped neatly behind his back and his eyes on Vice-Chancellor Lyndon.

The council continued to argue despite his interruption.

Lyndon gave up on trying to defend her and sank into his leather chair with his knuckles pressed to his brow. Julian's glower only grew darker with each passing second, and Petra tried not to flinch.

She swallowed against the tightness in her throat and glanced at Officer Cartwright again, who was now discussing something with his superior, the broad-shouldered man with the thick mustache. After a moment of quiet discussion, the elder officer nodded and gestured toward the council bench. Officer Cartwright stepped forward, his red uniform distinctive in the harsh overhead light. When the council finally noticed him, their arguments disintegrated into silence.

Vice-Chancellor Lyndon looked up from the council bench and adjusted his glasses on his nose. "Yes?"

"The Royal Forces has a suggestion for the Guild

council," said Officer Cartwright. "A proposition that may satisfy all parties involved."

Julian leaned forward in his chair and glared at the soldier, his gaze slowly sweeping across the chamber to the officers remaining to the side of the bench. Petra noticed the silent exchange between him and the mustached officer. The man nodded firmly, and Julian narrowed his eyes, slowly withdrawing back into his chair with a scowl.

"Well?" he prompted, gesturing for the soldier to continue. "What does the Royal Forces suggest?"

"I have conferred with my superiors and we believe that there is a way forward that will please both the Guild council and the designing engineer in a manner compliant with the interests of the Royal Forces," said the officer. "Both the Guild council and the attending officers have reviewed the proposed project that Miss Wade has brought forth and agreed that it is of an acceptable design, suitable for immediate development. Therefore, we can all agree that neither Miss Wade's knowledge nor her expertise are in question here, but her loyalty. Those of the council who voted against Miss Wade's application for a position within the Guild, you question her allegiance, correct? And it is on this basis that you wish to reject her application to the Guild, and yet retain her proposed project."

He waited for the dissenting councilors to nod their agreement before continuing. "Yet, according to the Guild bylaws, as supported by a few of the present councilors, you cannot commission her project without her consent—which she refuses to give without due involvement on the project at hand. To that end, I offer a solution:

"With the support of my superiors, I propose that the Guild council allows Miss Wade a probationary position on the quadruped project, where she can oversee construction of the machine and involve herself as required. However, as it suits the council, her access to Guild resources would be limited to the production of the quadruped, and her involvement would occur only under the observation of a trusted Guild associate."

His words lingered in weighted silence, the attending council members mulling over the suggestion as they conversed among themselves. Many of them shook their heads in quiet disagreement, but others seemed to consider the suggestion in earnest.

Petra felt her heart lift.

If Officer Cartwright could convince the council to let her join the project, even in a probationary position, she could ensure her sabotage progressed as planned.

The soldier's superior officer stepped forward then, taking up position in front of Officer Cartwright. "Let me remind you, gentlemen, that the Royal Forces is in need of advanced war technology to combat the anti-imperialist threat. This engineer's design is the only machine you have been able to offer to that effect. It would be imprudent to allow it to slip through your fingers based on nothing more than hearsay."

"Forgive me for questioning your judgement, Colonel," said Julian, leaning forward in his chair. "But what guarantees can the Royal Forces provide that Miss Wade will not take advantage of this probationary position and take treasonous action against the Guild?"

The colonel met Julian's stare. "None," he said plainly. "But the Royal Forces is in need of a war machine, and you now have the power to grant that to us. On behalf of the Royal Forces, I suggest that you do. Whatever consequences that follow will be a matter of further discourse."

Silence followed his words, clinging to the council chambers like cobwebs. Petra glanced at Julian and then Lyndon, trying to gauge their reactions to the proposal.

If a member of the council put the proposition to a vote, she had a chance—a *real* chance—to join the Guild, even if it was a highly restricted position. But if Julian rejected the idea, if her other detractors disagreed with the soldier's proposal, then she would be forced to make a desperate decision: allow the Guild to build the quadruped without her involvement, or formally withdraw her application and suffer Julian's wrath.

Neither would help her in her goal to delay the war.

Finally, Julian turned his attention from the colonel back to her. "Miss Wade," he said. "Would you agree to such terms?"

Petra stood a little straighter. "I would," she said with a nod. "If you allow me to oversee the project and have a part in the construction of the prototype, I will give my permission for the Guild to commission the quadruped, and therefore prove my loyalty to the council."

"Julian," said Mr. Fowler. "You can't seriously—"

Mr. Goss held up his hand, regarding Petra with a calculating gaze. "If anyone here wishes to call into motion the colonel's proposal, we will put the decision to another vote."

Petra locked eyes with Lyndon, silently pleading for him to help her, to do this one thing. If he called this motion, she would never blame him for not helping again.

The vice-chancellor sighed. "I call to bring the motion to the floor."

"Seconded," said another councilor.

She exhaled a breath of relief.

"Then we will put it to a vote," said Mr. Goss, standing with a measure of authority. "The Guild moves for Miss Wade's application to be accepted on a probationary level. She will be allowed to work on the quadruped in accordance with the Guild's conditions. As such, she will have limited access to the project, and only under the supervision of a senior member of the Guild, as chosen by the council. She must report her progress weekly, as is required of all our engineers, and she will not be allowed access to any other Guild office or workstation besides her own, except with the permission of the respective Guild employee, her supervisor, and a member of the council." He surveyed the room with a scowl. "Are these conditions acceptable?"

The entire bench exchanged glances with one another, some of the men nodding in agreement, others offering no more than a disinterested shrug, while the rest, including Mr. Fowler, remained sour.

"I would like to propose an addendum," said Lyndon.

Julian's mouth twitched. "Yes, Vice-Chancellor?"

"Should Miss Wade complete the quadruped as proposed, without any perceived treasonous action against the Guild during its development, I would like to suggest that she be offered a permanent position within the Guild, as an engineer of her caliber deserves."

Petra turned toward Julian, her heart racing.

He hesitated a moment before replying. "Very well. We will put the motion to a vote." He glanced around the council bench. "All in favor of allowing Miss Wade a probationary position during the production of the quadruped . . ." He raised his hand.

Petra held her breath. She needed only eight votes. Eight votes in her favor and she might actually have a chance to put a stop to Julian's war.

One by one, the councilors lifted their hands.

First two, then three.

A fourth, fifth, and sixth.

A grudging seventh.

Just one more vote . . .

A single vote to guarantee her position on the quadruped project, one more vote to ensure that her plan to delay the war could go forward. But if the vote stalled, if no one else voted to approve the amended application, she was doomed. Julian would not rest until she paid for this final defiance against him.

She swallowed thickly, glancing at the few members whose hands remained down. "Come on," she whispered, willing them to vote in her favor.

Then the colonel cleared his throat, and three other council members reluctantly raised their hands.

She had the majority.

She had won.

It was a probationary position, but still . . . Her cheeks started to ache from grinning, and it took all her effort not to jump up and down with excitement right there in the council chambers.

Julian inhaled a deep breath. "Very well," he said, his voice betraying only the slightest hint of a grudge. He turned toward Lyndon. "Vice-Chancellor? If you would like to conclude our business here . . ." He sat down in his chair, a sour look on his face.

"My pleasure." Vice-Chancellor Lyndon cleared his throat and stood up from his chair. "Miss Wade, should you agree to the conditions laid out in this meeting, you will be hereby instated as a probationary member of the Guild. Once you have completed the quadruped project, we will take another vote to determine if you have fulfilled the terms of your agreement and then decide if you should become a permanent member of the Guild. Do you agree?"

"Yes, sir," she said eagerly.

Lyndon turned toward the clerk. "If you would,

Mr. Connolly, have a contract drafted for Miss Wade to sign, listing the conditions of her new position. I will want to oversee the terms of the agreement before the contract is finalized and signed."

"As will I," said Julian, raising his hand.

"Of course, sir," said the clerk.

"Then this meeting is adjourned," said Lyndon, giving the other council members permission to leave. "Miss Wade, I will contact you when the contract is ready for your approval and signature."

"Thank you, sir."

Petra turned on her heel to leave but then paused, catching Officer Cartwright's eye. She nodded appreciatively, silently thanking him for his intervention, and he returned the gesture with soldierly precision, a flicker of a smile at the edge of his mouth. It didn't matter why he had stepped forward, only that it had swayed the council in her favor.

She left the council chambers feeling triumphant, unable to keep from smiling. She had done it. She had earned her place within the Guild.

Yet it was a bittersweet victory.

She was one step closer to joining the Guild, but Julian was now one step closer to having his war.

"Miss Wade."

Petra stopped dead in the center of the hall, the hair on the back of her neck bristling. She forced her face into a neutral expression and turned around, spying Julian Goss striding toward her without a hint of his usual pleasantries. She steeled herself against his anger, bolstering her resolve with her recent triumph over the council. "Sir?"

Julian gathered to his full height, a muscle twitching in his jaw. "Just because you delivered a war machine does not mean that you are no longer bound by our agreement." He leaned closer. "If you do anything to slow the construction of the prototype or sabotage production in any way, I will not hesitate to have you removed from the Guild and sent to the Royal Forces in chains. Do you understand me?"

"Quite," she said, not daring to let herself falter now.

She was done being bullied, done being scared.

It was time for her to fight back again.

Julian lowered his voice. "Make no mistake. This war machine will go into production, and I will have my war. Nothing you do will change that."

Petra held her tongue, glaring back at him with as much loathing as she could muster.

"Tread carefully, Miss Wade," he said. "Your defiance will cost you."

With that, he turned and left, leaving Petra alone in the middle of the hall, pulse racing.

Tread carefully, indeed.

CHAPTER 5

Another week passed, packed with tedious class assignments and studying for meaningless exams, Petra's late afternoons devoted to working on the mech with Rupert. The quadruped project hadn't progressed any further since she signed the Guild contract, and while she felt a sense of triumph when she wrote her name next to Lyndon's, there was a sense of trepidation also.

Once construction of the prototype began, she was certain Julian would try to find any and every excuse to blame her for whatever delays occurred—whether they were a result of her "mistakes" or not. At least she still had time to prepare for that eventuality. Her engineering team had yet to be assembled, so construction hadn't started yet—and wouldn't until her team was finalized and the designs confirmed—which was just as well to her. The longer construction was delayed, the better.

Until then, she had the mech to occupy her time.

Petra and Rupert sat in the floor of the subcity office, working on the mech's final systems. The first fight was only days away, and they had spent every afternoon entrenched in the hidden office, working to repair the busted machine, cobbling weapons together with whatever parts they could get their hands on, and adding as many modifications and attachments as they could cram inside. It looked a mess without its plating, a conglomeration of lifeless gears, cams, and linkage bars housed in the mech's bulky frame. Electric wires snaked through the machine like veins, affixed to various electric systems and powered by an electromagnetically charged battery. The machinery lacked elegance and order, but made up for it in power and versatility.

With Rupert's help, and both of them devoting as many hours as they could spare in the last two weeks, the mech was nearly complete. A few more adjustments to the mechanical systems, and they could start bolting the layers of plating to the frame.

"Hand me that screwdriver, would you?" said Petra, her voice muffled by the screws held between her lips. She took one of the screws and positioned it over the linkage joint, then held out her hand for the screwdriver. Rupert dutifully placed the tool in her palm, and she set to fixing the pieces together.

Rupert sat cross-legged beside her, his chin propped on his fist as he watched her work. "I wonder who you'll be facing first," he said. "It's supposed to be a random draw, but I bet Selby will arrange it so you're up against somebody like Darrow first, hoping to force you out early."

Petra nodded absently, concentrating on making sure all the systems in the left arm were lined up properly, slowly rotating one of the gears to test the movement of the main drive assembly. She frowned, turning the gears again. The transference could be tighter. Some of the connections were loose, causing the gear teeth to click upon engaging. Digging both hands into the bare systems, she loosened a few bolts and slightly shifted the gears before securing everything back into place. Testing the motion again, she listened for the steady whir of tightly fitted gears—no clicks or grinding—and withdrew her hands, satisfied with the result. She wiped her greasy fingers on a rag and stood, lifting her arms overhead as she stretched out her stiff muscles.

They'd been working for a few hours already, and though she wanted to finish the mech tonight, there was still too much to do. It would take the rest of the week to complete, even with Rupert's help.

But it *would* be ready.

All but one of her weapon concepts now augmented the machine, the final design lacking only the pneumatic fist, and only because it would have left the mech's arm useless for anything else. Instead, she had fitted the mech's limbs with a wide array of hidden weapons, hopefully versatile enough to combat anything her opponents threw at her.

Petra sat down at her desk and rubbed her eyes. "What time is it?"

"Nearly midnight."

She groaned, knowing she should probably head home. She had an exam in the morning and needed to cram in some last-minute studying before the test. If she failed, she'd be catching up for the rest of the semester, or else have to repeat the course. She closed her eyes and sighed, listening to the steady thrum of the subcity, the sounds of machinery playing a mechanical lullaby.

When she opened her eyes again, Rupert had moved to the wall beside her desk, arms crossed. He smiled, his face weary.

Petra was sure she looked just as tired.

She stood up from her chair and stretched, eyeing the mostly finished mech. "Do you think we'll win?"

"We have a fighting chance, at least," he said with a shrug, grabbing their things. "You're clever, and that will win you more fights than not. And with the surprises you've packed into this old machine, I feel bad for whoever you face first. Not one of them expects you to win—or to put up much of a fight." He laughed and held out his hand to help her onto the dumbwaiter platform. "Their mistake."

The night of the first fight, Petra stood at the base of the dumbwaiter shaft, less than an hour until the first match. She and Rupert had spent all of the previous night adding the final touches to the mech, hammering plating into shape and bolting it to the frame, staying up well past midnight as they made sure every system functioned properly.

She had been nervous testing the controls, worried she had made a mistake wiring the machine, especially the wireless receiver in the mech's brain chamber. Rupert's mech was corded like the others, but with a few adjustments, she had been able to house a wireless control receiver within the mech's body, a control apparatus like the one Emmerich had built for the automaton; though no one would know by looking at it. By all appearances, her machine was controlled via a direct wire between the control box and mech—the wireless control apparatus a hidden advantage should she need to use it. A gamble, considering her inexperience with electromagnetics, but one she was willing to risk.

"You ready?" asked Rupert.

She inhaled a deep breath and nodded. "Let's do this."

Petra helped him push the mech toward the dumbwaiter chute, and together they heaved it onto the platform. Rupert helped her onto the lift next, and she took a seat beside the hulking metal, glancing at the pulley cables that ran up the length of the chute.

"What's the weight limit on this thing?" she asked.

Rupert seemed to think about it for a minute, climbing up onto the platform on the other side of the mech. "Five hundred pounds?"

"You're not sure?"

He placed his hand on the lever that activated the pulley drive and swung it backward. "It'll hold."

The dumbwaiter motor whirred, and slowly, the platform began to rise, groaning under their combined weight, but holding.

Rupert smirked. "Told you."

Petra glared at him.

They reached the top of the chute and carefully lowered the mech to the floor before navigating their way to the dumbwaiter platform at the other end of the building. The second lift deposited them on the eighth floor, and as they neared the recreation hall, Petra's heartbeat quickened, pounding painfully against her ribs. She stopped a few feet from the door, the sounds of students and rumbling engines beyond. Several students milled about the hall, and a few of them cast snickering glances at her.

"What's wrong?" asked Rupert, slowing the mech to a stop.

She sucked in a deep breath. "Nothing. Just nervous."

Rupert laid a hand on her shoulder and squeezed. "Don't be," he said firmly. "You can do this, Petra. You can win."

She nodded, ignoring the snide comments from the other students. All she had to do was prove it.

"All right," she said, letting her breath out in a whoosh. "Let's go."

Pushing past the other students, Rupert keyed into

the recreation hall and shoved the door open, quickly navigating the mech into the room. Petra took another deep breath and followed.

The recreation hall had been cleared of furniture, the couches, chairs, and tables moved to the far side of the room. Already, the room had begun to fill with students and machines. Broad, hulking anthropoids of brass and aluminum stood at the edges of the room like metal sentinels, and Petra forgot her doubts and her fear, focusing instead on her potential opponents.

Some of the machines were crudely built, rough combinations of scrap parts. They looked as if they might fall to pieces with a well-aimed hit, but Rupert had warned her not to underestimate any of her opponents. As ugly as their machines might be, the engineers here were some of the best in the world. She would be a fool to forget that.

Then there were the other mechs, finely crafted works of mechanical engineering. These stood like gleaming titans, far superior to the rickety machines the other students had cobbled together. Petra was unsurprised to see Selby standing next to one of them, a smug grin on his face.

Most of the mechs were powered by combustion engines, but she did see two steam-powered machines among the combatants, hissing vapor in the far corner of the room. Of the smaller mechs, many were more vehicular than manlike, with wheels or treads instead of legs, and there were as many different types of weapons as there were machines—blades for arms, extendable saw-blades, broad-faced hammers, and heavy cudgels. By the time the last of the combatants arrived, there were more than a dozen mechs in the small space and three times as many students.

At eleven o'clock, Yancy Lyndon showed up. He jumped atop a stool in the center of the room, and all but one of the lights went out, quieting the crowd of students. "If I may have your attention, gentlemen . . ." His dark eyes swept the room until he found Petra, and he inclined his head with a tiny, mocking bow. "And lady."

Several of the other students snickered, but she refused to let it bother her, holding her chin high despite the flush in her cheeks. Let them laugh. A swell of prideful determination replaced the fear and doubt in her chest. She'd win this damn tournament and show them who was the better engineer.

Yancy spread his hands wide. "Engineers! If you will join me in the ring, I'll introduce our combatants."

Petra exhaled a shaky breath. This was it.

Rupert nudged her in the side. "You can do this."

"I know."

As the students formed a circle, the other mech engineers elbowed their way to the center of the room. Petra followed, taking up position at the end of the line, the last to enter the spotlight.

"So you decided to come after all," said the boy next to her—Selby.

"Well, I couldn't let you boys have all the fun," she said, keeping her voice low as Yancy introduced the first engineers to the crowd.

"You still have time to back out," he said.

"Not a chance."

Yancy reached the end of the line and introduced Selby to heightened applause. The engineer waved at the crowd. "I'm offering you the opportunity to preserve your dignity, Miss Wade," he said, leaning close. "Once you step out onto the floor tonight, there will be no mercy for you. Fight, and you'll only make a fool of yourself. You would be wise to back out while you still can."

The cheers and applause died down as Yancy introduced her to the crowd, the last engineer in the lineup.

"Funny," she said, ignoring their jeers. She turned toward Selby, her brows raised. "I was going to say the same to you."

He met her gaze with a scowl.

"Now if you'll excuse me, I have a tournament to win."

She left him standing in the spotlight and joined Rupert at the edge of the room, quickly checking over the mech's systems one last time.

Once all the mechs were primed and ready, Yancy drew a sheet of paper from his vest pocket and cleared his throat. "And now for the first of our preliminary fights, the combatants will be . . . Reynolds and Fletcher!"

Petra released the breath she had been holding and relaxed.

"Bring forth your mechs," said Yancy, "and let's get started."

Fletcher ended up winning the fight within a matter of minutes, the first to move on to the next round. Then two boys named Crosby and Morgenstern battled it out in the ring, the match going to the latter. Rupert had mentioned before that the German-born engineer was one of the top contenders for this tournament, and she could see why. Crosby's mech was nothing more than a smoldering heap of twisted metal by the end of the fight.

After Morgenstern's win, four more fights followed, impressive shows of mechanical force and clever maneuvering, adding Selby, Greer, Darrow, and Salamanca to the winning engineers.

Only two fights left.

"And now," said Yancy, stepping aside as one of the losing engineers carted his mech out of the ring. "Against towering odds, Miss Petra Wade and her wee mech will face Daniel Bellamy and his colossal mechanical construct, a titan of titans among machines."

Petra swallowed, her blood suddenly cold.

"So, lady and sir . . ." he said with a genteel bow. "Ready your mechs and prepare for battle!"

Sucking down a deep breath, Petra closed her eyes and tried to calm her nerves, curling and stretching her fingers, focusing on the movement of each joint, each muscle. She itched to put them to work.

Rupert nudged her arm and handed her the control box to her mech. "You'll do fine," he said. "Bellamy is a dolt. You'll win, no contest."

Petra absentmindedly nodded, her throat dry as she

took the control box. She tested the switches, going through the motions of maneuvering the mech as she mumbled the controls to herself. *Forward, back, right, left, crouch, dash* . . . The weapons interface was labeled with a square of paper beneath the array of switches. She glanced over the list, whispering the names under her breath.

"Miss Wade . . ." called Yancy. "If you care to join us?"

There was a scattered titter of laughter among the students.

Petra held the control box firmly in her hands. "Fire her up."

Rupert yanked the engine's pull-start cable, manually spinning the crankshaft with a violent tug. The gears locked together with a clunk, and Petra could hear the slow whir of the flywheel as it drove the motion of the pistons. Then, with a spark and a sputter, the engine rumbled to life. Rupert coiled the start cable and slipped it into a spot behind the engine where Petra could fetch it quickly if she needed to restart the mech midbattle—though she hoped it wouldn't be necessary.

The sound of the engine quieted to a low growl, and Petra focused on the gleaming electric spotlight illuminating the center of the room. She swallowed thickly. "Wish me luck."

"You don't need it."

"Rupert . . ."

He rolled his eyes, barely suppressing a smile. "Good luck," he said softly. Then he nudged her forward. "Go show them what you can do."

Petra flipped the mech's controls and led the machine to the center of the room, a glimmer of Bellamy's mech visible under the harsh light. The floor shuddered with each mechanical step, and the crowd of students parted in front of her, their eyes on her machine, and for once, no insults on their lips. The room was silent except for the growl of her mech's engine and its quaking footfalls.

Bellamy was waiting for her.

She had thought perhaps Yancy had overexaggerated in his description of Bellamy's titan construct, but the machine on the other side of the ring was nothing short of a metal colossus, standing over six feet tall and broad as an automobile, one of the brass sentinels she had first spotted when she and Rupert entered the recreation hall. Her mech was miniature in comparison, dwarfed by the monstrous machine. One hit would crumple her tiny construct into a brass pancake.

But despite the mech's enormous size, it had weaknesses . . . gaps in the plating, exposing the inner workings of the machine—namely, the engine and transmission. Most of the mech's joints were exposed as well, the best points of attack for her smaller machine. If she could disrupt the mech's movement and bring its main systems to a height level with her own mech, she might be able to penetrate the sparse plating and sabotage the machine's transmission, incapacitating it.

At Yancy's word, Bellamy stepped forward with his hand outstretched, and they silently shook hands before withdrawing to opposite sides of the ring. Bellamy took up his mech's control panel, poising his fingers over the levers and switches. Petra mirrored his movement, waiting for Yancy's signal.

She inhaled a deep breath, focusing on the titanic construct across the ring. She tuned out everything else, until there was only her mech and his. The spectators, the recreation hall, the other engineers and their mechs all faded into a distant quiet. They were distractions, and she needed to stay alert if she was going to win this fight.

Yancy stepped forward and spoke over the crowd, his voice muffled to her ears. In the corner of her eye, she saw him lift his fingers to his lips, and she tensed, ready and waiting for the sound of his whistle, determined to get the jump on Bellamy.

Then it came, a sharp blast that cut through the tense silence.

Petra slid her fingers over the controls, and her mech lurched forward with a burst of power, launching across the ring with a leaping stride. Bellamy advanced, and Petra thumbed the steering controls, maneuvering her mech around the metal titan. Her fingers danced across the control apparatus, and she ducked beneath a violent swing of the other construct's arm, aiming a quick jab to the back of the knee joint, where the gears were exposed.

There was a grinding crunch as her mech's fist fed into the whirring mess of gears. A belt snapped under the pressure, rubber slapping hard against the metal as it unraveled within the leg chamber. A discordant groan followed, and Bellamy's titan stumbled forward, landing on its damaged knee.

Petra withdrew and assessed the damage. The plating over her mech's right fist had shredded on impact with Bellamy's knee joint, only jagged barbs of twisted metal left, and some of the lower arm had crumpled, likely damaging the hidden weapons beneath.

Across the ring, Bellamy jiggled the switches on his control box and forced his mech upright, leaning all of its weight on its right leg. The left leg dangled uselessly, nothing more than an awkward crutch now. The main belt drive between the leg mechanisms and the engine must have snapped.

She frowned, deliberating her next move. Her only reliable offense now was in the left arm, but Bellamy would likely have her mech in a pulp before she could do enough damage. One step within reach of his mechanically muscled arms and her mech would be nothing more than a dented pile of scrap. She needed to play it smart, find another weakness, exploit it, and deliver a debilitating blow to ensure her victory. But the titan's engine was too far out of reach for her smaller machine. She would need to bring the torso closer to the floor in order to disable the transmission.

"Scared, Wade?" called Bellamy from across the ring.

A few of the other students laughed, but she ignored them.

If he thought his goading would make her do something stupid, he was wrong. The advantage was hers, albeit a small one: his mech couldn't move. Hers could, but if she got within range of the construct's massive arms, it would take only one strike to put an end to the fight.

Unless . . .

If she could maneuver her smaller machine fast enough, get close enough to his remaining good leg to push the mech off-kilter, she might have a chance.

She eyed Bellamy across the ring, his face drawn in concentration, waiting for her to act. She would have to distract him, break his guard.

"Hey, Bellamy."

"What?" he spat.

Flipping a switch on the control box, she activated the transport wheels on the bottom of the mech's feet. All she needed was a second or two, a slight delay in his reactions. If she could get past his defenses, knock the mech to the floor, the fight would be as good as hers.

She poised her fingers over the controls. "Tell me how it feels, knowing you're about to lose to a girl."

He scoffed, his arms relaxing slightly as he glared at her. "You wish."

She smirked. It was enough.

Diverting maximum power to the machine's legs, Petra launched her mech across the ring, using the transport wheels like supercharged skates—moving too quick for Bellamy to react in time. Her mech slammed into his with a crash and then careened wildly off to the side of the ring. With the flip of a switch, she retracted the mech's wheels, and its feet scraped across the floor with an earsplitting screech before finally drawing to a halt.

Bellamy's machine swayed from the force of the impact.

She darted forward again, her mech thundering across the ring with heavy footfalls. The titan aimed a swing at her, but missed, too off balance to land a square blow. Positioning her mech behind his, she reared back with her machine's damaged fist and punched through the back of the titan's uninjured knee, emitting a screech of grating metal as the gears tore through the remaining plating.

"Come on, come on . . ."

Finally, there was a wail of strained gears, a heavy clunk, and the damaged leg buckled under the weight of the machine, crashing heavily to its knees.

One small push, and the engine would be in range.

Petra directed her mech forward, but the thick cord connecting the machine to the control box had caught under the legs of the fallen mech.

She was trapped.

Seeing her predicament, Bellamy's fingers flew across his control panel, and before Petra could react, one of his mech's clunky hands grabbed the taut cord and pinned Petra's machine, the other arm pulling back for the final blow.

Petra pressed her mech forward, but Bellamy had given her too short a leash.

She couldn't move.

But she had one last trick up her sleeve—one no one would expect.

Sending a silent thank you to Emmerich and his automaton, she pressed a small switch on the back of her control panel and prayed the device would work. With a hiss, the coupling between cord and mech snapped free, and the cable whipped back as Petra's mech bowled forward—just as Bellamy's mech struck. The blow glanced off her mech's plating and crashed to the ground with thundering force, throwing her machine into the ring of spectating students.

Petra let out a breath. Step one complete.

Bellamy laughed, letting his control panel fall slack in his hand. "What was that about me losing, Wade?"

Petra yanked the remainder of the cord from the bottom of her control box and flipped a lever at the top of the panel, her heart pounding.

Now for step two.

Her fingers slid over the controls, and with a blissful whir of gears, her machine moved. The students at the edge of the ring jumped away in surprise as the mech rose to its feet and faced Bellamy's machine once more, the engine purring musically in the ensuing silence.

She allowed herself a smile.

Bellamy gaped at her. "How . . . ?"

She poised her fingers over the controls. "Science."

Using the wireless switchboard, she pressed her mech forward and maneuvered it under the other machine's lowered torso—just in range of the primary systems. She opened the mechanical fingers of her mech's one good arm and gripped the edge of the titan's sparse plating, peeling the metal away from the frame with a violent wrenching screech, and exposing the transmission gears.

Bellamy recovered from his surprise and tried moving his construct away, but too late. Extending the hidden retractable blade at her mech's wrist, she reared back and jammed the thick dagger into the transmission.

Gears grated against the metal edge, grinding to a crunching halt before the knife snapped cleanly in two, the broken blade stuck in the stalled gears. The machine groaned as Bellamy tried to push the mech to its feet, his fingers roaming across every switch affixed to his control box, but the mech only shuddered, smoke rising from its damaged torso.

Off to the side of the ring, someone began to count.

At four, the engine stalled, and with a shudder of straining gears and a sudden pop of electricity, the heavy machine groaned to a standstill, incapacitated.

Silence followed, the crowd gaping in soundless disbelief.

Petra smiled, a laugh bubbling up her throat.

She had won.

Rupert ran forward and collided into her, a giant grin on his face. "You did it!" He hoisted her into the air in a tight hug and spun her around in a circle before lowering her back to the floor, still grinning. "Told you."

She pushed her hair from her eyes and glanced at

Bellamy, gaping at her from across the ring, his control box limp in his hand.

Yancy stepped forward, running his fingers over his short hair. "Well . . ." he said, fighting back a tight-lipped smile. "It appears Miss Wade has . . . won."

Bellamy found his voice then. "She cheated!" he said, pointing an accusing finger at her. "I demand her disqualification."

"You know the rules," said Yancy. "She won—fairly, I might add."

"But she can't have," he said, his brows drawing into a frown. "She's a—she's a *girl*."

"Yes," he said, failing to suppress a laugh. "Yes, she is."

"But she isn't a real engineer. She shouldn't even be here," said Bellamy. "She should be disqualified!"

"On what grounds?" she challenged. "I beat you fair and square. I incapacitated your mech. The match is mine."

Bellamy glared at Yancy. "*You* said I'd beat her, that she had no chance of winning. This was supposed to be a bye match, a sure win."

"It seems I was wrong," he said, a smile twitching at the corner of his mouth. He glanced toward Petra then and nodded approvingly, the most acknowledgment she'd ever gotten out of any of the other engineers. Then he turned toward the crowd. "The match is decided!" he said, flourishing his arms with a sweeping gesture. "Miss Petra Wade will move on to the next round, and Daniel Bellamy is hereby eliminated."

Bellamy threw his control apparatus to the ground, where it split into a mess of metal and wires. Rupert wrapped his arms around her again, hugging her close, and she couldn't help but grin, her cheeks flushing from the excitement of winning the match. She could hardly believe it.

"Now, if the previous combatants will clear the floor," continued Yancy, "we'll move on to our final fight of the night!"

Petra took up her control apparatus and maneuvered the mech out of the ring, returning to the edge of the room. Rupert helped her push the machine up against the wall, the metal plating still warm from the fight.

"Impressive."

Petra turned to find Selby standing a few feet away.

"What do *you* want?" she asked.

"Merely to offer my congratulations," he said stiffly. "I didn't think you had it in you, Wade."

"Told you I'd win."

Selby scoffed. "You were *lucky*. Bellamy underestimated you and lost, a miscalculation on his part. No one else is going make the same mistake again."

Petra straightened, the taste of her victory souring slightly. "I'll win the next one too. You'll see."

"Perhaps . . ." he said. "But you'll need a lot more than luck to make it through the next round. You're up against Darrow next, and he's smarter than Bellamy." He glanced at her mech disapprovingly. "You had the element of surprise this time. You won't have it again."

"Thanks," she said, narrowing her eyes. "I'll keep that in mind."

"Then I'll see you at the next match." He nodded curtly and then turned away, pushing back through the crowd to where the final fight was in full swing.

"What the hell was *that* about?" she muttered, watching him go.

Rupert nudged her arm with a grin. "I think he's starting to like you."

CHAPTER 6

Petra knocked at the door to Vice-Chancellor Lyndon's office and peered inside. "You wanted to see me, sir?"

The vice-chancellor glanced up from his desk, a sheaf of paper in his hands. "Ah, Petra . . . Have a seat. I'll be with you in a moment."

She opened the door wider and stepped inside the stately office, planting herself in one of the hard wooden chairs across from his desk as she waited for him to finish. Shelves and cabinets lined the walls of his office, displaying various awards and certificates, photographs, trinkets, and small mechanical inventions. She hadn't forgotten the time she had torn this room apart, trying to find evidence pinning him as a conspirator within the Guild, the same night she discovered the truth of the conspiracy and failed to put an end to it . . . the night she lost Emmerich to his father.

"Now . . ." Vice-Chancellor Lyndon set aside the

stack of paper and regarded her over the rims of his glasses. "I asked you here because I received the list of engineers proposed for the quadruped project," he said, producing a thick sheet of paper from the top drawer of his desk. "I understand that your first review meeting for the quadruped design is scheduled for later this week, and I thought you might like to review the list before I signed off on it."

She took the list from his hands and immediately scowled at the name of her supervising engineer, scrawled in thick black ink at the top of the page. *"Calligaris?"* She dropped the list in her lap. "He's the one leading the project?"

"I'm afraid so," said Lyndon. "Professor Calligaris is Julian's personal appointment. Not my first choice of supervisors, but I couldn't actively challenge the nomination without—"

"I know."

If Lyndon openly challenged Julian in front of the council, Julian might begin to suspect the vice-chancellor of aiding Petra and working against him. Lyndon had told her as much before.

But Calligaris was Julian's spy, so deep in his confidence that whatever Calligaris might see or hear, Julian would know about it within the hour. She scanned the rest of the list, wondering who else was in Julian's pocket. How many more of his spies had been placed on the project? She paused at the last name on the list and glanced up at Lyndon.

"I didn't know Yancy was a Guild engineer."

"Student engineer. He devotes his workshop hours to Guild projects in conjunction with his studies."

"What does he specialize in?"

Lyndon sighed and removed his glasses. "Weapons," he said darkly, forcing a grim smile to his face as he cleaned the lenses of his spectacles. "My son is our resident weaponry specialist. He'll be designing the weapons for the quadruped, as he did for the original automaton."

Petra frowned. "I didn't know that was him."

The vice-chancellor nodded gravely, replacing his glasses on his nose. "It's certainly not the field I would have chosen for him."

She stared at the list of names in front of her, her stomach sinking.

"Does he know?" she asked. "About Julian and the war?"

The vice-chancellor shook his head. "No. He has too much else to concern himself with to question the Guild's leadership. He's only doing what he thinks he must, to protect his country, his family. For him, that means building weapons with which to defend ourselves. I'm sure he thinks it's noble."

"But you don't."

"No," he said. "There is nothing noble about war."

Petra pressed her lips together, biting back the urge to ask him why he made no effort to stop it, why he played so willingly into Julian's plans, letting this war happen without so much as a complaint. He had a part to play, so he said, and that involved faking ignorance of Julian's plot, but he had played the part so well she sometimes wondered if he was trying to stop the war at all. He needed to take a stand, to put a stop to Julian's madness, but he just sat behind his desk, ruminating over his inability to do anything.

The vice-chancellor cleared his throat and gestured to the list of names in her hand. "Do you find the proposed engineers acceptable?"

She handed him the paper. "Everyone but Calligaris."

The vice-chancellor leaned forward in his chair, his face stern as he took the list back from her. "You need to be careful, Petra—especially now. Julian already suspects you of planning to sabotage the quadruped project. After the stunt you pulled in the proposal meeting, withdrawing your project from consideration unless the council offered you access . . ." He shook his head. "If he catches you acting against him—"

"I know the risks, Vice-Chancellor," she snapped. "Everything I've done, everything I've *tried* to do to stop this war, I've done it on my own, knowing full well what will happen if I'm caught. And what have you done? You said you would help me, but all you've done is sit back and tell me to wait. You're the vice-chancellor, for goodness' sake. Why can't you *do* anything?"

"I've *tried*, but there is only so much I can do when I'm overruled on every decision we make. The rest of the council is all but convinced of Julian's cause. But you still have allies here, Petra. I'm on your side. Emmerich is too."

"And what exactly has he done?" she asked, her chest growing tight. "At least I'm *trying*. While you and Emmerich sit there, I'm still fighting, still trying to find a way to stop him. Which is more than I can say for either of you."

The vice-chancellor removed his glasses and kneaded the crease in his brow. "I know you're frustrated, Petra. I know you want to fight back, but it isn't the right *time*. We must be patient. We must wait until we have the evidence we need, only acting when the opportunity is right," he insisted, the same argument she had heard a hundred times before. "Emmerich understands this. I wish *you* would."

She glared at him. "And *when* will it be the right time? The longer this goes on, the harder it will be to stop him—don't you see that?"

"The time *will* come. We just have to be ready when it does."

Petra wanted to growl her frustration at him, but she bit back the urge. It was no use arguing. She wasn't going to change his mind. She had tried enough times before to know that nothing she said was going to make any difference.

She stood up from her chair and started toward the door.

"Just be careful, Petra," he said, his voice soft. "You're all that's left of your mother. She'd never forgive me if I let anything to happen to you."

Petra hesitated at the door, her fingers outstretched,

hovering over the curved handle. "I would think she'd rather you helped me."

"I'm doing what I can, Petra. I wish you could see that."

She swallowed against the tightness in her chest and curled her fingers around the rigid brass handle. "It's not enough," she whispered, pushing through the door into the hall.

It would never be enough.

Petra arrived first to the conference room, ten minutes before the scheduled review meeting with the rest of her engineering team. She took a seat at the far end of the table and waited, her stomach in knots. If the other engineers found her sabotage, if they recognized it for what it was . . . She clutched her bag in her lap, gripping the fabric until her knuckles turned white. No, she had been careful, deliberate. They wouldn't find it—*couldn't*. Her sabotage was meticulously hidden. She was safe.

As four o'clock neared, the others began to arrive, eyeing her with equal measures of curiosity and suspicion. She wondered what they'd been told, if they knew what project they would be working on, or who had designed it. Yancy was one of the last to enter. He spotted her at the end of the table and nodded in greeting before taking the seat across from her, a bemused look on his face.

At precisely four, Professor Calligaris entered the room, and conversation settled to a quiet murmur as he took up position at the head of the table. "Afternoon, gentlemen," he said, pointedly ignoring Petra. "Now that we are all here, I would like to—"

The door creaked open, cutting Professor Calligaris short, and everyone turned their attention to the man standing in the doorway. Petra's mouth soured, a cold chill creeping up her spine. *Of course he'd show.*

"Oh, don't let me interrupt you, Alonzo," said Julian, his charismatic smile almost venomous as he took the nearest open seat. He surveyed the assembled engineers with a genial expression, casually crossing one leg over the other. "I am merely here to observe on behalf of the council. Please continue."

"Of course, Minister," said the professor. "As I was saying . . . now that we are all assembled, perhaps we may make introductions. Then we can get on to discussing the project." He gestured to the nearest engineer. "If you please."

The engineers introduced themselves one by one, giving their name and expertise. When the circle of introductions reached Petra, Calligaris did the honors for her. "This, as you may have guessed, is Miss Wade," he sneered. "She is here on probationary appointment by the Guild to observe the development of the project and provide whatever input is required of her. Though I should like to impress upon you all that she is *not* an active Guild engineer—student or otherwise. She is our project consultant, nothing more."

"Consultant?" said one of the older engineers. "And what expertise could she possibly have for a project of this caliber?"

Petra bristled at his tone. "Well, I know exactly how it's supposed to work, for one. I'm the one who designed it."

Across the table, Yancy arched an eyebrow at her.

The engineer scoffed. "She can't be serious."

"She is," said Julian, regarding the engineer with a sedate stare before rising from his seat. He walked the perimeter of the room in silence, each step deliberate and precise. He stopped just behind Petra and rested his hands on the back of her chair. She heard him take a deep breath, his imposing presence drawing the attention of the entire room. "As the quadruped's designing engineer, the Guild believes her expertise will be vital to the project's success, and I am sure Miss Wade will more than prove herself in the months to come," he said, his words edged with double meaning—she would prove her loyalty, or else. "If you have any issue with her designs, now would be the time to address them," he went on. "We can afford *no* mistakes."

The pressure of his shadow loomed over her, and she struggled not to shy away from his close proximity, her skin prickling like mad. Finally, after an eternity of smothering silence, he withdrew and returned to his seat on the other side of the room, but the itch between her shoulders remained.

"I trust you will all do your part to ensure the production of the quadruped proceeds to the *best* of your ability," he said, surveying the table of engineers with languid ease. His copper eyes wandered to Petra then, and she felt the full impact of his weighted words. "Now, please . . ." he said, gesturing for them to continue. "I should like to see what you think of this machine and its capabilities."

With a nod from Julian, Calligaris withdrew the copies of her schematics from his leather portfolio and divided them among the engineers. The collected men examined the pages with undivided scrutiny, retrieving pencils and drafting paper, mechanical calculators, slide rules and mathematical compasses, writing notes in the margins of the schematics. Petra distracted herself from Julian's keen stare and glanced over the familiar designs. Her imperfect calculations and measurements were still there, the numbers determined within a hairsbreadth of an error. The failsafe remained intact.

No one had found the faults in the design.

Yet.

And if they did . . . she hoped her errors would seem genuine, not the deliberate mistakes of a desperate plan. The others already doubted her as an engineer; perhaps they would expect such faults, or write them off as a product of her supposed inexperience.

After several minutes of concentrated silence, Yancy was the first to speak up. "What sort of combat are we expecting this particular model to see? I assume active battle rather than defense, judging by its proposed mobility," he said, glancing at Julian and then Calligaris for affirmation before turning back to the designs. "In that case, according to these load calculations, we could mount two Agars on either side of the control cabin here," he said, pointing to the designs, "using rotating barrels to compensate for overheating. Without a gunner, I'll need to equip the interior with hoppers for reloading and maintenance, but I should be able to fit both guns with an automatic firing mechanism instead of a manual crank. For reload, we can design an automatic system to repack the shells and feed them back into the hopper at a rate of . . ." He scribbled some figures down on a piece of paper. "Sixty rounds per minute. Maybe ninety if I divided the reload between two chutes."

He drummed his fingers across the design. "Now, if we're looking for more firepower, we could hang a Gatling gun underneath, mounted to the base of the leg frame here," he said, pointing to the empty space between the machine's four crablike legs. "Anything larger and the recoil will knock it off balance, but a Gatling and a pair of Agars should be enough for general battle, with smaller sidearms attached for close-range combat. While the Agars are slower, the Gatling more than makes up for it. Up to ten times the rate of fire with an automatic ammunition feed."

Petra blanched at the thought.

Julian spoke up from the far end of the table. "That should suffice. The quadruped is intended for general combat, designed to equip one soldier with the firepower of a dozen."

Yancy nodded. "The Gatling will do that and more."

"Then we will focus on equipping the quadruped as you suggest," said Julian. "Does anyone else have suggestions for improvement?"

One of the older engineers adjusted his glasses on his nose and pointed to a roll of calculations printed by his mechanical calculator. "Not arguing the particular layout of the design, but some of these calculations don't add up. The error is slight, mere millimeters in most cases, but enough of a difference that it could lead to malfunction in the primary gear system."

Petra froze, heart pounding as she tried to keep her expression neutral. "Could I see your calculations?" she asked, reaching out her hand.

The man nodded, standing up from his chair and circling the table to where she sat. "See here," he said, pointing to the gear train between the transmission and the driving mechanism for the legs. "It's a simple mistake, but the alignment here is off, see? And these two gears don't quite match up."

She nodded absentmindedly, acutely aware of Julian glaring in her direction. "I see what you mean," she said, poring over the engineer's notes. "All right, so if we adjust this one here . . ." She glanced at his calculations, though she knew the exact adjustment that needed to be applied. " . . . a two-millimeter expansion in the gear's diameter should fix the drive issue. And if we lengthen this axle according to your numbers, that should fix the alignment issue, yes?"

The engineer nodded. "That's what I was thinking."

The meeting went on that way for hours, the engineers all working together to draft a fresh set of schematics to accommodate the adjustments to the quadruped's design, but with each mistake the engineers pointed out, Petra's heart sank a little lower in her chest. Every mistake they found was one less hiccup in the quadruped's manufacture, counteracting the extended deadline she had so desperately tried to buy herself.

She tried not to react, tried not to show her fear, but inside she was terrified, worried that Julian could see through her guarded responses and false excuses as the engineers found mistake after mistake.

If he suspected the truth, she was doomed.

When the meeting finally ended a few hours later, the quadruped design approved and finalized, Petra exhaled a shaky sigh of relief. Not one of the engineers had discovered the clockwork failsafe she had built into the machine. It was a bittersweet victory after the unfortunate discovery of her less subtle sabotage attempts, but a victory nonetheless.

As the other engineers gathered their things to leave the conference room, Petra slung her bag over her shoulder and stood, looking forward to spending the evening with Rupert, repairing the damage to her mech and preparing the machine for the next fight, just a few days away now. She felt Julian's eyes on her as she headed for the door, but she didn't slow down, hoping to escape him before he thought to threaten her again. She squeezed between two of the older engineers and pressed against the door, already thinking of how she might equip the mech against Darrow's underhanded tactics.

"Miss Wade . . ." Julian called after her.

Petra faltered, and the pair of older engineers brushed past and stepped into the hall. As much as she wanted to trail after them, her feet were cemented to the floor, a chill crawling up her spine as she lowered her hand from the door.

"Stay a moment," said Julian, his tone betraying nothing. "I would like a word in private."

She swallowed against the tightness in her throat, hardly daring to turn around for fear of giving herself away, but she could not hesitate, not now.

Clutching her bag with tight fingers, she strode away from the door and pressed herself against the opposite wall, Julian's gaze following her with the patience of a viper. The remaining engineers filed out of the conference room, until there was only Petra, Julian, and Professor Calligaris, who exchanged a few muted words with Julian before he too slipped out.

Julian closed the door behind him, and the latch clicked loudly in the empty conference room.

"Do you take me for a fool?" he asked, breaking the silence. His voice was calm, but there was a deadliness lurking beneath the surface. She could feel it. "Did you think I would not see what you were trying to do?"

Petra shook her head. "I don't—"

"Do not *lie* to me," he hissed, a muscle twitching

in his jaw as he drew away from the door and faced her. "I warned you what would happen if you tried to sabotage this machine, what would happen if you continued to defy me."

"I did as you asked," she said, her knuckles white. "I designed your war machine."

"A *faulty* war machine," he snapped. "You may have deceived the other engineers into thinking those *errors* of yours were nothing more than miscalculations, but I know you better than that. You do not make mistakes—not like this. No, this was intentional. This was sabotage."

"And why would I sabotage the design?" she countered, determined not to let her fear of him show. "You made it clear what would happen if I tried."

"Yet you seem to need a reminder," he said, his voice rising. "I offered you a chance to cooperate, Miss Wade. I offered you amnesty. And yet you continue to rebel, to defy me at every turn. That ends today."

She faltered, her mouth suddenly dry. "What do you mean?"

"I have allowed you too much freedom," he went on, his voice hardening. "But no more. From this point forward, you answer to me. No more distractions. No more opportunity for disobedience. You want to be a part of the Guild? Very well. But you will operate on *my* terms."

A soft knock sounded at the door, and Julian crossed the room and turned the handle, opening the door to reveal a pair of black-uniformed coppers in the hall-way, the chief enforcers of Guild justice—and fiercely loyal to Julian.

Julian turned toward her again. "It is time you face the consequences of your actions," he said, his voice firm. "Consider your studentship at an end. You are hereby transferred to the custody of the Royal Forces. Everything you do now will be reported directly to me."

Petra glanced from the coppers to Julian, her heart sinking. "You don't have the authority."

"I think you'll find that I do," he said with a grim smile. "And if I discover any further attempt to ob-struct the completion of the quadruped prototype, if any evidence of sabotage reaches me, I will not hesitate to have you hanged for treason." He let the weight of his words linger in the air for a moment. "Do we un-derstand each other?"

"You can't do this," she said, shaking her head. "Vice-Chancellor Lyndon—"

"The vice-chancellor has no power here," he said. "The Guild is my domain now, Miss Wade. You would do well to remember that." He turned toward the cop-pers waiting outside. "Take her to the Royal Forces office at once. Colonel Kersey will know what to do with her."

"Yes, sir."

Without further preamble, the two men grabbed her and ushered her away from the conference room, their gloved hands forceful, unyielding. She stumbled forward, risking a glance over her shoulder. Julian watched her go, his expression hard and calculating.

What did he mean to do with her now?

"Petra?"

The familiar voice wrested her from her thoughts, and she turned around to find Rupert leaning against a niche in the wall, his hands in his pockets. He stepped away from the wall as they approached, his eyes sweeping over the black uniforms of her two escorts, their tight grip on her arms.

"Petra, what's going on? What's happened?"

One of the coppers detached from her side and blocked him from coming any closer. "Nothing of your concern. This is Guild business. Move along."

Rupert ignored him, quickly sidestepping the officer. "Where are they taking you?"

"To the Royal Forces office," she explained, before either of her guards could stop her. "My studentship has been revoked. Julian, he—"

The guard to her right silenced her with a hard squeeze. "Quiet."

"Julian?" Rupert paled. "The minister?"

She nodded, wincing as her guards dragged her forward at a faster pace, their hands like iron vices on her arms. Rupert hurried to catch up.

"Petra, talk to me," he pleaded. He knew the implications of that name, knew the vendetta Julian had against her, the threats he had put on her life. "Tell me what's going on."

"I—"

"One more word, and I'll report both of you to the minister," answered the copper to her right. They came to the end of the hall and stopped in front of the lift shaft. The guard pressed a button to summon the lift.

But Rupert persisted. "Yancy said you stayed behind after the meeting. What happened?"

Petra stared at the blinking lights above the lift doors, her heartbeat quickening as the elevator sped up toward them, cables and gears whirring behind the metal gates. What could she say? What could she tell him that wouldn't land her in even more trouble? She couldn't tell him the truth, not here, not in front of her guards. Any word about the quadruped or her supposed sabotage would be equal to admitting treason.

The bell above the doors rang, and the lift slowed to a stop in front of them. The circular glass doors revolved open, pushing the lift gates aside, and the coppers shoved her forward, forcing her into the mechanical cylinder of glass and gears. Rupert watched helplessly, unable to stop them.

"What happens now?" he asked, his voice hoarse.

She shook her head as the two Guild coppers joined her in the lift. "I don't know."

"We'll fight it," he said, stepping forward as the glass door slowly closed between them. "I'll go to the vice-chancellor, appeal to the council if I have to. He can't take away your studentship just because it suits him."

The door slid shut, and Rupert pressed his fist against the glass, the line of his shoulders tense. "He can't do this to you," he said, his voice muffled. "He *can't*."

With a low hum, the lift gears whirred to life, and with a shuddering jolt, the platform began its descent, slowly sinking below the floor.

Petra met Rupert's eyes, her fate sealed. "He already has."

The quick consideration

With a low hum, the lift gears whirred to life, and
with a shuddering jolt, the platform began its descent,
slowly sinking below the floor.
Petra met Robert's eyes, her hate-seated "Hie of
ready for.

CHAPTER 7

Petra drifted through the University in a trance, faces
and voices blurring into an indistinct haze. The vi-
brant brass-and-copper world she had inhabited for the
last several months bled of all color and sound, leaving only the noise of her rapidly beating heart, pulsing
through her ears like an executioner's drum.

She stopped suddenly, held fast by the tight grip of
her twin shadows, and the world spiraled back into
motion. She faced the door to the Royal Forces office,
branded by the thin, brass plaque affixed to the door.
Her worst nightmare made real.

Julian had caught her in her sabotage, had seen
through the guise of her miscalculations and recognized the intent behind the mistakes.

She should have known it would never work.

One of her black-uniformed escorts knocked on the
office door. "Miss Wade for you, sir."

"Send her in."

The stoic officer turned the handle and pushed open the door, gesturing Petra inside. With no other choice, she sucked in a deep breath, gritted her teeth, and entered the room, the door shutting soundly behind her.

A large desk sat in the middle of the room, and behind it, the broad-shouldered officer she had often seen at her Guild proposal meetings, his red uniform decorated with a multitude of ribbons and medals. The nameplate on his desk read COL. KERSEY.

The colonel pushed aside his work and glared at her over his prominent mustache. "You're the one Goss sent?"

Petra nodded. "Yes."

"Stay here," he said, getting up from his chair. He circled around the desk, cracked open the door, and peered into the hall. "Miles," he barked. "Where's Cartwright? I have a job for him."

Petra glanced around. She knew that name.

"He's in his bunk, sir," answered the soldier in the hall. "I'll get him."

"Make it quick."

The colonel drew back into the room, leaving the door ajar as he shuffled back to his desk. He sat down and leaned forward in his chair, the seat creaking beneath his weight. "To business, then. By the minister's order, all activities in conjunction with your student-ship shall cease at once," he said dispassionately. "You will be moved into the engineer dormitories, where you will reside for the duration of the quadruped's production. A letter will be delivered to your family, informing them of your residency at the University, and your professors will be notified of your suspension. Henceforth, you will be accompanied at all times by a military escort, who will supervise and report your activities to me and the minister as necessary."

Just like that, her freedom was gone.

The few things she had worked so hard to achieve—her studentship, recognition, respect—gone. No more classes. No visiting family or Mr. Stricket now. No more nights working on the mech with Rupert.

There was nothing left to her but the war machine.

"Cartwright will keep an eye on you," continued the colonel. "He will ensure you obey the minister's restrictions and escort you to and from your workspace. He is a junior officer, but his word comes from me, and by that extension, the minister. You will obey any orders he gives, understand?"

Petra nodded slowly.

"Good."

There was a knock on the door. "Sir? It's Cartwright."

"Come in."

The soldier stepped into the office, his uniform jacket unbuttoned and golden-brown hair disheveled. His gray-blue eyes swept the room as he entered, focusing on Petra for a moment before turning his attention to the colonel. The corner of his mouth quirked up into a smile, but then he cleared his throat and assumed a rigid posture. "You wanted to see me, sir?"

Colonel Kersey appraised him with an arched brow. "I know you're off duty, lad, but that's no excuse for coming to my office in such a state. Button your jacket and do something about that hair."

"Yes, sir."

The junior officer raked his fingers through his hair, tucked in his undershirt, and did the buttons on his jacket, his movements fluid and precise. When he had his uniform to rights, he clasped his hands behind his back and stood at attention. "Sir."

Colonel Kersey assessed him with a gruff nod of approval. "Better." He rested his elbows on the desk and folded his hands together over the mess of paper and envelopes. "You've been temporarily reassigned," he said, not bothering with idle chatter. "You are now Miss Wade's official military escort for the next several months, effective immediately."

Cartwright frowned. "A military escort? What for?"

"A matter of internal security regarding the quadruped project," said Kersey. "The minister to the vice-chancellor informs me it is necessary to the interests of the Royal Forces that she be monitored for potential actions against the Guild and the quadruped project. Since you were the one to propose her probationary position, I leave her supervision to you. She is to be restricted to University premises, barred from all classrooms, offices, and workshops unless otherwise dictated by the Guild council. Once construction of the quadruped prototype begins, she is to report to her appointed Guild office to perform her duties under the supervision of Mr. Calligaris, and then you will return her to her room. Quarters are being cleared for her as we speak; nearby accommodations will be prepared for you as well."

"And my other duties?"

"Henceforth suspended," said the colonel. "Your primary concern is the supervision of Miss Wade. She must not do anything to jeopardize the success of the quadruped. Understood?"

Cartwright hesitated before answering, glancing at Petra with a flicker of suspicion. "Yes, sir. I understand."

"Good. Now escort Miss Wade to her dormitory—room 738," he said, turning his attention back to the letters on his desk. "I will update you as needed. You may go."

The soldier nodded stiffly and gestured to the door. "After you, Miss Wade."

She glanced back at Colonel Kersey, but he had already turned his attention back to his work. Despairingly, she left the office, and the junior officer followed, closing the door behind him.

The latch clicked loudly, punctuating the finality of her punishment.

She turned away, eyes stinging at the injustice of it all. Emmerich, her studentship, her friendship with Rupert, her *home*—all taken away because she refused to participate in Julian's war. Because of him, because of his dogged determination to use her, she had lost everything. And now she was a prisoner, a captive in the University she had so long strived to join, forced to work on a project that shouldn't exist—that *wouldn't* exist if not for her.

Officer Cartwright watched her warily, folding his arms across his chest. "Are you going to tell me what this is about?" he finally asked. "Or should I guess? From what the colonel said, it can't be good."

Petra glared at him. "By all means," she said, gesturing grandly to the colonel's door. "Ask him."

"I'm asking *you.*"

"Is that an order, *officer*?"

Cartwright uncrossed his arms, the tension in his shoulders easing. "No," he said, his voice gentler. "It's not an order, but—"

"Then forgive me for not answering."

She turned her back on him, cursing herself for being so careless, for falling under Julian's power yet again. She scrubbed her hands over her face and combed her fingers through her hair, her mind a fog. She was trapped, and there was no escape, no clever way to maneuver herself free of Julian's never-ending web. She was alone, and there was no one left to help her.

Sudden footsteps drew her attention down the hall, and she turned to find Rupert rounding the corner.

"Rupert?"

He collided into her with a tight hug. "I came as quick as I could."

"But what are you doing here?" she asked, pushing him away.

He withdrew a step, still clinging to her shoulders.

"I went to the vice-chancellor," he explained. "Told him what happened. He's gone to talk with the minister to set things right. You can't have your studentship taken away like that, not without reason."

Petra frowned. Julian *had* a reason, she thought bitterly, but she couldn't tell Rupert that, not with her military shadow hovering behind her. "Rupert . . ." How could she explain? Even if Lyndon spoke to Julian, nothing the vice-chancellor said could save her now. He had warned her not to cross Julian again, and now it was too late. "Thank you," she finished weakly, knowing it was useless. Nothing would change Julian's mind now.

Rupert glanced at the red uniform beside her. "Who's this?"

"*This* . . ." she said, gesturing toward him with a dismissive wave, "is my military escort."

The soldier straightened and formally offered his hand. "Officer Cadet Braith Cartwright," he said. "I've been assigned to supervise Miss Wade during the production of her Guild project."

Rupert eyed the officer but didn't shake his hand. "Your Guild project?" he said, turning toward Petra with the flicker of grin. She knew that look. "Where are they taking you now?"

"Engineer dormitories," she said quickly, before Officer Cartwright could interrupt her. "Room 738."

A brief smile lifted the corner of Rupert's lips, but he quickly suppressed it. "For how long?"

"I don't know," she said. "The length of the project, I think."

His expression faltered. "And then?"

She shook her head, her chest sinking as she considered the possible futures ahead of her. She croaked out an answer, barely able to force her voice above a whisper. "I don't know."

Rupert gripped her shoulders, a solid physical comfort anchoring her to the world. "We'll fight this, Petra. We'll get your studentship back. We'll set things right. You'll see."

Holding his gaze, she nodded, not daring to speak.

He pulled her into another tight hug. "If you get a chance," he whispered, "give him the slip and meet me in the office. We'll talk more then."

She hugged him back, breathing a little easier. "I'll be there."

He withdrew. "I have to go," he said gently. "But I'll send word if anything changes. Hopefully, the vice-chancellor can do something about this—and soon."

Petra nodded again.

"Take care," he said, offering her one last reassuring squeeze before letting go. He glanced once at Officer Cartwright and then departed, hurrying back down the hall and out of sight.

The junior officer watched him go. "Who was that?"

"A friend."

"What did he say to you just then?" he asked.

She swallowed against the tightness in her throat. "I don't know what you mean."

"He whispered something to you before he went. Don't think I didn't notice. What was it?"

"Nothing."

"Petra—"

"No," she said, whirling on him. A fire burned in her chest. "You do *not* get to call me that. Not now."

He didn't back down. "I'm not your enemy, Petra."

"No, of course not." She scoffed. "You're just my prison warden."

"I didn't ask to be," he said acidly. "So stop acting like it's my fault you're here. You seem to have managed that well enough on your own."

"You don't know anything about it," she snapped. "You haven't the faintest idea of what's really going on."

"Maybe not," he said, holding her gaze. "But I stood up for you. I risked my position and the esteem of my senior officers to help you convince the council—and the Royal Forces—of your allegiance. And now I'm supposed to make sure you don't sabotage your own project? Why? What did you do?"

"I didn't ask for your help."

"No, but I gave it anyway," he replied. "And maybe that was my mistake. You said you weren't what they claimed, and I believed you. I *wanted* to believe you. I thought you were different. Was I wrong?"

"What do you want me to say?" she demanded. "I'm not a traitor. I'm not what they say I am."

"Then why are you here?"

Petra pressed her lips together and glanced away. The answer was simple—Emmerich, the automaton, the decision to bring down a conspiracy, letting Julian turn her into a pawn for his war, and then trying to sabotage his plans . . . There was only person to blame for where she stood now.

"Bad choices," she muttered. "That's why I'm here."

And now she was paying the consequences.

Petra sat in the darkness of her new quarters, her pocket watch open in her hand, ticking soundly against her palm. It had been hours since Officer Cartwright led her up to the seventh floor and deposited her in the lonely dormitory—nearly midnight now. The hall outside was silent, her room so far removed from the rest of the students and engineers that she hadn't heard a single door shut or a pair of footsteps pass by, apart from her guard's pacing. She had the entire floor to herself.

She stared at the door to her room, considering whether or not she dared sneaking out to meet Rupert. Cartwright had retired to his room thirty minutes ago, and she hadn't heard a sound from him since.

If there was a time to escape, it was now.

She hadn't forgotten Julian's warning—she knew what would happen the moment he discovered her sabotage on the quadruped project—but the mech fights were not a part of that. Rupert was not a part of that. The respect she was so close to earning from the other students had nothing to do with it, nothing to do with the quadruped or Julian's plans for war.

She'd be damned if she'd give it up now.

The next fight was no more than a few days away, and she still needed to repair the damage she'd earned in the fight with Bellamy, as well as reconfigure the hidden weapons and replace the broken blade in its left arm. She couldn't do any of that as long as she was stuck in this room.

Steadily getting to her feet, she crept silently to the door and withdrew her mother's screwdriver from her pocket, twirling the familiar tool between her fingers. The bolt was locked from the other side, but it would take far more than a simple lock to keep her contained.

Using the point of her screwdriver, she carefully jimmied the lock, and a moment later, the deadbolt slid open with a loud click, the sound like a hammer in the drowning silence. Petra closed her eyes and waited, listening for any sign of Braith, but the seconds passed in silence. Nothing.

It was now or never.

Holding her breath, she turned the knob and edged the door open, silently praying for the hinges not to creak. When she had space enough to squeeze through, she slipped into the hall, eased the door shut behind her, and set off down the hallway, her stocking-clad feet padding silently across the hard floor. Behind her, the sound of a latch clicked softly, the gentle creak of unused hinges lighting a fire under her feet. She hurried around the corner and gripped the handle to the stairwell door and pushed inside, careful to ease the door shut behind her. Perhaps she had only imagined the sound. Perhaps it was nothing. But she did not dare slow down. She sped down the flight of stairs, skirting past floor after floor.

As she neared the fourth-floor landing, a door opened a few floors above her, and the sound of heavy boot steps drawing down the stairs was unmistakable. She quickened her pace, reaching the ground floor with sweat on her brow, the footsteps treading nearer and nearer. Swallowing against her rapidly beating pulse, she grasped the handle and swung the door open, the taste of freedom just beyond.

But then a slender hand forced the door shut.

Petra didn't need to turn around to see who it was.

"What do you think you're doing?" he hissed.

"Nothing to do with you," she said, not releasing her hold on the handle. "Now let me pass."

"No," he said, positioning himself between her and the door. Officer Cartwright pushed her back a step, no longer wearing his red military uniform, just a plain shirt and trousers. "I have my orders. Now, where were you going?"

"Nowhere."

"If that's true, then I'm sure you won't mind if I report this to the minister in the morning. Since you clearly have nothing to hide."

She glared at him. "If you report me, he'll think I was trying to sabotage the quadruped project."

"But you're not."

It wasn't a question.

"No," she said slowly. "I'm not."

The tension left his shoulders, and he leaned his back against the door, crossing his arms over his chest. "Then why not tell me what it is you're really doing?"

"Because I don't trust you."

"And if I promise not to report you?"

"Isn't that going against your orders?"

He shrugged. "That depends on what you were planning to do."

Petra stared at him, this peculiar officer with his blasé manner and suspicious familiarity. Any other soldier would have dragged her back to her room and reported her to Julian in an instant. But not him.

"What's your game?" she asked.

"Game?"

"Why not report me to the minister and be done with it? Go back to whatever it was you were doing before they assigned you to me. You must have more important things to do than follow me around for the next few months."

"Do you *want* me to report you?" he asked.

"Of course not," she snapped. "You know what will happen to me if you do. What I want to know is why you haven't yet."

He held her gaze a moment longer. "My orders are to prevent you from sabotaging the quadruped project—and I plan to follow those orders—but since the quadruped isn't in production yet, the probability of you doing anything to sabotage it is unlikely. If you can assure me that this has nothing to do with the quadruped, then I see no reason to report you."

"Why should I believe you?"

He considered it. "I could give you my word as a British soldier."

"Not good enough."

Cartwright shifted against the wall and studied her, his steely gaze unyielding. "It's clear you have enemies here, Petra. Why, I don't really know. But I don't have to be one of them, not if you don't want me to be." He unfolded his arms and offered his hand. "Let me prove it to you."

She drew back a step, regarding him warily. He seemed sincere enough now, but that didn't change the fact he was a soldier under Julian's direct authority. She couldn't trust him. Even if she did tell him the truth, there was no guarantee that he wouldn't report her mech and her subcity office to the Guild—and then that would be taken from her too.

"And if I refuse?" she asked.

He lowered his hand. "I'm not going to threaten you, Petra," he said, the familiarity in which he kept using her name irksome. "But if you *don't* tell me . . . if you insist on sneaking around and hiding things from me, I'll have no choice but to report your actions to the Guild. My orders are clear. If I don't know for certain what you're up to, how can I tell my superiors that you aren't doing exactly what they fear? Agreeing to keep quiet about something unrelated to the quadruped is one thing, but if you're caught out of bounds, it will be more than just you who gets in trouble. Now, I'm willing to risk that. But I need to know what I'm risking it for."

"You would be so willing to trust me?" she asked. "After everything you've been told?"

"You said you weren't what they claimed."

"I'm not."

"Then prove it."

There was a hint of a smile at the edge of his mouth, and she was reminded painfully of a warm summer day, when a dark-haired engineer had challenged her with those same words, daring her to prove her skill, to trust him when she had no reason to believe that he was telling the truth.

"We don't have to be enemies," he went on, offering his hand again. "You can trust me, Petra. At least give me the chance."

She stared at his outstretched hand. Could she? Could she trust him? This soldier, who was so willing to disregard his orders to keep a secret, not even knowing what it was? If she trusted him, and he betrayed her . . . it wasn't only her freedom she would lose. He could condemn her to death.

But if he was sincere, if he was willing to trust her, to keep her secrets as long as they had nothing to do with the quadruped, perhaps she could give him this chance. Perhaps she could even gain his loyalty, prove to him that she wasn't a traitor, that she wasn't an anti-imperialist allied against the Guild. It couldn't hurt to have an ally in the Royal Forces, not when everyone else in the world was against her.

"All right, Officer Cartwright," she said uneasily, stepping forward and taking his hand with a firm shake. "It's a deal."

He smiled. "Please . . . call me Braith."

Petra led Braith across the first floor, keeping to her usual paths as she navigated from the dormitories to the main workshop and down the stairs to the storage wing on the far side of the building. No one saw them. It was well after hours and no one was working or wandering the halls this late at night.

Neither of them spoke until they came to the end of the storage hall, where she found the panel to the dumbwaiter chute left slightly ajar. Rupert must already be in the subcity office, waiting for her. Not wanting to risk being caught by a stray engineer, she reached forward and swung the door open wide, the hinges creaking loudly.

Braith joined her at the open hatch and peered into the cavernous chute. "What's this?"

Petra couldn't help but smile, remembering Rupert's answer the first time he brought her here. "Our ride."

"To where?"

"You'll see." She pulled the lever and brought the dumbwaiter platform to their level, the gears and pulleys whirring loudly until the lift stopped with a loud clunk. Grabbing the edge of the opening, she hauled herself onto the platform and sat with her skirts tucked under her knees. She glanced up at Braith, still standing in the hall. "Well? Are you coming or not?"

He grinned briefly and climbed onto the platform next to her, admiring the exposed gears, wheels, and cables running up the length of the chute. "Up or down?"

She pulled the door shut and pressed the control lever forward. The drive motor hummed, the gear trains spinning into motion as the pulley cords whirred beside them. "Down."

The lift rumbled downward, sinking deeper into the subcity with each passing second. Braith raised his eyes to the shrinking square of darkness far above them, and Petra caught herself staring at him, trying to puzzle him out. He wasn't just another soldier in a red uniform, another of Julian's pawns. But what did that make him instead?

Electric light spilled into the dumbwaiter chute as the lift reached the bottom of the shaft, and Petra braced herself for the jerky stop. The platform clanged against the landing, and Braith knocked his head against the wall, the same as she had done the first time she rode down with Rupert. She bit back a smile and climbed out. Her damaged mech sat in the middle of the floor, the plating on its right arm snarled and twisted from the fight with Bellamy.

Rupert sat at her desk, slowly twirling a spanner in his hands. "About time," he said, jumping to his feet. "I was starting to think—" He spotted Braith and turned toward her with a frown.

"I know," she said, cutting him off before he could say anything. "I'm sorry. I didn't have much of a choice." She crossed the office and sank against the desk, folding her arms across her chest. "He caught me trying to sneak down here and it was either tell him what I was up to or give up on the fights, and I've worked too hard for this to quit now."

"You could have *lied* to him."

"Maybe . . ." she said, eyeing the soldier doubtfully.

Braith surveyed the cramped office, his gaze sweeping over the desk, the jumble of subcity equipment stacked against the other side of the door, the crates filled with mechanical parts, and finally the mech. "So this is what you snuck out for?" he asked, glancing up at her and Rupert.

She nodded.

"What is it?" he asked, circling the machine. "I don't recall you pitching anything like this to the Guild."

"That's because I didn't pitch it to the Guild," she said.

Rupert leaned close. "It's a risk getting him involved," he said, keeping his voice low. "What if he tells someone?"

"He won't," she said, hoping it was the truth. "He'll be in as much trouble as us if his superiors find out he was here. You're just going to have to trust me on this. I'll take full responsibility if it turns out I'm an idiot."

"Is it a prototype of some sort?" asked Braith.

Rupert shook his head warningly, but she ignored him. She pushed away from the desk and joined the soldier in front of the machine, resting her hands on her hips. "It's a battle mech."

Braith frowned. "A battle mech?"

She faced him, the truth sticking in her throat. Rupert was right. It was a risk telling him, but if she wanted to keep fighting in the tournament, she didn't have much of a choice. She needed Braith on her side.

"If I tell you . . ." she said slowly, "you can't tell anyone else, all right? You can't mention it to any of the other soldiers, not the colonel, not the Guild council or the minister—especially not the minister. Not a word. *No one* can know about this."

He regarded her with a frown. "But what's it for?"

"The other students . . ." she started, nervously wringing her hands. "They've formed a sort of fight ring in the recreation hall, kept secret from the professors and the Guild."

"A fight ring? *Here?*" A slow smile broke across his face, but then he narrowed his eyes, his gaze skeptical. "But what does that have to do with you? And this?" he asked, gesturing to the mech.

"Well," she said, a little hesitantly. "This is my fighter."

"Your . . . fighter?" He glanced from her to the machine, a frown inching across his brow. "Wait, *you* fight? With *this*?"

"How else?" she asked, trying not to laugh as she crossed the room to her supply of spare parts.

Rupert joined her, fetching a rod of welding metal,

goggles, and a portable blowlamp from the toolbox as she collected several small squares of plating from one of the open crates.

"I hope you know what you're doing," he muttered. "If he tells anyone—"

"I know," she whispered.

They exchanged frowns, and he dug through one of the drawers, fetching two pairs of gloves, a set of pliers, and a spanner. "I don't like it," he said, handing her the smaller pair of gloves.

"I didn't expect you to."

She set the fresh sheets of metal on the floor next to the mech, donned her gloves, and sat down to get to work. Rupert offered her the pliers, casting a suspicious glance toward Braith as she started peeling the plating away from the mech's arm.

Braith watched her pry the metal apart, exposing the hidden weapons and contraptions beneath the plating. "And you built it?"

She shrugged. "Rupert helped."

"Don't be modest," said Rupert. "I barely touched the thing. She's the mechanical genius here. Not me."

"So you fight against other machines?" Braith went on, pacing a circle around the mech. "Other engineers?"

"That's the gist of it," she said, assessing the damage to the inner mechanisms. There was a bolt loose in the mech's frame where she had taken the brunt of Bellamy's final attack against her. She held out her hand and gestured toward one of the spanners next to Rupert.

"Are you any good?" Braith asked.

"She's the best," said Rupert, passing her the spanner. "But not if we don't get this repaired before the next fight."

"When's that?" asked Braith.

"Saturday," she answered, tightening the bolt "We don't have a lot of time." She set the spanner aside and wiped her hands on a grease rag as she peered into the metal carcass, noting the bent rods and warped gears that would need to be replaced before the next fight.

Braith watched her work. "And the rules?"

"No projectile weapons or use of steel in construction," she said, returning to her work. She carefully removed one of the damaged gear trains and set it aside. "But once you're in the ring, anything goes. If your mech goes down—stalls out, keels over, whatever— you have fifteen seconds to resume the fight or the match is lost. Last mech standing is the winner."

The soldier nodded. "And how many fights have you done?"

"Just one," she said, digging back into the mech's inner mechanisms. "My next match is against Darrow. He's the third top contender in the tournament—lost to Selby in the semifinals last tournament. He's known to fight dirty." She dismantled another warped linkage and removed it from the machine. "I'll need everything I've got when I go against him in the ring."

And she still didn't have a strategy.

She had relied on the element of surprise for the first fight, but no one was going to underestimate her again, which filled her with a measure of pride. She had already shown that she could stand toe to toe with the best of them. Now she just needed to prove it a second time.

Braith stopped his pacing, drumming his fingers against his arm. "You know what will happen if you're caught with this, don't you? This is a weapon. A very dangerous and very illegal one."

"Yep." She turned another bolt and motioned for Rupert to hand her a different spanner, glancing up from her work to meet the soldier's eyes. "So let's make sure I don't get caught."

A slow grin broke across his face. "What can I do to help?"

begin, which filled her with a pleasure of pride. She
had already shown that she could stand toe to the wall
the best of them. Now she just needed to prove it a
second time.

Braith stopped his pacing, drumming his fingers
against his arm. "You know what we'll ...
tonight with this, don't you? This is a weapon. A very
dangerous and very illegal one."

"Yes." She turned another bolt and reached for
Rupert to hand her a different scanner, glancing up
from her wrist to meet the soldier's eyes. "So let's make
sure I don't get caught."

"A slow grin broke across his face. "What can I do

CHAPTER 8

The night of the second mech battle arrived, and Petra
sat in her dormitory, impatiently counting the minutes until she and Braith could escape to the subcity
office unnoticed. Rupert would be waiting for them
there, running the final checks on her mech before the
fight. They had finished the repairs only that morning,
working through the night.

It was almost ten o'clock when Braith finally
knocked. "You ready?"

Petra launched off her mattress and joined him in
the hall, already wearing her boyish disguise. Braith
was dressed down in a shirt and trousers, his hair tousled and face scruffy after a few days without shaving.
Out of uniform, he looked like any other student at
the University, and she could almost forget what he
really was. Still, he had kept his word so far. He hadn't
mentioned the mech or her secret subcity rendezvous

with Rupert in any of his reports, and she was starting to suspect that he enjoyed it, sneaking around, skirting the rules. He had that sort of anti-authoritarian air about him, an odd quality for a soldier, but perfect for Petra. In a different life, they might have been friends.

They reached the subcity office half an hour later. Rupert was waiting for them, the repaired mech ready for transport.

"You checked all its systems?" Petra asked him.

"Twice. Everything is in order." He glanced at Braith with a frown and leaned close, lowering his voice. "You sure we can't ditch him? The other engineers won't be happy about an outsider attending the fights—especially if they realize who he is."

"He promised not to tell anyone," she whispered, examining the repaired arm. The plating rippled under the light, dented by the many hammer strokes that had reformed its shape. She tested the manual release on the newly added claw, and four sharpened metal fingers unfolded from the mech's fist. "Besides," she said, retracting the claw. "I don't have much of a choice. Either he goes with us, or I can't fight. That was the deal."

"I still don't get why the Guild put you under watch like this. Taking you out of your classes to focus on the project, I can understand, but a military guard? What are they afraid you'll do?"

She shrugged, the truth burning behind her teeth. She couldn't tell Rupert what was really going on— not about the quadruped or her hidden sabotage, not

Julian's suspicions or his threats. The truth was far too dangerous, and she wasn't about to drag him into it too. Rupert was her best friend. She wouldn't condemn him to that fate.

"I know that look," he said, his voice barely above a whisper. "What aren't you telling me?"

She tried to maintain a straight face, but Rupert knew her too well. "I'm sorry," she said, shaking her head. "But I can't. Not this time."

"Why not?"

She pressed her lips into a firm line and glanced over her shoulder at Braith, leaning against the desk with his arms crossed. "I just can't."

"Petra—"

"Is everything ready?" asked Braith, stepping away from the desk.

"Looks to be," she said, swallowing against the feeling of guilt in her chest as she turned away from Rupert. "We should make our way to the recreation hall. I don't want to be late."

She moved aside and Rupert met her eyes over the mech, the tightness in his brow suggesting that the conversation was far from over. She hated to keep secrets from him, but she had no choice. The truth would only make him an accomplice in her sabotage, and she refused to drag him into this, knowing what would happen if she was caught.

Braith and Rupert wheeled the mech to the dumb-waiter chute and hefted it onto the platform, pushing the machine into the far corner.

"There," said Rupert, wiping his hands clean. "We should all fit now."

"Can the lift hold this much weight?" asked Braith.

"You could always take the stairs," suggested Rupert.

Petra rolled her eyes. "We'll fit."

The three of them squeezed around the mech, huddled together shoulder to shoulder. Rupert pulled the lever, and the dumbwaiter inched upward, the additional weight putting a strain on the drive motor. Petra could feel the tension in the pulley cables as they climbed. The gears groaned and whined, the lift creaking and vibrating as they ascended, but the cables held, and after a slow, stifling crawl, they reached the top of the chute and climbed out onto the sixth floor, mech in tow. Then they piled into the next lift and ascended two more floors before emptying out again.

Petra stopped outside the door and laid a trembling hand on the arm of her mech, her heart thumping heavily in her throat. Facing Darrow in the ring wouldn't be easy. He was one of the best engineers in the school and not afraid to fight dirty; the carnage of his last match was ripe in her mind. She would have to be smarter, faster, and a hell of a lot luckier to win. The slightest mistake could lose her both the match and what little respect she had earned since winning the first fight.

She exhaled slowly, letting go of her uncertainties. She could win this. She had to. After what had happened with the quadruped, the mech fights were all she had left. She could not lose, not now.

Rupert took her hand, bolstering her confidence with a tight squeeze. "You ready?"

She nodded. "As ready as I'll ever be."

"**D**ammit!" Petra gritted her teeth, desperately flipping switches across the control panel. "Get up, you stupid thing!"

Darrow's heavy block of a machine had hers pinned, its long, prong-ended arms holding her to the floor. His mech was a hunkered down contraption, a trapezoidal mass of metal on tracked wheels, with three layers of reinforced plating around the engine and a fully rotational swiveling cabin.

While she uselessly tried to wrest her mech free from Darrow's grasp, a pair of panels slid open in the front of his mech, revealing a hefty straight-pane sledgehammer fastened to a pulley drive. Petra heard the grinding lock of a gearbox from inside the machine, and the hammer slowly began to spin. Faster and faster it went as Darrow increased the power output to the drive, until it was nothing more than a circular blur of metal aimed at Petra's mech.

"Petra, move!" shouted Rupert, standing off to the side of the ring.

"I'm trying," she growled, pushing the controls back and forth, trying to break free of the grapple.

The spinning hammer edged closer to her mech's hull, dangerously close to pounding the outer plating of her main fuel tank. If the hammer broke through . . . at best, she would have a fuel leak to deal with; at worst, an explosion. She pressed her lips together and tried to think through the chaos of noise all around her. If she could push his mech off balance, give herself enough of an opening to maneuver her machine into a better position . . .

"Use your legs," she heard Braith shout, his voice cutting through the excited cheers of the gathered students. "Break his stance."

The hammer struck the plating with a cracking blow, sparks shooting off between the two mechs. Petra cringed against the sound, the rat-a-tat-tat of hammer blows shuddering through her bones as she focused her attention on her mech's lower half. The mech's legs were tangled beneath the front of Darrow's machine, but not pinned. Sending a silent thank you to Braith, she rerouted power to the lower half of the machine, her thumbs dancing across the switches of her control panel.

With a deep breath, she planted her mech's feet at the base of Darrow's machine and kicked. Engines strained and tires spun, and with a wrenching scrape of metal, the sharp prongs holding her mech to the floor broke away, and the spinning sledgehammer veered off target, striking nothing but air.

And Petra was ready for it.

Flipping a switch, she extended the mech's newly added claw—four thick blades crafted to withstand well over a hundred pounds of force—and forced the arm into the open panel in the mech's body. Sparks flew as the spinning hammer glanced off the arm's plating, but she held fast, using the edges of her sharpened claw to cut through the hammer's pulley belt, shredding the rubber into paper-thin strips. The sledgehammer fell slack and crashed against her mech's freshly plated arm, crumpling the metal.

That she could deal with. The leaking fuel tank was another problem.

She pulled back, and Darrow recovered, folding his mech's prong-ended arms across the gaping hole left in the center of its body. The sledgehammer dangled uselessly, but it had done its damage. A trickle of petrol leaked from her mech's body, the dark liquid dripping steadily onto the floor. The plating across its chest had buckled and split. Another hit, and she would lose.

She needed to finish the fight—and quickly.

Her best point of attack was the open sledgehammer panel, but she would never avoid Darrow's prongs long enough to do any substantial damage. He'd trapped her twice already, and with her fuel tank leaking, she couldn't survive a third grapple. But if she could jam the mech's arms, prevent him from pinning her again, she might be able to break through the maintenance panel at the rear of its base and disable the mech with an electric shock.

It was the best plan she had.

Before Darrow could prepare a defense, she launched across the ring, reinforced claw at the ready. She slammed into the trapezoidal frame and shoved the claw into the machine's shoulder joint, tearing through the mess of gears and wire beneath. Darrow tried to maneuver out of range, his rubber treads squealing, but Petra had the advantage. She curled her mech's arm around the damaged joint, the harsh grating of metal and gears splintering the air. Then, with a crack like a gunshot, the prong-ended arm snapped free, tumbling to the ground with a clatter of gears.

Rupert let out a cheer, and Petra allowed herself a grin. She hadn't expected that.

Darrow's machine careened toward the edge of the ring, its remaining arm swinging dangerously off balance. Darrow fought for control, rubber treads spinning uncontrollably across the petrol-soaked floor as he aimed the machine toward hers. Petra sidestepped the reckless charge, but Darrow twisted around at the last second, swinging wildly with the one good arm. Not enough time to dodge, she flicked the mech's controls to brace for impact, but her mech wouldn't move. She pressed harder on the switch, but no use.

Metal crunched against metal, sending her machine sprawling across the ring. It crashed hard against the floor and skidded to a screeching, sputtering halt at her feet, smoke rising from the hot metal. A heartbeat passed in tense silence, and behind her, Rupert cursed.

Petra jiggled the controls, pressing the switches to their limit, but nothing. Not even a twitch. She kicked the machine, and a flare of pain throbbed through her foot. "Come on, dammit, get up!"

But the engine only spluttered and wheezed, choking on fumes. The air was thick with it, the smell of leaked petrol and exhaust clouding the room. And then nothing. Just dead silence.

Then someone started to count.

"Shit."

She had fifteen seconds.

Fifteen seconds to get back on her feet.

Fifteen seconds to stay in the fight.

Petra dropped to her knees and grabbed the start cable from its holster, quickly threading the cord around the crankshaft. Sweat dripped from her brow and sizzled on the hot metal plating, her blood thick in her throat, fingers stiff and clumsy as she fed the cable through.

Ten seconds.

Bracing her foot on the mech, she yanked hard on the cable, praying she still had some fuel left. The cord ripped free, and a faint guttering answered, but not enough. *Blast.* She threaded the cable again, exhaling a slow, steady breath as she looped it through, careful to wind it tight. She clutched the cord with both hands and breathed, her rapid pulse outpacing the dwindling countdown.

Three . . .

Two . . .

She pulled, yanking as hard as she could.

The cable ripped free with a metallic whirr, and she stumbled backward into the ring of spectators, falling hard to the floor. Strong arms dragged her to her feet, and the count dropped to zero, the whistle at Yancy's lips. But then the engine rumbled musically, and the sound breathed life back into her bones.

She was still in the fight.

Someone thrust the control box back into her hands, and a familiar voice whispered in her ear. "He'll strike hard and fast to catch you off guard. Be ready." She felt a breath of warmth touch her cheek and then a gentle shove at her back, forcing her back into the ring.

She had less than a heartbeat to prepare before Darrow pressed his mech forward again, not waiting for her to regain her bearings. Reacting almost instinctively, she drew her mech to its feet, fingers flying across the controls as she narrowly dodged the first attack and pivoted hard, targeting a quick jab to the maintenance panel at the rear of his machine. The craggy, damaged claws of her mech's right fist swiped across the plating and ripped the panel free. The square of metal clattered to the floor, exposing a number of wires and glinting metal within the machine's base.

Darrow countered, lashing out with his remaining arm, but she was ready this time. She braced and absorbed the force of the attack, plating crumpling like a metal bruise as she locked her mech's arm around his shoulder, applying maximum pressure to the weak linkage joint.

The two machines skidded across the floor, treads squealing and metal screeching. Petra pressed her machine to the brink, engine whining, praying it would hold on just a little longer, and then, with a twist of the controls, the arm snapped loose, dangling by nothing but a bent rod.

Petra didn't hesitate. His last defense compromised,

she moved her mech into position and dug her bladed fist into the machine's base, not daring to electrocute the systems lest a fire ignite all the leaked petrol in the ring. Darrow tried to escape, but he couldn't gain traction on the petrol-slicked floor as she ripped through gears and wires with brute force, tearing his carefully crafted machine to pieces, not relenting until the telltale sound of engine failure brought the match to its end. She withdrew victorious, warped gears and bowed linkage rods littering the floor at her feet, soaked in petrol and glimmering iridescent in the electric light.

There was no coming back from that.

Petra expelled a sigh of exhausted relief and lowered her control panel as Yancy stepped forward.

"We have our winner!" Yancy gestured to Petra with a grand flourish. "Miss Petra Wade will move on to the semifinals! And Carbrey Darrow is hereby eliminated!"

A cheer rang out, and Rupert joined her in the ring with a tight hug. "Bloody well done," he said brightly. "Best fight I've seen—hands down."

"Are you kidding?" She laughed nervously. "I almost lost."

"You pulled through in the end. That's all that matters."

Students swarmed the ring then, a chaos of cheers, congratulations, and praises all around. She was swept up in the joy of it, bolstered on all sides by the respect and admiration of her fellow engineers. She had done it. She *beat* Darrow.

Yancy shepherded the crowd out of the ring for the next fight, and a pair of wash boys took to the floor to clear the mess Petra and Darrow had left behind. The rest of the students chatted enthusiastically about the fight as she carted her mech out of the ring, some of them calling out further congratulations as she passed by. She hadn't even won the tournament yet, and already she was gaining their approval, their respect.

Even Selby.

As the room cleared, she caught his eye on the other side of the ring, arms crossed, regarding her critically. Then he nodded, a flicker of approval in his usual dour expression. She just grinned.

The next fight began in a racket of clashing metal and groaning engines, and she left the recreation hall with Rupert and Braith, floating on her victory. Winning the second fight put her another step closer to the respect she so desperately desired. She belonged here, and she'd prove it one match at a time if she had to. Eventually, they'd see.

Once the mech was safely tucked away in the subcity office, Petra and Braith left Rupert behind to finish up some last-minute homework and then rode the dumbwaiter back up to the main floor. As they navigated the overstuffed storage wing, the excitement of her win started to wear off, and she yawned, feeling the weight of sleep steal over her.

"You fought well tonight," said Braith, holding the door open for her. It was the first he had spoken since the match.

Petra shrugged. "I wouldn't have won if not for you. When he brought out the sledgehammer, I thought I was done for. You deserve *some* credit."

"It wasn't me who managed to restart an engine in under fifteen seconds or win a fight with a cracked fuel tank," he said, following her down the hall. "You earned that win. You were smarter than him, quicker to execute your attacks—the better engineer hands down."

She smiled, a flush creeping into her cheeks. "Thanks."

"I mean it," he said. "It suits you, Petra—the engineering, building things. I see now why you fight so hard for it. You belong here."

She really did blush at that, unable to articulate a response. She was so used to being challenged, so used to having to fight for approval, she didn't know how to respond. Only one person since Emmerich had accepted her for what she was, and he was sitting three floors below, studying up on advanced aerodynamics. She never expected to find that kind of recognition in a soldier.

The sound of footsteps broke the awkward silence, and Petra stopped, the steps drawing nearer. "Someone's coming," she whispered, touching Braith's arm. She stood, waiting, listening. Then voices followed, distinct in the dark, abandoned halls, and her body went rigid, every muscle turning to lead. She knew that voice, smooth and rich as honey but deadlier than snake venom.

She turned to Braith, a tremor coursing up her spine. *Julian.*

Braith heard him too.

He raised a finger to his lips and gently grabbed her hand, his touch like a jolt of electricity up her arm, unsticking her feet from the floor. Silent as a shadow, he dragged her back down the hall toward the wide staircase that led to the upper levels of the University and the main building. Nestled beneath the stairs was a narrow storage closet, the door ajar. They took refuge there.

Petra stumbled inside, squeezing between a pair of shelves, and Braith followed, leaving the door open just enough to let a crack of light in. There was hardly room enough to stand, much less to breathe, and she was aware of how close she stood to him, pressed together in the cramped storeroom, his clothes smelling of tobacco smoke and boot polish.

The men's conversation soon neared, and Petra shifted toward the door, brushing against Braith to better hear them, but he grabbed her firmly by the arm and held her there, as immobile as a statue. She glared up at him. His grip was almost painful, but she could barely make out his face in the dark, his jawline highlighted by the dim light filtering through the door. She didn't dare speak, but after a moment of rigid stillness, his grip on her arm eased and she turned her attention to the men's voices, growing louder by the second.

" . . . having difficulties pursuing the usual paths for

commissioning a project of this nature," said another man, hesitant. "If we waited until the prototype was closer to completion—"

"No," Julian insisted, the anger in his voice evident. "Contact the manufacturers again and remind them of our agreement."

"But without the proper authorization—"

"To hell with the paperwork!" said Julian, drawing to a stop mere paces from their hiding place.

Through the crack in the doorway, Petra recognized the lividness in his dark eyes, and she shrank back into the safety of the closet, pressing closer to Braith. He touched her arm again, gently this time, and eased her away from the door, turning his face toward the light.

"I have spent too long preparing for this to be stalled by such miserable excuses," Julian went on. "They have the designs now. They've long had their money, the materials, and the connections they need to build what I asked. We have an arrangement. See that it is done."

The other man mumbled something unintelligible in reply, and their footsteps continued—not further down the hall, but up the stairs. Their shoes thudded heavily against the steps as they climbed, shaking trickles of dust from the ceiling.

"What of the French machines?" asked Julian.

Petra frowned, turning her eyes to the cobwebbed ceiling. The men's voices were already beginning to fade as they climbed higher up the stairs, their conversation punctuated by their heavy footsteps. She craned nearer to listen.

"On schedule," said the other man, his tone considerably more eager. "The manufacturers have already begun production, and the first consignment should be ready for deployment within the month."

"Good," he replied. "And Emmerich?"

Petra's breath caught in her throat and she stiffened.

"Cooperating as promised," answered the other man.

"Nothing to suspect?"

"No, sir."

Petra searched the dark shadows above her, aching to hear more, but the conversation slipped out of range. She sank down onto her heels, mind racing as she considered what Julian had said. Something about authorization issues, problems with a manufacturer—that could be anything—but the mention of French machines . . . and Emmerich . . . That could only mean one thing: his plans for war were advancing, and here she was wasting time with the mech fights.

Pressed against her in the cramped quarters, Braith cleared his throat, his breath close enough to brush her hair from her cheek. She started, realizing her fingers were twisted in the folds of his shirt, so wrapped up in her thoughts, her fears, she had forgotten he was there. She let go and flattened against the shelf behind her, bumping into a row of paper boxes. Her skin tingled where she had touched him, and a flush crept up her cheeks, the air in the closet suddenly impossibly warm.

"Sorry," she sputtered. "I didn't—"

"We should go," he said softly, his hand suddenly guiding her toward the door. "Before someone else comes this way."

Petra nodded, grateful he couldn't see her face in the dark. "Right."

Braith peered through the gap in the door, waited a beat, and then ushered her out of the closet and down the hall. Their steps were quick and fleeting over the hardwood floors as they hurried back to the dormitories in tense silence, taking care not to make any noise as they crept up the stairs to the seventh floor. It wasn't until they reached the door to her room that either of them dared to speak.

Braith slid his key into the lock, releasing the deadbolt with a loud click. "We need to be more careful," he said, pushing the door open. A muscle twitched in his jaw, his mouth set in a firm line. "We could have been caught."

Petra only nodded, her stomach still in knots. If Julian caught them out of bounds together, they could both lose their heads.

"What was the minister doing here so late?" he went on, turning toward her. "What were he and his associate talking about?"

Her heartbeat slowed to a crawl.

"You know something about it, don't you? The way you reacted . . . I'm not blind."

Petra chewed on her lip. What could she say? When Julian had mentioned machines in France, and Emmerich . . . She swallowed thickly, a pressure rising up her throat. How could she not react?

"I don't know what you mean," she said stiffly, her voice breaking. She pushed past him into her room, but he touched her arm, holding her in place.

"You do," he said gently, releasing her arm. "And I hate that you don't trust me enough to tell me what it is."

"It has *nothing* to do with you."

He regarded her carefully. "I'm not your enemy, Petra."

"No? Last I checked, you take your orders from Julian."

"What does that have to do with it?"

She seethed. "Everything! That's what you completely fail to understand! That man has taken *everything* from me. You know *nothing* of what he's done, what he plans to do. He—" She bit off the rest of her words, her hands shaking. She could almost tell him everything—about Julian's plans, the conspiracy, the false accusations against her—but she didn't. She couldn't. Braith was a soldier. He couldn't be trusted. Not yet.

He held her gaze, his touch gentle. "I'm not him, Petra."

"No. You just do what he tells you to," she snapped, jerking her arm away. "You're not on my side, Braith. You're on *his*, whether you want to be or not."

"I didn't realize there were sides to choose."

Her anger faltered then, and she searched his face,

his blue-gray gaze like a bleak morning rain. She wanted to trust him. She did. But he was still a soldier. If it came to choosing between her or his duty to the Royal Forces . . . she knew which one he'd pick.

"There are always sides to war," she said quietly, the fight gone from her voice. "You're a soldier, Braith. You should know that by now."

He leaned against the doorframe and crossed his arms, standing less than a foot away. "And what makes you think we're at war?"

"What makes you think that we aren't?"

2 · SECOND POSITION

CHAPTER 9

Just a few days later, Petra received the official summons to begin production of the quadruped prototype—three weeks ahead of schedule.

She should have had more time to prepare, but Julian had plans of his own. Barely a fortnight since the Guild approved the flawed designs, she now stood on one of the upper catwalks of her new workshop, taking in the spectacle of engineers and equipment below. The room was packed full of construction vehicles, crates, toolboxes, and supply carts, the nearest wall lined with rows of desks and cabinets.

"Should we head down to the floor?" asked Braith. He stood rigidly beside her, hands clasped neatly behind his back. He wore his full military garb today—jacket and trousers crisply pressed, boots polished, his hair combed, and face clean-shaven—the perfect image of a dutiful soldier.

Petra wrinkled her nose and headed down the service ladder, her shoes clanging loudly against the metal rungs. She preferred him off duty.

She reached the ground floor and surveyed the busy workshop. Her engineering team unpacked sheets of plating, linkage rods, wires, gears, axles, and pistons from the collection of crates, sorting the machinery by system. Leg mechanisms to the east workstations, electrical and engine parts to the center, control cabin to the west. Yancy Lyndon directed the handling of the weapons, placing the massive cylinders and automatic hoppers against the north wall, where they would remain until the final stages of production.

Overseeing their progress was Professor Calligaris.

Yancy caught sight of her and hurried over. "Glad to see you could make it," he said, tucking a stack of papers under his arm as he reached out and shook her hand. He glanced at Braith beside her, taking in his spotless red uniform and polished boots. "And you are? I don't believe we've formally met."

"Officer Cadet Braith Cartwright, Miss Wade's military escort for the quadruped project."

Yancy turned back toward Petra with a frown, the furrow in his brow so like his father's. "He wasn't the one with you at the last match, was he?" he asked, his voice low.

Petra winced. "About that . . ."

"You've got to be kidding me," he said flatly. "If the other blokes found out you dragged a Royal Forces officer to—"

"You won't tell them, will you?"

"The fights are supposed to be a student thing. If he tells anyone . . ."

"He won't," she said. "Trust me. We'll both be in trouble if anyone finds out about that." She glanced at Braith beside her, his stoic posture betraying nothing. His gaze remained on the working engineers, but she knew he was listening to her every word. She turned back to Yancy, keeping her voice to a whisper. "Having him along is the only way I get to fight, and he's risking a lot even letting me do that. Please don't tell anyone. I can't quit the fights, not now."

Yancy eyed the soldier with a deep sigh. "Fine. I won't say anything. But I can't stop anyone else from finding out themselves. You're on your own there."

"Thank you," she said.

He waved the comment away. "If that's what keeps you in the tournament, so be it. You're a good fighter. I'd hate to see you quit before you're beat."

"Who says I'll be beat?"

"John, for one. And others. Bellamy isn't happy with your win against him in the first round."

"Well, maybe he should have fought better."

"Maybe," he said with a shrug. "But you're up against Fletcher next, and he took second place last tournament. Just don't get ahead of yourself. You still have one fight to go before the finals, and I'd bet my stipend that John will be in the final round. He's the best we have."

"We'll see."

Yancy shook his head with a laugh. "Anyway, Calligaris has already briefed the team on the agenda for today, but if you want, I can catch you up on everything."

Petra scowled at Calligaris across the workshop. Just like him to start without her. "Thanks," she said. "I'd appreciate it."

Yancy guided her through the workstations then, explaining the engineers' initial assignments. "Once we finish unloading the crates, we'll split into two groups and start on the leg mechanisms. Calligaris estimates a week to build up the frames and fit the inner cables. Then we'll move onto the base. We're estimating a month for the first stage of production."

She nodded, calculating estimates of her own. Assuming the engineers didn't run into any complications, the quadruped prototype would be completed within three months.

She had that long to find a way to stop Julian's war, that long to come up with a better plan—or else face the consequences of her sabotage.

They moved on to the north side of the workshop as Yancy explained the latest developments to the quadruped's weapons—an improvement in the automated hopper mechanisms—but they were soon interrupted by a courier, one of the messenger boys that ran letters and missives within the Guild.

"Message for you, sir," he said, thrusting a letter into Yancy's hand. "Urgent. From the vice-chancellor."

Yancy turned the letter over and tore it open. A

small envelope slipped free and tumbled to the floor as he read.

Petra knelt to retrieve it, inadvertently reading the address stamped across the brown paper. She froze, her pulse stuttering in her chest as she reached out and touched the thick black ink.

119 Farringdon Crescent

Emmerich's house.

"Petra, are you all right?" Braith crouched beside her and touched her arm. "You're shaking."

She collected herself and nodded, forcing a feigned smile to her lips as she stood, the telegram clutched in her trembling hand. "Of course. Sorry, I—" She hesitantly offered the telegram to Yancy. "You dropped this."

Yancy met her eyes. "Actually, it's for you."

"What?"

He offered her the letter, and she looked it over, the message written in the vice-chancellor's familiar lean scrawl:

Y—

　　Please deliver the enclosed telegram to Miss Wade. I understand the matter contained within may be of some urgency to her. Inform her she may use my office telephone at her earliest convenience, should she wish to make enquiries about its contents.

　　　　　　　　　　　　　　　　　　—HL

Curious, she turned her attention to the telegram, cautiously removing the yellowed paper from its envelope, the seal already broken. The telegram itself was addressed to the Goss household, sent from a telegraph office somewhere near Taverny—wherever that was.

The thick letters glared up at her from the crinkled paper:

Urgent information. Phone telegraph office at once. Caution. Uni comms monitored. E.

She stared at the words, her pulse echoing mutely in her ears.

The telegram was from Emmerich. She had no doubt of that. Only he would send her something so cryptic, or go to such lengths to avoid Guild interception, routing the message through someone at his household, then through the vice-chancellor, who had sent it to Yancy rather than risk sending it to her directly, not with Calligaris watching her every move.

But what could be so important? Something he didn't want the Guild or the Company to know . . . Something about the war? The conspiracy?

"What does it say?" asked Braith, suddenly standing at her shoulder.

She clasped the telegram to her chest. "It's nothing. I—" She swallowed thickly, considering her next words. If Braith thought she was doing anything to undermine his orders, anything to do with the quadruped or her previous crimes, however indirectly, he would report her to Julian. And if Julian discovered that Emmerich had contacted her . . . "I need to make a telephone call," she said, forcing her voice flat. "Personal business."

"Is something wrong?"

"I don't know," she admitted. "It doesn't say, but I should go now. I don't think this can wait."

"Would you like me to escort you to the public telephones?"

"No," she said, glancing from the telegram to the letter from the vice-chancellor. Every telephone call in the University was directed through the Guild switchboard, which Julian was certainly monitoring, but if the vice-chancellor had offered his telephone, knowing her and Emmerich's situation, he must have a secure line out of the University, hidden from Julian and his allies. Perhaps Lyndon was not as submissive as she once thought.

"The vice-chancellor has a telephone," she said finally, folding the telegram and the letter. She stuffed them in her pocket. "We'll go there."

Braith stopped her not far from the door to Lyndon's office. "Petra, what is this really about?" he asked. "What did the telegram say?"

She looked him in the eye, her heart beating like a drum in her chest. What could she say? She couldn't tell him the truth. She couldn't risk him reporting her to Julian for this. If Julian found out she had telephoned Emmerich, if he thought they were conspiring against him, it would be her head.

"Petra, who sent the telegram?"

"I can't tell you," she whispered.

Braith let out a frustrated sigh. "Why not?"

"I just can't."

"You realize how suspicious that is, don't you?" he asked. "Why can't you just tell me what's going on? What are you so afraid of?"

She didn't answer. She couldn't. But the fear in her eyes must have given her away.

"You're afraid of *me* . . ." he said, his voice breaking. "You are, aren't you? Afraid of what I might do, what I might say." He drew away from her, a pained look on his face. "Petra . . . don't you know me better than that? You know I wouldn't report you to the Guild unless I had to, unless I had no other choice. Have I not earned at least some small measure of trust by now?"

She bit her lip. "It's not that I don't trust you, Braith," she whispered, a knot stuck in her throat. "It's just . . . It's better you don't know."

"Because it's something to do with my orders?"

"I didn't say that."

Braith combed his fingers through his hair. "Damn it, Petra . . . Think about what this looks like. If anyone found out about this, if they suspected you of conspiracy or sabotage . . . There's only so much I can do."

"You could choose to trust me," she said. "I never said this went against your orders, only that I couldn't tell you. That's not a crime."

He turned away with a shake of his head and let out a deep sigh, slowly kneading the center of his brow. "Sooner or later, Petra . . . there's going to come a time when I have to choose between you and my responsibilities as a soldier. Don't force me to make that choice. Please."

She started to say something in reply but then stopped herself. She could make no such promise, and he knew it as well as she did. There would always be that dividing line between them, the threat of that choice—and they both knew which one he would choose, as blatant as his red uniform.

"I have my orders," he said. "If you say anything suspicious, anything at all about the quadruped, I will have to report it." He stepped aside and gestured down the hall toward the vice-chancellor's door. "Just remember that."

"You're letting me use the telephone?" she asked.

"You asked me to trust you," he said. "All I ask is that you afford me the same courtesy in the future." He softened then. "You have enough enemies here, Petra. Don't make me into one too."

She nodded without speaking, the sincerity in his gaze achingly clear. She had no idea what awaited her at the other end of the telephone call with Emmerich, if it had anything to do with the quadruped or his father's conspiracy, but in her heart, the last thing she wanted to do was make an enemy of Braith Cartwright. She needed someone like him on her side.

"Just be careful," he said. "For your own sake."

"I will."

Braith gestured toward the door again, and Petra

turned toward the vice-chancellor's office, her heart pounding fast at the thought of contacting Emmerich after all this time. It had been too long.

Exhaling a steady breath, she walked up to the door and knocked.

"Enter."

She turned the handle and went inside.

Vice-Chancellor Lyndon glanced up from his desk as she walked in, his brows drawing together as he spotted Braith behind her. "I gather Yancy delivered my message?"

She nodded. "Can I use your telephone?"

"Of course," he said, standing up from his desk. "Let me connect you through. Do you have the address?"

She withdrew the telegram from her pocket and handed it over.

The vice-chancellor glanced at it briefly and picked up the handset from the telephone box on the wall, turning the crank to ring the switchboard. He waited a moment and then smiled. "Hello, darling. Yes, the reserved channel, if you please." He looked down at the telegram again. "A telegraph office in Taverny." He recited the address. "Bypass the congested channels if you can. Thanks, Maude."

He lowered the telephone receiver and glanced at Petra, his gaze flitting suspiciously toward Braith. "She's connecting us through now. It shouldn't be long."

Petra nodded, nervously twisting the stem of her mother's pocket watch, the familiar motion a comfort to her. It had been months since she had last spoken to Emmerich, months since she had last heard his voice. Would she even recognize it now? So much had changed since he left. Had he?

Finally, Lyndon spoke again into the telephone, first in French, then English. "Yes, I received a telegram from your office this morning and I believe there may be a young man expecting a telephone call in return?" The vice-chancellor paused and then gestured for Petra. "Yes, she's here."

Petra stepped forward and took the handset from Lyndon, her hands trembling as she raised it to her ear. "H-hello?"

The line crackled in response, and a familiar voice emerged out of the hollow static. "Petra?"

She weakened at the sound, as if time and distance were nothing, the sound of his voice soothing an ache in her heart she had long tried to ignore. "Emmerich . . ." She touched the side of the telephone box with trembling fingers, wishing she could see his face. "I'm here."

"Are you alone?" he asked.

The directness in his voice sobered her, and she glanced over her shoulder at Braith, now leaning against the wall with his arms crossed. "No," she answered softly.

"One of my father's?" asked Emmerich.

She met Braith's cold gray eyes across the room. "Yes."

Emmerich cursed. "I was afraid of that," he said. "Perhaps we should—"

"No, don't," she said, fixating on the telephone again. "Please don't go."

"The last thing we need is for my father to find out I contacted you. I know I shouldn't have risked it, but—" He sighed, the sound of it a crackle in her ear. "It was worth it just to hear your voice again. I know it's been a long time, but . . . I've thought of you every day."

She bit down on her bottom lip. "Likewise."

"I'm sorry I haven't been able to telephone until now. I suspect my father has—" A high-pitched ringing sound cut through the telephone speaker, and his next words were lost in the pop and snap of the long-distance connection. Petra held the receiver closer to her ear, trying to hear through the noise, when his voice suddenly returned. "—realized he must be contriving to keep us apart."

She nodded, remembering too late that Emmerich couldn't see her.

"But that isn't why I wanted you to telephone."

Petra stood a little straighter, remembering the telegram. "Why did you?"

"I have information," he said. "About your mother's family. I've been researching their whereabouts since I arrived in France. Most of the records were lost in the University fire. It's been a nightmare tracking the information down, but I think I may have finally found someone—your mother's sister, your aunt, here in Taverny."

Petra gripped the receiver more tightly. "You *what*?"

"I telephoned you as soon as I could," he said apologetically. "With communications being monitored between the Company and the Guild, this isn't something I dared put in a letter, not with the risk of my father intercepting it. So I waited until I could contact you privately.

"That's why I'm in Taverny," he went on. "To meet her. And, Petra . . . if this woman is truly your mother's sister, if she knows of you, knows of the circumstances of your birth, the truth of who you are . . ." He paused. "We might be able to prove it to the Guild, to the city. You can claim your mother's name and take your rightful place as head of the Guild—as you deserve."

Petra's heart stilled. "This is what you've been doing, all this time?"

"Yes. If we can prove who you are, the Chroniker name will protect you from my father, from the council. And then we can end this ruse and stand against him. Together."

"You think that would work?" she asked.

"It's the best plan we have," he said, his voice distorted by the static hum. "But, Petra . . . in the meantime, you need to tread carefully. My father isn't happy with the way you've acted since we agreed to cooperate with his plans—and now he has it in his head that you're trying to sabotage your war project." He paused. "Whatever it is you're doing, you have to stop. You can't put yourself at his mercy, not again. He needs only the barest of excuses to follow through on his threats."

"I can't sit here and do nothing."

"That is *precisely* what you must do."

She chewed on her bottom lip. "It's too late."

It was too late to stop her rebellion, too late to take back what had already been done. As soon as her engineering team found her sabotage, Emmerich's warnings would no longer matter.

"What do you mean?" He hesitated. "Petra . . . what did you do?"

"What I thought I had to," she said more firmly.

Emmerich cursed on the other end of the line, and she felt his anger through the tenuous connection. "Why?" he demanded.

"I didn't think I had a choice," she said. "You left, remember?"

"To protect you!"

"And look where that got us."

The connection fell silent, interrupted only by the occasional crackle and low hum of static. Then Emmerich's voice came clearly through the speaker, as if he stood right there beside her.

"That isn't fair," he said.

"No," she said thickly. "It isn't. But you left me here. Alone. To figure things out on my own."

"I didn't—"

"I did what I had to," she went on. "To survive, to make a life for myself, to *be* someone." She swallowed against the tightness in her throat. "Without you."

He stayed quiet a moment, the distance between them seeming to multiply tenfold, held together only by the fragile static link between the two telephones.

"I did what I thought was right," he said finally, his voice strained. "Everything I have done here, every order I carry out, every design I hand over to the Company . . . I do it for *you*. For *us*. To keep you safe. To keep you alive. To make it back to you someday." He wavered a moment, and she heard him inhale a deep breath as the telephone line popped and fizzled, the speaker crackling in her ear.

"I love you, Petra," he said quietly. "I don't want to lose you."

Petra bowed her head, gripping the telephone receiver with both hands, wishing she could see his face, smooth the frown from his lips. Life had been better when they were together, when she was wrapped up in his arms, the two of them caught up in a world of their own. He never should have left, never should have agreed to his father's plans.

"You haven't lost me," she whispered, wondering if he could even hear her through the crackling connection. "I'm still here."

But there was a distance between them now. She could feel it.

Emmerich sighed on the other end of the line. "I never should have left you," he said wearily. "And I wish I could be there now, that I could come home and be at your side again, but until this war is put to an end, until my father is stopped, I can't—I *won't*—not until I'm certain you are safe, that *we* are safe." He paused. "So please, *be careful*. Now that my father has the war machine you promised him, anything you do, any stand you take against him could be your last. You'll only get yourself killed, and I—" His voice faltered then, and he cleared his throat. "I couldn't bear for that to happen," he said more softly. "I can't lose you, Petra. Not now."

The telephone connection crackled and whined.

"Just let me be the one to take care of things," he said. "Let me be the one to protect you. I have a plan. I just need you to stay alive long enough for me to see it through."

She stared at the telephone box, her chest pinching with guilt.

"Promise me," he said. "Promise me you'll stay out of trouble."

Petra bowed her head, knowing she could make no such promise. The moment the engineering team discovered the hidden sabotage within the quadruped, that would be the end of it.

"I'll try," she said, certain he knew it was a lie.

"Just stay alive," he said, his voice heavy. "Promise me that, at least. I need to know you'll be there when I return."

She nodded silently, hoping against hope that she would be. "I'll try."

A deadly silence stretched between them, painful in its vastness.

Finally, he spoke. "There's someone waiting for the telephone. I'm sorry, I have to go," he said, his voice breaking. She couldn't be sure if it was the pain in his voice or the poor connection. The handset speaker crackled and popped against her ear. "Be safe, Petra."

"You too."

The line clicked and he was gone. She lowered the receiver, her knuckles whitening around the handset as a deep void opened up in the center of her chest, the sound of Emmerich's voice still ringing in her ears. The happiness she felt just moments ago turned to a harrowing ache, the bitterness of their separation growing within her like a malevolent seed. She closed her eyes, gritting her teeth until her jaw ached. She hated that she could feel this much pain, this aching absence that consumed her from the inside.

All she wanted was for him to come home. Nothing else mattered. Not the war. Not his father. She just wanted to see him again, to kiss him, to wrap herself in his arms, to punch him in the chest and tell him what a coward he was for leaving, for surrendering, for thinking he knew what was best for her.

"Petra?"

She turned to find Braith standing next to her. She felt bled dry, the very center of her gouged out with a knife. She was suddenly exhausted, and she wanted nothing more than to lock herself in her dormitory for the rest of the day and sleep off the pain in her chest.

He touched her arm. "Are you all right?"

"Let's just go," she said wearily, turning toward the door.

He stepped out of her way and she brushed past,

ignoring the vice-chancellor as she left the office. Emmerich's words weighed too heavily on her mind for her to care about anything else. Had he really found someone from her mother's family? Her mother's own sister? If he had, and the woman knew the truth of Petra's identity, if she could prove that Petra was a Chroniker, Adelaide's heir . . .

Petra shook her head. It was too much to hope for. As much as she wanted to believe that Emmerich had found her family after all this time, she couldn't stake her freedom on it, hinging everything on a feeble hope that this woman might know the truth about her. No . . . if she wanted to protect herself from Julian, it would take more than a name. Surely Emmerich knew that.

Braith fell into step beside her, remaining silent as they walked from the Guild offices and headed down the stairs to the main floor. She wondered how much he had overheard, how much he might have guessed, and a slight panic rose in her throat as she wondered whether he suspected her of anything.

It wasn't until they climbed the stairwell to the dormitories and reached the door to her room that he finally spoke. He withdrew the room key from his pocket and turned it over in his hand, staring at the number stamped into the metal. "Petra, who was that on the phone?"

She pressed her lips together, the urge to lie pushing against her teeth.

"Look . . . I understand that you don't trust me," he

went on. "But you don't have to be afraid of me, Petra. I'm on your side."

Petra bit her lip, wanting to believe him, wanting to believe that she could trust him. But he was a soldier. He was the enemy. If she told him the truth, if Julian found out she had contacted Emmerich, it wouldn't matter that it had nothing to do with the quadruped, nothing to do with her sabotage. All that mattered to Julian was her defiance, that she had disobeyed him. How could she tell Braith the truth, knowing that? Knowing what it might cost her?

"How can I not be afraid?" she asked, her voice shamefully weak. "How can I allow myself to trust you when you wear that uniform? One wrong word from you is all it takes for me to lose everything. Don't you see that?"

Braith glanced down at his jacket, the stiff collar unbuttoned. "Because I'm a soldier?"

"You said it yourself," she said. "If it came to a choice between me or your orders, we both know which you would choose."

"Is that what you think of me?" He scoffed. "Damn it, Petra. What more must I do to prove myself to you?"

She held his gaze. "I don't know that you can."

He stared at her a moment longer, and then raised his hands to the collar of his coat, unfastening the top button and then moving to the next, his fingers working quickly down the front of his jacket.

"What are you doing?" she asked, following the movement of his deft fingers. He reached the last button and then jerked his sleeves from his arms, tossing the scarlet jacket to the floor.

"There," he said, gesturing to the heap of fabric at his feet. "Is that it? Is that what I have to do to gain your trust? I am more than just a uniform, more than a nameless soldier who follows orders without question. Have I not proven that?" he asked, his voice cracking. "Damn it, Petra . . . I'm not asking you to put your faith in me as a British soldier. I'm not asking as your military escort . . . I'm asking as your *friend*."

She swallowed hard. Braith was the enemy. He couldn't be trusted. She had told herself that often enough to believe it, but in that moment, laid bare in front of her, she wondered if she'd been wrong.

"And if I trust you?" she asked, her voice shaking. "If I tell you the truth? What will you tell your superiors? What will you put in your report?"

He hesitated. "Nothing."

"What?"

"Whatever it is you're afraid of, I won't breathe a word of this to anyone. You asked me to trust you, to let you make that phone call, and I did. Now I'm asking you to trust me."

Petra stared at him, her throat tight. She had trusted him with the mech, had trusted him with the mech fights and her nightly rendezvous with Rupert, and he had yet to betray her for that. Maybe she could trust him with this.

She bowed her head, slipping her hand into her

pocket where her fingers brushed the edge of Emmerich's telegram.

Maybe she could even convince him of the truth.

Inhaling a deep breath, she closed her hand over the folded paper and withdrew it from her pocket, hoping she wasn't making the biggest mistake of her life. "His name is Emmerich," she said, handing Braith the telegram. "Emmerich Goss."

Braith unfolded the paper with a frown. "You mean—"

"Julian's son," she said, a sudden weight leaving her chest. "He's been in Paris since the end of last summer, working at the Continental Edison Company as a Guild associate."

"And what business does he have contacting you?" he asked.

"A private matter," she said, shaking her head. "Nothing to do with the quadruped."

"Then why go to such lengths to hide it? Why not just tell me this from the start?"

"Because I wasn't sure you would understand," she said quietly. "Emmerich and I aren't supposed to be in contact. His father has been blocking our attempts to communicate for months. If Julian found out about this, he would think it had something to do with the quadruped, some plot to undermine his authority and conspire against him."

"But why? What does his son have to do with it?" Braith gestured with the telegram, his brow tight. "What's his connection to all this?"

Petra sucked in a deep breath. "Emmerich and I . . ." She trailed off, wondering how she could possibly summarize everything that had happened in those few short months. It felt a lifetime ago now. "We worked on the failed automaton project together," she said, sharing as much of the truth as she dared. "You've heard mention of it before. It was a restricted project, its true purpose as a war machine unbeknownst to either of us until it was too late. Emmerich involved me in the development, thinking we could work together in secret, but the Guild found out and when I was no longer useful to them, they tried to frame me as an anti-imperialist spy, accusing me of passing information to Guild enemies. When they came to arrest me, Emmerich destroyed the prototype to help me escape, but he failed. I was captured, and Julian used the destruction of the automaton as further evidence that I was an anti-imperialist, a spy working to sabotage the project. But it wasn't true. None of it was." She frowned, remembering the events that followed—the trial, her escape, their utter failure to stop his father's conspiracy.

"I was tried for crimes of espionage and treason. Julian fabricated evidence to prove my guilt. It was only because of the vice-chancellor that I left that courtroom alive. He and Emmerich did everything they could to clear my name, but by the time I was pardoned of my supposed crimes, it was too late. I had already made an enemy of Julian. I had caused the destruction of his automaton and turned his son against him. After that, he made it his solemn vow to make sure that I repaid him for the damage I caused."

"And that's why he suspects you of wanting to sabotage the quadruped?" asked Braith. "Because of the automaton?"

She nodded.

"And Emmerich?" he said, his voice tentative. "I overheard what you said—about him leaving. There was something between you, wasn't there?"

She stared at the floor, a pang of heartsickness gripping her chest. "I wouldn't be here if it wasn't for him," she said softly, remembering everything they had gone through for her to be here now. It wouldn't have been possible if not for Emmerich. "I owe him that at least."

"But he isn't here now."

"No," she said, more bitterly than she intended. "He isn't."

"What happened?"

She sighed heavily, a swell of resentment rising in her chest. "He left," she said simply. "His father offered him a job at the Company, and he went."

"Just like that?"

"Just like that."

CHAPTER 10

Construction of the prototype continued without delay, the first week passing without even the slightest hiccup in production. Petra watched the engineers' daily progress with a worsening sense of despair. Every wire, gear, and linkage the engineers bolted to the frame was yet one step closer to war, one step closer to the discovery of her sabotage.

She needed more time.

Standing at the edge of the workshop, she watched as her team of engineers measured cables, fitted pulleys, and bolted axle plates and gear trains in place, testing each mechanism in turn. Sparks soon lit up the far edge of the workshop, arcing off the hot steel as the team of welders fired their blowlamps against the quadruped's larger joints, melting metal to metal.

Time was the one thing she didn't have.

Three months until the prototype's deadline.

Three months to find a way to end this war.

If only Emmerich had given her something more useful. Claiming her mother's legacy might protect her from Julian in the short term, but she doubted even the Chroniker name could save her once her sabotage was discovered. Taking her rightful place as her mother's successor wouldn't delay the production of the quadruped. It wouldn't stop the war. Part of her worried nothing could, that no matter what she tried to do, Julian would find a way to beat her.

She let out a heavy sigh and leaned against the nearest drafting table, her eyes on the white-hot sparks on the other side of the workshop. That didn't mean she intended to make it easy for him.

But sabotaging a war machine in a room full of engineers was no easy task, especially with a Royal Forces officer always at her side.

She glanced at him now, standing next to her with his hands clasped behind his back, face trained to stoic indifference. With Calligaris as Julian's spy in the workshop, they had decided to keep things strictly professional during work hours—no idle conversation or easy banter. If anyone suspected Braith of fraternizing, he would be removed from her detail and replaced by someone far less forgiving of her secrets.

No more working with Rupert. No more mech fights.

No possible chance of sabotaging Julian's plans.

At least Braith was willing to bend the rules a little. He had his orders, but at least with him, she had a chance. He trusted her, misplaced though it might be, and while part of her hated the thought of using that trust to her advantage, what else could she do? Julian had to be stopped. This war had to be stopped. And she was getting desperate.

Keeping an eye on Braith, she edged toward the nearest filing cabinet and eased one of the drawers open behind her, careful not to make a sound as she reached in and withdrew a thick folder. She set it on the table next to her, just out of sight of Braith and the other engineers, and nonchalantly sifted through the file—a parts order for the second phase of construction, scheduled to go out at the end of the week. She slipped a few pages into her trouser pocket, returned the folder to the cabinet, and slid the drawer shut again.

Pretending to observe the ongoing construction, she wandered along the edge of the workshop to one of the engineer's tables nearby, feigning interest as a few of them argued over the correct assembly of the tension supports within the machine's base. As one of them whipped out a tapeline to measure the cables, she leaned against the desk and rifled through a folder of notes, carefully tearing a few pages loose before stuffing those in her pocket as well.

She started to walk off, intending to displace the schematics from the drafting tables, when someone grabbed her arm and whirled her around, her blood turning to cold iron as she met with Braith's steely gray eyes. Before she could utter a word of protest, he dug his fingers into her wrist and dragged her across the workshop floor, pulling her behind a stack of crates, hidden from the rest of the engineers.

"What the *hell* do you think you're doing?" he hissed, pushing her toward the wall. She stumbled backward, surprised by his forcefulness.

She held her chin a little higher and glared at him, a fire blazing in her gut. "I don't know what you mean," she said, opting for ignorance.

Pressing his mouth into a frown, he stepped closer and reached into her pocket. "And this?" he asked, holding the torn notes and parts orders in front of her face. "This is sabotage, Petra; this is *treason*." The papers crumpled in his fist, and he lowered his hand; his face still just inches from her own. "Why?" he asked, his voice breaking. "Why would you do this? You know what will happen if you're caught."

She stared back at him, betraying nothing.

He drew away with a shake of his head and threw the crumpled pages to the floor at her feet. "You lied to me. You're exactly what they said you were."

"Braith—"

"You know my orders," he said. "I should report you for this."

Her pulse slowed. "Will you?"

"Give me one reason why I shouldn't."

She pressed her lips together, a thousand excuses crawling up her throat. But the seconds ticked by in silence, all her lies failing to form into words. "Because I'm not a traitor," she said finally.

"Your actions prove otherwise."

"If you turn me in, they'll have me hanged," she said, her heart beating faster. "Is that what you want?"

He held her gaze a moment longer and then glanced away, a frown pinching his brow. "Damn it, Petra. This isn't a game."

"You think I don't know that?" she asked, her voice rising. "I know the risks, Braith. I know what's at stake."

"Then *why* are you so determined to put a noose around your neck?"

"Because I'm not ready to let the world go to war for my mistake!"

Braith faltered. "What are you talking about?"

She clamped her mouth shut and swallowed hard, the fear of what he might do if he knew the truth of what she had done battling against the urge to tell him everything.

"Petra . . . what mistake?"

"The quadruped," she said abruptly. "I never should have designed it, never should have pitched it to the Guild. And now because of me, the Royal Forces will build an army of them, and it's only a matter of time before it comes to war."

"And you think that sabotaging the project will . . . what? Stop the war?" he asked. "The animosity between France and Great Britain goes back decades. Nothing you do is going to change the outcome. It isn't your responsibility."

She curled her hands into fists.

But it was.

Great Britain was on the brink of war because of her. If she had never helped Emmerich with the automaton, if she hadn't been so stupid, she never would have become the catalyst Julian needed to start this war. Everything since then—her arrest, the trial, the bargain she and Emmerich had struck to save themselves—had only brought them closer to war. And now she had given Julian another machine, a *better* machine, more devastating than the first.

"I can't sit by and do nothing."

"Why not?"

She inhaled a deep breath and let it out in a puff, words failing her. "You wouldn't understand."

"What is there to understand?" he asked, his voice rising. "This is treason, Petra. Plain and simple."

"Nothing about this is simple," she said, meeting those cold gray eyes. The look he gave her cut her to pieces. "It's not what you think."

He laughed, a hollow sound that sent chills up her spine. "What I *think*? God! They told me what you were, what you would try to do, and I . . ." He trailed off, shaking his head. "Damn it, Petra, I trusted you! I vouched for you. I *lied* for you." He turned away with a snarl, pacing like a caged tiger. "I thought you were better than this."

"I'm trying to do the right thing!" she said, taking a step forward. "Can't you see that? There is so much more to this war, so much more to what's going on here—with me, with Julian, with this damned war machine—more than I could *ever* make you understand. I'm trying to stop them, Braith, trying to stop this war. If that's treason, then fine!"

"What could you possibly hope to accomplish?" he asked. "Sabotaging the quadruped won't stop the war. It will only get men killed. What do you think will happen when France attacks and the British are left unarmed because of your sabotage? Soldiers will die because of you. British soldiers. My *friends* . . ." he said, his voice cracking. "Your war machine is the only thing standing between us and the French. Don't you see that? Why do you think the Royal Forces is so desperate to get their hands on it? Why the deadline was advanced? The French are building an army, a legion of war machines not unlike your failed automaton. Without your quadruped, we cannot hope to stand against them."

Petra clenched her jaw, a knot forming in her chest. "No," she said, shaking her head. "The war . . . it's not—you're wrong. Julian—"

"*Julian?* It's always the bloody minister with you," he said, cutting her off. "At least he understands the severity of the situation. You, on the other hand . . . I see now why they wanted you under military supervision. You're a risk to everything—to the war effort, to the Empire, to *me*—and for what? War is coming, Petra. Nothing you do is going to change that."

"But you don't understand," she said. "If this war happens—"

"If this conflict does turn to war—and I pray every day that it doesn't—but if the worst does happen . . .

men's lives will be at risk because of you, because of this misguided notion that you and you alone can stop a war. I won't stand by and let you jeopardize their lives. This has to stop. *You* have to stop. You have to accept that this is not your fight."

"But it is my fight," she said weakly. How could she make him see the truth? It burned within her—to tell him everything—but how could she tell him now, when he suspected her of treason and sabotage and worse?

"This has to end, Petra," he said. "*Now*, before you do something that cannot be undone. I will not be responsible for their deaths, not because of you. Do you hear me? Do anything like this again, and I *will* report you. I'll have to. Do you understand?"

Petra met his commanding gaze, any challenge bullied into silence by the look in his eyes. He meant it, every word. "I understand."

He stepped away from her then, roughly kneading the center of his brow. "Damn it, Petra, I don't want to see you hang," he muttered, the line of his shoulders tense. "I couldn't live with myself if . . ." He dropped his hand. "Please, just . . . don't do anything like this again. Don't force me into that position. I couldn't—I couldn't bear it."

Her heart ached at the sight of him like this, the guilt of her betrayal sharp in her chest.

And if what Braith said was true, if the French were building an army of their own war machines, what hope did she have of stopping this war? Sabotaging the quadruped would never be enough. Julian had planted the seeds of war and those seeds were now bearing fruit, spawning armies of war machines to carry out his deception. A battle between mechanical armies would be all the technological spark he needed to fuel this war, to burn the modern world to ash and build anew, securing a position of power out of the chaos and industrial advancements of war.

How had she failed so utterly?

This war would happen no matter what she tried to do.

Panic climbed up her throat as she stared at the torn and crumpled notes at her feet. How had she failed to see the truth right in front of her? Sabotaging the quadruped wouldn't solve her problems; it would only make things worse. But she could not stop what had been set in motion. She could not take back what she had done.

The quadruped prototype would fail, and when her engineering team uncovered her sabotage, she would pay for her hubris, for thinking she could stop this war on her own. She would be charged a traitor, and Braith would discover just how right the Guild had been about her.

Was that the justice she deserved? For putting lives at risk?

She glanced up to find Braith studying her, his gaze filled with some inner torment. She deserved his anger, his resentment. And maybe she deserved to stand trial before the Guild for crimes of sabotage. She certainly didn't deserve his loyalty, or his trust.

But perhaps she could come to earn it.

If there was a way to make this right . . . If she could find a way to settle the war before it began, before her mistakes manifested into outright sabotage . . . She had to try, didn't she?

Braith was right: delaying the quadruped was not going to stop the war. She had stupidly focused all her efforts on the idea that slowing the production of the war machine would somehow change the course of a conflict that had been brewing for decades, long before she had become involved with the Guild, before Emmerich and the automaton, before she had become the catalyst to Julian's schemes. If she was going to stop this war, she had to root out the direct cause—Julian Goss. If she could find a way to expose his hand in the conflict, reveal the conspiracy that had been building for far longer than she had been involved, perhaps she could convince the Royal Forces of the folly of this war and put an end to it before it ever began.

Not that she expected it to be easy.

Emmerich had told her as much before, the first time they had devised their ridiculous plan to expose the Guild conspiracy, his eyes alight with a feverish excitement, infecting her with the naïve hope that the two of them alone could root out the corruption within the Guild. How foolish they had been. Yet they had tried. Even knowing the unlikelihood of their pursuit, still, they had tried.

"Of course it won't be easy. Nothing worth doing ever is."

Petra sat on the floor of her subcity office, slowly tightening the bolts around the mech's fuel tank—newly repaired and no longer leaking after the damage it had taken in the match against Darrow. In just the last week, she and Rupert had reequipped the machine with freshly sharpened blades and new plating, every wire and linkage retightened and examined for even the slightest damage. Just a few final touches, and it would be done. She twisted the final bolt into place and withdrew her hands from the mech's innards, wiping the sweat from her brow with the edge of her sleeve.

"Finished?"

Petra glanced up from her work to find Braith sitting astride her desk chair, his arms folded over the back.

"Almost," she said distractedly, averting her gaze as she wiped her hands on a stained grease rag. "I just need to replace the plating."

She stood up and went to the toolbox to fetch her welding supplies, turning her back to him. She let out a sigh, a steady headache gnawing at her brow. Things had been uneasy between them in the last week, ever since their argument in the workshop. She couldn't even look at him for more than half a second, waiting for the moment he decided to turn her over to the Guild for trying to sabotage production. But for whatever reason, he hadn't yet. And it was like a constant storm brewing between them, just waiting to let loose. At any moment, it would break, and she would drown in the torrent.

Some days she wondered if she deserved it.

She donned her welding gloves and lowered a pair of goggles over her eyes, turning back toward the mech. She had doubts now, about what she was doing—about what she had already done—but there was no taking it back, no stopping it. All she could do now was try to find a way to stop the war before anyone found out.

Sitting down in front of the mech, she fired up the portable blowlamp, and began welding the last square of metal into place, focusing on the bright flare of fire against metal. She hadn't tried to sabotage production again, not since the argument with Braith, though it pained her to see the prototype coming together so quickly. Already, some of the engineers had begun constructing the piloting controls, and the gyroscopic sensors were scheduled to arrive with the next shipment of parts. There were still months of work ahead—weeks of testing each system and ensuring everything worked in perfect synchronization—but the quadruped was slowly beginning to take shape.

She was running out of time.

Finishing the weld on the mech's plating, she switched the portable blowlamp off and slid the goggles off her face, reveling in the sore muscles earned from another night's hard labor. She stretched her arms overhead with a satisfied sigh. She had missed this.

The rattle of the dumbwaiter chute made her jump, and she slipped off her gloves, swallowing hard to smother her rapid heartbeat. Probably just Rupert again. He had left a couple of hours ago to finish up some last-minute homework in the library, but said he might be back later, if she and Braith were still here when he finished.

The dumbwaiter clattered to a halt at the bottom of the chute, and Rupert climbed out, the sight of his sandy-blond hair and familiar smile putting Petra at ease.

He joined her beside the mech and looked it over. "Nice work."

Petra wrinkled her nose. "It's passable," she replied, scrutinizing the irregular edges of her amateur welds. "But it'll have to do. The fight's tomorrow."

"Nervous?"

She shook her head. "Not this time."

"Fletcher's certain to put up a fight."

"Well, so am I."

She turned toward her battered little machine, broken and repaired three times over now, and fought hard not to smile. Already, her metal fighter had won her the respect of her fellow engineers, more than she ever could have dared to hope for at the beginning of the semester. She had shown them what she could do, what she could build. Now all she had to do was win the tournament and prove herself to the few who still doubted her.

"Before I forget . . . I brought you something," said Rupert, producing an envelope from his pocket. He held it out to her with a genteel bow. "For you, milady."

She snatched the envelope from his hand with a

playful shove. "What's this?" she asked, glancing at the writing scrawled across the outside of the thick paper: *For Miss Petra Wade.*

"Just open it."

Arching her brow, she flipped the letter over and broke the seal—the Guild signet imprinted in the metallic wax—then unfolded the paper and read:

To Miss P. Wade,

Regarding your request to visit Hasguard Airfield under the supervision of your assigned military escort, Officer Cadet Braith Cartwright, and student engineer Rupert Larson for purposes of recreation, the Guild council has agreed to temporarily alleviate the restrictions placed upon your person, in consideration of your continued cooperation in matters concerning both the Guild and the Royal Forces.

Providing that your cooperation continues, you are hereby permitted to travel to the Hasguard Airfield as requested, via the Chroniker City–Milford Haven ferry and by carriage to the airfield, on the date of May 27th, 1882, to return that same evening. Some limitations will remain in place while you are abroad, and upon returning to the University, you will revert to your prior restrictions. If you have any additional concerns or questions regarding your upcoming trip, please bring them to my attention.

Sincerely yours,
Vice-Chancellor Hugh Lyndon

Petra glanced up at Rupert. "What's this for?"

"You didn't think I forgot, did you?" he asked, a huge grin on his face. "Your birthday is next month."

She blinked at him and ran the dates through her head, realizing that he was right; her eighteenth birthday was only a few weeks away. She had almost forgotten. She glanced down at the letter again. "They're letting me go to the mainland?"

"By special request," said Rupert, nodding toward Braith. "Courtesy of our resident officer cadet. It wouldn't have been possible if not for Braith."

She glanced away from Rupert and turned toward Braith. "*You* did this?"

"It was Rupert's idea," he said, standing up from his chair. "But I was the one who petitioned the minister for approval, filing a request through Colonel Kersey on your behalf."

"But why would you do that?"

There was more to the question, but she didn't need to elaborate. He knew what she meant.

"We put the request in weeks ago."

"Oh," she said, deflating a little bit. "Before—"

"Yes."

"And now?"

He held her gaze with icy clarity. "That's up to you."

There was a challenge in his words, and she knew the threat that hid there without him having to say another word. If she made any further effort to sabotage the quadruped, their tenuous friendship would end and he would hand her over to Julian without a second thought.

Rupert nudged her arm, breaking the silence. "So what do you say?"

She held Braith's stormy gray gaze—one minute as tumultuous as the ocean, the next as hard as solid steel—the unspoken question still lingering in the air.

Finally, he spoke. "As long as you promise to keep yourself out of trouble, I see no reason we shouldn't go." His eyes narrowed a fraction of an inch, the tiniest shift in his expression. "But you have to promise me, Petra," he said. "Promise me you'll stay out of trouble, and we can forget what happened the other day—on my word as . . . as your friend."

She swallowed hard and nodded, her throat tight. "I promise."

And she meant it.

Trying to sabotage the quadruped further was a wasted effort. If playing the part of the compliant, subservient girl was what she needed to do to earn a trip to the mainland for her birthday, so be it. But in the meantime, she would wait. She would watch, and she would listen, learn what she could about the war, about the conspiracy and the politics behind the conflict, and hopefully discover the evidence she needed to bring Julian down from the inside.

If not . . .

Well, she'd rather not think about that.

CHAPTER 11

The recreation hall was full to bursting with students and engineers by the time she arrived for the semifinals. There were only four fighters left now—herself, Fletcher, Morgenstern, and of course Selby—their mechs an impressive display of engineering skill in the center of the room. She took her place among them and awaited the coin flip that would decide which pair of opponents took the first fight of the night.

The energy in the room was palpable as Yancy stepped into the middle of the ring. "All right, lads," he said, readying the heavy coin. "Heads to Selby and Morgenstern; tails to Wade and Fletcher."

He flicked the coin into the air and it landed on the floor with a ting.

Tails.

Petra let out a slow breath as Selby and Morgenstern withdrew from the ring, leaving her and Fletcher on either side of the wide circle.

Fletcher had fought against Selby in the finals in the last tournament, and she could see why. The mech standing before her was a towering display of brute force; it had two stocky legs, a cylindrical rotating center, and a terrifying turbine of an engine roaring in the center of its massive chest. Dozens of dents and scratches ornamented the plating where previous opponents had tried to pierce the multiple layers of metal—but to no avail. The machine was an impenetrable vault on legs. Well-armed too.

Sharpened blades augmented its right hand, attached to the arm at twisted angles, and a massive spiked pincer completed the left arm, large enough to crush her mech in half if she got herself caught between its jaws. The jagged barbs glimmered menacingly in the electric spotlight.

There was one peculiarity to the machine: a thick, mechanical tail jutting out of its backside, its use unknown.

Yancy stepped forward, quieting the crowd with a wave of his hand. "Fighters at the ready?" Both Petra and Fletcher nodded, and Yancy raised his fingers to his lips, inhaling a deep breath.

Petra honed her focus to a fine point as across the ring Fletcher's machine crouched, ready, waiting. Her throat tightened, her heavy pulse drowning out all other sound. Then came the whistle, sharp and clear, and the two mechs launched into battle.

Petra dived to the right, testing Fletcher's maneuverability as she narrowly ducked beneath the first snap of its lethal pincer, and then weaved around its broad pelvis, activating the supercharged blowlamp in her mech's arm and scoring a deep mark into the cylindrical waist. But before she could pull out of reach, Fletcher turned on a pin, and the mech's massive tail whipped around and caught her machine's legs, blocking her movement as a spinning bladed fist slammed into her from behind.

The sound of crumpling, tearing metal echoed through the room, the attack plastering her mech to the floor. Her machine screeched forward on its face and skidded to a stop, a great dent where its right shoulder used to be. Petra jimmied the controls and forced the machine to stand before Fletcher could mount another attack, but the movement in her right arm was jerky and slow, the joint severely damaged.

Fletcher's machine roared again, and Petra tensed, an electric rush thrumming through her veins as she readied her mech for another charge. She dodged the first attack and landed a swipe across the mech's chest with her bladed fist, but the blades only scraped across the fortified plating, showering sparks on the floor. And then her machine was knocked off its feet again, caught off guard by the mechanical tail. She gripped the edges of her control panel, her fingers digging into the hard metal as she thumbed the controls, barely evading being crushed beneath Fletcher's massive legs before getting to her feet again.

The two machines met blow for blow, landing solid punches and glancing strikes, leaving crumpled dents and jagged gouges in their wake. The smell of scorched metal singed the air, and the heat from the two straining engines roasted the room.

After narrowly dodging another hit from Fletcher's bladed drill, Petra withdrew and assessed the damage to their machines. The two mechs stood on either side of the ring, both of them scored and scratched, spouting thick black smoke and leaking traces of oil and petrol onto the scuffed floor—wounded but not yet beaten.

Fletcher's mech looked worse for wear. Half its tail hung at an odd angle, nearly sliced in half by its own pincer. Sparks crackled from torn wires as it dangled behind the machine. A swath of plating had been carved from its torso where she had landed a swipe of her bladed fist, and deep gouges marked the mech's central cylinder from her efforts to weaken its structure—but she had paid for it dearly. Her mech's right arm was wrecked, the shoulder joint busted to hell and the connecting linkages and gears pummeled to scrap—the protractible saw, bladed claw, and blowlamp brutally damaged.

She needed a better strategy. Brute force wasn't going to win this fight.

A spark from the mech's broken tail caught her eye, and she had an idea—one that might win her the match. But if she failed . . . she wouldn't get a second chance. This was it.

Pressing her fingers to the controls, she darted forward, feinting right as if to aim another attack against the mech's narrow waist, but as Fletcher braced for the attack, she veered left, utilizing the wheels on the bottom of her mech's feet to change direction quickly. Taking him by surprise, she wheeled under the bladed arm and readied the electrified prong with a flip of a switch, diverting all mechanical power into a violent punch, right into the center of the machine's body.

The hooked prongs pierced the plating, and, activating another switch, she emptied the maximum voltage her portable battery could hold, straight into Fletcher's machine. The plating sizzled, and the acrid tang of scorched metal burned the air as smoke filtered out of the cracks in the machine's armor. The mech shuddered and twitched, the jagged pincher snapping open and shut. The twisted blades on its right arm spun wildly, both arms swinging wide as its torso twisted out of Fletcher's control.

Petra's mech jerked forward, tethered to the malfunctioning machine by the prongs buried in the plating, unable to break free. The bladed fist whipped across her mech's already damaged shoulder, the jagged blades scoring through the plating with an earsplitting screech. Linkages and cables snapped. Crumpled gears and shreds of torn metal clattered to the ground.

Across the ring, Fletcher fought to regain control, and the machine's pincer swiveled around, snapping violently over the heads of the watching crowd. Petra fumbled with her control panel and ducked her machine, avoiding the blow by inches. If she didn't break loose now, Fletcher's mech would tear hers to pieces.

Activating another of her hidden weapons, she fired up the supercharged blowlamp in the injured arm and tried aiming the flame at the smoking prongs still buried in Fletcher's mech. The damaged arm's jerky movements made it difficult enough without the faulty mech dragging her across the ring. Still, she concentrated on keeping the flame steady, slipping with every halting step of Fletcher's mech, melting through the tubing and copper wire a fraction of a millimeter at a time, until finally, the blue flame bit through the thick rod and the mech snapped free with a loud crack.

Fletcher's mech teetered, and the circle of students scrambled backward, shoving each other in an effort to get away from the falling machine before it crashed to the floor. It landed with a shuddering boom, limbs still twitching and groaning from the surge of electricity.

Shaking, Petra eased her mech to its feet. It was broken and beaten and falling to pieces, but still standing.

Someone to the side of the ring started to count, but despite the engineer's efforts to get the machine back on its feet, Fletcher's machine remained inert. Smoke poured out of its damaged plating, clouding the room in a gray haze, and fifteen seconds later, the match was over.

She'd won.

Petra lowered her control panel, heart hammering against her ribs as the students cheered her victory. She ran a trembling hand through her sweaty hair, a smile working its way onto her lips.

Yancy stepped forward. "After a thrilling and unexpectedly brutal match, Fletcher is hereby eliminated, and Wade moves on to the finals, her opponent to be decided after our next match: Selby versus Morgenstern."

Fletcher caught her eye across the ring, and with apparent reluctance, he nodded. "Well fought," he said, his voice carrying over the excited din of the other students.

She fought back a smile. "You too."

Students swarmed the ring, congratulating her on her win. She grinned back at them through the handshakes and the pats on the back, buoyed by their adamant praise, but when she saw what was left of her mech, the triumph of her win died in an instant.

Half the mech's plating had been torn to shreds, scores of gears and linkages twisted and warped, pieces still falling from its gaping wounds. The right arm was a shattered husk, dangling from the flattened shoulder joint, and the left arm, though mostly intact, was now without the electrified prong, sacrificed to escape Fletcher's flailing machine.

Rupert elbowed through the crowd and wrapped her in a tight hug, his grin faltering at the look on her face. "What's the matter?"

She gestured hopelessly toward the damaged mech.

"There's no way I'll be able to repair it before the finals. I might as well have lost."

"Don't say that. We'll have her fighting fit again in no time."

Petra conceded with a sigh, too exhausted to argue the point after such an intense match. She didn't even care to stick around and watch the fight between Selby and Morgenstern next, even though she'd be facing one of them in the final round. Assuming she had a mech to fight with. She certainly didn't share Rupert's optimism on that account.

As the floor finally started to clear for the next match, Braith helped her and Rupert cart the battered mech out of the ring, pieces still falling from its gaping wounds. Every clink of metal set her teeth on edge, more gears, axles, and linkages lost in this one fight than she could afford to replace before the finals. It would take a miracle to fix it—if it could be fixed at all.

They pushed the mech halfway across the room, when suddenly, the door to the hallway slammed open. Bright light streamed into the room, followed by a squad of men in stark black uniforms.

Coppers.

Petra shrank back from the doorway as none other than Julian's right-hand man, Mr. Fowler, walked into the room. Braith was at her side in an instant, his body blocking her from view.

"Tell me there's another way out of here," he said.

She shook her head, her heart sinking. They were trapped.

"By order of the Guild council," said Fowler, his voice cutting through the student's chatter, "this circus of engineering is banned forthwith. These machines are to be confiscated immediately, and—"

A din of outrage followed, drowning out the rest of Fowler's words, and then Rupert appeared beside her, Yancy with him.

"Yancy knows a way out," he said, glancing from Petra to Braith. "He'll show you."

"What about you?" she asked, grabbing his arm.

"I'll stay with the mech and make sure they don't follow you." He held her gaze a second longer. "Go. I'll be fine."

Yancy touched her arm, pulling her away from the crowd, still in an uproar. "Follow me." He led them to the back of the recreation hall, putting as many students and engineers as possible between them and the Guild coppers. He stopped and crouched beside the stacks of tables the students had pushed against the wall to make room for the mech fights. "It's just this way," he said, gesturing toward the far corner. "There's a loose panel near the window. It's where we stash our contraband, but if you squeeze in and swing a left, you'll find a service ladder that will take you down to the maintenance room for the library, two floors down."

He glanced toward the door, Fowler's men already combing through the crowd. "I'll hang back and keep them busy. I expect a few mentions of my father ought to stall them for a while," he said with a wry grin.

Fowler's voice cut through the noise. "Where *is* she?"

The room quieted, and Petra froze, clinging to Braith's arm beside her. He took her hand and squeezed, the force of his fingers anchoring her to him.

Selby spoke first. "Where is who?"

"The Wade girl," answered Fowler. "We had word that she was participating in this . . . tournament of yours. Where is she?"

"I haven't the slightest idea," replied Selby.

"Go," said Yancy, ushering her toward the back wall. "I don't know who snitched on you, but no one here will give you up. I can promise you that. You're one of us now," he said with a wink. "Just don't get caught."

Braith squeezed her hand again. "Let's go."

The hidden passage was right where Yancy said. Braith found the panel and carefully pried it loose, ushering Petra inside. She crawled in through the square gap, squeezing between half-empty whiskey bottles, cigarette cartons, and tobacco tins. The space was small, and she had to pull herself into an awkward crouch to make room for Braith, standing on tiptoe to avoid knocking any of the students' contraband over. One wrong move, and the collection of bottles and metal tins would topple, alerting everyone in the next room to their hiding place.

"Careful," she whispered as Braith slipped in behind her. "There's a lot of stuff in here."

Braith pulled the panel shut and stood, bracing his arms against the wall behind her as he found his footing. Petra barely dared to breathe, aware of how warm her skin was, the two of them pressed tightly together in the cramped quarters, close enough that she could feel the rise and fall of his chest. He smelled of tobacco and sweat and something else decidedly masculine, and for a brief moment, she wanted nothing more than to stay there, her body pressed against him in the dark, protected in the shelter of his muscled arms.

There, she felt . . . safe.

"We should go," he whispered, his voice close enough to stir the hair against her cheek. "Before they search the room any further."

She swallowed against the tightness in her throat and nodded, prying herself away from the solid protection he provided as she inched toward the empty passage. Braith held her steady as she crept over the collected contraband, not releasing her until she reached the vacant safety of the access tunnel, the feel of his hands still burning into her skin long after he had let go. The absence of his touch left her strangely empty.

She rubbed the sensation away and crept down the narrow passage, the back of her throat prickling with a sudden sense of loneliness—of guilt and longing. She'd forgotten what it was like to be held like that, to feel safe in someone's arms, to forget herself at someone's touch, and she ached at the memory of Emmerich's embrace, standing in his arms without a care for anything else in the world. Every day, she felt his absence, wanting to feel that alive again.

For a moment, she had.

On the other side of the wall, a man reported that she wasn't among the students, and Fowler flew into a rage. "I want her found immediately! Search the rest of the building if you have to. I don't care if it takes all night. Find her." He paused a moment, the sound of heavy boot steps trailing away. "As for you lot, if I find out you are lying to me, or that you are hiding her whereabouts from me or my men, you will face *severe* punishment. The Wade girl is no longer a student here and fraternizing with her outside of her restricted Guild duties is a criminal offense."

A heavy silence followed his words, and he went on. "So if any of you know something, I advise you speak now."

She paused midway down the narrow corridor and listened.

But no one spoke.

Not one word.

The tension in her body eased. She was safe, for now.

A few steps further and she found the access ladder, six inches wide and bolted into the wall. She stepped off the mesh walkway and descended into the inky black darkness below. Soon it swallowed her up, and she closed her eyes against the shadows, focusing on the feel of the rungs beneath her sweaty palms, descending deeper one foothold, one handhold at a time.

Then the world seemed to open up around her, and her shoes met thin carpet, the air here suddenly cooler, laced with a musty, stale scent. Feeling her way along the walls, her fingers brushed over electrical panels, switches, and shielded cables until finally, she found the exit. Turning the handle, she eased the door open, allowing a tiny chink of light into the room just as Braith reached the bottom of the ladder. He crossed the tiny maintenance room and peered out.

"It's clear," he said.

The maintenance room opened to the second floor of the library, the tiny room tucked behind a row of disused shelves, each one filled to the brim with dusty books. The rest of the library was empty and dark, lit only by the dim glow of a few desk lamps left on in the wide atrium below. The hour was late, well past student curfew, and the library was closed.

Petra breathed a sigh of relief, safe from the coppers and Mr. Fowler for the time being. She deflated against the nearest shelf of books and glanced at Braith. "What do we do now?"

He shrugged, worrying at a thick scar at the edge of his bottom lip. "All we can do: get back to the dormitory before anyone finds us missing, and hope to hell no one catches us on the way."

"But how? The entire school is probably crawling with coppers now. You heard Fowler. They'll search the whole University until they find me."

"Then they'd better find you in your room, where you're supposed to be. I shouldn't need to remind you what happens if we're caught out."

Petra muttered a curse, fighting the urge to kick the shelf behind her. "There's no way we'll make it there without being caught."

"We can if we hurry. They can't cover the entire University at once, and they'll focus their search on this building first, starting with the eighth floor and spreading outward from there. We just have to get to the dormitories before they do."

"And if we don't?" she asked, her voice breaking. "If we're caught?"

The lines of his face hardened. "Let's just hope it doesn't come to that."

From the library, they made their way to the dormitories, pausing at every corner, every doorway, descending quickly down a remote stairwell and stealing down long, abandoned hallways, praying in silence that the coppers stayed far behind them.

Soon, they reached the corridor joining the main building to the dormitories. The night sky was cloudy and moonless beyond the high arching windows. The shadows here were thick and dark, no electric light to alert anyone to their passing. They crept along in deathly silence, neither of them daring to speak. Taking the stairwell furthest from the dormitory lobby, they climbed the steps to the seventh floor. With each flight of stairs, a feeling of dread wrapped like a noose around Petra's throat, pulling tighter and tighter with each step she climbed. As they reached her floor and opened the door into the hallway, she realized why.

Julian Goss was standing at her door, waiting for her.

Braith cursed under his breath and jerked her back

into the shelter of the stairwell, his grip firm on her waist. Petra flattened herself against the wall, every muscle rigid with the need to flee. But there was no way out of it now, no chance she could escape.

"I want her found *now*," said Julian, his melodious voice thin and sharp. "Her and her damned military guard. Search the Guild workshops next, and when you find her, bring her straight to me."

She frowned up at Braith. "What now?"

His eyes flashed in the low light of the stairwell. "I don't know."

Petra swallowed hard. "If Julian suspects I was anywhere near the Guild workshops . . . if he suspects me of sabotage—"

"I *know*." Braith gritted his teeth and curled his hand into a fist, pressing his knuckles into the wall. "We can't let him think you were in the workshops—or at the mech fights," he whispered. "Even if you weren't off sabotaging the quadruped like he suspects, you aren't supposed to be out this late, especially not off fighting in a very illegal mechanical combat tournament." He drew away from the door and ran his fingers through his wavy golden-brown hair, tugging the length away from his brow. "Damn it! We can't just sit here and wait for his men to find us. We need a plan."

She shook her head. "I doesn't matter what we do," she said, her voice sticking in her throat. "He'll suspect me anyway. I disobeyed him. That's all the justification he needs."

"Then we'll just have to convince him otherwise," he said. "He can't accuse you of sabotage without proof."

She scoffed. "You just don't get it, do you? What we say doesn't matter. The *truth* doesn't matter. Julian will convince himself of whatever reality benefits him most, and if that means accusing me of sabotage to further his aims, then that's what he'll do. I'm nothing but a pawn to be moved and sacrificed as needed, a cog in his grand machine. As soon as I outlive my usefulness, he will do whatever it takes to dispose of me."

"Petra, one man can't just do as he pleases without consequences. The real world doesn't work that way."

"*His* world does."

"Well, *mine* doesn't. I don't care who he thinks he is, I will not let him apprehend you for something you didn't do." He turned toward the brightly lit hallway and peered through the door, his brow furrowed.

"And if he orders you to?" she asked. "If he tries to convince you of my guilt? What then?"

Her heartbeat quickened, the real question lurking just beneath the surface, the same question that had divided them ever since he had the misfortune of becoming her guard . . .

Which will you choose, Braith—me, or him?

"You're still a soldier," she said, risking a step closer. "He could order you to arrest me."

Braith hesitated. "He might," he said, turning toward her. "But I would rather lose my uniform than let him arrest you for a crime you didn't commit."

Petra stood a little straighter. "You mean that?"

The twitch of a smile raised the corner of his mouth. "Damned if I do—but for you?" His eyes met hers for the span of a heartbeat, the blue-gray of his irises like dawn breaking through a storm. "I would—gladly."

A flush burned her cheeks, and she bit back a smile. "I assume you have a plan?"

"Part of one," he said, edging toward the hall. "Just follow my lead."

"Wait. What are you—"

But he was already slipping through the door and down the hall, heading toward Julian and the coppers.

Petra had no choice but to follow.

Julian stood outside her dormitory with his back to them, facing a pair of black-uniformed coppers, their faces rapt with attention. "One of you go wake the colonel and tell him one of his officers is missing, the one assigned to Miss Wade. Inform him—"

"Is there a problem, sir?" Braith interrupted.

Julian turned, his eyes sweeping over the two of them with dark calculation in his gaze. "I see Mr. Fowler was not mistaken in sending for me," he said coolly. He turned to the coppers at his side and waved them forward. "Take her into custody."

Petra shied away, but Braith grabbed her by the arm and stepped in front of her, shielding her from the two men.

"I beg your pardon, sir, but on what charges?" he asked.

"For suspicion of illicit activities," he said evenly,

glancing over Petra's boyish attire. "Miss Wade is suspected of being involved in an illegal mechanical fight ring in the student recreation hall. An activity, I would surmise, that you allowed—and even attended yourself, given your lack of uniform. I should remind you that such activities are in direct opposition to your orders, *Officer* Cartwright. As such—"

"I'm sorry, minister, but I'm afraid I don't quite follow," Braith interrupted, drawing to his full height. He stood almost eye to eye with Julian now, the effect of his usual stolid manner somewhat stymied by his lack of uniform, but he commanded an air of authority nonetheless. "Miss Wade and I were in the library this evening."

Julian faltered. "The library?"

"Yes, so you must understand my confusion," Braith went on. "I know nothing of a mechanical fight ring—should such a thing exist. We have been in the library for the better part of the last two hours, and I can assure you there has been nothing of incidence to concern you with."

"Nothing of incidence?"

"That's right."

Julian regarded Braith with a newfound measure of suspicion. "I see . . ." he said, the glint of a hard smile at the edge of his cruel mouth. He would punish Braith for this; Petra was certain of it. She had lived long enough in Julian's shadow to know that there was nothing he hated more than disobedience. To stand against him was suicide.

And yet Braith stood firm, undaunted by Julian's dark gaze. "I would have included this in my report to the colonel tomorrow, if that's your concern," he went on. "Though I don't understand what the fuss is about. Miss Wade is within her rights to visit the library."

"Miss Wade has no rights," Julian snapped, his voice barely above a hiss. "She is a criminal and a threat to the security of the Guild. It is *your* responsibility to ensure she remains confined to her quarters unless otherwise dictated by her contractual agreement with the Guild. I should not need to remind you who you receive your orders from, Officer, but know this . . ." He leaned close and his voice dropped a few degrees. "If I discover that you have neglected your duty—or worse, I discover you are *lying* to me—this will be the last assignment you ever have as a soldier of the Royal Forces, *boy*. Do not cross me."

Braith didn't flinch, meeting Julian's dark gaze. "Of course, sir."

"Good." Julian withdrew then. "In the meantime, I will inform Colonel Kersey of your failure to comply with your orders and see that your pay is docked for the remainder of the month, for your insubordination."

Braith stiffened, but said nothing.

"Should something like this happen again," the minister went on, arching his brow high, "rest assured—swift punishment will be made."

"Understood, sir."

Julian clasped his hands behind his back and glanced at Petra. "As for you, I would remind you to behave yourself, Miss Wade. You would not want to risk the revocation of your temporary release." He smiled acidly. "I hear the weather is rather fine in Pembrokeshire in the late spring."

Petra swallowed hard, aware of Braith's tight grip on her wrist.

"Should I not see you again before, do enjoy your birthday venture to Hasguard next month," he said pleasantly, starting toward the door. With a quick gesture, his two coppers went ahead of him, and he paused just long enough to meet Petra's eyes. "I am sure it will be *most* diverting."

behave yourself, Miss. We do. You would not want to
risk the revocation of your temporary release." He
smiled archly. "I hear the weather is rather fine in Fort
Brocklehurst in the autumn."

Petra swallowed hard, aware of Brath's tight grip
on her arm.

"Should I not see you again before, do enjoy your
birthday visit to Brightfield next month," he said
pleasantly, marching toward the door. With a quick
gesture, his guards went ahead of him, and he
paused just long enough to meet Petra's eyes. "I am
sure it will be well diverting."

CHAPTER 12

With the fights canceled, her mech confiscated, and
Rupert stuck in detention with the rest of the students
caught at the tournament, Petra had nothing to do in
her spare time but work toward exposing Julian's conspiracy. She spent her days working on the quadruped,
the prototype advancing rapidly toward completion,
and her nights trying to scrounge up enough evidence
against Julian to put a stop to this fraudulent war.

When she was permitted outside her dormitory,
she collected whatever outside information she could,
newspapers and gossip mostly, searching for clues of
what was going on beyond the walls of the University. But after three weeks of trying to gather evidence
against Julian, she was no closer to finding a way to
stop the war than before.

In just the last week, there had been an anti-
imperialist attack on a British embassy in France,

claims of anti-imperialists arming themselves and preparing an assault on Buckingham Palace, arrests of supposed imperial detractors, but no clear evidence or convictions. Always, there were rumors of France's involvement with the anti-imperialist movement, claims that the French government was financing their rebellion.

Rumors and propaganda—that was all she could find. Nothing concrete. Nothing factual. And nothing to tie Julian to any of it.

Three weeks passed with zero progress, and Petra had finally run out of time. She had no substantial evidence, the quadruped prototype was nearly finished, and war was lurking on the horizon like a steadily advancing storm. All it needed was one final spark to light the conflagration.

Her days were numbered.

The quadruped would fail.

Julian would find her sabotage.

And that would be the end of Petra Wade.

There was only one way out of it now, and though she hated the thought of admitting defeat, of running away, she could see no other way, not if she wanted to survive the aftermath her sabotage would bring.

She had to leave the city.

Tomorrow.

The day of Petra's birthday celebration dawned bright and cool, and Petra dressed with special care, wearing her sturdiest work clothes beneath layers of petticoats and skirts, a change of clothes tied around her waist and bundled at her back to act as a bustle. She covered the ensemble with one of her more modest dresses, hidden pockets sewn into the skirt. She put her few items of value there—her mother's pocket watch, a reticule containing what little money she had saved back, her mother's wooden screwdriver and design journal, and the clockwork butterfly Emmerich had given her before he left for Paris. To complete the outfit, she opted to wear her work boots instead of something more fashionable, not knowing what sort of travel she had ahead of her once she skipped Milford Haven and headed east.

Everything was in place, her one chance for escape unwittingly approved by the council for her birthday. All she had to do was slip away at the last minute, board the last train east, and not look back, not for a second. If she looked back, if she hesitated, they would find her. And she would not be trapped by Julian's hand again. She would not give up her freedom, her life, not when she had a chance to save herself, not when she had a chance to live.

A knock sounded at her door, and she frowned at her reflection in the mirror, seeing only how badly she had failed, how low she had come. A year ago, she had the world at her feet, a fire in her heart, and a dream worth fighting for. Now she had nothing.

Braith knocked again. "Petra? Are you ready to go?"

"Coming," she said, her voice hollow.

She checked her pockets, patting the solid weight of her reticule and the smooth surface of her pocket watch, her fingers grazing over the screwdriver and the tiny box where she kept Emmerich's gift—too precious to leave behind. Inhaling another deep breath, she glanced around her spartanly furnished room, bed made, desk neat. But there was nothing here for her anymore. She wondered if there ever had been.

Leaving the room behind, she met Braith in the hallway. He was dressed up in his formal military attire, his hair combed, face clean-shaven. She smiled at him and exchanged the usual pleasantries, but her heart wasn't in it.

By the end of the day, she'd leave him behind too.

They left the University without delay. Never before had she left the shores of Chroniker City, and after today, she might never come back. This city was her home—every street, every alley, every nook and hollow as familiar as the lines of her palms; the heavy thrum of engines beneath the streets beat with the pulse of her own heart. This city was hers. It was in her bones.

She belonged to it.

The thought of leaving it behind ripped her apart, but she had no choice, not if she wanted to survive. She walked on, one step after the other, and then they were at the gates to the city, the open harbor and waiting ferry just beyond.

Petra stopped in her tracks, the echoes of the sub-city engines vibrating through the cobblestones beneath her feet, singing to her, calling her back, begging her not to leave.

"Petra?"

She looked up to see Braith at the open gate, his golden hair tousled by the seaward winds as he glanced back at her, and she remembered Emmerich suddenly, his dark hair, his copper eyes, the touch of his arms around her, remembering the day he left, how much it had ached to lose him, as if a part of her soul had left with him.

This was worse.

She breathed deeply of the city air, inhaling the rich scents of coal smoke and tangy metal, clouds of hot steam rolling lazily over the cobblestone streets like an early-morning fog. She filled her lungs with it, with the breath of this city, holding on to it like a talisman.

I'll come back, she promised. A whisper of a prayer. *Someday.*

And then she stepped forward, striding up to the gate without looking back. If she looked back now, she'd never leave.

They boarded the first ferry to Milford Haven and she held on to the deck rail with shaking hands, trying not to think of the life she was leaving behind. The ferry drifted away from the pier with the chime of a bell, and then they were sailing away from Chroniker City. Only then did she dare look back at the city she'd lived in for almost eighteen years, slowly slipping toward the horizon as the ferry puttered east. Its high walls and brass towers glimmered brightly in the morning sun, birds soaring over angled rooftops and blackened smokestacks, a haze of steam and coal smoke rising steadily overhead. And then it was gone, lost behind a mist of sea spray and fog.

She closed her eyes and sighed, breathing freely for the first time in months—free of the Guild, free of the University, free of Julian's long reach. She turned eastward, a weight lifting from her chest as she breathed the salty air, filling her lungs with the taste of it.

Julian could not touch her now.

When the ferry docked a couple of hours later, Petra and Braith disembarked, following the crowd of passengers off the boat and up the wide walkway into the town proper, the air ripe with the briny tang of the harbor and the scents of cookery from the nearby restaurants. The smell of steam exhaust and burning charcoal was barely noticeable here, nothing more than an afterthought. Shops lined the shorefront street, interspersed with restaurant patios, alfresco boutiques, and a pair of stately hotels. Trees, grass, and shaped hedges filled the empty spaces between, the heady scent of fresh soil and trimmed leaves a stark contrast to the atmosphere of brick, metal, and steam of Chroniker City.

Braith led the way up the street, Petra close behind. Passersby filled the footpaths, milling about the shops and gossiping among themselves, and carriage and steam-car alike clip-clopped and puttered up and down the street, pausing briefly to allow the foot traffic from the docks to pass. Petra stopped for a passing carriage and wiggled her toes in her shoes, the stone pavers beneath her feet still and quiet. There were no engines under the streets, no mechanical structures or mechanisms of any kind—just solid earth, as if the city itself was dead.

It was unnerving.

They met Rupert at the train station. He had traveled ahead days ago, leaving the city at the end of the semester to start his official internship at the airfield. It had been a dull few days without him, but seeing him now dragged her out of her melancholy mood in an instant. He lifted her with a tight hug and kissed her cheek, making her blush. "Happy birthday, Petra."

She smiled in return. "So what's the plan for today?" she asked, trying not to think of the fact that she would be leaving in a few hours.

"An airship tour, of course," he said with a grin, producing a brightly colored flyer from his pocket. A lithograph of an airship emblazoned the handbill, artistic lettering decorating the rest:

Visit Scenic Chroniker City Aboard Britain's First Aerial Cruise Ship!

"After that, I thought we might take a tour of the airfield," he went on. "I wanted to show you the airship I designed for the Royal Forces. It's on the military side of the airfield, but Braith says he can get us access with his identification."

Petra glanced up at him. "Really?"

Braith nodded, a crooked smile on his face. "Consider it a birthday gift."

Just then, a public omnibus rolled up to the train station, stopping with a hiss.

"This is us," said Rupert, fishing in his pocket for three bus tickets.

He handed a ticket each to her and Braith, and then the three of them climbed aboard the vehicle, handing over half of their ticket stubs before taking their seats by the wide windows. The rest of the passengers quickly boarded, and then the bus trundled away from the station with a kick, leaving a puttering cloud of black smoke behind them.

They traveled from Milford Haven through a few outlying towns and then onward to Hasguard, passing endless fields and blue sky, so vast and open and green compared to the crowded streets and towering buildings of Chroniker City. Eventually, the road narrowed, and the broad, flat landscape disappeared behind leafy trees and wild hedges. The omnibus slowed, weaving through low hills and gentle curves, the carriage swaying and shuddering as they delved deeper into the countryside, trees and branches whipping past the open windows. Then they took a sharp right up a narrow road and passed another busload of passengers heading back to the harbor town.

The omnibus puttered steadily up a low rise, and as they came to the top of the hill, Petra saw the first of the airship balloons in the distance, hovering low over the grassy plains. She rose in her seat and leaned out the window, her eyes on the floating dirigibles, like lazy wooden birds hovering over the horizon—so high and far away as they sailed through the open sky, untethered to the earth.

Then the bus took a turn, and she stumbled back into her seat, landing soundly against Braith. He caught her by the waist, and their eyes met for a brief moment before she cleared her throat and inched away, a knot of guilt in her chest as she turned her attention back to the window. She focused on the familiar putter of the omnibus engine, watching the distant ships float through the sky. In just a few hours, she would be leaving, and she still didn't know how to tell him—or if she would tell him at all.

Moments later, Hasguard Airfield appeared ahead, a sprawling meadow of landing docks, anchoring equipment, and rows and rows of hangars. The bus rolled through the open gate and onto the airfield grounds, chuffing to a stop in front of a small collection of booths and tents erected atop the grass.

Petra, Braith, and Rupert quickly disembarked and set off through the tents, the canvas and fabric flapping loudly in the high wind. The camp was packed with people, bustling with passengers, crewmen, and soldiers.

"I already have our tickets," said Rupert, ushering them past the large ticket stall at the far end of the camp. He pointed to one of the anchored ships ahead. "We'll be flying on the *Diantha*, the first of a new class of aerial tour cruisers; this will be her maiden tour."

The *Diantha* was a majestic sight, built like an old seventeenth-century sailing ship, with a balloon instead of sails and two short wings protruding from the hull, each fitted with a pair of electric propellers. An ornately carved figurehead ornamented the prow, and decorative balustrades stood in place of standard deck rails at the top deck. Banners of silk brocade and embroidered flags hung from the inflated balloon, fluttering prettily in the breeze, while a large windowed cabin claimed the bow of the ship, the glass panes glinting like gold in the bright morning sunshine. Already, a crowd gathered below, a team of crewmen preparing the ship for boarding.

Rupert pointed to the sun-gilded windows. "That's the dining room there. I've reserved us a table for tea, once we're over the bay. I thought we might have dinner at the harbor after we get back to Milford Haven. The last ferry doesn't leave until eight, so that gives us plenty of time to spend in town before we have to head back."

Petra forced a smile to her face, knowing she wouldn't be returning with them. At least she had a few hours until that eventuality. "Sounds perfect."

They hiked across the spongy grass to the airship dock, passing a military steam-lorry parked nearby. A group of redcoats lounged around the back, smoking and talking among themselves, their eyes roaming over the assortment of passing ladies. One of the soldiers caught Petra's eye and winked, taking a long draw off his cigarette. She rolled her eyes and ignored him, turning back toward Braith and Rupert as another steam-car pulled up to the airship, leaving deep ruts in the grass.

The car jolted to a stop and out stepped another officer, a tall, bearded man with dark hair and a severe expression on his face. The soldiers quickly stamped out their cigarettes and saluted him.

"Which one of you is Cartwright?" he barked.

Petra stopped and glanced at Braith. "Is he looking for you?"

"I'm not sure," he said, taking a tentative step forward. "But I'll find out. Stay here. I'll be right back." He strode across the grass and stopped in front of the officer with a salute. "Lieutenant-General, sir? Officer Cadet Braith Cartwright reporting."

"You're the one who reports to Julian Goss, yes? One of Colonel Kersey's boys from the Guild?"

"Yes, sir."

"Good. I need you to come with me." The lieutenant-general turned on his heel and started toward his steam-car, gesturing for Braith to follow. "Quickly now."

Braith wavered. "Sir?" he said tentatively. "I have prior orders."

The lieutenant-general paused halfway to his vehicle and slowly turned around, his hands clasped behind his back. He glared at Braith, his steely gaze as hard as the pistol he carried at his hip. "I assume you are referring to the supervision of Miss Wade? It is my understanding she will be occupied for the next few hours aboard this airship, and as such, your services will not be needed. There are far more important matters that require your attention, Officer *Cadet*." He spat the word as if it were an insult. "Once Miss Wade has returned from her airship tour, you may resume your duty, but until then, you shall attend to *me*. Understood?"

"Will another officer be assigned to her in my absence?"

"I don't see why that is necessary."

Braith frowned. "Forgive me, sir," he went on, hesitation in his voice. "But did Minister Goss approve of this—the minister to the vice-chancellor? My orders come directly from him, and I received no word that those orders should change upon arriving at Hasguard."

The ranking officer squared his shoulders with a deep breath, exuding an air of authority that commanded attention. "My orders supersede the minister's, but if you must know, when I petitioned the Guild for an officer familiar with Guild affairs to help me with some . . . particular military matters, the minister offered you by name."

"He did?"

"Just so. I assume that answers your question?"

Braith hesitated before answering. "It does, sir."

"Good. If that's all? Then, follow me."

As the officer returned to his vehicle, Braith turned back toward Petra. "I'm sorry," he said with a wince. "He's right. His orders supersede the minister's. I have to go."

"What do you think it's about?" she asked, keeping her voice low.

He shook his head. "I don't know, but . . . something doesn't seem right about this." He met her eyes, a frown etched across his brow. "Wait for me when you get back?"

She nodded once, swallowing against a pang of guilt as she realized the opportunity this could present. If she returned from the airship tour and Braith was not back yet, tied up in whatever business the Royal Forces required of him, her escape was all but secured.

All she had to do was slip away.

"See you then," he said.

He turned and left without another word, joining the lieutenant-general at his vehicle. She felt a slight twinge in her chest as he climbed into the cab and drove away, the prospect of escape quickly souring at the thought of what might drag him away from his duties at Julian's command.

Nothing good, she suspected.

Rupert stepped up beside her. "I wonder what's going on."

"I wish I knew."

"I'm sure we'll find out when we get back," he said gently, turning her toward the *Diantha*. "Come on. Let's get in line to board. We don't want to miss our flight."

The airship cruiser was far more extravagant than Petra expected. They stepped off the hydraulic lift, through a pair of gilded doors, and into a lavishly decorated room, spreading down the full length of the ship like a long, low-ceilinged ballroom. The floor was bedecked with painted tile and plush carpets, with curtains of shimmery brocade pulled back from the wide casement windows. Twin spiral staircases curved up from the floor to the upper decks, and at the far wall stood an electric lift, its gilded gates flanked by a pair of attendants in crisp black livery. Another dozen attendants stood at intervals along the cream-colored walls.

The other boarding passengers flocked to the wide windows overlooking the airfield, but Rupert grabbed Petra's hand and tugged her toward the stairs.

"Come on. You'll want to be up top when we take off."

They pushed past satin skirts, lace fans, and voluminous bustles and hurried up the metal stairs, a velvet rope guarding the top. Rupert held it up for Petra to duck under, and then they came face-to-face with a narrow door, a "No Passengers Permitted" sign nailed to the wood. They ignored that too, quickly pushing through to the uppermost deck, the massive dirigible balloon floating weightily overhead.

Ropes creaked and banners fluttered in the wind as a breeze rushed over the balustrades and swept across the deck, tugging at Petra's skirt and hair. The air was cold and clear atop the airship, smelling of grass and earth and sky, without even a hint of smoke or grease or hot metal, so alien and strange . . . but comforting somehow.

Standing here, floating above the ground, she was free.

At the foredeck, they watched the busy airfield, thick with ships and pedestrians. Then a bell rang somewhere below, and the airship surged upward with a smooth leap. Petra held tightly to the railing as the grassy airfield fell away and the crewmen and visiting public diminished into tiny scurrying dots across the busy pasture, the airships and hangers soon nothing more than distant spheres and metal prisms.

The ship leveled out and Petra laughed, her skin alive with the boundlessness around her. She leaned against the balustrade, watching the landscape slip away beneath her. The world seemed smaller from the height of the airship: vast squares of farmland stretching out for miles, endless grassy hills, and countless trees. Little hamlets and villas dotted the countryside in clusters of steep roofs and stone walls, and to the south, the gray streets of Milford Haven lined the blue stretch of waterway, turned hazy by the distance, with the shores of southern Pembrokeshire just beyond.

Rupert slid up next to her. "I'm sorry Braith couldn't come."

She sighed, a feeling of unease settling in her chest. "Me too."

Despite everything with the quadruped and her sabotage and the fact that he was a soldier of the Royal Forces, she liked Braith—which only made things worse. Guilt pricked at her chest at the thought of leaving without telling him. He had trusted her, despite it all, blindly dragged into this web of lies and conspiracy and sabotage.

She rested her elbows against the railing, wondering what the lieutenant-general wanted with him. The fact that Julian had offered him up by name worried her more than anything else. Braith had stood up for her, had lied to Julian to protect her. His sudden transfer of duties was no coincidence—she was certain of that—but what did it mean?

What was Julian planning?

Once the ship sailed beyond the Welsh coast and over open water, Rupert led Petra belowdecks, where they enjoyed the view of the ocean from the dining room. But all through tea, Petra's mind brewed tirelessly, preoccupied with thoughts of Braith, of Julian, the quadruped and the conspiracy. The war. Her escape. She barely ate any food, a dark cloud hanging over her despite Rupert's best efforts to brighten her mood.

Finally, a half-hour later, an airship attendant announced they would be arriving over Chroniker City soon, and she was spared from her mire of dark thoughts. Rather than follow the rest of the passengers down to the lower viewing decks, Petra and Rupert climbed the spiral stairs once again to the upper deck, left to enjoy the view alone, except for the few crewmen lounging near the stern of the ship.

Petra leaned against the decorative balustrade, enjoying the brief freedom of the sun on her face and the wind in her hair, flying so high above the rest of the world. But then she spied Chroniker City ahead, looming out of the ocean like the sunken city of Atlantis, sea-green waves breaking against the walled shore. The University, forever a beacon of technological prosperity, glimmered brightly in the afternoon sun, the rest of the city in its shadow.

It was beautiful, really.

But what had once been her home had become a cage.

She could not go back there, not if she wanted to survive.

The airship dropped low on its approach and circled the city walls. The many buildings were nothing but a collection of shingled roofs, pipes, and smokestacks from this height. They passed over the south of the city, dropping lower as the dirigible eased toward the brass walls of the University. Petra could see the street divisions between the four quadrants—the white-walled buildings and wide windows of the second quadrant, the darker brick and wood of the fourth, and between, the low, stone buildings and bright greenery of Pemberton Square in the first. She could see the gentle curve of Medlock Cross as it cut through the fourth quadrant, and she spied the windows of Mr. Stricket's pawn shop far below, the fateful steps where she had met Emmerich only a year ago.

So much had changed since then.

Rupert nudged her with his elbow. "Happy birthday, Petra," he said quietly, wrapping his arm around her in a hug.

She leaned into him with a sigh and rested her head

on his shoulder, grateful for his companionship. She wondered if she would ever see him after today, if she would ever return to the University and walk those familiar halls again, Rupert at her side. He was her best friend—for a long time, her *only* friend within those walls. She hated to leave him now, after everything he had done for her, but what choice did she have? The war had finally caught up with her, and there was nothing left to do but run.

Maybe, if she was lucky, she'd find another way to bring Julian to heel, end the war from outside the Guild's constraining walls, outside of Julian's influence. If she could make it to Paris, perhaps there she could find Emmerich, and maybe together they could bring his father down, just the two of them—as it should have been from the very beginning.

And maybe then, she could come home.

Maybe then, she could claim her family name, take up the mantle her mother had left behind. But not before, not while the world was still in turmoil, not while the Guild still sowed so much corruption.

Not yet.

On the return trip to Hasguard, Rupert and Petra remained top deck, even as the airship began its descent. As the ship approached the airfield, a group of crewmen climbed over the balustrades and rappelled down the side of the hull, landing masterfully on the grass below before guiding the airship to anchor.

"See Braith anywhere?" asked Rupert, peering over the rails.

Petra searched the airfield for Braith's familiar features, but she didn't see him among any of the redcoats. "Not yet. He must still be with the lieutenant-general."

She swallowed hard, a knot forming in her throat. With Braith gone, this could be the best time to escape. She could be halfway back to Milford Haven before he even realized she was gone, and by the time he returned to the harbor, she could be on a train to Cardiff, putting as many miles between her and Chroniker City as a steam locomotive could take her. But only if she left now, before he returned from his business with the lieutenant-general.

She slipped her hand into her skirt pocket and touched the solid weight of her reticule, easily enough money to buy passage to London by train. From there she could make for Paris.

Would he guess where she was headed?

Would he come after her?

Her fingertips brushed over the front of her pocket watch, the ornate design so familiar to her after all these years. She withdrew it from her pocket and checked the time.

Three hours until the last train left the station at Milford Haven. Three hours to slip away and leave Chroniker City behind for good, but not yet. She couldn't bring herself to leave, not without . . . not without some sort of goodbye. She owed him that much, didn't she?

"What if we went ahead without him?" suggested

Rupert, startling her out of her thoughts. "He knows where we'll be. He can find us there when he's finished."

"But how?" she asked, putting her pocket watch away. "Without Braith, we don't have the military clearance to get into the hangars. They'll never let us through."

Rupert shrugged, a sly grin on his face. "Then we'll just sneak in."

"And if we're caught? You know I'm under a lot of restrictions, even here."

"Then we won't get caught." He hopped down from the loading dock and extended his hand. "Trust me. I know a way in."

Petra fought back a smile, knowing she couldn't deny that mischievous look in his eye. Sneaking into the hangars without Braith wasn't exactly what they had planned, but she only had three hours to spend with Rupert before she had to leave—possibly for good, if things didn't turn out the way she wanted—and she intended to make the most of what little time she had left.

Besides, Rupert was right. Braith would know where to find them.

"All right, then, Mr. Larson," she said, elegantly taking his hand with a grin to match his own. "Lead the way."

They left the loading dock behind, weaving around docked ships and huddles of crewmen, making their way to the north side of the airfield.

The military hangars stood on the other side of a

barbed fence and a barred iron gate, but they skirted past the heavily guarded entry, heading toward a hangar on the civilian side of the airfield. Rupert pulled her behind the building and led her to the fence on the opposite side, hidden from sight.

Rupert pried a section of fence away from the nearest post and opened a gap through to the other side. "After you, milady."

Petra slipped through, and Rupert quickly followed. Footsteps echoed off the hangars' corrugated tin walls as they snuck through the compound, pausing at the occasional chatter from nearby soldiers. Once, a military lorry rumbled down an access road toward the gate, and Petra and Rupert shrank into the shadows of the nearest building until the sound of its boiler engine faded.

Finally, they reached the largest hangar in the complex, each bay door at least forty feet wide. Rupert opened a smaller side door, letting Petra in first. For a brief moment, she had an impression of vivid red, but then Rupert came in and shut the door behind him, plunging the hangar into darkness.

"Just a moment," he whispered, his voice bodiless in the dark hangar. Petra heard him shuffle away, and a minute later, a tiny flame flared into the bright orange glow of a lantern, steadily growing brighter. Rupert held it aloft, illuminating the base of the nearest structure.

A ship.

Petra gaped at it, the immense hull painted a deep

scarlet, built of wood, with brass ornamentation at its prow. She could see nothing beyond that, the rest of the ship lost in the darkness of the massive hangar. It was the size of a frigate, the hull at least fifty feet broad and five or six decks tall, sitting on wooden frames to keep from tipping.

Rupert grabbed her hand. "Come on. Let me show you the inside."

Petra followed wordlessly, gaping as they passed another two ships, identical to the first. Then Rupert turned between two of the enormous hulls, and they stopped at a rope ladder not far from the front of the ship.

"I'll go first," he said. "Follow close."

The climb took a few minutes. Petra worked up a sweat under her thick layers of clothing by the time she reached the top and climbed over the railing onto the deck. Rupert's lantern cast long shadows, illuminating distant structures, the shapes floating eerily in the darkness. The deflated dirigible balloon hung overhead, held up by a thick rope net.

Petra wandered across the deck, her footsteps echoing loudly in the silence of the dark hangar. Rupert followed, the flickering lantern revealing the indistinct structures as she approached. Light glinted off the nearest object. Weapons.

"This is a warship," she said quietly, touching the nearest one.

Rupert nodded. "It was meant to be a cargo ship. But with the anti-imperialist threat, the Guild decided to repurpose the design for war. Add a few guns, a couple of bomb bays, and what was once a cargo ship is now a warship." He gestured toward the collection of weapons with a grim frown. "Construction started last month. Four ships have been completed, and the Royal Forces have commissioned another dozen."

A chill spread down her spine. "But what are they for? Defense? Patrol?"

"Deployment. They're meant to deliver soldiers to the battlefield and provide backup artillery if needed. Here . . ." he said, gesturing toward the rear of the ship with his lantern. "I'll show you." He led her through a door and down a flight of stairs to a narrow hallway.

Signs lined the doors here—Auxiliary, Bridge, Captain, Officer on Deck—but Rupert passed them by, turning down another staircase, heading deeper into the ship.

"Originally, the bays were meant for cargo drops—supplies, rations, ammo—whatever the soldiers on the ground needed," he explained. "But with tensions rising with France, the Guild and the Royal Forces decided our priority was to build a warship first, outfitted for deploying soldiers. And here was a ship ready-made. All they had to do was change the cargo—soldiers instead of supplies—and mount enough guns to provide aerial artillery. No one is equipped to combat a ship like this, not in the air. The Royal Forces could deploy soldiers almost anywhere, with little to no resistance from opposing ground forces."

They traveled down two more flights of stairs and

pushed through a set of double doors at the base of the ship's hull. Rupert walked a few steps ahead of Petra, his lantern illuminating the wide metal walkway.

"The hold was refitted to carry a new weapon, another Guild project intended for ground combat. I'm told the . . ." He slowed to a stop and lifted his lantern, the light glinting off great hulking machinery to the side of the walkway. "That's not right," he said, holding his lantern toward the nearest machine. "I was told the prototype wasn't supposed to be completed until next month. These should be months from manufacture."

Petra followed his gaze, a ringing in her ears. Her heartbeat slowed to a crawl. "Rupert . . ." she said slowly, eyeing the sharp angles of the machine, the structure disturbingly familiar. "Give me your lantern."

He did as she asked, and she took the lantern to the edge of the mesh walkway, her hand shaking as the light spilled over metal joints and taut cables. She shook her head and backed away a step, plunging the machine in darkness again. Her chest constricted. She couldn't breathe.

"No . . ."

"Petra, what's wrong?"

"These shouldn't be here," she whispered.

"What do you mean?"

She inhaled a trembling breath and lifted the lantern higher, illuminating the familiar domed cabin, the twin Agars on either side and the Gatling gun underneath. Four spidery legs supported the massive frame, towering over her like a great mechanical beast. This was her war machine, her quadruped, complete and armed and ready for battle.

She walked further down the walkway, shoes clanging against the metal as she raised her lantern to another of the deadly machines, and beyond that, another one. She walked faster, her footsteps echoing loudly through the hull as she broke into a run, stopping only when she reached the other end of the hold.

"No . . ." she panted, her blood rushing in her ears. "This can't be."

Rupert joined her at the end of the walkway and touched her shoulder. "Petra," he said gently. "What's wrong? Talk to me."

"This is my project," she said quietly, tears burning the corners of her eyes as she stared down the row of machines. "The war machine I designed for the Guild—the quadruped."

"But how?"

"I don't know," she said, shaking her head. "This doesn't make any sense; the prototype isn't finished yet. We were supposed to finish next month, but—" She glanced around the cargo hold, the lantern illuminating half a dozen of the deadly machines, the rest obscured in darkness. She faced Rupert. "How many are there? How many is the ship designed to hold? Do you know?"

"Um . . ." He blinked, combing his hand through his sandy hair. "Eighty, I think."

"Eighty?" she repeated, her voice shrill. She couldn't

breathe. Her knees gave way, and she slumped, trembling, to the floor.

"'There's another bay next to this one," he explained, kneeling beside her. He gestured to the doors behind them. "Just through there."

She shook her head, unwilling to believe it. This wasn't possible. The prototype wasn't done yet. Her engineering team was still weeks away from finishing the initial design, from finding her sabotage, and even if they completed testing and repaired the system she had put into place, it would still take *months* to construct this many quadrupeds, entire factories working to complete the finished machine. How could this have happened? How could so many quadrupeds already exist?

And then it struck her.

"Julian."

She gritted her teeth, a fire flooding her veins as she realized the truth of what he had done. Lantern in hand, she climbed to her feet and went to the nearest machine. She pressed a trembling hand to the smooth metal, the plating buffed to a polished shine, and looked up into the face of this thing, this monster *she* created, grotesque in its actuality.

"He built an army."

CHAPTER 13

Petra curled her hand into a fist against the cold metal, clenching her fingers until her knuckles ached. "Dammit!" She punched the domed cabin and a shock of pain jolted up her arm, the acute sting bringing her thoughts into sharp focus.

Julian must have planned this all along.

"Hold on . . ." said Rupert. "*This* is the machine you've been working on for the Guild? You're sure?"

She drew away from the machine with a nod, her hand still throbbing with pain. "I don't know how," she said, looking over the familiar domed cabin and jointed legs. "But this is it, Rupert. This is my machine. Down to the bolts."

"But you said the prototype isn't finished yet."

"It's not," she said darkly. "To already have an army of them . . . He must have bypassed protocol, advanced manufacture."

"But how? Wouldn't he need the Guild's approval?"

"Not if they don't know about it." She had her doubts about Lyndon's efforts to stop the war, but she at least trusted him enough not to sign off on something like this—at least not without telling her. "No, Julian did this on his own somehow, circumventing the Guild and submitting the designs directly to the manufacturers, likely sometime after the engineering team approved the . . ." She trailed off. " . . . the original designs."

Her heart sank. "Oh, no."

"What?"

Petra thrust the lantern into Rupert's hand. "Hold this."

She climbed up the access ladder of the nearest quadruped, opened the pilot's hatch at the top of the control cabin, and slipped inside. The cramped compartment was dark, lit only by the dim glow of Rupert's lantern through the narrow window.

"Can you bring the light in?" she called to him, tracing her fingers over the pilot controls, the smudged pencil marks she had designed all those months ago suddenly made real before her eyes.

Rupert climbed to the top of the ladder and lowered the lantern into the cabin, illuminating every bolt and screw. Petra moved across the compact compartment, running her hands over the plates in the floor.

"What are you looking for?" he asked.

"Access panel," she said, finding the hidden latch.

She curled her fingers around the handle and disengaged the locking mechanism, pulling the heavy panel open. The door crashed against the cabin wall, and she lowered her head through the opening, fingers gripping the metal edge as she peered through clusters of linkages and wires, the systems of gears and sensors that powered the entire machine.

Part of her hoped she would not find it, that Julian or his engineers had somehow found the sabotage and removed it, but she knew it had to be here, that it was in every single machine aboard this airship. Had he found it, she'd have been strung up as a traitor to the crown in an instant. But she was alive, which meant Julian didn't know. Yet.

She just had to make sure, had to know.

And there . . . sitting innocently among the assembly of gears and axles—the mechanism that would shut the entire machine down once the quadruped was activated.

Damn.

She lifted herself out of the opening and stared at the wall, absently drumming her fingers against her thigh as she tried to think, leaving greasy spots on her skirt. There were eighty machines on this airship. *Eighty.* Four ships had been completed, with a dozen more on commission. She could only assume there were eighty quadrupeds in each one, totaling well over a thousand of the deadly war machines. A thousand soldiers.

If war began and her quadrupeds were sent into battle, every one of those soldiers would die. She could see it in her mind's eye—marching against the French in droves, each machine wielding the firepower of a dozen men, victory certain, and then . . . the opposing gear trains would break the tension spring within the regulator, activating the system of gears and springs that would systematically jam every single system within the quadruped. They'd have nothing—no power, no weapons—only the hard shell of the quadruped's dome to protect them from French fire.

Tears stung her eyes and she pressed her palms to her face. Julian had been so confident in his army, so convinced that nothing she did could stop him. Now she understood why. He must have planned to build the army the moment he had the approved designs. He never wanted her on the project, never wanted her involved. He just wanted a weapon, and here it was. An army of them. How could she have been so stupid?

How could she have believed she could run away from this, that she could escape Julian and turn her back on her mistakes? How could she leave now, knowing that men would die because of her?

Rupert hooked the lantern on a peg near the hatch and lowered himself into the control cabin. He crouched beside her and touched her shoulder. "Petra, what's wrong?" he asked, his voice soft. "Talk to me."

She glanced away with a shake of her head. How could she tell him? How could she explain? This was treason, sabotage—everything the Guild accused her of.

How could she drag him into it?

"I made a mistake," she whispered, staring at the open access panel at her feet. "A stupid, terrible mistake. And now . . ." She inhaled a shaky breath. "They're going to fail, Rupert—all of them."

"What?"

"The quadrupeds . . . I—" She glanced up at Rupert. "You have to believe me . . . If I had known, if I had realized . . ."

"Petra, what are you talking about?"

"I sabotaged it, Rupert."

"You *what*?"

"It wasn't supposed to happen like this!" she explained. "I never meant for it to go this far. I never meant for— The prototype should have been *tested* first, the fault found and repaired, not . . . not replicated a thousandfold! These machines never should have been built. The quadruped project never should have been approved, not with the device still intact."

"What device?"

She pressed her lips together. "A jamming device," she said with a sigh. "I'll show you."

Leaving Rupert at the open access panel, she moved across the cramped compartment and fetched a screwdriver from the toolbox bolted to the side of the cabin, curling her fingers around the weighty handle. Then she delved back through the opening and removed the faulty axle plate from the machine's gear systems. Twisting the last screw loose, the solid metal fell into her open palm, and she slowly withdrew from the access hatch, the device heavy in her hand. She stared at the connected gears, glimmering faintly in the yellow lantern light.

"You have to understand," she said quietly, her voice barely above a whisper. "I thought that if I caused the prototype to fail, if it malfunctioned while in production, I could delay its approval, set the Guild back a few months, delay the war long enough to find another way to stop it altogether, but now . . ." She tightened her grip around the axle plate, the sabotaging gears cutting deep into her palm. "I only ever meant to delay the prototype, not sabotage an entire army."

"What does it do?" he asked.

She turned it over in her hand. "Once the quadruped activates, this will trigger systematic failure throughout the quadruped's main systems, rendering the machine inoperable within minutes."

"Can you fix it?"

"Maybe." She sighed. "Yes. But . . . every single quadruped on this ship has the fault, built right into the infrastructure. All of them." She tossed the faulty axle plate to the floor and scrubbed her hand over her face. "And if the Guild finds out what I've done, if Julian finds out I sabotaged his war machines, they'll—" She swallowed hard, her throat tightening around the words. "They'll hang me."

Rupert regarded her in silence. "So this is what you've been hiding from me these last few months, what you wouldn't tell me?"

She kneaded her brow. "Yes."

"Damn it, Petra, why didn't you say something?"

he asked, his voice rising. "You could have trusted me with this! I could have helped you!"

Petra scoffed. "And condemn you too? How could I? This is *treason*, Rupert. If I'm caught, I'll hang, and I'll be damned if I condemn my best friend to hang beside me."

"And I'll be damned if I let you hang at all!"

She frowned at him. "This is exactly why I *didn't* tell you. This isn't your fight, Rupert. If anyone found out you were involved—"

"Well, it's too late for that, isn't it?" he said, glaring back at her. "What are you planning to do?"

She rubbed her hand over her face. "I don't *know*," she admitted, sinking against the cabin wall. She pressed her fingers to her forehead, a headache forming in the ridge of her brow. "I was going to leave. Today, after dinner. I was going to run, slip away when you and Braith weren't looking, board the last train out of the station, and get as far away from the Guild and Julian as I could before they discovered what I had done. But now . . ." She pulled her knees to her chest and sighed. "I can't run from this—I know that—but if I go back now . . . if I report the fault to the Guild, if I try to fix them, Julian will see it for what it is and have me arrested for sabotage. I can't win, Rupert. No matter what I do, they'll kill me for this."

Rupert sat down beside her and wrapped his arm around her shoulders. "I won't let that happen," he said, the anger gone from his voice. "Braith wouldn't—"

"Braith?" She scoffed. "Braith will follow his orders."

"You give him too little credit."

"And you give him too much," she said, drawing away. "He's still a soldier. His loyalty is to the Royal Forces. Not me."

"He might be able to help you."

"And he might turn me in."

"You don't know that."

"Yes, I *do*," she said, getting to her feet. She kicked the access panel shut and ran her grease-streaked fingers through her hair. "Why do you think he was ordered to follow me in the first place?" she asked, whirling on Rupert again. "He might not know what I've done, but he suspects. He's known all along I might try to sabotage the project. That's the whole reason the Guild assigned him to me."

Rupert regarded her from the floor. "Even if that's true, you know he would never turn you over to the Guild, not if he knew the truth."

She shook her head. "I can't risk that."

"Then what are you going to do?"

Petra ran her fingers through her hair. She knew the answer, had known it the moment she found the faulty axle plate. "I have to fix them," she said, turning toward him with a shrug. "I just wish I knew *how*."

Rupert stood and laid his hand on her arm. "We'll figure it out."

"We have to. If I don't fix this . . ." She buried her face in her hands. "If this army goes into battle, they'll die because of me, because of what I've done. There's too much at stake for me to fail."

He squeezed her shoulder. "Then we won't fail. Now, come on," he said, gently pushing her toward the ladder set into the back of the pilot's chair. "We should find Braith and head home. We'll figure out a plan from there."

Petra snatched up the discarded axle plate and stuffed it in her pocket, following Rupert out of the control cabin. They left the platoon of quadrupeds behind and quickly crept out of the cargo hold, climbing up the narrow stairs to the upper deck. They were halfway to the main deck when a loud boom thundered in the distance, the aftershock rumbling through the ship. The walls creaked around them, the floor shifting beneath Petra's feet.

She clung to Rupert's arm. "What was that?"

"It sounded like an explosion," he said, turning his eyes to the ceiling.

Then a second boom answered the first, closer this time. The hangar quaked, rattling the metal walls and wooden beams. It shuddered through the airship, and Petra stumbled into Rupert as memories of the Luddite attack on the University sprang to mind—dozens dying in the square, burning, twitching, bleeding, Emmerich pierced with shrapnel, his blood on her hands, reddening the alleys as they stumbled away from the carnage. She dug her fingers hard into Rupert's arm, her throat closing up.

Not again.

Rupert grabbed her by the shoulders and forced her to look him in the eyes. "Petra, listen to me," he said gently. "We need to find Braith and get out of here." He took her hand with a comforting squeeze. "We need to find out what's going on."

Finding an anchor in the pressure of his hand, she focused on Rupert's determined gaze and nodded, pushing the fire from her mind.

It wasn't the Luddites this time. This was war. She could feel it.

Rupert dragged her to the top deck, hurrying quickly toward the rope ladder, when on the other side of the building, the hangar side door slammed open and the lights flickered on, the electric bulbs buzzing dimly overhead.

"Petra? Rupert? Are you in here?"

Braith.

Petra turned away from the rails and clutched Rupert's hand. "Rupert, please . . . Braith *can't* know about this. You can't say anything—not about the quadruped, not about the sabotage or this army . . . *Nothing.* If he finds out what I've done . . ." She trailed off, fear creeping into her chest. "Please," she begged. "Promise me you won't say anything, not until I've set things right. Promise me—"

"He might be able to help you, Petra."

She shook her head. "I can't take that risk. Not until I know what to do. Please, Rupert. Promise me you won't say anything."

Rupert held her gaze a moment longer. "I promise," he said quietly. "But I wish you'd change your mind about him."

Braith's steps echoed off the walls as he hurried across the hangar floor, his heavy boot steps accompanied by a string of curses. "Damn it, Petra, where the hell are you?"

"Up here," Rupert called, leaning over the railing.

Braith's footsteps quickened. "Rupert? Is Petra with you?"

"She's here." Rupert pushed her toward the ladder. "Go."

Petra clambered over the rails and climbed down the ladder, her hands sweaty on the coarse rope. She reached the floor just as Braith rounded the corner, his cap gone, hair disheveled, the top of his uniform jacket unbuttoned. Then his eyes met hers, and a dozen emotions ran across his face in an instant.

She gravitated toward him, drawn forward by an irresistible pull until they met halfway, stopping just short of reaching out and touching one another. He held her gaze without speaking a word, his face completely disarmed as he slowly raised a hand to her cheek, his fingers hovering mere inches from her skin. She swallowed hard, paralyzed by the crack in his demeanor.

He had never looked at her like that before.

Then he curled his hand into a fist and withdrew, falling behind the mask again. "Tell me this wasn't you," he said quietly, lowering his hand.

The world rushed back into motion, and she shied away. "What do you mean?"

"Tell me this wasn't your doing," he said more urgently. "That you aren't a part of this."

"A part of what?" she demanded, her pulse thundering in her ears. "Braith . . . what's going on? What's happened? We heard—"

Another explosion thundered outside, even nearer than before, and the floor trembled, the entire hangar shuddering with the aftershock. Petra stumbled forward, and Braith caught her by the shoulders.

He steadied her and forced her to look into his eyes, his grip firm. "Petra, tell me you had nothing to do with this," he said, his jaw tight. "Swear to me you aren't behind this attack."

She blinked. "An *attack*? How could you think—"

"You *disappeared*," he said, his voice hardening. "You said you'd wait for me, but instead you snuck off and left me to come find you . . . and then *this* happens," he said gesturing toward the hangar doors. His voice cracked. "What were you thinking? Why didn't you wait?"

"We *did* wait," she said. "You didn't come."

"You should have waited longer!" He pressed his lips together and tore away from her. "Of all the *stupid* things you could have done . . . Don't you realize what this looks like? If anyone finds out you snuck away, that we were separated in the midst of an attack . . ."

Petra blanched. "But I didn't—I wasn't—I had nothing to do with this! I've been with Rupert the entire time. I swear it. Braith . . . you have to believe me," she said. "I'm not an anti-imperialist spy. I'm not a traitor. I had nothing to do with the attack. If anyone thought . . . If you said anything to make them think—"

"I believe you." He touched her shoulders, silencing her fears. "I just . . . I had to ask."

She closed her eyes with a sigh, relief flooding her veins.

"Despite what you may think, Petra, I'm on your side. I trust you."

She glanced up at him, her gut wrenching with guilt. *You shouldn't*, she wanted to say—but she didn't. He still didn't know what she and Rupert had found in the belly of that airship. He didn't know she had already sabotaged the war machines, that she had lied to him—was still lying to him. But he couldn't know the truth, not yet, not until she knew what to do, not until she knew how to stop the Royal Forces from sending those machines into battle. Not until she had fixed her mistake.

"What now?" she whispered.

"We need to get you out of here," he replied. "Away from the hangars, away from the airfield. Whatever is going on here, you need to be as far away as possible before you're dragged into it somehow. We can't let anyone think that you were involved. Where's Rupert?"

"He's—"

"Here." Rupert dropped down from the ladder and jogged up next to them. "Braith, what's going on? Who's behind the explosions?" he asked. "Is it the French?"

Braith shook his head. "I don't know, but whoever it

is, the military hangars may be their prime target. We should go. It isn't safe here."

"Right. Let's get out of here."

The airfield was chaos.

Petra, Braith, and Rupert stood at the northern edge of the airfield, their backs to the military hangars as black smoke billowed across the sky. Sirens blared as a pair of water trucks sped toward the fires. Droves of military vehicles rolled across the grassy field, soldiers in uniforms of red and navy wielding rifles as they headed toward the source of the explosions. All around them, people clambered to safety, away from the smoke and flames.

Braith withdrew his pistol from its holster and held it aloft, his finger resting against the trigger guard as he scanned the airfield ahead.

She grabbed him by the sleeve of his red uniform, her throat suddenly dry. "Don't leave me," she said, a tremor in her voice.

A faint smile lifted the corner of his mouth. "Wasn't planning on it."

The earth shuddered as another explosion rattled the airfield—dangerously close. The deep boom ripped through the air, and the resounding shockwave clapped the breath from her lungs as it passed. She stumbled into Braith, and the world plunged into thick silence as he caught her against his chest. A white haze clouded her vision, and ringing filled her ears, dust and smoke clogging the air, making it hard to breathe. Hands touched her shoulders, and she looked up into Braith's face, his voice muffled and distant as he steadied her on her feet.

Then it pierced through the noise, like static through a telephone. "—a way off the airfield." His brows drew together, and he searched her eyes. "Petra? Are you all right? We need to get out of here."

She met his gaze and nodded.

"There are still some vehicles at the southern gates," said Rupert, standing on his toes. He pointed toward the encampment of booths and tents to the south. "We might be able to catch one if we hurry."

Another explosion sounded, further off than before—another hangar up in flame.

Braith grabbed Petra's hand. "Come on. Let's go."

The three of them headed toward the other side of the airfield, weaving through the panicked crowds as fires burned through hangars and airships, dark smoke curling into the open sky. The sound of popping gunfire pierced the noise of disorder all around them, and Petra gritted her teeth against the sound.

Rupert ran ahead a few paces, and Petra and Braith shoved after him, buffeted and elbowed by the rush of people around them, all running away from the heavy smoke and curling flames. Many headed toward the few remaining airships, escaping the burning airfield by taking to the air, while others hurried toward the airfield entrance to the south, silk hats and lace fans discarded, crumpled beneath muddy boots.

Halfway to the southern gate, Rupert paused and turned toward both Braith and Petra. "I'll run ahead and hold one of the buses before it leaves, get us a way out of here." He sprinted toward the departing vehicles, leaving Braith with Petra.

Braith tugged her forward. "Let's hurry."

They ran forward as quickly as the two of them could navigate over the trampled tents and booths, passing the few people that still remained as they headed toward the gates. Steam boilers hissed and combustion engines rumbled to life as passengers piled into the scattered automobiles and through the gates, escaping the airfield grounds in a flurry of footsteps and squelching tires.

Petra spotted Rupert several yards away, waving at them from the back of an idle omnibus, the passengers all leaning out the windows as they looked toward the columns of smoke rising to the west. The explosions had stopped for now, but the fires still raged, black smoke spilling into the sky, the sounds of collapsing structures punctuating the cacophony of panic.

Braith and Petra caught up to the bus, and Braith quickly scaled the ladder and held out his hand for Petra to follow.

She hesitated next to Rupert, noticing the lack of space within the omnibus. Her heart sank. "You're not coming."

Rupert shrugged. "I'll catch the next one."

"Don't be stupid. There won't be a next one," she said. "All the other buses have gone."

"I'll be all right."

Petra reached out and grabbed his hand. "Come with us."

He raised a hand to her cheek, his touch gentle. "I can't. Go with Braith. Get back to the city. I'll message you as soon as I can, let you know what's going on."

The omnibus driver shouted something from the front of the vehicle, and Rupert pulled her into a tight hug.

Tears burned her eyes and she hugged him back. "Be careful."

He sighed against her neck, holding her close. "You too."

Then he let her go, and Braith pulled her onto the carriage, his hands secure on her waist. Rupert closed the carriage doors behind her and drew the deadbolt shut, stepping away from the carriage with a frown. Not a moment later, the driver shifted the vehicle into gear and they rolled away from the airfield, leaving him behind.

Petra gripped the carriage doors as the omnibus wheeled down the long, dusty road and out of sight of the airfield. Airships floated overhead, drifting aimlessly above the burning airfield, their colorful banners fluttering in the smoky breeze, until they too disappeared from sight, obscured by tree and hedge as the bus drove on.

"He'll be all right," said Braith, his voice close and quiet, the two of them pressed tightly together in the overcrowded carriage.

All around them, the other passengers exchanged frantic worries in hushed tones, speculating the cause of the explosions, who might be behind them. But it didn't matter whether it was anti-imperialist radicals or French soldiers, not really.

Either way, the result would be war.

Petra curled her hands into fists, fighting back tears.

Hours ago, she had believed she could escape this war, escape Julian and the quadruped and her sabotage, but she should have known escape would be impossible. Julian would always find a way to drag her back into his web. And now he had an army, soon to have a thousand quadrupeds at his command, ready for whatever war might come—an army that would fail in battle because she was stupid enough to think she could stop him.

Braith had been right.

This war would happen with or without her.

There was only one thing she could do now: she had to fix the quadrupeds. Whatever it took. Whatever the cost.

She would not let men die because of her.

CHAPTER 14

Petra stood at the bow of the overcrowded ferry, a cold stone of nausea settling in the pit of her stomach as they approached the brass towers of Chroniker City. She gripped the rail with shaking hands, her fingers and toes soaked through by the relentless mist of sea spray crashing against the hull of the ship. A chill wind gusted over the choppy ocean waves, bringing dark clouds in from the west. Braith stood at her back, the only source of warmth on the deck of this godforsaken ship, but nothing could warm the chill that had settled deep in her bones.

She saw her fate now with the utmost clarity. When she left the city that morning, she had thought she could escape it, but there was only one way forward now. If she wanted to repair the quadruped before war struck, then she had no choice but to expose her sabotage, and if that meant surrendering herself to Julian, so be it.

The ferry docked and Petra hurried off the ship, Braith not far behind. She shouldered through the crowd, the docks bustling with redcoats, coppers, bobbies, and pedestrians alike, everyone swarming toward the arriving ships as droves of passengers came ashore. News of the attack circulated through the crowd—panicked exchanges and whispered speculation, questions of war, fear of other attacks, worries of whether the attackers had targeted more than the airfield, if this was part of some greater scheme against the British Empire.

Petra shoved past them all, pausing only to show her papers to the guards at the gates before hurrying up the street toward the University, towering high above the rest of the city.

Braith finally caught up to her on the other side of Pemberton Square and grabbed her arm, jerking her to a stop. The busy main-street crowd bustled around them, a confusion of voices and bodies, faceless and ghostlike.

"Petra, slow down," he said, holding her steady. "Why are you in such a rush?"

"I need to speak to Julian," she said, trying to tug free of his grasp. "As soon as possible."

"Why?"

She faltered. How could she explain? If he knew what she had done . . . There would be no going back after that, no returning to the lies that had kept her safe until now. To tell him the truth would break down every last wall she had built to protect herself.

Could she trust him with that?

He laid a hand on her shoulder. "Petra, what's wrong?"

She met his concerned eyes, her resolve starting to crack. What point was there in hiding the truth from him now? After today, that would be the end of it, the end of her rebellion, proof of her sabotage handed over willingly. Julian would have everything he needed to get rid of her, and there was nothing Braith could do that she wasn't about to bring down on herself.

If there was a time to trust him, it was now.

"There is something I need to tell you," she said slowly. "Something you're not going to like. I—" She choked on the words, the truth sticking in her throat.

"What is it?" he asked. "Petra . . . you can tell me."

"I made a mistake," she whispered, her voice quavering. "I—I was wrong to think I could stop this war, to think—" She swallowed thickly and closed her eyes, seeing again the rows and rows of quadrupeds in Rupert's airships, just waiting for an excuse to go to war. "I have to fix them, Braith. Whatever it takes. If I don't . . . men will die because of me, because of what I've done."

"What do you mean?" he asked. "What mistake?"

She pressed her mouth shut, glancing up and down the heavily congested street. Too many eyes. Too many ears. "Not here." She grabbed his arm and pulled him down a side street to a less populated area of the city, between the first and fourth quadrants. She stopped at the mouth of a derelict alley, the brick and cobblestones grimy with soot and dirt.

"Petra, what—"

"I told you before, of my involvement with the automaton," she started, worrying at the stem of her pocket watch as she paced across the narrow alleyway. "How Emmerich destroyed it trying to protect me from his father."

She remembered that day with perfect clarity—the fire in Emmerich's eyes as he turned the frightening machine against his father, how he used the automaton to smash a hole through the floor so she might escape. "Well, there is a bit more to the story than I let on . . .

"I tried once to stop this war, to stop Julian when I realized the truth of what he was trying to do, but I failed. The automaton was his first attempt to create a war machine, long before there was any conflict with the anti-imperialists. It was proposed as a preemptive measure, but that was a lie. All along, he planned to replicate the automaton, create an army, and use it to mount an attack on the French once his plans to fuel a war were in motion. When we discovered the truth— Emmerich and I—we intended to destroy the prototype and reveal his conspiracy, hoping to stop the war before it ever began, but before we could prove anything, I was arrested and accused of being a spy and a traitor, of being involved with the anti-imperialists. Emmerich helped me escape, but by then, it was too late. The damage had been done. The destruction of the prototype was all Julian needed to fuel the conflict between Great Britain and the anti-imperialists. By trying to stop him, I played right into his hands.

"By the time I was cleared of any crimes, the designs had already been prepared for manufacture. There wasn't enough evidence to prove that Julian was behind the war. There was nothing we could do to stop him. We failed."

Braith stared at her. "Hold on . . . You think the *minister* is behind the war? What possible reason—"

"He wants to create a new world," she said, the words bitter on her tongue. She still remembered the glint in Julian's eyes the night he told her his plans. "He'll burn this one and build a new one from the ashes, with him in power and all the world at his mercy."

"That's madness."

"That what's I've been trying to tell you," she said. "This war isn't what you think. Julian is behind everything—the automaton, the rising conflict between Great Britain and France. All along, he's been the one pulling the strings. He forced Emmerich to present the automaton project to the Guild. He perverted it into a war machine. And when Emmerich and I destroyed the prototype, he turned it into an anti-imperialist attack on the Guild. Everything he's done, everything he's worked for, he only ever intended to start a war, to fuel the fire between Great Britain and the anti-imperialists."

"Petra, one man can't orchestrate an entire war. The conflict between Great Britain and the anti-imperialists has been brewing for decades. It only needed—"

"A spark," she said, finishing for him. "A catalyst. *Me.*"

"But why you?"

"Because I was the one stupid enough to design his war machine," she said bitterly. "I was the one stupid enough to try to stop him."

He remained silent for a moment. "That's why you feel responsible for this . . . for the war. You think you're the cause."

She nodded. "Which is why I have to stop him, why I've fought so hard to end this. I never wanted to build a war machine, I never wanted to be a part of this war, but after what happened with the automaton, he threatened to turn me over to the Royal Forces as a traitor and a spy unless I cooperated with him, unless I built him a new war machine. If I agreed, he promised to withdraw his statement about my anti-imperialist ties; he promised me a position within the University and the Guild—as long as I did as he asked. All I had to do was keep my mouth shut, build his war machine, and do nothing else to sabotage his plans. I resisted as long as I could, trying to earn a position in the Guild on my own terms, but in the end, building the quadruped was the only way to keep my freedom—to keep my *life.* The day you and I met outside the council chambers, he threatened to repeal my pardon and send me to the Royal Forces to answer for my crimes, unless I delivered on our agreement. I thought that if I cooperated, it might buy me the time I needed to expose his conspiracy, to expose him for what he was, but—"

She paused, the truth of what she had done sticking in her throat. "After failing with the automaton," she went on, "I knew I needed a contingency plan, in case I couldn't find a way to expose the truth about the war and Julian's hand in it. A surefire way to stall the production of the quadruped and delay the war."

Braith regarded her with a frown. "How?"

"I . . . You have to understand," she said thickly. "I thought I could delay his plans, put off the war long enough to find another way to stop him. I thought I had more time. I never meant for it to—" She broke off, shaking her head. "If I had known what he was planning . . . if I had realized . . ."

"Petra, what did you do?"

She swallowed against the tightness in her throat. "I sabotaged it," she said bluntly. "The quadruped design. From the very beginning."

Braith took a step back. "You didn't."

"I thought it was the only way. I didn't—" She glanced away, an ache spreading through her chest. "I didn't *think*. You were right, Braith. I can't stop this war. I was wrong to think that I could. I realize that now."

"After all this time . . . after everything I did for you . . ." The muscles in his jaw twitched, and he turned away from her with a shake of his head. "I *lied* for you, Petra," he said, his voice barely a hiss. "I stood up for you. And now you tell me you already sabotaged it? Why?"

"I didn't think I had a choice."

Braith scoffed.

"I thought I could stop him before it came to war, but now—"

"But now what? Why are you telling me this now?" he demanded. "What changed?"

"Because after today, I may not get another chance," she said. "I have to fix it. *Today*. If I don't . . . Julian, he—" She pressed her lips together with a frown, her mouth suddenly dry. "He built an army of them, Braith," she said thickly, her voice cracking. "An army of quadrupeds, built from the sabotaged design."

"What?"

"I saw them, at Hasguard, sitting in the cargo hold of one of Rupert's warships. We found them right before the attack on the airfield—eighty to a ship, with more being commissioned as we speak."

"How?"

"I don't know," she admitted, shaking her head. "But you have to believe me—those machines were never supposed to exist; the schematics were never meant for mass production. The prototype was designed to fail, delaying manufacture until the fault was repaired. But Julian must have bypassed the council somehow, ignoring Guild protocol to advance construction before the prototype could be approved." She swallowed hard. "And now, because of what I've done . . . if the quadrupeds in those ships are deployed, every one of them will fail."

The sky darkened a shade, the smell of rain on the air.

"That's why I have to fix them," she went on. "Before it's too late. I may not be able to stop this war, but I can fix my mistake."

He looked up at her. "How?"

"There is an axle plate," she explained, reaching into her skirt pocket and withdrawing the faulty device. "A part of the regulatory system linking the intersecting mechanisms. Without it, the quadruped will function as intended, the sabotage rendered inert." She gripped the device in her hand—this tiny thing, a weapon in its own right, capable of disabling an entire army within mere minutes. All because she was stupid enough to believe she could stop Julian's schemes. "You have to believe me, Braith," she went on, her voice quiet. "I never meant for it to go this far. All I ever wanted was to delay the war, stop it if I could. Not this."

They stood there in silence for a moment, distant thunder echoing across the sky. The sky turned a slate gray, casting the city in shadow.

"Turn me in if you have to," she said. "Report me to the Guild. I don't care. But first, let me fix my mistake. Let me make this right."

Finally, he spoke. "What do you plan to do?"

"The only thing I can do," she said. "Tell Julian of the fault and hope it's not too late to fix them."

"Petra, if the minister learns what you've done—"

"He'll have me arrested—I know—but he's the only one who can have the army repaired in time. I don't have any other choice."

Braith shook his head and turned away, slowly running his fingers through his hair. "No, there has to be another way," he said, starting to pace. "You can't just waltz into his office and tell him you sabotaged the quadruped . . . or what's more, that his entire army—an army you shouldn't even know about—is defective."

"What else am I supposed to do? If the quadrupeds aren't repaired in time, those men will die."

He stopped pacing. "And if you tell the minister the truth, *you* will die," he said, his voice surprisingly soft. "You realize that, don't you?"

Rolling thunder punctuated his words, and a cold shiver crawled down her spine. She knew what would happen when she told Julian of her sabotage—she had known from the very first day she decided to sabotage the quadruped—but there was no other way to stop the Royal Forces from sending the faulty machines into battle.

"I have to fix this," she said quietly. "Whatever the consequences."

"So you're going to hand yourself over? Just like that?"

"If that's what it takes to repair them, then yes. I know what needs to be done; I've known since I first saw the quadrupeds sitting in Rupert's warship. So either you can help me, or—"

"What do you think I'm trying to do?" he asked.

"I'm trying to figure out a way out of this that doesn't end up with you dead. You need a plan."

"I told you—"

"A *better* plan." He turned away from her, kneading his forehead as he paced up and down the alley, his brows knit in concentration. "What about the prototype?" he finally asked, turning toward her. "How long would it take you to fix it?"

"A few minutes. Why?"

He started pacing again. "Say you repaired the prototype and removed the sabotage, would that not accomplish what you want? The minister would learn of the repair in the weekly production report, and he would have no choice but to forward the repair to the Royal Forces, or else their failure would be on him."

"But it could takes days for that to happen," she countered. "There are hundreds of these machines, Braith, with even more in production. If there are any delays, if war starts before the repair is fully implemented . . ." She shook her head. "It's too much of a risk."

"It is a risk, yes, but one we can afford. Wars don't happen overnight. Once the Royal Forces is aware of the fault, they'll have no choice but to repair the machines—all of them. They can't knowingly send faulty machines into battle. We just have to make sure the minister never suspects the truth of what you're actually trying to do."

"You think that could work?" she asked, her heart beating faster at the possibility.

"There's only one way to find out."

Petra hurried to her dormitory and ditched her dress in her room, no need to change since she was already wearing her work clothes underneath. She delayed only long enough to grab a hat and change into a dry pair of socks and shoes before fetching her copy of the quadruped schematics from her desk. She riffled through the stack of pages until she found the design for the machine's base, where her sabotage connected through the primary gear systems. It had seemed so simple all those months ago. Sabotage the prototype. Delay the war.

How naïve she had been to think it would be that easy.

Stuffing the designs in her pocket, she left the bedroom and met Braith in the hall, pulling her hair back into a braid as she walked.

"You got them?" he asked, falling into step beside her.

She nodded, tying off the end of her hair. "We need to hurry, before Calligaris sends everyone home for the day. Someone has to be there to confirm the fault and verify the repair, or else Julian will cry sabotage and bury me for trying to fix it."

Braith stopped her. "I won't let that happen," he said, his voice full of conviction. "Petra, listen to me . . . Whatever happens now, I'm on your side. I'm with you."

An hour ago, she wouldn't have believed it, but she had no doubts about his loyalty now. The choice she had feared for so long had come, and despite everything, he had chosen her.

Not his duties. Not the Royal Forces. Not the Guild. *Her.*

"I know," she said, her voice cracking.

She only hoped he wouldn't come to regret it.

From the dormitories, they made their way to the workshop, the University halls still abuzz with engineers and students, the mood somber after the news of the airfield attack. Petra's heart beat like a drum in her chest, afraid that Julian would see through their fragile plan and figure out the truth of what she had done. If she failed to remove the sabotage, if she failed to pass it off as a legitimate repair . . . there were so many things that could go wrong, so many ways she might fail.

But there was more than her own life on the line now. Failure was not an option.

She turned the corner down the long hallway that led to the Guild workshops, determined to stop for nothing until the quadruped prototype was repaired, when she ran smack into another engineer.

Braith caught her by the arm before she fell.

She brushed him off and glanced up at the engineer, relieved when she recognized him. "Yancy? What are you doing here?"

"I suppose I could ask you the same," he said, looking her over. "I thought you were on leave today, a trip to the airfield."

"We just got back a little while ago. Have you heard what happened?"

He nodded. "We just got the news. I was on my way to see if my father knew anything more about what happened. No one's saying much, but there's talk of anti-imperialists behind it."

"Where did you hear that?"

"Minister Goss," he said "Just a half-hour ago. We've been ordered to expedite production in light of the attack; the deadline has been moved to next week. We're scheduled to work in shifts until it's done."

Petra glanced at Braith, the rigid line of his jaw all she needed to know that he understood the severity of the situation. "We need to get the workshop," she said, her pulse racing. "Now."

She turned to go, but Yancy touched her arm.

"Petra, wait. You should know . . ." He leaned close, lowering his voice to a whisper. "When the minister came by the workshop, he mentioned you. He seems to think you're involved."

"Involved?"

"In the attack."

"*What?*"

"I didn't catch everything he said, but before he left, he told Calligaris to telephone if you turned up. Something about the bombings on the airfield. That's all I know."

Petra turned away, eyes searching blindly as her mind raced ahead of her. This couldn't be happening. Not now. Not so soon. She pressed a hand to her brow, their plan to repair the quadruped suddenly narrowing to an impossibly fine line. A single misstep and they would fail. She glanced up and her eyes met Braith's.

"We have to do it now," she said. "Before it's too late."

"You can't. If the minister thinks you're involved in the attack—"

"Then this is the only chance we'll get."

Braith frowned. "Petra . . ."

"It's over for me," she said, shaking her head. "It was over the moment I stepped foot in the city. You know it as well as I do. But I still have a chance to make this right. I still have a chance to fix it. I have to *try*."

He regarded her stonily. "Are you sure?"

"Yes," she answered, not a hint of reservation in her voice. "And you?" she asked. "Are you still with me?"

"You know I am."

"Then we need to hurry." She turned toward Yancy, the frown on his face so like his father's. "Yancy . . . I wouldn't ask this of you if it wasn't important, but I need your help with something."

Yancy arched an eyebrow. "Go on."

"There's a repair that I need to make to the prototype," she said, retrieving the quadruped designs from her pocket and offering him the pages. "An error I found checking over the schematics again. With production accelerated, it's important we fix it as soon as possible."

Yancy took the pages from her. "An error?"

She nodded, showing him the faulty axle plate. "If you look here, where the trains overlap through the regulator, the gears are connected to conflicting drive systems. If left intact, once the quadruped is fully operational, these will rotate in opposition. With enough pressure, the tension springs linked to the regulator will snap." Causing the sabotaging clockwork system to set off, but she didn't mention that. "Complete immobilization of the primary systems in a matter of minutes. It wouldn't have shown up in the initial tests because—"

"Because the intersecting systems aren't connected yet," he finished for her, drawing his finger across the paper to the main transmission in the war machine's base. "I see what you mean." He glanced up from the schematics. "But why do you need my help?"

"I can repair the fault," she said. "But with the council's suspicions and Julian out for my blood . . . If the Guild arrests me before I can finish the repair and file the report myself, someone else will need to do it in my stead—someone I trust. Will you help me?"

Yancy regarded the schematics again. "Shouldn't we go to my father with this? He could—"

"We don't have time," she said. "I've already wasted enough as it is."

"Petra, if you return to the workshop now, with Calligaris waiting for you—"

"I know," she said. "Trust me, Yancy. I wouldn't risk it if I thought there was any other way. I can't tell you why, but it's imperative the repair is filed today, as soon as possible. Can I count on you?"

"Of course you can," he said with a nod, giving the schematics back. "Just tell me what to do."

Petra paused at the door to the workshop, her heart in her throat as Yancy slipped inside and disappeared over the edge of the catwalk, his footsteps loud on the rungs of the access ladder. She gripped the edge of the doorframe, the sounds of electric-power tools whirring beyond her sight—the hiss and flare of a lone blowlamp, the deep knell of a sledgehammer driving a peg—her quadruped coming together piece by piece. She inhaled a shaky breath.

Repair the prototype. File the report. Fix the army.

That was the plan. She just hoped it worked.

"Petra, are you sure about this?" asked Braith, standing at her elbow. "If the minister thinks you had a hand in the airfield attack—"

"What choice do I have?" she spat, more anger in her voice than she intended. She turned away from the workshop floor, her chest tight. "If I don't fix the quadruped—"

"Then someone else will," he said, taking her arm and pulling her away from the door. "Let someone else repair the fault. Let Yancy take care of it. Show him how to fix it, and we can get you out of here before—"

"No," she said, pulling herself away. "I can't leave this to someone else. I *won't*. This is *my* mistake, *my* responsibility."

"Petra—"

"I *have* to do this, Braith," she whispered. "I have to make this right. Whatever the cost."

He let out a heavy sigh. "Then do what you need to

do and get out of there," he said. "We may still have a chance to escape if you act quickly enough. Don't give up yet."

She glanced up at him, the urge to say something itching at her throat, but she didn't have the words—only fear. And regret. She didn't deserve such loyalty, not from him. "I'll try," she said quietly, and then she was through the door and over the catwalk, sliding down the ladder to the workshop floor.

Her feet hit the ground hard and she turned on her heel, holding her hat firmly to her head as she walked slowly toward the quadruped. It stood like a great metal spider in the center of the room, the harsh electric light glinting off its sharp, angled legs and smooth brass dome.

Yancy was already at the base of the machine, talking animatedly to one of the elder engineers, his welding goggles pushed above his brows as Yancy gestured toward the quadruped's base. Another engineer lay underneath, busily welding sheets of plating to the underbelly while two others began mounting the left-hand Agar to the piloting cabin. It was terrifying really, the unfinished edges and fragmented construction almost grotesque compared to the neat rows of completed quadrupeds she had found in Rupert's warship. Frankensteinian. Emmerich would have found some sort of ironic poetry in that.

Yancy caught her eye as she approached and joined her beside the machine, leaving the other engineer to his work. "Merle's going to run the numbers again," he said to her, "but it will take Calligaris's approval before they can investigate the possibility of repair—if the fault does show up."

Petra frowned. "We don't have time for that."

"Not likely." Yancy gestured over her shoulder. "Looks like Calligaris knows you're here."

"Dammit." She turned toward Calligaris's desk. Already he had the telephone receiver to his ear, his eyes fixed on her like a hawk. She swallowed hard. "How much time do you think we have?"

"Ten minutes? Five?"

She grabbed a screwdriver from the nearest toolbox, curling her fingers around the heavy wooden handle. "Give me a hand with the ladder."

Yancy helped move the ladder to the quadruped, and then she was up the rungs and inside the unfinished cabin, landing on the exposed floor beams with a clang. Her eyes swept the chamber, taking in the chaos of uncompleted mechanisms, the unmounted control panel leaning against the wall, the dashboard a tangle of wires and linkages. The pilot's chair was absent, the floor nothing more than a frame of metal crossbeams, but the array of gears beneath the cramped dome had the look of a finished machine. The engine transmission and connecting drive systems had been completed nearly a month ago. Every single axle, linkage, and gear fitted together according to Petra's flawed designs—down to the sabotaging axle plate.

"Yancy, you there?" she called.

Outside the dome, the ladder creaked under his

weight, and a few seconds later, Yancy hung over the open hatch, blocking the overhead light. He heaved himself over the edge and dropped into the cabin with a thud.

"Need some help?"

"Just pay attention," she said. "I can only show you this once."

She crouched over the exposed floor and pointed out the faulty axle plate with her screwdriver. "This is the axle plate here," she said, reaching down into the machine's base. "Removing it will prevent the mechanical failure, but it will also deactivate the regulator. Without it, the pilots will have to adjust power distribution manually, likely leading to a drop in mechanical efficiency, but the quadruped will function as intended."

She pulled the first screw loose and passed it up to Yancy.

"Could we not reconfigure the axle plate to adjust for the rotational disparity?" he asked, watching as she removed the next couple of screws. "If we implemented a secondary transmission between the interconnecting mechanisms, or maybe added another gear train to redirect the load from the main drive, we could bypass the tension issue and still keep the regulator intact."

"If we had more time, perhaps," she said, passing him another screw. "But with the deadline moved up, this is the best fix we have."

Even if they could reconfigure the drive trains, the repair would take days to complete on the prototype, possibly even weeks, and with the army of quadrupeds sitting in a hangar at Hasguard, they didn't have the time or the manpower to implement such a complicated repair to over twelve hundred machines. Removing the axle plate was the simplest option. The only option.

She wiped a trickle of sweat from her brow, the cabin swelteringly hot this close to the freshly welded underbelly.

Three more screws.

And then maybe she and Braith could get out of here.

She hadn't twisted the next screw more than a few turns when she heard a shout at the far side of the workshop, someone banging on the supply door, then footsteps treading nearer. The ladder beside the prototype creaked, rattling against the quadruped's shell with each step, and Petra froze as she looked up at the open hatch door, wondering whose face she would see.

Braith appeared overhead. "He's here," he said with a frown, his voice tense. "I barred the supply door and cut the wires for the mechanical lock upstairs, but it's only a matter of time before they break in. You need to hurry."

Petra clenched her jaw and stared at the exposed floor. She had no *time*. "Yancy? I need you to do something else for me," she said, leaning back into the machine's base. She removed the final two screws and yanked the faulty axle plate free, tossing it to Yancy before wiping her greasy hands on her trousers. She fetched the schematics from her pocket and pressed the crumpled pages into his hands, hardly breathing as she heard the slam of the supply door banging against the wall and the sound of boot steps echoing off the workshop floor. "I need you to take these to your father," she said. "Don't wait. Go straight there. File an official repair order with his signature and have it delivered it to the Royal Forces at once."

"What are you going to do?"

Braith dropped into the quadruped. "We're going to run."

"Wait," she said, Braith already hauling her to her feet. "There's something else . . . Yancy, there's an army of faulty quadrupeds at the Hasguard Airfield, built according to the prototype's flawed design," she said, resisting Braith's grasp. "Rupert knows where they are. If the report isn't filed, they'll fail—all of them. You have to tell your father. You have to make sure—"

"Damn it, Petra . . ." Braith shoved her to the ladder. "We have to *go*."

"You have to fix them," she said, stumbling up the ladder. "Yancy—"

"I'll take care of it," he said, pocketing the schematics. "Just go."

She nodded in gratitude and let Braith push her up the rest of the narrow access ladder, clambering out of the quadruped and down the other side.

The coppers were already on them.

She landed hard on the floor, barely evading the first copper as Braith landed next to her. He grappled with one of the black-uniformed men as she kicked another in the shin. Then she scrambled back and ducked beneath the machine's massive frame, hoping to slip between the quadruped's legs to escape, but there were too many of them.

Someone struck her in the back and drove her to her knees, twisting her arms behind her. She tried to jerk free, but then a pair of manacles bit hard into her wrists, and she was unceremoniously hauled to her feet, dragged away from the quadruped by two grim-faced coppers, their grip on her arms unbreakable.

"Bring her here."

The tone of satisfaction in that familiar melodic voice set her teeth on edge, and she looked up to see Julian Goss standing among the black-uniformed officers, triumph in his eyes. Beside him stood Calligaris and the rest of her engineering team, not one of them stepping forward in her defense.

"I demand to know what this is about," said Braith, struggling against two of Julian's men. "You have no right to come in here and—"

"I have every right," said Julian, stepping forward. "Miss Wade is under arrest by the authority of the Guild council."

"On what charges?" he demanded.

Julian smiled handsomely. "For conspiring against the Guild and the Royal Forces. She is a prime suspect in the anti-imperialist attack on the Hasguard Airfield and accused of—"

"I had nothing to do with that attack on the airfield," she spat, twisting in her captors' grasp. "And you know it."

"Unfortunately, Miss Wade, you have no one to corroborate such a claim. According to key witnesses, you were seen trespassing on military property just moments before the first explosion."

She clenched her jaw, her heartbeat quickening. If that was true, if someone had seen her . . . "I didn't do it."

"I'm afraid the evidence suggests otherwise."

"What evidence?" said Braith, coming to her defense. "You have no substantial proof, no grounds for this arrest. She didn't conspire with the anti-imperialists. She wasn't involved in the attack."

Julian's smile stretched thinly as he turned his gaze on Braith. "And would you be willing to testify to that, Officer Cartwright?"

"Yes," he said firmly. "I would."

"Yet as I understand it, you were absent from your assigned post around the time of the attack, or is that not so? In fact, you were attending to other military duties with Lieutenant-General Stokes at the time." The minister slipped a piece of paper from his pocket and held it up for all to see. "I have here the lieutenant-general's signed statement that you were with him in the final moments before the attack occurred. Testifying to the contrary would be perjury."

Braith twisted in his captors' grasp. "You set this up," he spat. "She was right all along about you."

Petra faltered, mind racing with Braith's accusation, realizing the truth of his words. Letting her visit the airfield, dragging Braith away from his duties, giving her the opportunity to incriminate herself by sneaking off with Rupert, the timing of the attack . . . every step of it planned, as if she was truly nothing more than a pawn in his plot for world domination.

Julian had manipulated everything.

"As for evidence," he went on, "I have proof enough to see her hanged by the end of the week. And to find her here, attempting to sabotage the quadruped prototype mere hours after the attack on the airfield—"

"I wasn't trying to sabotage your bloody machine," she said through gritted teeth, hot rage welling up in her chest as she realized just how far he had gone to implicate her in all this. "I was *trying* to fix it. There's a fault in the design, an error that—"

"Any error in the design is of your own making," he hissed, drawing close. "Admit defeat, Miss Wade. Give up this pointless effort."

She glared back at him, breathing hard. He might have manipulated her every move, but there was one thing he hadn't planned for. "I know about the quadrupeds at Hasguard," she said, her voice low. "I know about your army. You want to know where I was when the attack occurred? I was sitting inside one of your machines."

There was the briefest falter in his triumphant smile, but he soon recovered, leaning close enough that only she could hear him. "Then you see how futile your rebellion has been," he said, his breath hot on her face. "Whatever sabotage you thought you could achieve, you were mistaken. Now that I have my army, there is nothing you can do to stop me."

"You don't understand," she said, struggling against her captors. "They're faulty. All of them. If the error is left unrepaired, every single one of your quadrupeds will fail." She searched his dark copper eyes, pleading to his sense of humanity. "You have to fix them."

He held her gaze a moment longer and then gestured to the two coppers holding her. "Take her to one of the third-level cells. I do not want any chance of her escaping."

Petra's captors jerked her forward, but she struggled against them. "You can't do this," she said, a vice tightening around her throat. "You can't—"

"It has already been done."

The finality in his voice struck her cold.

"He won't get away with this, Petra," said Braith. "I'll speak on your behalf to the council, try to clear your name before the trial. I'll testify to your innocence."

"Oh, but I am afraid there will be no testimony, Officer Cartwright," said Julian, folding his hands behind his back. "There will be no trial. The evidence against her is insurmountable."

"What?"

"And because you failed to prevent Miss Wade from committing these crimes, you are hereby stripped of your rank and henceforth transferred to Hasguard for combat training under Lieutenant-General Stokes, effective immediately."

Braith faltered. "You don't have the authority."

"Oh, but this order doesn't come from me," he said, withdrawing a parcel from his vest pocket. "I have the transfer order right here. Signed by the lieutenant-general himself."

Petra paled, her throat dry as she looked from Julian to Braith, the realization of what he intended slowly sinking in. "No . . ." She met Braith's eyes, and her heart crumbled at the defeat, the sudden fear in his ashen gaze. She shook her head. "You can't."

"Take her away."

Her guards jerked her forward, leading her away from Julian and the quadruped—and Braith. She twisted in their grasp, refusing to go willingly, refusing to let Julian dictate their lives as he pleased. Braith didn't deserve to die because of her, because of what she had done.

Tears burned her eyes, streaming down her cheeks as she fought against the two men holding her. But she could not escape, could not change what her treachery had bought them.

As she struggled, she spied Yancy among the other engineers, his arms folded tightly across his chest. He met her eyes briefly and nodded, a resolute frown on his face, and she stilled, one last feeble hope rising in her chest. If he could carry the repair order to his father, convince him to file the report with the Royal Forces, they might still have a chance.

He was their only hope now.

CHAPTER 15

Days passed in lonesome solitude, reminding Petra of the time she had spent locked away in the first-quadrant jail the previous summer. Only this time, there would be no trial. There would be no escape. No one had come to visit since Julian's men deposited her in the tiny cell, not even Julian himself. She was starting to go mad from the isolation, left to pace her windowless cell for hours on end, lying awake on the floor night after restless night, wondering what was going on beyond the walls of her prison.

There could be a war raging between Britain and France by now and she wouldn't know. Braith could be piloting a faulty quadruped into battle—he could *die*—and she wouldn't know. She had no idea if Yancy had succeeded in delivering the repair to his father, or if the vice-chancellor was able to convince the Royal Forces to repair the fault in the existing machines—or if they had even listened. For all she knew, the sabotaged army was deploying at this very moment, minutes away from shutting down and trapping those soldiers on the battlefield.

For a week, she had paced her prison, worrying, waiting, a thousand plans formulating in her mind of how to free herself, repair the quadrupeds, save Braith from the front lines, and somehow stop Julian's war, but she was stuck in this godforsaken cell like a rat in a cage, unable to do anything more than kick and scream and fruitlessly interrogate her guards any time they brought her daily meal or changed her chamber pot. But they would tell her nothing of the war, nothing of Julian, their footsteps heralding nothing but stoic silence.

She heard them now, as familiar to her as the low thrum of the subcity below, and she slammed her fists into the door at their approach.

"Let me out of here, you bastards!"

"Now, now, Miss Wade," came a smooth, familiar voice from the other side. "There is no need for such hostility."

Petra scrambled away from the door. "Julian?"

"Open her cell," he ordered.

There was a jangle of keys, and the door to her cell slid open with a clank. Two Guild coppers swept into the cramped room, cuffing a set of shackles around her wrists before leading her out the door and into the hall.

Julian was there waiting for her.

"You tell me what's going on," she said, curling her hands into fists. "Tell me right now, or—"

"You are being transferred," he said.

She faltered. "Transferred? Where?"

"I would not want to ruin the surprise," he said, gesturing down the hall with a sinister smile. "Shall we?"

"I don't suppose I have a choice."

"No. You do not."

Her guards shoved her forward, and they headed up the stairs from the prison cells, stopping only to unlock the bolted security door to the Guild's police force offices. Stark yellow light glared overhead, the electric bulbs sizzling in their metal housings, unforgivably bright compared to the dim light of the prison hall. Without pause, Julian steered her across the first floor, guiding her down familiar halls and across the main workshop, eerily empty.

Their footsteps echoed harshly across the lobby floor, heading purposefully toward the University entrance. The doors cracked open on their approach, and Petra blinked against the startling brightness of the early-morning sky, the sun barely rising over the city walls. Clumsily, she staggered down the stairs into the square, driven like a mule in front of her two guards.

Her destination was a steam-powered vehicle sitting idle in the middle of the square, another handful of Guild coppers flanking either side.

"Where are you taking me?" she asked, twisting around to face Julian. She struggled against her captors. "What are you planning to do?"

But Julian said nothing, regarding the waking city with a serene expression, even as she was unceremoniously forced into the back seat of the car, the door slammed behind her. The hard manacles cut into her wrists as she tumbled onto the leather seat, the sting of fresh blood burning her skin. Julian opened the opposite door and slipped inside, leaning forward to rap against the driver's window before settling comfortably in his seat.

The car pulled away from the University with a putter and turned down Chroniker Main. Petra forced herself upright and jiggled the car door handle, but it would not budge. She curled her hands into fists and reared back to strike at the window with the iron manacles, but a hand reached out and gripped her by firmly the wrist.

"I would advise against that," said Julian.

"Where are we going?" she demanded, jerking her arm away.

He said nothing, peering out the window as the first-quadrant shops slipped past the rumbling steam-car. They drove past the cafés near the square, then through the shadows cast by the Towers Hotel, rolling by the Guild offices and the public police station. They continued on to the greenery of Pemberton Square, where she and Emmerich had once spent their summer afternoons, and further still, the morning stalls and rotund fountain vanishing behind another row of buildings as the car approached the city gates.

With a hiss, the vehicle rolled to a stop, just in sight of the harbor.

"Did you think I would not discover your last pathetic attempt to thwart me?" asked Julian. His voice was light but it cut through her with the deadliness of a knife.

She swallowed thickly. "I don't know what you mean."

"I do not know how or when you managed it, or what lie you offered the vice-chancellor to persuade him to your cause, but no matter. War is upon us. Nothing you do will change the outcome. You have failed."

A chill crawled down Petra's spine, a hard fist crushing her chest as she realized what he meant. She had failed . . . Lyndon had failed.

"Do you realize what you've done?" she asked, her voice breaking. "I wasn't trying to sabotage your army. I was trying to *fix* it. There's a malfunction in the regulator, a rotational disparity that will lead to system-wide failure within minutes of the machine's activation. If you don't repair them, they *will* fail."

"So you say. Though I don't suppose you care to explain how such a malfunction slipped past the notice of your engineering team," he said coolly, turning in his seat to face her. "Because if such a malfunction does exist, that would mean you sabotaged the quadruped project of your own volition, and that, my dear, would make you a traitor."

Petra glared back at him, breathing hard.

"I offered you the opportunity to cooperate," he went on, withdrawing back to the window. "Yet you will never give up this misguided rebellion of yours, no matter how many times you are beaten; I see that now."

The guards at the city gates waved them forward, opening the wrought-iron gates to let them through. The steam-car rumbled loudly and then lurched forward with a putter, rolling steadily through the city gates and onward to the harbor docks.

"It seems I must *show* you the futility of your efforts," he said, the pleasantry now gone from his voice. "Threats, it seems, are not enough."

The car rolled to a stop at the edge of the furthest pier, and Julian stepped out of the car, graciously holding the door open for her.

She shrank away, her jaw clenched, throat tight.

"Come now, Miss Wade," he said. "It will do no good to put off the inevitable."

Hesitating a moment more, she swallowed against her pounding heart and followed him out of the vehicle, her wrists still bound by the thick manacles. The roar of the ocean waves assaulted her ears, crashing against the jetties on either side of the harbor. Wind whipped over the shore, catching her disheveled braid in its early-morning gust as Julian took her firmly by the arm and dragged her away from the steam-car and down the pier.

That's when she saw the airship.

It hovered over the harbor waters, the sigil of the Royal Forces painted on its wooden hull, the prow tethered to the end of the pier. And there at the end of the dock, a group of redcoats waited.

There was only one reason he would bring her here.

She planted her feet and tried to twist out of his grasp, fighting against his steady pull, but he was too strong.

"Oh, no, Miss Wade," he said, dragging her toward her fate. "It is too late for escape now. I warned you what would happen should you defy me again." He shoved her toward the group of soldiers, and she stumbled to her knees. "I am not a man to tolerate disobedience."

Petra glanced up, her eyes trailing over the polished boots and crisp uniform of the nearest soldier, standing at attention, his hand poised in salute.

"Deliver her to the lieutenant-general as soon as you arrive," Julian ordered.

The soldier nodded. "It will be done, sir."

Petra climbed to her feet and turned around, the seaward wind spraying her cheeks with mist. "You aren't coming with me?"

Julian smiled handsomely. "I'm afraid I have more important matters to attend to at present," he said, his voice carrying over the crashing waves. "Though I do regret the necessity of my absence. I would take *such* pleasure in seeing you break."

She swallowed hard, a shiver crawling up her spine. "Where are you sending me?"

"You will find out soon enough." He held her gaze a moment more. "Goodbye, Miss Wade."

Then he turned and left.

Petra took a few steps after him, but two soldiers grabbed her and pulled her back, their hands strong and firm. She struggled, but they dragged her away, toward the airship and up the swaying gangway, the plank tethered precariously between the ship and the dock.

"Make ready for takeoff," shouted one of the soldiers, handing her off to another red uniform. "We leave as soon as the passenger is secure."

"This way, miss," said the soldier.

She jerked away from her captor and ran to the deck rail. "Julian, you bastard! Where are you sending me?" she shouted, clinging to the rail as another soldier restrained her. "You can't do this!"

Two soldiers peeled her away from the railing, dragging her backward.

"Julian!"

But her voice was ripped away by the wind and crashing waves.

He did not look back.

Julian returned to the steam-car and climbed inside, pulling away from the docks in a skitter of gravel as she struggled against her captors. Then she stumbled through an open door and the bright morning sky disappeared behind paneled hallways as the soldiers dragged her belowdecks. They threw her into a small cabin, shut the door, and slid the bolt behind them, locking her inside. She banged against the door, but no one answered.

Less than a minute later, the ship creaked around

her, bobbing gently as it untethered from the dock and rose into the sky, snapped up by the wind.

They were airborne now, any hope of escape gone.

Tears stung her eyes, and she dashed them away with a closed fist, bitterness roiling up her throat as her failure ate through her chest. The quadrupeds would fail. Julian would have his war. And she was trapped on a Royal Forces airship, heading God knew where, and there was absolutely nothing she could do. She had failed. Utterly.

She pressed her fists into the door until her knuckles cracked and then shoved away, her chest burning as she found a seat in the corner of the cabin. She slid to the floor and tightly hugged her knees to her chest while the airship creaked and groaned around her, steadily carrying her to her fate.

Their destination was Hasguard.

The airfield was in a frenzy when they arrived—a chaos of Royal Forces soldiers scrambling from airship to airship, supply lorries zipping across the muddy pasture, hangar doors thrown wide open. Petra stared at the churning field from the edge of the airship deck, held fast between two soldiers as the ship prepared for landing. There were no civilians milling about the airfield now—no lace fans or feathered hats, no satin skirts or long coattails—just the red and navy colors of the Imperial Royal Forces, a swarm of ships and soldiers, all preparing for one thing . . .

War.

The ship shuddered to a halt as it landed on the soft grass, and her military guards led her down the gangway to the landing dock, where an omnibus awaited them. They boarded quickly and sped across the bustling airfield, eventually rolling to a stop in the shadow of a colossal airship. Her heart sank as she stepped out of the vehicle and recognized Rupert's design—its scarlet hull and brass ornamentation at its prow. Another seven of the massive warships sat alongside the first, identical from bow to stern, each equipped with an army of her faulty quadrupeds.

She clenched her jaw as she climbed the steps to the landing and boarded the deadly ship, led between two Royal Forces soldiers. She stumbled ahead of them, the narrow halls familiar. She had walked this passage just a week ago, with Rupert at her side and no idea of what lurked in the cargo hold beneath her feet.

She had no such illusions now.

The soldiers pushed her up a flight of stairs and down another hallway, and she winced at the ache in her wrists, stinging from the scrapes and bruises wrought by the heavy iron manacles. A fire brewed in the pit of her stomach, arcing through her every nerve. Julian would pay for this. He might have his war, and there might be nothing she could do to stop him now, but she'd be damned if she went down without a fight.

If she survived this, she would find a way to make him answer for what he had done—for the automaton, for Emmerich, for every threat he had given her, for the quadruped and the army now sitting belowdecks, for every life lost because of his greedy machinations . . . for Braith.

She would make him pay.

At last, they came to the bridge, and Petra was ushered inside the low-ceilinged room, the curved walls lined with windows from port to starboard, overlooking the whole of the airfield—still busy with activity. The late-morning sun beamed through the glass, highlighting dust motes in the air. An array of gauges and instruments stood at either side of the wide deck, a display of lights, wires, switches, and tickertape manned by a small team of military engineers. Near the front of the ship stood the captain's wheel. A handful of men in red uniforms were standing at the forward windows, a few of them in deep conversation over a thick stack of paper.

But it was the soldier standing off to the side of the others that drew her eye. He stood with his back to her, the sun reflecting harshly off the side of his face as he peered out the dusty window, his copper-gold hair almost luminescent in the sunlight. She'd know him anywhere.

The soldier next to Petra cleared his throat. "Lieutenant-General, sir?"

One of the men huddled near the captain's wheel glanced up at the address, his shrewd gaze cutting from the soldier to Petra as he straightened to his full height, towering well over the rest of the men—the same bearded officer she had seen the last time she was at Hasguard.

"I see Julian sent the girl," he said, the distaste apparent in his voice.

A few of the other men shifted their attention in her direction, but she had eyes only for Braith. He slowly turned around, and his gaze held hers like an anchor in a storm, no words between them, just worry, fear, helplessness. Then he noticed the manacles on her wrists, the disheveled state of her hair, the rumpled clothes he had last seen her in a week ago, and he pressed his mouth into a tight frown, his expression suddenly hard as steel.

"I suppose I should welcome you aboard my ship," said the lieutenant-general, drawing her attention away from Braith. "I am Lieutenant-General Stokes, First Ardian of Her Imperial Majesty's Royal Forces. For as long as you remain on this ship, you are under my authority."

"Then maybe *you* can tell me why I'm here," she said, raising her chin.

"All in due time," he said, turning toward the soldier beside her. "Take Miss Wade to her quarters. She is to be guarded at all times until we arrive at our destination. No visitors."

"Sir."

"What destination?" asked Petra, resisting the soldier's pull on her arm. She glanced between the lieutenant-general and the other officers, their faces dour. "Where are we headed? Where are you taking me?"

Lieutenant-General Stokes arched his brow. "The brig, for now. Where you will stay until I have further need of you. That is all you need to know at present—and this: attempt any sort of sabotage while you are aboard this ship, attempt to thwart our mission in any way, and your disobedience will be swiftly punished." He gestured to her guard. "Take her away."

She struggled against the soldier as he pulled her toward the door, searching the bridge until she found Braith again. He stared at her with his hands curled into fists, knuckles white, but he did not move, did not speak. There was nothing he could do for her now; he knew it as well as she did. Yet his eyes held on to hers with a raw determination that sparked a flame of hope in her chest.

This fight wasn't over yet.

Petra's guard shoved her into the cell furthest from the brig entrance and slammed the metal gate shut with a bone-shuddering clang. She staggered inside, bracing against the opposite wall with her bound hands as the key turned in the lock behind her. She whirled around, but her guard was already stalking away, taking the lantern with him.

She pressed against the bars. "Wait! Where are we going?"

He shut the brig door behind him without reply, locking her in darkness with a resounding clunk as the handwheel secured the deadbolts back into place.

She was alone.

A bell sounded somewhere beyond her prison, and

she felt the ship shift and creak around her as it left the ground far behind, still no idea where they were headed—or why. She slammed her palms against the metal bars, wincing against the pain in her wrists, rubbed raw by the hard iron.

"Dammit!"

She pushed away from the cell door and pressed her back against the opposite wall, an ache spreading through her chest as she closed her eyes and slid to the floor. She had no idea what Julian had planned, why she was aboard this ship, what fate he intended for her. She was alone and in the dark, with no idea where she was headed or what she would find when she got there.

She hugged her arms around her knees and sighed.

All she could do now was wait.

Hours passed in dark solitude.

The ship groaned all around her. Intermittent footsteps trailed overhead. Doors creaked open and slammed shut as soldiers traversed the airship's many halls, and underneath it all, the heavy thrum of the ship's distant propeller engines pulsed through the wooden floor like a familiar heartbeat, reminding her achingly of home.

It must have been late afternoon by the time she heard someone outside the brig again. Footsteps approached, then muffled voices, a scuffle. Something slammed against the door with a hard thud, and then the handwheel spun open.

Petra clambered to her feet as the heavy door creaked wide and lantern light spilled into the room, revealing a familiar face.

"*Braith?*" She gripped the iron bars of her cell, curling her fingers around the smooth metal. "What are you doing here?"

Braith barely made a sound as he hurried down the narrow hall, lantern held aloft. "I'm here to get you out," he whispered, withdrawing a short iron key from his pocket.

He hooked the lantern on the wall, the flickering light casting a dim glow throughout the brig as he slipped the key into the lock and retracted the deadbolt. The hinges creaked loudly as he pulled the door wide and stepped inside the cell, quickly dispatching the manacles on her wrists.

The iron cuffs fell to the floor with a clatter, and he took her hands in his—warm and firm as he looked over her wounds. He glanced up at her, worry etched across his face.

"Are you all right?" he asked.

She couldn't help but smile, relieved at the sight of him. "I am now."

"Then let's get out of here." He held tightly to her hand, his firm grip anchoring her to him as he dragged her from her cell toward the open brig door.

She followed carefully, aware of the sounds of footsteps on the deck above. "Braith . . . What's going on?" she whispered. "Why am I here?"

He stopped at the door and peered down the hallway with a frown. "I don't know," he admitted. "But I intend to get you off this ship before we find out. We're about a mile out from London now—our best chance to get you clear of whatever the lieutenant-general has planned."

Braith pulled her forward and they stepped out of the brig, tiptoeing past an unconscious soldier outside the door, a reddening welt coloring his brow. Hurried footsteps sounded ahead, and Braith quickly redirected their steps, dragging her down another hallway, another flight of stairs. He opened a narrow door and ushered her inside.

"Quick. In here."

They ducked into a storage closet, filled with shelves of spare uniforms. The two of them squeezed together in the tight space, neither of them daring to breathe as another set of footsteps came and went.

When they passed by, Braith let out a relieved sigh.

"Why are we going to London?" she asked him, her voice low.

"To pick up reinforcements," he said. "Pilots for the quadrupeds."

Her heartbeat quickened. "So it's war?"

"Seems that way."

"But how? Why? What happened?"

"There was an assassination a few days ago," he said darkly. "Some British dignitary on a diplomatic mission from the queen was killed en route to Paris, supposedly by French soldiers stationed near Calais." He tensed as another pair of footsteps neared the storage closet, his hand resting on the grip of his pistol. Only when the footsteps faded into silence did he relax. "It was all over the papers," he continued. "After that, there were threats of retribution unless France paid recompense and claimed responsibility for the attack. When they didn't, Parliament urged the queen to declare war and send a military force against them before they attacked us from across the Channel."

"Is that where the ship is headed next? After London?"

He nodded. "There's said to be a force of French soldiers there, war machines in tow, planning to head across the Channel into England."

Petra's breath fell short. "Then we've failed," she said weakly. "*I* failed."

"This wasn't your fault, Petra. You can't blame yourself for—"

"You don't understand. The quadrupeds, they're—" She bit down hard on her bottom lip. "Braith, they were never repaired. Yancy got the repair order to his father, but Julian found out somehow. He stopped the report from ever reaching the Royal Forces." She shook her head, her throat tight. "They're all going to fail."

He swallowed hard, his face pale. "You're certain?"

"Julian said as much before he put me on this blasted airship," she said, a cold fire blazing in her chest. "He thinks I was trying to sabotage them, and he was right. I did. I sabotaged it, without him ever knowing. All because I was stupid enough to think that I could stop him, that I could stop this war. I was wrong. And now . . ." She pressed her lips together. "Men will die because of me, because of what I've done."

"No, Petra, you didn't know. You couldn't—"

"I should have known!" she snapped, a deep ache settling in her chest. "I should have known."

"You did what you could to fix them. You can't fault yourself for—"

"Don't try to justify it, Braith," she said wearily. "It's my fault the army is defective; you know it as well as I do. I never should have sabotaged the design."

Braith exhaled a deep breath, and she was aware of his steady heartbeat, the two of them pressed so close together in the confined space that she could feel the rise and fall of his chest. "There may be another way to fix them," he said, his voice soft. "It may not be too late."

She glanced up. "How?"

A bell rang somewhere above.

"We're about to land," he said, taking her hand and pulling her toward the door. "We need to get to an exit and get you off the ship before the rest of the soldiers come aboard."

Petra grabbed his arm. "Braith . . . tell me how to fix them."

He met her determined gaze and let out a heavy sigh. "There are engineers here in London," he said quickly. "If I can convince the lieutenant-general to repair the fault, the military engineers stationed here could come aboard and implement the repair before the quadrupeds are deployed. It's a few hours from here to our drop point in France. That should be plenty of time to fix them all."

The airship landed with a heavy thud, and a shudder rippled through the hull.

"You think that will work?" she asked, barely daring to hope.

"It might, but *first* we need to get you off this ship," he said, laying his hand on the door. "This is the last place you need to be right now."

"But I can help," she said, holding him tightly by the arm. "I know the quadruped better than anyone. Let me stay. Let me fix this."

He pressed his lips into a frown, his expression softening as he looked into her eyes. "I can't," he said, shaking his head. "I'm sorry."

"But—"

"I'm not going to argue with you, Petra. Not about this."

He clasped her hand then, tightly lacing his fingers through hers, and before she could utter another word of protest, he opened the door into the vacant hallway and hauled her forward. They hurried down the hall and swept down a flight of stairs, steadily heading toward the base of the ship. She recognized the familiar passages—they were close to the cargo bays now—but then Braith took another turn and opened a panel in the wall, revealing a narrow flight of steps leading down to a hatch in the hull wall.

He guided Petra inside and closed the door behind them before heading down the stairs. When they reached the hatch door, he let go of her hand and gripped the heavy handwheel in the center of the door, and then slowly, painstakingly, it started to turn.

"There shouldn't be anyone on the ground near here," he said with a grunt of effort. "Once the way is clear, head straight for the fences to the south of the airfield. Keep your head down, talk to no one, and you should be safe. Once you're free of the airfield, make your way into London." He paused and handed her a folded piece of paper from his pocket. "Go to this address. There's someone there who will help you. Just tell them I sent you."

"You're not coming with me?"

He hesitated. "No," he said, lowering his hands from the door as he turned around to face her. "The lieutenant-general will be looking for me soon, and I need to get back to the bridge before he realizes you've escaped." He frowned. "I'm sorry. I have to stay."

"Why?"

"Someone needs to make sure the quadrupeds are repaired."

"Then let me stay too."

"Damn it, Petra. *No*," he said. "I don't know what they're planning to do with you, but you can't be on this ship when we get to France. We're about to go to war, and I don't want you anywhere near it when we do. You're an engineer, not a soldier. You don't belong here."

"And you?" she said, taking a step closer. She hesitated, the question she most feared to ask on her lips, too afraid to hear the answer; though she was certain she already knew. There was only one reason he could be on this ship; she had feared it the moment she saw him on the bridge. "You're going to pilot one of the quadrupeds, aren't you?"

He deflated slightly. "Yes."

"Braith, you can't."

"I don't have a choice," he said more firmly. "I swore an oath, Petra. This is what I signed up for—for good or ill."

Seconds ticked by in silence, her heart twisting painfully in her chest at the thought of him in one of her machines, moments away from malfunction.

"I don't want you to die because of me," she said, her voice cracking.

His expression softened, and he slowly raised a hand to her cheek. "I'll be all right, Petra."

"You're lying," she whispered.

A pale smile lifted the edge of his lips. "I learned from the best."

He turned the handwheel the last few clicks, and the hatch cracked open behind her. Sunlight spilled onto the narrow staircase, and she could hear shouting outside, the indistinct sounds of men preparing for war.

She curled her hands into fists, unable to tear herself away. "Just make sure you fix them," she said, her trembling voice full of conviction. "Fix the quadrupeds, Braith. Whatever it takes."

"I will. Now go," he said, pushing her toward the open hatch. "Go! I'll come find you when this is over."

Petra clenched her jaw, fighting back tears. "You better."

She turned away, hating herself for running away, for leaving him to fight her battles for her. There was no guarantee that he would repair the quadrupeds in time, no guarantee that he would survive, and she couldn't . . . she couldn't bear the thought of losing him, not now.

She stopped and turned back around. "Braith—"

But then the hatch door swung open and sunlight flooded the corridor, blindingly bright. Petra shielded her eyes against the afternoon sun, barely making out the dazzling red uniforms and glinting rifles in the open doorway.

Braith let out a curse behind her, grabbed her arm, and dragged her away from the open hatch, scrambling back up the narrow stairs, but then the door above them slid open, revealing more soldiers between them and escape, the ends of their rifles aimed to kill.

They were trapped.

CHAPTER 16

Petra stood again in the brig, arms folded tightly across her chest as she glared at the pair of British soldiers now guarding her prison cell, their gleaming rifles ready at hand.

She and Braith had been separated the moment the soldiers found them trying to escape the airship. Lieutenant-General Stokes had ordered her back to her cell, but Braith . . . she had no idea where they had taken him, if he remained on the ship or somewhere in London, if he was even all right. She should have been quicker to leave. It was her fault they had been caught, that Braith's plan to help her escape had failed.

She gritted her teeth, cursing her selfishness, her stupidity. If she hadn't been so reckless, so determined to do *anything* to stop the war, this never would have happened. But she had meddled. She had tried to sabotage the quadruped, tried to stop Julian's plans, and now Braith was being punished for it—because he had dared to trust her, despite everything he had been told.

And she had let him.

For an hour, the airship stayed anchored outside of London, but no one came to escort her off the ship. No arrest. No threats. No transfer to a mainland prison to await sentencing. Nothing.

Finally, a bell rang, and the ship suddenly shifted around her, the walls groaning heavily as the warship lifted off the ground. She pressed her hand to the wall, feeling the subtle change in the ship's engines as it turned away from London, the mechanical vibrations pulsing musically through the wood.

To France, then.

But why? Why send her to France with the warships?

What was Julian planning?

An hour after the ship departed, there came a knock on the thick metal door. "Another prisoner for the brig."

Petra stepped across her cell and pressed close to the iron bars, curling her fingers around the smooth metal as one of her guards went to answer the door. The other stepped closer to her cell, holding his rifle steady as his compatriot turned the handwheel and opened the heavy door. The hinges creaked loudly as three red uniforms entered the brig—one of them Braith, held fast between the others. His hands were cuffed, and a shallow cut bled beneath his left eye, his bottom lip swollen and bruised. He winced with every step, his breathing hitching as his guards dragged him down the hall.

Petra clenched her jaw, gripping the bars of her cell until her knuckles turned white. She remained silent as they shoved him into the cell next to hers. He fell hard against the opposite wall and slowly slid to the floor. Then the deadbolt slammed shut with a deafening clang, and the guards exchanged a few muted words before all four soldiers left the brig and closed the door behind them with a heavy clunk.

They were alone.

She hurried to the other side of her cell, crouching low. "Braith?" She leaned against the bars, taking in his disheveled, sweaty hair, the shallow scrapes on his jaw, the rumpled disarray left of his uniform. "What happened?"

Groaning with effort, he lifted himself off the floor and turned so his back rested against the wall, breathing hard. He glanced up, the tempest gone from his gaze. "I'm sorry," he said, his voice hoarse. "I should have gotten you out."

She swallowed hard and gripped the bars between them, watching the stuttering rise and fall of his chest. "What did they do to you?"

He shrugged. "The usual," he said with another wince, lifting a hand to the cut on his cheek. "The lieutenant-general gave me what for and then chained me to a post for a couple of hours for good measure." He shifted against the wall, gingerly pressing against his upper ribs. "I'm no stranger to it, but . . . he can throw a hell of a punch, the lieutenant-general."

"Braith, I'm so sorry."

He actually laughed. "It's not your fault."

Petra pressed her back to the wall, settling in the corner of her cell. "Yes, it is," she said quietly, an ache spreading through her chest. "We wouldn't be here if it wasn't for what I did. It's my fault we're here, my fault you were punished. Because of me—"

"Petra—"

"You never should have trusted me, Braith," she said, shaking her head. "I never should have let you."

"Petra, I'm here because I chose to be," he said. "More than once, I made the choice to trust you, to help you, even when it went against my orders—*especially* when it went against my orders. But I made that choice myself. I didn't have to keep your secrets. I didn't have to trust you. But I did."

"Why?"

He inhaled a deep breath, wincing slightly as he let it out. "Do you really have to ask?"

She swallowed hard. "Braith . . ."

"I don't regret the choices I made," he said. "Not for a second."

"Even now?"

With a weary, stitched sigh, he slowly edged toward her cell and settled against the wall beside her, just on the other side of the iron bars. Then he reached out his hand. "Even now."

She glanced down at his outstretched hand, his

wrists just as scraped and bruised as hers beneath the heavy manacles he wore. Delicately, she placed her hand in his, and their fingers entwined—as naturally as anything could. His touch didn't send shivers over her skin or make her breath fall short, not like the rush she felt with Emmerich. It just . . . *was*, like breathing, or a heartbeat, steady and constant and familiar, as if it had always been. She leaned her head against the wall, a painful ache twisting her chest as she listened to Braith's unsteady breathing beside her.

"What now?" she asked, her voice thick.

"I don't know," he said quietly, rubbing his thumb over her knuckles. "Once we reach Amiens, they'll ready the ship for battle, deploy the quadrupeds, and then . . ." He trailed off into silence, both of them aware of what would happen when the quadrupeds were deployed.

"But what are they planning to do with us—with *me*?"

"I don't know," he admitted. "The lieutenant-general never said, but . . ." He dropped his gaze to their joined hands and cleared his throat. "Whatever happens now, I've got your back, and I . . . I'll fight for you, to whatever end. All you have to do is ask." He glanced up at her then, his eyes bright in the shadows of the brig, studying her face with surprising gentleness. "I'm on your side," he said softly. "Always."

She offered only a pale smile in reply and held tightly to his fingers, the only thing keeping her from sinking into the pit of despair that threatened to swallow her whole.

Whatever happened now, at least she had Braith.

It made facing the darkness ahead easier to bear.

Sometime later, they heard footsteps outside the brig. Braith let go of Petra's hand and slowly pulled himself to his feet, still wincing with every movement. She stood next to him, gripping the bars of her cell as the handwheel set into the brig door started to turn.

"We must be over France," whispered Braith.

Petra leaned close and reached for his hand, not ready to face this alone. Their fingers entwined, both of them holding tightly to the other.

"It'll be all right," he said, his voice low. "This isn't the end. Not yet."

She swallowed thickly. "How can you be so sure?"

"Because I'm not ready to give up on living yet. You shouldn't either."

The door creaked open on squealing hinges, and suddenly his touch was gone, her hand cold where his had been. She mechanically flexed her fingers and curled her hand into a fist, mustering the last of her inner fight as she raised her eyes to the redcoats now standing in front of her cell. She may be afraid, but she'd be damned if she let them see it.

One of the soldiers approached her cell, producing a key from his pocket. "You've been summoned to the bridge," he said, quickly unlocking the door. He pulled the door wide and gestured one of the other men forward while he moved on to Braith's cell. "Both of you."

Petra and Braith had a moment to exchange a wary glance, and then she was being ushered from her cell and out of the brig, shoved step by step down the now-familiar passages to the warship bridge.

Lieutenant-General Stokes was waiting for them.

He stood at the front of the cabin, his back to them as they entered. The orange glare of the setting sun bathed the bridge in reds and golds, the fading light slipping steadily across the green countryside—what Petra assumed was northern France. Ahead, a river snaked through a wide stretch of trees and dark ponds, and thin lines of road wound through farm-land and open pastures, the brief image of a small town highlighted by the setting sun. And then the sun dipped below the distant horizon, plunging the land in shadow.

Their guards dragged them to the front of the bridge, stopping at the wide windows overlooking the dark landscape below.

"Your prisoners, sir."

The lieutenant-general turned briefly, his shrewd gaze sweeping over the two of them before he turned his back to them once again. "Remove their shackles and leave us," he said to his officers. "Report to your stations and await my command. We will arrive at our destination shortly."

"Yes, sir."

The soldiers removed Petra and Braith's manacles and then left the cabin as ordered, shutting the door solidly behind them.

"I apologize for the strict measures," said the lieutenant-general, turning away from the window. He walked the perimeter of the deck, carefully observing the flickering lights and spill of tickertape emitting from the nearest dashboard, his hands clasped neatly behind his back. "But given your previous actions against the Guild and the Royal Forces, your containment during our flight was deemed necessary for the success of our mission."

Petra rubbed the bruises circling her wrists. "And what mission is that?" she asked, flexing the stiffness out of her hands.

"A matter of military concern," he said dismissively, glancing up from the table of mechanical instruments. "You are here to observe, Miss Wade. Nothing more."

"Observe?" She narrowed her eyes. "Observe what?"

The lieutenant-general straightened. "The results of your hard work, of course," he said icily, continuing his path down the line of tables mounted to the floor. "This mission would not be possible if not for you, after all."

She shivered at his words, a cold chill stealing up her spine.

"We're ten minutes out, sir," said one of the nearby officers, sitting in front of a display of flickering gauges and instrument panels.

"Good," said the lieutenant-general, turning toward another officer. "Signal the other ships. It's time to give the order."

Petra turned toward Braith. "We have to do something," she hissed, a last desperate plan shaping in her mind. "Now. Before it's too late."

"But how? What can we do?"

She pressed her lips together. "Tell him of the fault. Beg him not to deploy the quadrupeds. Beg him to fix them. I don't know . . . but we can't just stand here and do nothing," she whispered. "We have to stop this."

"Petra—"

"I have to try." She left Braith behind and stepped between the lieutenant-general and the communication's dashboard. "Wait," she said, her voice desperate. "Don't give the order. Not yet. The quadrupeds, they're—"

"Step aside, Miss Wade."

"They're faulty," she said. "If you deploy those soldiers—"

"I will not ask you again."

Braith stepped forward and gently pulled her away. "Petra . . . it's too late."

She wilted at his touch, at the sound of defeat in his voice. "No . . ."

The lieutenant-general spared her one last withering glare, stalked to the other side of the cabin, and plucked a black telephone from the wall. He drew the receiver up to his lips, and his voice pierced through every single deck with alarming volume. "This is Lieutenant-General Stokes, First Ardian of Her Imperial Majesty's Royal Forces," he said, his heavy voice transmitted through the entire ship by the electric speaker system. "We are presently approaching our designated target. Estimated time to arrival . . . eight minutes. Man your stations and prepare for deployment."

Petra's heart sank, seeing her last chance to set things right slipping through her fingers. She pulled away from Braith. "Don't do this," she said, curling her hands into fists as she approached the lieutenant-general. "The quadrupeds aboard your fleet will fail unless you fix the fault. If you send those men to battle now, they will die."

"Stand by for my command," he finished crisply, his voice ringing with authority. He returned the telephone receiver to the wall and faced her. "A wasted effort, Miss Wade," he said. "You will not sabotage this mission."

"I'm not trying to sabotage anything! The quadrupeds are faulty," she explained, panic twisting around her chest like a vice. "There is a defective axle plate in the quadruped's base, one that will lead to systematic failure in the quadrupeds if it isn't removed. You have to stop them from launching."

"I will do no such thing," he said dispassionately. "I have my orders. I intend to follow them."

"If you send those machines into battle, your men will die!"

The lieutenant-general's expression did not change. "This is war, Miss Wade. Men die. That is the way of things." He turned toward the control dashboard. "Status report."

"Signal received, sir," said one of the officers. "The

other ships are preparing for deployment. Five minutes from drop point."

"Good."

The darkening sky provided a cloak of concealment as they neared their destination. Ahead of the ship, Petra could see the dim glow of a sprawling camp on the other side of a copse of trees, numerous tents, shanties, and heavy lorries parked alongside. Standing sentinel at the forward of the camp was an army of humanoid machines, beautifully constructed, like brass titans out of ancient myth—so unlike the clunky, heavy design of her quadruped.

The fleet of British warships slowed to a halt in midair, stopping a mile north of the French camp. A large town claimed the distant countryside, following the curve of the river. The yellow glow of gas lamps illuminated the streets and bridges and the clusters of riverside buildings, and a great cathedral loomed high in the center of the city, its windows and narrow arches glowing almost silver in the moonlight.

"Prepare the quadrupeds for deployment," said the lieutenant-general, his gaze on the camp of soldiers and war machines, men scrambling to mobilize in response to their arrival. The banners of the British Empire flew from the sides of each ship, proudly declaring their allegiance.

There was no question as to why they were there.

"Should we signal the other ships to begin their approach, sir?" asked one of the bridge officers.

The lieutenant-general nodded. "See that it's done."

The officer flipped a few switches across the dash, typed his message, and waited. A few seconds later, a light flickered from the window of the nearest ship, the flash of a shuttered spotlight. "Message received, sir," reported the officer; then, after another sequence of flashes, "All ships ready to deploy."

As if in response, the ships visible from the bridge inched forward, drifting ahead of the flagship as they descended toward the ground.

The lieutenant-general stepped forward and stood at the front of the bridge, clasping his hands behind his back. "Forward sail, Captain, and lower the ship for deployment."

"Yes, sir."

Petra watched, horrified, as her worst fear unfolded right in front of her. She shifted toward Braith and sought out his hand, clasping his fingers tightly as the hum of spinning engines thrummed through the cabin. The warship lurched forward, sailing downward at a steady speed. The landscape rose up around them as they approached the French camp, the towering brass titans now crawling with men in navy uniforms. Between the camp and the advancing ships, a line of soldiers marched forward with rifles at the ready.

"Nearing one hundred feet above ground," reported an officer.

Another officer grabbed a second telephone from the communications dashboard and listened intently to whoever spoke at the other end. "Soldiers at the ready, sir. They await your command."

"Not all of them." The lieutenant-general slowly turned around, his shrewd gaze landing on Braith. "I believe you have somewhere to be, Private."

Petra whirled toward Braith, holding tightly to his hand. "Braith, no . . ." she whispered. "You can't."

"I don't have a choice," he muttered, his face hardened by the practiced stoicism she was so used to, his inner turmoil betrayed only by the tense line of his shoulders. He let go of her hand and saluted the lieutenant-general, the line of his jaw hard, resolute. "At your command, sir."

"Then I suggest you get into position." The lieutenant-general turned and nodded toward one of the attending officers, who brought him the telephone receiver. He raised the mouthpiece to his lips. "Open the bays."

A bell rang overhead, and a heavy thrum burrowed through the floor.

"Bay doors open," reported one of the officers.

"Steady the ship."

The captain pulled the pilot's controls in reverse and halted the advancing warship, the French camp close now. The sound of rapid gunfire popped far below, but their bullets pattered harmlessly off the hull.

The lieutenant-general cleared his throat. "Private Cartwright? I should not need to remind you the penalty for desertion."

Every muscle in his body seemed to tense. "On my way, sir."

"Braith . . ."

He turned toward the door, pausing only to spare her a passing glance. He parted his lips as if to speak, but no words came. Clenching his jaw, he tore himself away, heading through the bridge door without another word.

Petra started after him, but one of the lieutenant-general's men grabbed her by the arm, pulling her away from the door as Braith slipped out of sight. She struggled against his hold. If Braith launched from the ship in one of her quadrupeds—

"Let her go." Lieutenant-General Stokes's harsh voice cut through the bridge. "Let her say her goodbyes. She can't do anything to harm our mission now."

The soldier let go of her arm, and she hurried through the door without looking back. She raced down the hall and clambered down the stairs to the cargo bay, praying he hadn't deployed yet.

She reached him at the bottom of the landing. "Braith, wait. Please . . . Don't do this."

He hesitated with his hand on the door, the line of his shoulders rigid. "I have to," he whispered. "I'm a soldier, Petra. These are my orders. I have to follow them. You heard the lieutenant-general. I have no choice."

"Braith . . . you could die down there."

He clenched his jaw. "I know."

"One minute to drop point," said a voice over the bay's loudspeaker.

"I have to go," he said, hesitancy in his voice.

"Don't." She reached forward and took his hand. "We can still fight this. Together. Please."

Braith held her gaze for what felt like an eternity.

There was regret in his eyes—regret and something else, reflecting the storm of emotion she felt in her own heart at that moment, wondering if she would ever see him again.

"*Thirty seconds.*"

He glanced down at their hands with a frown. "I'm sorry," he whispered, his voice hoarse. "I can't. I . . . Goodbye, Petra." Then he let go, pushing through the door into the cargo bay.

Wind gusted through her hair and slammed the door against the stairwell wall as Braith hurried across the catwalk ahead, halting at one of the few remaining machines. A pulsing red light bathed the metal dome and spidery limbs in flashes of blood-red light, while below lay a dark green pasture, yet untouched by the ravages of war.

"*Twenty seconds,*" blared the loudspeaker.

Petra left the safety of the stairwell and hurried forward, her footsteps clanging against the metal walkway, fingers sliding over the smooth railing. Braith stood at the foot of the access ladder, both hands gripping the railing, his eyes on the deadly war machine. He turned as she approached, and she stopped mere inches away, no words on her lips, only the ache of fear in her chest as the red light pulsed overhead.

"*Fifteen seconds.*"

He wavered in that moment. "Petra—"

She stepped forward and crashed into him, throwing her arms around him in a tight hug. "Don't die, you idiot," she said. "Don't you dare die down there."

Braith gathered her into his arms with a weak laugh and hugged her close, breathing into her hair with a sigh. "I won't."

"Promise?" she asked, her voice breaking.

The voice over the loudspeaker began to count the final seconds before the drop. *"Ten seconds . . . Nine . . . Eight . . ."*

He drew away, his hand resting on the curve of her jaw, the two of them standing barely a breath apart. "I promise."

He held her there for a second more, and then he turned away, climbing up the ladder and into the quadruped, hesitating only as he closed the hatch. Their eyes met for too brief a moment, and then he was gone.

"Prepare for launch."

Petra stepped back, and Braith's quadruped jolted violently toward the bay doors. As the machine rumbled downward, she caught a glimpse of him through the narrow cabin window, strapping himself into the pilot's chair, and then he sank out of sight, joining the rest of the war machines below the central walkway, ready to drop through the bay doors and engage the French.

Petra clung to the railing, her knuckles white as she peered over the edge, her heart failing to beat as the red light pulsed ominously overhead.

"Launch."

CHAPTER 17

The quadrupeds plummeted, falling like missiles to the ground.

Petra braced herself against the catwalk railing as the warship lurched upward, a terrible wrenching boom twisting through her gut as thunder awoke from the earth, several thousand tons of metal impacting the ground all at once.

A cloud of dust rose from the impact site, shrouding the army of war machines in a thick haze. Seconds ticking by in tense silence. Then, as the dust began to settle, there was the distinct discord of combustion engines igniting, the quadrupeds rearing to life in a cacophony of gears and pistons.

Petra watched as the first machines shifted forward, the pilots testing the controls one halting step at a time. The quadrupeds' brass hides glimmered in the ambient light of the airship fleet as they marched toward the French camp. She followed them along the catwalk, even as a bell rang overhead and the bay doors began to close, her view of the battlefield steadily shrinking. She couldn't tell one machine from the other, couldn't know which one was Braith. Then the doors shut with a loud thump and she could no longer see the army of quadrupeds below.

The airship started to rise.

She tore herself from the railing and hurried back up the stairs, trying not to think of whether or not Braith would survive this battle, if he would survive her sabotage, survive the war. She slowed to a stop halfway up the metal steps and gripped the railing, her stomach roiling as her every effort to stop this war crumbled down around her ears. Rapid gunfire sounded far below, peppering the airship's wooden hull with heavy thuds, the metal clank of her machines audible despite the distance of the warship from the battlefield.

How had it come to this?

Petra bowed her head, her hands shaking as she fought not to cry.

Even if the soldiers survived, even if the British forces somehow won this battle despite the quadrupeds' inevitable failure and returned to England in one piece, her sabotage would still be known. Julian would know the truth about what she had done—the *world* would know—and despite her every effort to reverse the damage, there was no hope of surviving the aftermath to come.

She closed her eyes, holding steady to the railing.

But even so, even if she was doomed to whatever dark fate Julian intended for her, she could not give up, not yet. As long as there was a chance—however slim— that she might find a way to stop his plans from going further, she had to try.

She could not leave the world at his mercy, not without a fight.

She sucked in a shaky breath, a deep calm settling over her—the kind of serene quiet that heralded the coming of a storm. Even though she had failed to stop the first battle, there might still be a way to stop the war.

There might still be a way to beat him.

Petra let her doubts and fears fall away, no time for them now, and she hurried up the rest of the stairs, renewed purpose pumping through her veins.

Rather than return to the bridge, she made for the lieutenant-general's office on the opposite side of the hallway and tested the handle, finding the door mercifully unlocked. Once inside, she shut the door behind her and moved swiftly to the desk, the only furniture worth investigating in the sparse quarters. She sifted through drawer after drawer, digging through military briefings, missives, and official reports, searching for anything connecting the lieutenant-general to Julian's conspiracy, anything that might give her a hint of his next move.

She stumbled across a telegram marked CONFIDENTIAL in the top drawer, addressed from the Guild to the airfield at London, dated just hours ago.

Proceed as planned. Keep her under guard and ensure she does nothing to subvert the mission. Imprison the officer until it is time to deploy. Make sure she is present during the battle. She needs to see how futile all her efforts against me have been. —J.G.

She paused, staring at the words on the page, reading the message again. Was that why she was here? To see the battle? To see just how badly she had failed to stop his war? A bitter taste filled her mouth, and she gritted her teeth. *Bastard.*

A door opened somewhere down the hall, and Petra quickly folded the telegram and stuffed it into her pocket, returning her attention to the desk. She searched the rest of the top drawer and found another letter mentioning her by name, warning the lieutenant-general that she might attempt to sabotage the mission if given the chance, and in another drawer, she found a missive detailing a rather large munitions shipment received by the lieutenant-general the day before, as well as a dated update on the progress of some unexplained project.

She stuck the letters in her pocket with the telegram and crouched low, digging through the bottom drawer last. There she found a logbook of updates, a record of the growing conflict between Great Britain and France. Several events had been underlined, including the attack on the airfield just a week ago. She flipped ahead a few pages to today's date, and another telegram slipped from the logbook and fluttered to the floor.

She snatched it up, addressed from the Guild to the lieutenant-general at Hasguard:

Prototype complete. Prepare the ships.

Petra read the date, the message sent in the late hours of the previous evening according to the time-stamp. So they had finished it. The last piece in Julian's plan for war, finally completed.

For all the difference it made. The army already existed, ready to launch at a moment's notice. Why wait until the prototype was complete?

As she stood there with the telegram in hand, trying to puzzle it out, the lieutenant-general's voice blared over the ship's loudspeaker, crackling with authority.

"Approaching French lines. All hands prepare to engage."

Petra hastily placed the telegram back in the event log, knowing she needed to return to the bridge before anyone came looking for her, when she noticed the lieutenant-general's entry for today's date: _Attack at Amiens_. _Quadruped army destroyed by French aerial assault. Sabotage suspected. Aerial counterattack successful. Significant losses. British deaths estimated at _____.

The last of the note was left blank, waiting to be written.

She read the words again to make sure she hadn't misread. Then her hands started to shake.

The attack on the French had only just begun, and the lieutenant-general had already written how the battle would end . . . but none of this had happened yet. The quadrupeds still stood. They hadn't yet lost.

Heart pounding, she closed the journal and tucked the thin book into her pocket with the rest of the evidence she had gathered from the desk.

What on earth were they planning?

Petra slipped into the hallway from the lieutenant-general's office and carefully latched the door behind her, no plan except to keep moving forward. It was only a matter of time before the quadrupeds failed, and she needed to find out what Julian and the lieutenant-general were planning. The evidence in her pocket was useless otherwise. She needed to know, needed to see it for herself. And then? Maybe she'd live long enough to escape the ship and find Braith . . . if he survived.

Exhaling a slow, steady breath, she faced the bridge door, curling her fingers around the handle. She had to believe he would. She couldn't bear the thought of losing him now, not after everything they had been through together, after everything he had done for her. She had to believe she would find him again.

She turned the handle and pushed inside.

Lieutenant-General Stokes turned at her approach, his gaze sharp. "Miss Wade. Good of you to finally join us. I trust Private Cartwright left you well."

"He's down there fighting your war," she spat. "If that's what you mean."

"As he should be."

Petra bit back her anger, a hot fire prickling up her

spine as she joined him at the front of the bridge cabin, the windows providing full view of the battlefield below. Praying for Braith's safety, she gripped the railing and watched the battle unfold in morbid fascination, counting down the seconds until the quadrupeds failed. How many minutes had passed since the machines launched? How long until her sabotage revealed itself?

The quadrupeds showed no sign of slowing down. They scuttled forward ahead of the British ships and fanned out around the French camp, men and machines reduced to miniature at such a distance. The muffled crackle of the Gatling guns and heavy boom of the Agars turned Petra's stomach, but the French machines easily deflected the quadrupeds' rapid gunfire. The hail of bullets ricocheted harmlessly off the smooth metal armor as the French machines raised their weaponized arms against the quadrupeds to return fire. Guns whirled out of hidden chambers, their arms jolting backward with the recoil before rotating ninety degrees with a freshly loaded barrel, volley after volley hailing on the quadrupeds. But the British pressed on, even as a barrage of cannon fire rained down on the metal domes.

Petra watched, horrified at the wake of destruction these machines left behind, several tons of metal and artillery storming across the battlefield. The rapid volley of automatic weapons punctuated the night with cracking gunfire and heavy blasts, the bullets pinging off reinforced hulls and ripping through weakened plating, rending the machines apart when they found their mark.

This was no longer a battle between men and nations; this was a battle of technology, the future of war—the future of the *world* if Julian wasn't stopped—displayed in all its brutal glory.

Her knuckles whitened around the railing. Every quadruped that fell, every French machine that split apart with the well-aimed strike of an Agar . . . that was another man dead, another man who would not be returning home from battle.

And then it stopped.

The quadrupeds staggered, the sound of bullets dropping by half as one by one, the machines groaned to a halt. Petra leaned closer to the glass, her forehead pressing against the cool window as the French machines continued to advance, their heavy footfalls thundering across the earth as they rained bullets on the British. Hatches crashed opened as many of the British soldiers fled. They climbed out of their smoking quadrupeds, the glint of rifles and pistols in their hands as they fired on the advancing metal titans, but their bullets had no effect against the superior war machines.

"Sir . . . the quadrupeds have halted their advance. They've stopped."

The lieutenant-general eyed the battlefield, his broad hands gripping tightly to the brass railing as he surveyed the mired army, a muscle twitching in his jaw.

Petra swallowed hard. "I told you not to send them

to battle," she whispered, her voice wavering slightly as she wondered if Braith was among those to flee, if he was even still alive. "I told you they would fail."

The lieutenant-general stared out the window, the lingering silence in the cabin seeming to last an eternity. "It doesn't matter," he finally muttered. "It will all end the same way."

Petra faltered. "What?"

"What are our orders, sir?" asked one of the bridge officers. "Do we proceed?"

Stokes turned from the window and faced the bridge officer. "Proceed as planned. Signal the other ships and tell them to initiate blackout," he ordered. "This changes nothing."

"Yes, sir."

The captain turned the wheel and directed the flagship away from the quadrupeds, away from battle. Across the sky, the lights aboard the other ships flickered out as the warships sank into darkness and drifted away, dark blots against the starry evening sky.

Petra turned to the window. "What are you doing?" she demanded, watching as the quadrupeds shrank away beneath them. She faced the lieutenant-general. "You can still get them out of there! You can still save them!"

The lieutenant-general glared down her. "Those are not my orders."

Petra balked at the sheer malevolence in his voice, backing away a few steps. "This was your plan?" she asked weakly. "Leave them to die?"

"All ships ready, sir," reported the bridge officer. "On your command."

"Hold," he ordered, staring down at the distant battlefield.

Far below, the French machines approached the rows of quadrupeds, a host of foot soldiers creeping up behind, rifles at the ready. Then, all at once, the French machines stopped, halting just short of the British lines.

Not a single one moved.

"Sir, the French are not engaging," reported one of the officers.

"Damn it, I can see that," the lieutenant-general barked.

Petra pressed her forehead against the window and breathed a relieved sigh, her breath fogging the glass as every last bit of tension melted from of her body. *Emmerich.* This was his doing; she was sure of it. He had rebelled against his father's war after all, fighting the only way he could: by sabotaging the French war machines—just as she had done.

"What are our orders, sir?"

The lieutenant-general peered out the window again, flexing his hands across the brass railing. "Signal the other ships," he said at last. "We proceed."

The soldier nodded. "Yes, sir."

Suddenly, out of the dark sky, the other airships flared to life, but for the ships on the south side of the battlefield, gone were the red and gold flags of the British Empire and the Royal Forces. The French *Tricolore* fluttered across the sky, banners of blue, white, and red dancing in the wind.

"Signal fire," ordered the lieutenant-general.

Weapon discharges rocked through the airship in a discordant rhythm, the metallic boom and clank of heavy guns firing and reloading overhead.

Petra gaped at him. "What are you doing?"

"Engaging the enemy, Miss Wade."

Far across the open sky, the ships flying the French flag returned the assault with a vengeance, their cannons flaring like match-lights in the dark. Petra braced against the railing, preparing for impact, but the shots went wide, bullets and cannonballs firing uselessly into the night. Empty cartridges rained down on the battlefield, falling past the bridge windows in a hail of smoking brass as black smoke clouded the sky in a gray haze, but if either side of the British fleet took any damage from the onslaught, the ships showed no signs of ruin. Far below, however, the soldiers fighting on the ground exchanged rifle shots and pistol fire, the battle between the two mechanical armies suddenly devolving into a desperate gunfight while the airships mimicked return fire overhead.

After a few minutes, the lieutenant-general turned toward his communications officer. "Tell all ships to prepare mortar shells for drop," he ordered. "And stand by for my command."

"Yes, sir."

Petra blanched. "Mortars?" She stared out the window at the battlefield, her heart pounding as she realized what he was planning to do. "You're going to bomb them."

"A necessary measure," said the lieutenant-general, his voice flat. "We cannot allow the French to gain the upper hand."

"But they're not—" She cut herself short, gasping as she realized what was happening. "This was his plan all along," she whispered, her mind racing. "He never intended to let them live."

"All ships ready to launch the attack," reported one of the officers.

"You would murder them? Your own men?" she asked. "Why?"

The lieutenant-general inhaled a deep breath and raised his chin. "This is war, Miss Wade. Sacrifices must be made." He nodded sharply to one of the men standing nearby. "Do it."

"No!"

She started toward the communications officer. If she could stop him from sending the order, maybe she could save them. Maybe she could save Braith.

"Restrain her."

Two soldiers grabbed her by the arms, reining her back before she could reach the communications officer. She struggled against them as he reached forward and pressed the switch.

"No . . ." she whispered, wilting in her captors' arms. "You can't."

"It is already done, Miss Wade."

The warship lurched upward, and she felt, more than

heard, the explosions that followed. The sound ripped through the bones of the airship, and her heart withered inside of her as fire and smoke lit up the night sky.

And then there was nothing. No sound. Only silence.

Only death.

Braith . . .

She collapsed to her knees, her body shaking with rage and fear and grief, blinded by her own tears.

"Bring her here."

Her captors forced her to stand, dragging her toward the window. She shook her head, feebly attempting to free herself from their grip, but her strength had left her.

Lieutenant-General Stokes lifted a hand to her chin. She recoiled at his touch, but he dug his fingers into her jaw and forced her toward the window. "See the power of the British Empire," he said, turning her face toward the ground below. "See the power of the Guild and the Royal Forces combined."

Petra inhaled a shaking breath.

The world *burned*.

The battlefield was aflame, a crater of fire and blood marring the once idyllic landscape, the corpses of quadrupeds and French machines rent asunder by the barrage from above. Tears slid down her cheeks and she pressed her shaking hands to the glass, searching for some sign of life below, any sign of movement on the ground . . . But there was nothing. Only deathly silence.

They were dead, and it was all her fault.

"You cannot stop this war, Miss Wade," said the lieutenant-general, jerking his hand away from her face. "You were a fool to try."

"Why?" she whispered, her voice strained. "Why would you do this?"

"For a better world."

She tore herself away from the window, breathing hard as she leveled a glare at the officer. She had no words, only anger—and grief. The pain of it raged through her like a storm, fire and lightning crackling through her bones. She curled her fingers into fists, pressing her nails into her palms until her hands ached.

"You're mad," she spat. "Both of you."

The lieutenant-general regarded her coldly. "All a matter of perspective. Such a tragedy that the British soldiers could not retreat from the onslaught of French artillery, stalling midbattle due to a fault in the machine's system. Perhaps if the designing engineer had not tried so hard to sabotage the war effort, those men might still be alive."

Petra shook her head and backed away. "No . . ." she whispered. "I didn't do this. I didn't—"

Her breath fell short as she realized the truth: Julian meant to pin this massacre on her. The French flags, the bombing of the airfield, the timing of the quadrupeds' failure . . . She staggered away, shaking her head. How could she have ever believed she was capable of stopping him, of stopping this war?

"Sir, should we send in the recovery ships now?"

asked one of the officers, his voice quavering slightly. "For the survivors?"

The lieutenant-general glanced away from Petra and focused on the bridge officer. He hesitated a moment and then nodded. "Send the order," he said. "Question any surviving soldiers for their account of what happened, and should any man attempt to undermine our mission, he is to be labeled a detractor and a traitor—and killed on sight."

Petra's heartbeat pulsed heavily in her throat. She had to find Braith. If he survived, if he still lived, then she had to get to him first, before they killed him for knowing the truth.

She turned away from the window and ran for the door, but she hadn't gone two steps before the pair of bridge officers seized her again. She fought against them, managing to free one of her arms and twist away before tumbling hard to the ground. Her head slammed sidelong into the nearest control panel. Not stopping to regain her bearings, she winced against the sharp pain and blundered forward, crawling under a raised dashboard before scrambling to her feet again, her vision still swimming with spots. She blinked, the ache spreading through her skull. Two men blocked her path to the door, and in her moment of hesitation, someone grabbed her from behind and twisted her arms behind her back, quickly securing her wrists with a pair of manacles. She struggled, every nerve in her body burning to break free, but she was trapped.

The lieutenant-general approached, leaning close

enough that his breath rustled against her cheek when he spoke. "The minister sends his regards," he said icily, his voice low enough that only she could hear. Then he straightened and addressed the men holding her. "Take her to the brig and remain there as her guard until we reach London. The Royal authorities there will know what to do with an anti-imperialist saboteur."

"That's a lie," she snarled, fighting against the two soldiers.

"I'm afraid it is my word against yours, Miss Wade."

She bit back a frustrated scream, trying to wrench herself away from her two captors, even as they led her out the door and down the hall toward the brig. Her mind raced, wondering how she might get off the airship and find Braith before the lieutenant-general's men did—if he wasn't already dead. And if he was . . . No. She had to believe he still lived, that he survived.

They stopped outside the door to the brig once more, and Petra considered her options. Her hands were cuffed behind her back, and both her guards outsized her by a hefty margin, but she refused to admit defeat, not now when Braith needed her, not now when she finally had the evidence she needed to bring Julian down. The logbook weighed down in her pocket like an anvil.

She glanced around, inching slightly away from the brig door. There would be no escaping once the soldiers locked her in her cell. The hall was narrow, not much room to maneuver free, but she needed only the barest of head starts to escape, just enough to flee down the stairwell to the cargo hold and assume control of one of the remaining quadrupeds.

There was no other way off the ship, no other way to escape.

It was the only plan she had.

As one of her two guards turned the handwheel to open the heavy brig door, she made her move. Pivoting away from the remaining soldier, she kicked up her legs and pushed her feet against the wall, shoving them both toward the brig and the other soldier. They staggered backward, all three of them toppling to the floor. Petra landed on one of the men, knocking the breath out of him with a satisfying wheeze. Trapped atop a heap of tangled limbs, she struggled to stand, her arms still bound behind her back by the heavy manacles, the metal biting painfully into her wrists as she tried to get to her feet.

One of the soldiers cursed and tried to grab her, but she managed to get free, throwing enough of her weight forward to escape his outstretched hands. She scrambled to her feet and stumbled into the wall, tripping over the soldier's legs as he tried to stand. Staggering away, she landed a well-aimed kick to the soldier's groin for good measure, and ran for the stairs.

She reeled left around the corner and slipped past the hall to the bridge, not daring to slow down. She hurtled down the stairs, shoes clanging loudly against the metal steps as she tried pulling her hands free of the manacles, but the rings were too tight. At the bottom of the stairwell, she stopped and turned her back to the door, awkwardly twisting the knob with her bound hands before shoving through to the cargo hold.

There were a pair of unused quadrupeds at the far end of the chamber—her only chance of escape now—but the bay doors were tightly shut, and with her hands still bound behind her back, she couldn't operate either.

One thing at a time.

Searching the cavernous hold, she found a large mechanical lever set into the floor not far from the stairwell, but she needed the use of her hands to activate it. Breathing hard, she leaned against the catwalk railing and forced her arms down her legs, wincing at the bite of metal against her already bruised wrists. Slowly, she brought the manacles low enough that she could step over the chain and bring her hands in front of her. A trickle of blood ran down her arm, and her wrists stung, but at least she had the use of her hands again.

She gripped the lever for the bay doors and put all of her weight against it, dragging the switch toward the floor until it locked into place. A bell rang out overhead, and with a mighty crack, the bay doors began to part.

Not wasting any time, Petra ran down the narrow catwalk to one of the few remaining quadrupeds, the red light pulsing ominously overhead as wind whipped up through the widening gap in the floor. Fires and broken quadrupeds lay scattered across the battlefield below.

She reached the nearest quadruped, and the lieutenant-general's voice blared through the bay's loudspeaker, making her jump out of her skin.

"I do not know what you expect to accomplish, Miss Wade," he said, "but you will not escape this ship."

Petra climbed the access ladder to the quadruped. "Watch me."

She dropped into the quadruped's body and pulled the hatch shut, the deadbolt clicking into place with a turn of the handle. Moving across the cabin, she fetched a large spanner from the toolbox next to the pilot's chair and braced her left hand against the dashboard, pinning the heavy manacle in place. Gritting her teeth, she slammed the head of the spanner down on the manacle lock and broke the tension spring inside, releasing the catch. The broken shackle fell from her wrist, dangling by the chain still attached to her right hand. Settling in the pilot's chair, she activated the descent mechanism, and the machine jerked violently, descending one lurching inch at a time.

Gunfire popped across the cargo bay and a spray of bullets pinged harmlessly off the quadruped's hull. Petra leaned forward as she strapped herself into the pilot's harness and peered through the narrow viewing window at the front of the cabin. There was a squad of redcoats at the other end of the bay, an assortment of rifles and pistols aimed directly at her. An officer signaled fire, and a second volley of bullets deflected off the quadruped's metal plating as she came to an abrupt halt. Then the ship shuddered all around her, and she heard the heavy groan of the bay doors activating. She looked through the window and saw a soldier standing at the mechanical switch near the cargo bay exit as the others advanced toward the quadruped. They were closing her in.

She sat back in the pilot's chair and curled her fingers around the quadruped's controls. Well, she certainly wasn't going to let that happen. Reaching across the control panel, she flipped the ignition switch and felt the rumble of the quadruped engine roar to life. Power flooded the machine, and she tested the controls she had designed all those months ago, knowing she had only a matter of minutes before the quadruped stalled.

Activating the weapon controls, she turned the wheel and pointed the Gatling gun straight at the band of soldiers on the other side of the cargo bay. She lowered the barrel and fired a spray of warning shots beneath them, striking the gears that powered the door mechanism. The bullets deflected harmlessly off the slowly rotating gears, but the soldiers predictably fell back from the catwalk and through the door, withdrawing into the stairwell.

Reaching above the pilot's chair, Petra gripped the release handle connecting the quadruped to the ship, her fear suddenly catching up with her, like a thousand pistons churning in place of her heart.

But she couldn't turn back now.

Inhaling a deep breath, she twisted the handle and fell.

CHAPTER 18

The quadruped slammed against the closing bay doors with a bang, tilting Petra sideways before finally tumbling over the edge, plummeting fast.

Her heart lurched into her throat, and she nearly choked on her own pulse as panic flooded her veins. Wind whistled through the gaps in the quadruped's plating as the machine righted itself midair, the shrill hiss of air punctuated only by the pounding rush of blood pulsing through her ears. She squeezed her eyes shut and gripped the straps of her harness, imagining the earth opening like a great maw beneath her, ready to swallow her whole.

Then the world crashed around her ears.

Her body jerked side to side. Her bones shuddered and the breath left her lungs. The crush of metal was deafening as the quadruped flipped and the cabin spun violently. She banged her knee on the dash, and hot blood ran down her shin, the pilot's harness biting into her skin as the straps strained against her weight. She retched suddenly, hot bile burning her mouth and throat raw.

Then the pressure from the harness eased and she leaned back into the pilot's chair, her head swimming, a cold sweat on her brow. Every muscle in her body ached, her skin already tender beneath the wide harness straps. Her head pounded, and she winced against the pain in her neck, aware of the gasp and sputter of the quadruped engine spitting beneath her, the sharp tang of petrol filling the cabin.

Swallowing against the raw ache in her throat, she unclasped the harness buckle and spat the acrid bile from her mouth, drawing herself to her feet. The quadruped had fallen onto its side, the floor tilting at an awkward angle, and she stumbled into the side of the cabin, stomach still reeling.

Pain whorled through her head in steady beats, and she reached a shaking hand to her forehead, blinking against the flickering light within the quadruped, the orange flames of the battlefield illuminating the inside of the metal cabin through the cracked window. Blood reddened her wrist where her manacles had been, the shackles now lying on the floor. The lock must have broken on impact.

Groaning against the ache in her bones, she blinked hard, her thoughts slowly reorganizing in her head as she remembered what had happened, why she was here—Braith. Escape.

She inhaled a sharp breath and opened her eyes wide, a renewed burst of energy burning through her veins. The smell of petrol was sharper now. The fuel tank had likely cracked, not that it mattered. She couldn't pilot the quadruped across the battlefield with the sabotage still intact.

She clambered toward the access hatch and hoisted herself out of the cabin, a gust of fresh air filling her lungs with the taste of smoke and gunpowder and blood as she slid to the ground on the other side of the dome, landing hard on the dirt. Her trousers stuck to her leg where her knee still bled, and fresh bruises ached beneath the fabric of her shirt where the harness straps had been. But she was alive.

Which was more than she could say for the grave-yard of machines and soldiers before her. Yet not all of them were dead.

A few men walked the battlefield, searching for sur-vivors, supporting the injured as they headed north, away from the French camp and the destruction that had befallen the two armies.

If they lived, perhaps Braith did too.

Checking her pocket to make sure she still had the evidence against Julian, Petra left the wrecked quad-ruped behind and headed across the burning battle-field. She passed dead soldiers and sundered machines, calling Braith's name as she went, peering into fallen quadrupeds, searching for any sign of him among the dead and dying, asking any survivors if they might have seen him, but he was nowhere to be found. She walked for what felt like miles through mud and ash, and as night crept on, any hope she had of finding him began to wane. She feared he had been in the center of the attack where the bombs had fell hardest, obliterated into nothing without even a chance to escape.

A lump hitched in her throat, and she tried not to think about him dead.

She called for him until her throat ached.

No one answered.

Eventually, she reached the French machines, toppled and broken, the beauty of their artful design marred by the destruction of the mortar shells, smoking metal ripped apart and smoldering. Here, French soldiers lay just as dead as the British, the only difference the color of their uniforms.

But none of them were Braith.

Petra sank to her knees in the mud, the earth trampled by the soldiers and war machines, soaked through with blood and oil. This was all her fault.

She reached out and touched her hand to the warm metal of the nearest French machine, recognizing Emmerich's influence in the design. The thought of him put a knot in her chest—their lives torn apart because of his father's conspiracy, both of them turned into pawns for his war. She gritted her teeth, fighting back tears.

It never should have come to this.

Something rustled nearby, and she glanced up to see a French soldier standing a few yards away, the barrel of his rifle pointing straight at her. She swallowed hard and shakily raised her hands in surrender, absently noting the blood soaking the soldier's dark uniform and the deep gash across her brow.

He said something to her in French, but she didn't understand.

She shook her head apologetically, and he gripped the rifle tighter, shouting something at her as he took a step forward. She squeezed her eyes shut, cursing her foolishness for wandering so close to the French camp. Not all the British troops had died in the attack; she should have known there would be survivors among the French as well.

The cold barrel touched her forehead, and she shivered, knowing she should be afraid, but all she could think about was how, for so long, she had feared dying at Julian's hands, sentenced to die at the gallows for her crimes, for sabotaging his plans. To be caught in the aftermath of a brutal battle, with a Frenchman holding a gun to her forehead and her hands raised in surrender . . . she didn't know how to be afraid of this. All she could think about was home, how much she missed it, how badly she wished to see her brothers and sisters again, visit Mr. Stricket in his shop, breathe in the smell of metal and hot steam and coal smoke and feel the subcity machines beneath her feet one last time . . .

And Emmerich. *Oh, God . . . Emmerich.*

Tears slid down her cheeks in steady streams.

She should have listened to him, should have heeded his warnings.

Now she would die here, with all the rest of them. And maybe she deserved it—to die for what she had done. Every man now lying in the ash-streaked mud had died because of her mistakes, because of her self-ishness, for thinking she could stop this war. They had died because of her sabotage. And Braith . . .

Braith was likely just as dead, and it was all her fault.

Footsteps approached from behind, and the gun left her brow, a split-second reprieve that shocked the world back into motion. She breathed in a shallow gasp, her heart pounding as a renewed need to live flooded her veins.

Then a solitary gunshot rang through the night, jolting the breath from her lungs.

Someone collapsed in front of her, and she opened her eyes to find the French soldier lying on the ground, bleeding from an open wound in his chest. She stared at him unblinkingly, the wheels of her mind slow to understand what had happened.

Then a hand touched her shoulder and she inhaled sharply, instinctively reeling away as she climbed to her feet.

"Petra, it's me."

She stopped and blinked, the light of the dying fires illuminating his face and bronze hair, reddened by the smoldering flames. Her chest tightened painfully, hot tears streaking down her face. She glanced at his hand, where he held a pistol, still smoking. "Braith?"

There was such pain in his eyes as he looked her, but then he sighed and the tension left his shoulders.

He dropped the pistol in the mud, and the next she knew, his arms were around her, holding her close.

He didn't say anything. He didn't need to.

She shuddered with relief and buried herself in his chest, clinging to his uniform as the last of her remaining strength left her. He was alive. He was here, and he was alive, and she had found him.

"I thought you were dead," she whispered. "I shouted for you, but—"

"I know," he said, his voice strained. He raised his hand to her face and gently brushed back her hair. "That's how I found you."

A shiver stole through her, and she tightened her grip on his uniform, curling her cold fingers in the folds of his jacket, the body beneath warm and real and alive. She could still feel the chill of the gun barrel pressing into her skull, and she shuddered, closing her eyes against the burning battlefield, the countless dead that surrounded them.

She had almost been one of them.

Braith drew away suddenly, holding her firmly by the shoulders. "Petra, why are you here?" he asked. "Why aren't you on the airship?"

She swallowed hard, her heartbeat quickening as the events of the last hour finally caught up with her— the lieutenant-general's orders, Julian's plans, the evidence against them, her escape.

"I had to come find you," she said, her chest tight. "I had to know if . . . if you were still alive, if you survived the attack. After the bombs fell, I thought—I thought you were dead, Braith. The battlefield, it . . . it *burned*. I hardly dared to believe anyone could have survived, but . . . if there was a chance, the slightest chance you still lived, I had to know. I had to come find you—warn you if I could."

"Warn me? Of what?"

She bit her lip. "The battle, it . . . This was their plan all along—the bombs, the deaths. You were supposed to die here, Braith. You weren't meant to survive." She swallowed against the tightness in her throat and glanced toward the smoldering battlefield. "None of them were."

"What are you talking about?"

"Julian . . . the lieutenant-general . . . . they orchestrated everything. They knew the quadrupeds would fail. knew I had sabotaged the army, but it only furthered their plans in the end, giving them someone to blame for the deaths they caused." She shook her head, a shiver stealing through her. "All along they meant to bomb the battlefield, to lay waste to both sides of the skirmish."

"But the French—I saw—"

"No. You didn't." She withdrew the lieutenant-general's logbook from her pocket and showed him the day's entry. "Those were British ships, Braith, disguised as the French. You only saw what they wanted you to see. All a part of their plan."

He read the lieutenant-general's handwriting, his frown growing deeper.

Somewhere in the distance, a gun fired.

"We should move," he said suddenly. "We're too close to the French camp. It isn't safe here." He left her side and retrieved his pistol from the mud, wiping the barrel clean on his trousers. "Let's find somewhere to talk. Then you're going to tell me everything."

They left the French machines behind and found refuge in the shadow of a fallen quadruped, its dome rent apart by a mortar blast.

"Now . . . what happened?"

Petra sucked in a breath and then launched into a full account of the battle, everything that happened after the quadrupeds failed—the airship blackout, the appearance of the French fleet, the exchange of fire, and the lieutenant-general's orders to drop mortars on the battlefield.

"*This* was their plan from the start," she finished, gesturing to the burning debris all around them. "All along they intended the battle to end in massacre."

"But *why*?"

"Why do you think? For their war. 'For a better world.' "

He glanced down at the pages of the lieutenant-general's logbook. "Where did you get this?" he finally asked.

"From the lieutenant-general's desk. After the quadrupeds deployed, I thought I might find some evidence of Julian's plans in his office, something tying him to Julian's conspiracy, and I did," she said, gesturing to the journal. "But even with the logbook and the other messages I found—"

"What other messages?"

She dug the bundle of letters and telegrams from her pocket and handed them over. "Even with the evidence I gathered, I can only prove they were planning something together. I'm not sure it's enough to convince anyone of a conspiracy, especially of this magnitude."

"It's a start," he said, glancing over the collection of papers in his hand. "But we need to get this evidence to someone who can put a stop to the minister's plans before he does this again. He cannot be allowed to orchestrate a war as he pleases. We have to stop him."

Petra frowned. "Don't you know that I've *tried*?" she said, her voice breaking. "I tried before to stop him, but—"

"This time will be different."

"How can you be so sure?"

"Because this time, you have evidence," he said, holding up the lieutenant-general's logbook. "We may not be able to convict him outright, but we might have enough to launch an investigation into his affairs. If we can find someone who already suspects the minister, someone who will listen to our claims, perhaps they can bring an accusation against him in our stead. I don't know who, but—"

"I know someone," she said suddenly. "Someone who might be able to help."

"Who?"

"Vice-Chancellor Lyndon, the head of the Guild." She had her misgivings about Lyndon, but at least he would believe her—and she might even convince him to finally make a stand against this war. "If we bring him evidence of Julian's schemes, he will do what he can to get it into the right hands. He'll help us."

"You're sure?"

She swallowed hard and nodded. She had to believe he would.

"Then that's where we'll go." He shut the logbook and tucked the rest of the evidence inside the cover. "But first we need to get out of France."

"How?" she asked. "We can't go back to the airships."

"We have to," he said, handing her the slim leatherbound journal. "Otherwise we'll be captured and killed by the French before we ever make it out of the country."

"Braith, the lieutenant-general gave the order to kill anyone who knows the truth of the mission. If they find us, if anyone realizes who we are, what we know . . . They'll kill us."

"Not if they don't recognize us." He started to remove his uniform jacket, wincing slightly as he peeled the fabric away. It was then that she noticed the blood on his coat.

"You're hurt," she said, reaching out and touching the damp fabric.

"A bit of shrapnel," he said, peeling the shirt away from the wound. His skin was pierced through with a shard of metal. "It's fine."

"Braith . . ."

"It looks worse than it is," he said with a grimace, handing her the blood-stained jacket. "Here. Put this on."

She took the bloody uniform from his hands and slipped her arms into the sleeves, the warmth of his body still lingering in the fabric.

"Anyone looking for you will be looking for a girl, not a wounded soldier," he explained. "We need to disguise you." He gingerly touched the bright red stain of his shirt and pressed against the wound with a sharp intake of breath, fresh blood soaking his fingers in red. He stepped closer and gestured toward her face. "May I?"

Her stomach turned at the thought, but she gritted her teeth and nodded.

Braith pressed his fingers to her brow and wiped a sticky smear of blood down the side of her face, staining her jaw with red. Using the blood from his chest wound, he painted her neck and collar red, carefully combing the sticky blood through the hair at her temple. Then he stepped back. "There's one more thing . . . Your hair. I'll need to cut it."

Petra raised her chin, the blood already drying on her face. "Do it."

Drawing close, he slipped a knife from his belt and lifted the blade to the braid at the back of her neck, breathing steadily as he sawed through the thick plait. Her long tangled hair fell away in amber ribbons, landing in the mud at her feet.

"Braith . . ." she said quietly. "What if this doesn't work? What if we don't make it out?"

He paused a moment, not quite meeting her gaze; then he cut the last of her hair and withdrew, returning the knife to his belt. "We will," he said firmly, quickly buttoning her jacket for her. His fingers trailed up the front of the bloodied uniform, slowing down only as he fastened the final clasp at her collar. "We just have to get aboard one of the recovery ships and lie low until we reach England."

"And then?" She ran her fingers through her shortened hair, sticky with Braith's blood. "Even if we manage to escape, the Royal Forces will blame me for the massacre, accuse me of weakening the British army with my sabotage. If we're caught, if something happens and—"

"Nothing is going to happen, Petra," he said, his voice steady as he reached forward and took her hand. "We have evidence against the minister now. All we have to do is get it to the right people. If we can make someone listen, we have a chance to stop the minister's schemes and stop this war before it spirals out of control." He squeezed her hand. "We have to try."

Petra frowned, letting her gaze fall to their joined hands, sticky with blood and dirt. Of course they had to try.

She just hoped they survived the effort.

They smuggled themselves onto one of the recovery airships, slipping past the notice of the Royal Forces officers and taking refuge among the many injured soldiers packed into the low-ceilinged cabin. A team of field medics hurried from pallet to berth, applying bandages and distributing morphine among the more severely wounded—men who were unlikely to make it back to London. Petra and Braith skirted the edge of the makeshift infirmary and settled in the corner of the cabin, still in sight of the rear bay doors. The battlefield smoldered beyond, embers of red and gold flickering across the ashen wasteland, the grave silence of night yielding to the groaning of dying men.

Petra sat against the wall with her knees hugged to her chest, the smell of blood and antiseptic sharp in her nose. A headache burrowed deep beneath her brow, and she ached all over, a deep pain that carved its way into the marrow of her bones, yet sleep seemed unlikely any time soon, not with the constant fear of discovery lurking just over her shoulder. Every footstep, every grunt of pain and sudden cry from the injured soldiers, every creak and whisper of the wooden ship exacerbated her unease. She jumped at every sound, Braith's solid presence little comfort to her.

She still had the evidence against Julian and the lieutenant-general tucked away in her pocket, the weight of it burning against her leg, but so much could still happen between here and London. So much could still go wrong.

There was movement at the bay door, and Petra glanced up to see a redcoat jog up to the officer stationed outside the ship. "The French are starting to remobilize," he reported, swallowing a gulp of air to catch his breath. "They've had reinforcements from the south."

"Then it's time we take off," said the ship's officer. "Deliver the order to the other ship and signal the medics back. We leave in five minutes."

"Yes, sir."

Another soldier approached. "What if there are more survivors?"

"Then they're on their own now," said the ranking officer, throwing a switch on the wall. A red light pulsed across the night, throwing the battlefield into sharp relief. "If they can make it to the ships before we take off, God be with them, but our priority has to be getting the rest of these men to safety."

"And the girl? Did anyone find her?"

Petra tensed, her pulse slowing as Braith's hand found hers. She squeezed his fingers and leaned hard against the wall, her ear trained on the soldiers.

"Not that I heard," answered the officer. "She's probably dead after that fall from the airship. We were up almost three hundred feet when she launched. There's no way the quadruped survived impact. But no matter. Even if she did survive, she won't last long out there. Once the recovery ships are clear, the lieutenant-general plans to launch a second counterstrike against the French. Anyone left alive will soon be dead."

"To think she sabotaged the entire battalion. Why would—"

But their conversation was cut short by a shout

somewhere beyond the ship, the last group of medics and wounded soldiers approaching.

Petra pressed the back of her head against the wall, heat welling up behind her eyes. Already, the lieutenant-general had spread word of her sabotage. The rumor would burn through the Royal Forces fleet like wildfire until every single soldier aboard the British ships knew of her sabotage. The blame for their failure would be on her head. They wouldn't know that she had tried to fix her mistake before it came to this, wouldn't know that she repaired the prototype, that it was Julian's machinations that led to the quadrupeds' failure on the battlefield. In their eyes, she was a traitor—and maybe rightly so. The failure would not have happened if not for her.

Once the rest of the medics and wounded soldiers were aboard, the bay door closed and the recovery ship took to the air, leaving the ghastly battlefield behind. Echoes of it remained in the rasps of shallow breathing, the muttered opiate dreams, the tortured cries of pain . . . and in the deep red stains that seemed to seep through everything, the stench of blood and sweat and soot on the air. It clouded the cabin like a dense plague.

This was the cost of Julian's war, the cost of his new world, painted in such vivid detail, Petra would never fully erase it from her mind. This was the war she had to stop, this needless sacrifice of life, this lust for progress that left only death in its wake. It was worse than she ever could have imagined.

The distant booms of mortar shells rippled through the ship, and Petra hugged her knees tighter to her chest.

She had to stop him.

Whatever the cost.

Petra awoke to the sudden jolt of the airship landing on English soil, startled out of dark, ashen dreams she would rather soon forget. The bay doors cracked open at the far side of the cabin, letting in a cool gust of crisp morning air, the early glow of dawn peeping over the distant horizon.

Braith laid a hand on her arm and gestured toward the door. "We should hurry," he whispered, his voice the first human thing she had heard since they left the battlefield behind. "Before anyone has a chance to recognize us."

She nodded and climbed to her feet. Her breath stitched in her chest, and she winced, tender bruises where the quadruped harness had grappled with her on impact. She gingerly touched the line of her collarbone, grimacing as she did.

Three hundred feet.

She never should have survived such a fall.

Petra followed Braith through the cabin, and they came to the bay door, where they gave false names to the officers tasked with identifying the surviving soldiers. Then they moved through the makeshift hospital that had been erected near the landing zone, the area already crawling with surgeons, nurses, and wounded soldiers. The first medical tent they passed, a nurse took one look at Braith's bloodied shirt, streaked with a thick swath of red from chest to hem, and quickly ushered him inside. He protested at first, but the nurse dragged him to a bed and ordered him to lie down with the authority only a nurse could command, and he grudgingly obeyed.

Petra touched his shoulder, the close quarters making it hard to breathe. "I'll be just outside," she said, offering a gentle squeeze. Then she slipped out of the overcrowded tent, thick with the stench of injured men and disinfectant.

While Braith had his shrapnel wound cleaned and stitched, she waited by the entrance to the medical tent. The sun climbed steadily higher over the London skyline to the east, casting a warm yellow glow over the dewy airfield, and she breathed in the fresh air, listening to the idle chatter of the less wounded soldiers passing through the camp.

Most of the soldiers here were not part of the wounded from Amiens—she quickly learned—but from Calais, part of a second attack force meant to take the port city in the night. The quadrupeds had failed there as well, taking heavy damage from the French naval forces in the ensuing skirmish, but with the artillery support of the British warships, they eventually emerged victorious, claiming the port for the Empire and driving the French further inland. But they weren't without their losses. The airfield was littered with wounded, far more than the injured from Amiens, despite the smaller attack force.

And then she realized . . . that was because most of the soldiers who fought at Amiens were still there, lying dead in the mud and ash, sent into dark oblivion at the hands of the lieutenant-general. All at Julian's command.

She curled her hands into fists, shaking with the sudden wave of anger that flooded her veins. He would pay for this, for every life lost because of his madness. All she had to do was get the evidence against him to the right people, and despite her misgivings, Vice-Chancellor Lyndon was the one person who could help them now. No matter Julian's accusations, he would believe her.

He had to.

A touch on her shoulder made her jump, and she whirled around to find Braith at her side, his chest freshly bandaged. "Time to go."

They left the medical tents behind, and when they were certain their escape would go unnoticed, they slipped past the airfield borders and stole a parked steam-lorry at the edge of the city. They stopped only to ditch their bloody military garb in the Thames before abandoning the vehicle some thirty miles west of the airfield.

It took two days to travel from London to the furthest reaches of Wales, catching rides from passing carriages when they were fortunate enough to find a kind driver near some of the larger towns, but mostly, they walked, taking long dirt roads and crossing expansive farms, resting in barns and wayside hovels when they were too tired to keep going. They had no money to spend on a pair of rooms in a pub house, or to buy train tickets that might have hastened their journey cross-country. But eventually, they came to Milford Haven train station, battered and exhausted after two days of travel, but alive.

News of the massacre at Amiens had spread quickly across the Empire, the impending war on everyone's mind, and by the time Petra and Braith reached the Milford Haven train station, the local papers had printed several dreadfully accurate lithographs of the charred battlefield—corpses of quadrupeds alongside French war machines, a tattered British flag flying overhead.

BRITAIN AT WAR!
France Mobilizes Against British Empire
Six Hundred British Soldiers Dead

Petra unfolded a discarded newspaper and began to read.

The article reported over five hundred dead at Amiens, and another one hundred at Calais. Officially, the cause of the failure of the two armies was unknown, but according to the article, the Royal Society was launching an investigation into the matter, sending a delegation of engineers and police officials to consult with the Guild and discern the technological cause behind the failure, in case the rumors of sabotage were true.

She lowered the paper with shaking hands, crumpling the images of war-torn machines in her fists. "We have to get back to the city," she said to Braith, sitting beside her on the bench. "Tonight."

"How?" he said, rubbing his eyes with a weary sigh. "There's no ship that will take us until morning."

"Then we have to leave first thing tomorrow. As soon as possible. The Royal Society is launching an investigation into the quadruped failure," she explained, shoving the paper into his hands. "They start their trials tomorrow. We have to get to them before Julian or the lieutenant-general. We have to tell them what really happened at Amiens. If Julian or the lieutenant-general convince them that I sabotaged the army, that I was the reason the battle was lost . . . This could be our one chance to expose them, our one chance to set things right."

Braith sat up and squinted at the crumpled newspaper, quickly scanning the article. "Do you think we could convince them?" he asked, glancing up at her. "Do you think we could get them to listen?"

"Maybe," she said. "If we can get the vice-chancellor on our side. But we have to get there in time for the trial. After that . . ." She leaned forward with a frustrated sigh and kneaded her brow. "If we're too late, and Julian convinces the Royal Society that I'm the one to blame . . . We won't have a chance."

"We'll make it," he said, laying a hand on her shoulder. "As soon as the harbor opens, we'll find a ship and get back to the city before the trial begins. We'll deliver the evidence in time. But right now, we need to rest, wait until morning. There's nothing else we can do until then."

Petra stared at the empty train tracks at the edge of the platform, chewing hard on her bottom lip. Even with the evidence against them, she feared it still wasn't enough. That it would never be enough. It would be her and Emmerich's failure with the automaton all over again.

She sighed, burying her face in her hands. "What if we still fail?"

"We have evidence enough to prove that the minister was involved somehow with the attack at Amiens," he said, "as well as evidence to prove he commissioned the quadrupeds without Guild approval. With the other letters and telegrams you collected from the lieutenant-general's office, we have enough to make a case against him, at least enough to warrant suspicion."

"You think so?"

"We have a chance," he said. "We have to try."

She ran her hands through her shortened hair and leaned back against the bench, her gaze on the distant harbor waters to the south. "You know you don't have to come with me," she said quietly. "You'll be in just as much danger as me if we're caught, if we fail. I'd understand if—"

"I'm not leaving you to fight this alone, Petra," he

said, taking her hand with a squeeze. "I'm on your side. Always. You should know that by now."

"We might fail," she said.

"We might."

"And they'll hang you right next to me, you realize."

A smile twitched across his lips. "They'll try."

CHAPTER 19

Morning dawned quick and cold, the rising sun hidden behind a mask of gray clouds as Petra and Braith left the train station and headed for the harbor. They found passage on a steam-powered supply boat that had stopped in from Cardiff the night before, en route to Chroniker City with a coal shipment for the subcity boilers. Braith negotiated their fares, and before the first hour of morning had passed, they were setting sail out of Milford Haven, the sky steadily lightening to a chalky gray as they puttered down the waterway and into the open ocean beyond the borders of Wales.

Petra stood at the bow of the ship, her eyes trained on the distant horizon, nothing but choppy blue waters ahead, the Welsh coast and neighboring isles gradually slipping behind as the ship puffed on. Braith stood beside her, the line of his shoulders tense, rigid and silent as a statue.

The two of them looked worse for wear after their long trek from London. Their shoes were worn with holes and scuffs, their clothes muddy and stained with sweat. Braith still wore his military boots and trousers, but they were unrecognizable now, his dark slacks caked with mud and his shoes no longer polished to a shiny black. His red uniform jacket was somewhere at the bottom of the Thames now, along with the rest of any identifying military regalia; though he had kept his pistol, tucked into the calf of his right boot.

Petra hoped he wouldn't need it.

Too soon, the city loomed into view, the University standing like a golden spire atop the waves, the walls shrouded in a misty haze. Petra swallowed hard and gripped the deck railing with both hands, her stomach twisting in knots. There was no guarantee that this would work, no guarantee that their evidence would be enough, but they had to try.

Not an hour later, the ship anchored in the harbor, and they disembarked, marching steadily down the pier until they reached the rocky shore that formed Chroniker Isle. Petra paused, just in sight of the city gates.

This was her last chance to turn back, her last chance to save herself and escape Julian once and for all. Yet she knew she wouldn't. Emmerich had offered her the chance to run once, to walk away from this, but she had chosen to stay, to keep fighting, to try to stop the war before it began.

She could not turn back now.

Petra glanced at Braith, his eyes sharp in the bleak

morning light, the seaward winds tossing his hair. At least whatever happened now, she wouldn't be facing it alone.

She turned toward the city gates and peered at the gleaming University beyond. Those brass towers were the start and end to everything—everything she had ever wanted, everything she had ever hoped for. Only a year ago, she had stood at the foot of the University steps, hoping to earn a position there—the same fateful day she met Emmerich and soon found herself embroiled in his father's conspiracy.

Today, she would see the end of that conspiracy. One way or another.

Exhaling a deep breath, she clenched her hands at her sides and stepped forward, her feet sure and steady—her heart less so.

As she neared the gates, she reconsidered her plan. The guards at the gate had been doubled since she was last here. Four Royal Forces soldiers now stood on either side of the city entrance, the doors barred shut. They'd never let her through—not without asking far too many questions. And the more time they spent at the gates, the less time they had to get to the trial. She slowed, holding out a hand to stop Braith.

"Maybe you should take the lead on this one," she said, meeting his gaze. "You're military. If you say you have orders to be here, maybe they won't question it. And if they do, well . . ." She trailed off with a frown, a deep sense of unease growing in the pit of her stomach as she considered what she was about to say. "Use me if you have to. Say I'm the one who sabotaged the quadrupeds. They're certain to listen to that."

"Petra—"

"We have to get to that hearing," she said firmly. "Whatever it takes."

He pressed his lips into a hard frown. "I won't turn you over to them."

"If that's what it takes to get us inside, then that's what you'll do," she said, holding his gaze. "If we don't get to the hearing and deliver this evidence, they'll blame me for it anyway. At least this way, we might have a chance to prove what really happened in France . . . *before* they hang me."

Braith clenched his jaw. "It won't come to that."

"It might," she said. "Braith, you have to accept that I may not make it out of here alive. And if that happens, I won't have you dragged to the gallows with me."

"And won't have you dragged there at all. I would die first, before seeing you hanged a traitor," he said, his voice cracking. "We're in this together, Petra. I told you that. Where you go, I go. So if you want to have yourself hanged for sabotage, fine. But know that I'll be right there beside you."

She exhaled sharply. "Dammit, Braith—"

"We do this my way," he said firmly. "Or not at all. We didn't come all the way here for you to take the fall for the minister's schemes. I didn't come this far to let you die. So don't you dare turn yourself over now. I haven't given up on getting you out of here alive, Petra. You shouldn't give up on that either."

She held his gaze a moment longer. "Just get us through those gates and to the Royal Society hearing," she said. "Do that, and then we can talk about getting out of here alive."

He nodded once. "Just follow my lead."

They turned again toward the gates, the guards standing tall and statuesque, their faces drawn into rigid frowns as Petra and Braith came to a halt in front of them.

"State your business," said the shorter of the two soldiers, his expression hard as he appraised their travel-worn clothes.

"We're here for the Royal Society hearing," said Braith. "We have information regarding the failure of the war machine army in France."

"Do you have identification?"

"Of course." Braith crouched and withdrew a leather wallet from his boot. "Officer Cadet Braith Cartwright of the British Royal Forces," he said, handing the booklet to the guard. "We're here to deliver evidence."

The guard looked over Braith's identification, briefly scrutinizing his grimy appearance before shutting the passport with a frown. "We have had no word of your impending arrival."

"I wouldn't be expected," he said. "I was at Amiens. My superiors likely believe me to be dead."

The soldier gaped at him. "You were at the battle?"

Braith nodded. "I piloted one of the war machines."

"Blimey . . . What happened?" he asked, staring at

Braith with a measure of awe. "We heard it was sabotage. Is that true?"

"It was . . ." He clenched his jaw. "It was a massacre," he whispered, his voice breaking. "So many men—" He broke off with a frown, real pain etched into his every word, cracking through the stoic mask he so often wore as a soldier. He cleared his throat, meeting the other soldier's gaze. "You must understand. I have to tell the Royal Society what happened there. It may aid their investigation and bring those responsible for the failure to justice."

The soldier frowned, shifting the position of his rifle to his other shoulder. "I'm sorry, but I have orders not to let any soldiers into the city, not without prior approval. Had we been informed . . ."

"You must make an exception, surely. If I don't testify—"

"Those are my orders," he said. "You're a soldier. You understand. This goes above me."

"Then I should ask to contact your superior officer," said Braith, standing a little straighter. "If you telephone Colonel Kersey at the Royal Forces office and give my name, I am sure he will grant us entry."

The Royal Forces guard exchanged a frown with his fellow soldier, and then turned his back to Braith, conversing in low tones with another soldier on the other side of the gate.

He nodded once and then faced them again.

"Very well. Wait here while one of our men telephones the office."

The moment the soldier turned his back again, Petra leaned close, turning away from the gate. "What are you doing?" she hissed. "Kersey is on Julian's side. We can't trust him."

"No, but he can get us past the gates. That's what you want, isn't it?"

"And I thought *you* wanted to keep me out of the Royal Forces' hands," she said, her voice rising. "If we go to Kersey for help, he'll hand me straight over to Julian the moment we step foot in the city."

"You really think I'd let that happen? After all we've been through?"

There was movement on the other side of the city gate, and they both fell silent as one of the soldiers returned, quickly conversing with the others through the bars.

The shorter soldier faced them again. "The colonel wishes to speak with you to verify your identity before admitting you into the city. If you come with me, I can take you to the gatehouse telephone, where you can speak with him directly."

Braith nodded and turned toward Petra. "Let's go."

"Wait," said the guard, standing in their way. "The colonel will speak to Officer Cartwright only. But he did ask for the identity of your companion. Who is this with you?"

"I'm—"

"A Guild engineer," answered Braith. "We crossed

paths in France and decided to travel here together as our destination was the same."

"Your name?" asked the soldier.

She paused, racking her brain for a name that wouldn't give her away. "Rupert," she finally answered, careful to disguise her voice. "Rupert Larson. I'm a Guild engineer, a resident of the University. I was previously stationed at Hasguard."

"Do you have identification with you?"

She shook her head. "I lost my papers on the journey here," she said. "But if you contact the vice-chancellor, he can confirm—"

"The vice-chancellor does not have the authority to allow anyone through the gates. Only the colonel," said the soldier. "Without proper identification or the colonel's permission, I cannot allow you to enter."

"But—"

"Don't worry," said Braith, laying a hand on her arm. "I'll discuss the situation with the colonel and get his approval. Just wait here. I'll be right back."

Petra clenched her jaw. If this was a trap . . . if Colonel Kersey guessed the truth and had them arrested before she could reach the Royal Society hearing . . . "Be careful," she whispered.

"I will."

The soldier gestured toward the narrow guard gate. "This way, Officer."

Braith hesitated, holding her gaze for a moment longer. Then he left, the gate shutting behind him with a clang.

She whirled away from the door and curled her hands into fists, exposed and vulnerable in sight of the city walls; she could feel the eyes of the Royal Forces soldiers following her every step, and she forced herself to calm down, to breathe. She sucked in a deep breath and peered up the road through the barred gates, the gleaming University visible at the top of the street, its brass towers looming over the rest of the city. So close now. The clock tower in the square chimed half past seven, and the citizens of Chroniker City slowly filled the cobblestone streets, going about their daily business as if a war hadn't started just days ago.

The minutes ticked on, inching steadily toward the top of the hour, and still, Braith did not return to the gate. Petra kept her eye trained on the corner where he had disappeared, every nerve in her body strung taut. The sea churned at her back, waves crashing on the shore as more ships arrived in the harbor—traders, fishermen, industrial supply ships, craftsmen, and grocers from the mainland—but no passenger ships. No ferries. Workers passed her by, congesting the harbor plaza as they approached the city gates. All around the mood was glum, somber, heads bowed and backs bent.

Finally, Braith appeared again, his expression a little more rigid as the soldiers unlocked the side gate and let him through. She stared at him, her throat dry, waiting for him to speak.

"Let them pass," said the familiar soldier, brusquely waving them forward. "By order of Colonel Kersey. Official military business."

Braith nodded crisply to the officer and gestured Petra through the gates, his lips pressed tight. She obeyed without question, passing from the rocky island shore into the city proper. Despite her unease, the moment her feet touched the familiar cobblestone streets, she breathed a sigh of relief, the vibrations of the subcity engines flooding her with life.

She was home.

The gates clanged shut behind her, and Braith took her firmly by the arm, leading her steadily up the street. "We need to move quickly," he said, keeping his voice low. "The colonel may have given us entry into the city, but I think he suspects I might be lying to him. I wouldn't be surprised if he sent someone to intercept us." He covertly glanced over his shoulder at the Royal Forces guards at the gates. "He asked about you."

She swallowed against the sudden tightness in her throat. "What did you tell him?"

"That you were dead, killed at Amiens, as the lieutenant-general would have everyone believe. The soldiers at the gate informed him that a Guild engineer was with me, but I denied that it was you, or that I had any knowledge of what happened to you in France. Then I told him I had information about the attacks at Amiens and Calais, specifically regarding the failure of the quadrupeds. He requested I come to him directly, before reporting my evidence to the Royal Society. I insisted I needed to see them immediately, but . . ." Braith sighed. "He said it was too late. The hearing is already in session."

Petra stopped in her tracks. "No . . ."

All Julian had to do now was convince the Royal Society that she had been the one behind the failure of the quadrupeds—cite her previous anti-imperialist involvements, make sure no one raised their voice to defend her—and the investigation would be over, a dead girl blamed for the machinations of his conspiracy. Julian would be free to do as he wished, his plans for the war and the future sealed with her demise.

"What should we do now?" he asked.

"What do you mean? It's over . . . isn't it?"

Braith shrugged. "We still have the evidence. We still may have a chance to stop him."

"Do you think we could?"

"We have to try, don't we?"

She held his gaze and nodded, knowing he was right, but her heart stilled as she recognized the defeat in his eyes, the fear, the concern. He knew where this path led, just as well as she did. If they failed now . . .

"Still think we can make it out of this alive?" she asked, her voice breaking.

"Only one way to find out."

Petra and Braith quickly made their way into the University, the somber halls quiet as they navigated through the empty workshops and up the stairs to the Guild offices, pausing at every slight sound, every flicker of light. If anyone caught them now, prevented them from delivering their evidence to the Royal Society . . . that would be the end of it. Her rebellion ended, once and for all.

Petra exhaled a deep breath, slowing her steps as they neared the end of the long hallway, the council room entrance flanked by two men in red uniforms. She stopped in the middle of the hall, a chill settling in the pit of her stomach as she eyed the heavy wooden doors.

This was it.

Everything she and Emmerich had worked for, every failure they had suffered in their fight against his father, every setback, every defeat—it all led to this moment, one last attempt to stop this war and finally make Julian pay for his crimes. She was more than aware that she could fail again, that even with her evidence, Julian might still come out of this unscathed, but she could not turn back now, even if it meant she might lose her life in the process.

She glanced at Braith beside her, glad he was on her side for this. She wasn't sure she had the heart to do it on her own.

"You ready?" he asked.

"Ready as I'll ever be."

Not wasting another second, she strode up to the council room doors, Braith not a step behind.

The two guards intercepted them.

"We need to speak to the Royal Society," she said. "Immediately."

"No one is allowed to enter the council room while the Royal Society is in session," said one of the guards, keeping his voice just above a whisper. "The Society is currently in the middle of a hearing, and—"

"I know," she said. "That's why we're here. We have evidence."

The guards exchanged a frown. "Evidence of what?"

"Regarding the failure of the quadrupeds at Amiens and Calais," she said evenly. "So if you would just let us pass—"

"Not possible. The hearing is already in progress, and there are to be no interruptions to the proceedings, as dictated by—"

"You're not listening to me," she said, her voice rising. "I have evidence regarding the failure of the war machines in France, a failure leading to over six hundred men dead—soldiers, like you. I know the cause of the failure *and* the identities of the ones responsible. You *will* let us into that council room."

"Any evidence you may have can be directed to the Royal Society after—"

"Damn it, man, do you not hear her?" said Braith, stepping forward. "If we do not deliver this evidence to the Royal Society—"

"My orders are clear," said the soldier, arching his brow. "No one is to interrupt the hearing. For any reason."

Braith squared his shoulders. "And whose orders are those?"

The soldier began to respond, but then the door cracked open behind him.

Braith's hand twitched toward his pistol, and Petra's heart leapt into her throat, not sure if she should stand her ground or run, when Yancy Lyndon stepped out into the hall.

"What the devil is going on out·here?" he hissed, closing the door behind him with a heavy thud. "You had better—" He stopped when he saw her, and his mouth fell open.

"Hello, Yance," she said, a wry smile on her lips.

"Petra?" He stepped past the two Royal Forces guards and walked up to her. "But you're . . . you're dead. The minister said—"

"He's lying, Yancy. About all of it. I didn't die at Amiens. I didn't sabotage the quadrupeds. You know that as well as I do."

"Petra, he's in there now blaming you for everything, for sabotaging the quadruped army, causing the failure, saying you're the one responsible for all the lives lost in France. He says he has evidence against you, testimony from Royal Forces soldiers, other engineers, claiming you are an anti-imperialist, a French spy planted here to steal Guild secrets and sabotage the British war effort. He—"

Petra reached forward and gripped him by the shoulders, startling him into silence. "That's why we're here. We have evidence to prove who was behind the massacre at Amiens. We need to present it to the Royal Society as quickly as possible. Is your father inside?"

Yancy nodded slowly. "He is, but—Petra, if you go in there, they'll arrest you on the spot. The minister has everyone but the magistrate and my father convinced of your guilt."

"That's why I need your help—your father's help," she said, letting go of him. "We have evidence to suggest that Julian was involved in the attack, that he ordered the massacre of all those men. It wasn't just the quadruped failure, Yancy. He *bombed* them. *He* is the one responsible for those deaths. Not me. You have to help me prove it. You have to help me bring him to justice. We can't let him get away with this."

He clenched his jaw. "All right. Let me get my father."

Yancy turned his back on them, ignoring the two soldiers as he pushed through the doors into the council room. Petra dared take a few steps forward. She could hear the distinct sound of Vice-Chancellor Lyndon's heavy, gravelly tones beyond, a sliver of light illuminating the council chambers through a crack in the door.

"—and we have reason to believe the failure was *not* a result of sabotage as the minister claims, but . . ." He trailed off, a heavy silence falling on the council chambers. "*What?* Are you certain?"

"What is the meaning of this interruption?" asked another man, a voice Petra didn't recognize. "Lest I remind you, we are in the midst of a hearing."

"My apologies, Magistrate," said the vice-chancellor. "I have an urgent matter to attend to, relevant to the proceedings. If I may—"

"Vice-Chancellor, we are in the middle of a trial. You cannot—"

"I am well aware of the trial at hand," he replied,

his voice drawing nearer to the doors. "And I assure you, Magistrate, I would not leave if the matter were not of the utmost importance. This should only take a moment."

"Sir, if you leave the council chambers now, you forfeit the floor."

The vice-chancellor paused a moment, his shadow blocking the light from within the chambers. "Forgive me, Magistrate, but I believe you will make an exception upon my return."

"Vice-Chancellor—"

But he was already pushing through the door and into the hallway.

The door shut soundly behind him, and he stopped in the middle of the hall, standing stock-still as his steely brown eyes met hers. "Petra?" He took a tentative step forward. "Is it really you?"

"Hello, Vice-Chancellor."

"You're alive," he breathed, the tension melting from his shoulders in an instant.

"Seems that way."

He stared at her a moment longer. "We thought you fell at Amiens. We thought you were dead. I—" He cleared his throat, a hard frown weighing on his brow as his gaze swept over her face and hair, taking in the state of her dirty, tattered clothes, stained with mud and soot and blood. "What happened to you? How did you get here?"

Petra glanced at Braith beside her. "We escaped," she said, remembering the aftermath of the mortar attack in vivid clarity—the blood and death, the smell of it still in her clothes, everything burning, the world cloaked in ash. Her throat tightened, a shiver snaking down her spine. "We came as quickly as we could," she said. "We need to speak to the Royal Society. We know what really happened at Amiens. The quadrupeds didn't fall under French fire. It was Julian. All of it was Julian." She swallowed hard. "We have to tell the Royal Society. Before it's too late."

Lyndon sobered a bit. "Yancy said you had evidence. Where? How?"

Petra reached into her pocket and withdrew the lieutenant-general's logbook, the rest of the letters and telegrams tucked inside its pages. She clutched the smooth leather cover, every piece of evidence she had against Julian contained in the tiny, nondescript journal.

"It's here—all of it," she said, holding tight to the little book. "Letters, telegrams, what little I could gather from the lieutenant-general's office tying Julian to the attack. I don't know if it's enough to convict him, but . . ." She swallowed hard, a lump rising in her throat. "We have to *try*. He can't be allowed to continue like this, not after what he did at Amiens. We have to stop him, Vice-Chancellor," she said, meeting his hard gaze. "Today."

Lyndon pressed his lips together with a weary sigh. "I know."

"Then you'll help me?"

"I promised you a long time ago that I would help

you put an end to Julian's conspiracy, and I meant it. Which is why I called the Royal Society here—to bring him to justice once and for all."

"That was you?"

"When I heard what happened at Amiens, I knew I had waited long enough—and foolishly so." He cleared his throat. "I thought you were dead," he said, his gravelly voice breaking. "And I blamed myself for not acting sooner. Perhaps I might have saved you had I not been so cautious. Perhaps I might have saved them all."

Voices sounded from within the council chambers, and Petra tensed at Julian's familiar dulcet tones, the sound of his voice driving needles through her spine. She swallowed hard.

"We have a chance now to make it right," she said, her chest tight. "We have a chance to stop him. We have to try."

"And we will. Just wait here a moment. I'll—"

"No." She stepped forward, meeting Lyndon at the council room doors. "I'm done waiting. I'm done hiding. If we do this now, then I want to be the one to look him in the eye and tell him that he's lost."

Lyndon let out a heavy sigh and turned toward the door with a shake of his head, the sound of muffled conversation beyond. "You're just like your mother," he muttered, curling his fingers around the door handle. "Damn stubborn woman."

CHAPTER 20

The council room doors opened wide, and Petra followed Lyndon inside. She paused at the threshold as she spotted Julian Goss in the center of the hall, his back to the doors as he argued with one of the men now presiding behind the council bench—five of them in all, their faces stern and lined with age. Sitting along the walls were a few familiar faces, some pledged to Julian's cause—Fowler, Calligaris, a few of the more unsavory engineers she had met in her time at the University—and others more friendly. She recognized a few members of her engineering team sitting off to the side, Yancy among them, and beside him . . .

"Rupert . . ." she gasped, her feet carrying her forward before she could think otherwise.

Yancy nudged him in the arm and he glanced up as she approached. His eyes met hers, and half a second later, he was on his feet, hugging her close.

"We thought you were dead," he whispered, breathing into her hair.

"You're not getting rid of me that easily."

He laughed, drawing away to look at her again. There were tears in his eyes, and his hands shook on her shoulders, but the smile on his face was unbroken. "Never should have doubted you."

"It's good to see you," she whispered, her voice breaking.

"Better to see you."

Raised voices drew her attention back to the center of the room.

Julian glared up at the council bench, pointing accusingly at Lyndon. "Whatever evidence he claims to have is too late in coming. You cannot—"

"It is for *me* to decide whether his evidence is admissible or not," said the man behind the bench, sitting where the vice-chancellor usually presided. "I will hear his claim and decide then if this new evidence of his is permissible. Now then . . ." He turned toward Lyndon. "Explain yourself. What is this new evidence of yours?"

Lyndon faced the bench. "It is with regard to the failure of the quadrupeds at Amiens, further evidence of the persons responsible for the deaths that—"

"We know who is responsible," said Julian. "As I have already—"

"Yes, the young female engineer, as you have already claimed," the magistrate interrupted, his voice firm. "But until you can provide substantial evidence to support your claims, your words are meaningless in my court. *Nullius in verba*, Minister . . . 'On the word of no one.' Evidence will determine our course of action, *not* hearsay."

"You want evidence?" Julian went on. "There are nearly six hundred men dead, and more than a thousand inactive war machines now sitting on French soil, utterly destroyed because that girl—"

"You mean me?" Petra stepped forward, a fire raging in her chest. She clenched her hands into tight fists. "You want to blame *me* for their deaths? After what you did?"

"Petra . . ." Braith whispered, gently holding her back.

Julian's shoulders tensed, and he turned, slowly at first, his face lit in profile as he glanced over his shoulder—the familiar line of his brow, the angle of his jaw highlighted by the electric sconces set into the walls.

She gritted her teeth and stepped forward, ignoring Braith's warnings. "Answer me, you bastard. You want to blame me? Do it to my face."

He turned toward her then, recognition flashing across his dark copper eyes in an instant. A muscle twitched in his jaw.

"What is the meaning of this?" asked the magistrate. "Who is this person?"

Lyndon stepped forward and cleared his throat. "This is the engineer—"

"Petra Wade," she answered, breaking away from

Julian's fierce gaze. "The engineer who designed the quadruped."

"Who *sabotaged* the quadruped," said Julian, finding his voice. "This is the girl responsible for their failure, Magistrate. If not for the effects of her sabotage, the British soldiers now lying dead on foreign soil might have escaped that battlefield before the French launched their deadly attack against us. Those men died as a direct result—"

"They died because of *you*," she said, raising her voice over his. "They didn't die because the quadrupeds failed; it wasn't the fault that led to their deaths. It was *you*."

"You see the level of her delusion? To think that I—"

"It's no delusion. The British army didn't fall under French fire. They fell because *he* ordered it—disguising half the British fleet as French ships and bombing the battlefield to destroy both armies, killing what few survivors knew the truth. All to secure a war against France."

The magistrate arched his brows. "That is a tall accusation."

Julian clenched his jaw, his face reddening a shade. "It is hearsay," he announced, turning away from Petra with a dismissive wave. "What would I have to gain from such a plot? This is preposterous, a fanciful invention to further her anti-imperialist agenda, a pale attempt to undermine the Society's investigation. Miss Wade is the one responsible for the quadrupeds' failure. She is a traitor to the empire, a known anti-imperialist conspirator and saboteur. We should be *arresting* her, not listening to whatever falsities she would attempt to have you believe."

"I can prove it." She withdrew the lieutenant-general's logbook from her trouser pocket, the collection of telegrams and letters stashed inside. "I have evidence to suggest Julian was involved in the attack at Amiens, that he was in communication with the lieutenant-general, and that he knew the quadrupeds would fail before the British fleet ever left Hasguard."

"What evidence would that be?" Julian sneered. "This is an absurdity! Nothing more than a desperate attempt to subvert the investigation at hand. Miss Wade is the one behind the failure of the quadrupeds. To entertain otherwise is a waste of the court's time."

"I will be the one to decide that," said the magistrate. "If she has evidence to support her claims, then I should like to review it."

"To even consider these accusations is folly," said Julian, his voice sharp. "She is nothing but a lying saboteur, and any evidence she claims to possess is a grotesque falsification, an inexcusable attack against my very character. If you think I shall stand here and allow her to spout such slanderous statements without recompense—"

"You *will* stand there, Minister, and if you wish to remain for the rest of our proceedings, you will do so quietly," said the magistrate, his voice stern. "I will hear no more outbursts from you. I was brought here to investigate the failure of the quadruped army and bring any persons responsible to justice, and I intend to do my job. You have made your claims against Miss Wade very clear, and I have reviewed your statements regarding the quadruped failure quite thoroughly. Now I shall give Miss Wade the same consideration and judge the validity of her evidence myself. Is that understood?"

Julian gathered to his full height and glared up at the magistrate, sitting tall behind the council bench. "This is a mockery of British justice."

"This is how things are done." The magistrate leaned forward in his chair, folding his hands together under his chin. He regarded Petra with a measure of cold reservation. "Now, let's start with your accusations. You say you have evidence of the minister's involvement in the massacre at Amiens?"

"That's right."

"Let's see it, then."

Petra clutched the lieutenant-general's logbook in her hand and stepped forward, approaching the magistrate and the council bench. Julian glowered at her, his jaw set in rigid determination, but he did not make any move to stop her. He couldn't, not without incriminating himself further.

The magistrate regarded her coldly as he took the leather-bound journal from her outstretched hand. "This is everything?" he asked.

She nodded. Every last scrap of evidence against Julian was bound in that tiny book, her only hope of revealing the truth of his conspiracy.

The magistrate opened the front cover and set the stack of telegrams and folded letters aside, reading the lieutenant-general's neat scrawl as he turned the first few pages. "Where was this evidence of yours obtained?"

"From the lieutenant-general's office, aboard the Royal Forces flagship," she said. "I suspected the lieutenant-general was conspiring with the minister, so I decided to investigate."

"Why were you aboard the flagship?" he asked, scanning the next page.

"The minister put me there."

"That is a lie," said Julian, drawing the magistrate's attention away from the logbook splayed in front of him. "Miss Wade was not aboard that airship by any means of mine. She snuck onto the airship herself in order to attempt further sabotage of the quadrupeds' mission. I have a written statement from the lieutenant-general of that flagship, detailing her efforts to—"

"I was on that airship because *you* put me there," she said. "You wanted me to see how badly I failed to stop you and your war. You wanted me to see those soldiers die, to see what you were capable of. Well, I did." She resisted a shudder, the stench of blood and death still ripe in her nose, burned into her memory with acrid clarity. "I saw everything. You want evidence?" she asked, facing the magistrate again. "Turn to the entry for June 5th and see what's written there."

The magistrate flipped halfway through the thin journal and stopped suddenly, his eyebrows rising steadily higher as he read. " 'Attack at Amiens,' " he read. " 'Quadruped army destroyed by French aerial assault. Sabotage suspected. Aerial counterattack successful. Significant losses. British deaths estimated at—' " He glanced up. "The rest is left blank."

"I found that in the lieutenant-general's office just moments after the quadrupeds launched from the airships," she said. "That entry was written *before* the battle commenced, long before the quadrupeds malfunctioned or the army fell. Yet he knew how it would end. He knew the quadrupeds would fall."

"All lies," said Julian. "Clearly, the girl forged the entry to disguise her own guilt. How could the lieutenant-general know what would happen?"

"Because it was planned," she said. "All of it."

"Preposterous."

The magistrate glanced up. "You wish me to believe the minister conspired with Lieutenant-General Stokes to massacre his own men?"

"Julian knew about the fault in the quadruped design," she went on. "He knew the quadrupeds would fail, knew they were faulty, and yet he did nothing to prevent their failure. Instead, he used the fault to orchestrate the massacre of those men, bombing the battlefield to cover up his conspiracy and burn away the evidence, killing anyone who knew the truth. All along, he planned to destroy the quadrupeds and lay the blame of their failure on me—accuse me of sabotage and treason and worse—but it wasn't the fault that killed those soldiers. It wasn't sabotage. It was the bombardment of mortar shells, dropped from British airships, that killed those men."

A heavy silence followed her words.

"An absurd accusation," said Julian, finally breaking the silence. "Those men died to protect their country. To suggest anything less—"

"Those men died because you wanted a war!"

The magistrate held up his hand before Julian could respond, staring intently at the lieutenant-general's logbook. "It's clear there are discrepancies between your two accounts of what happened at Amiens, but while these accusations are troubling, I am afraid I do not have the authority to further investigate such matters at this time."

Petra frowned. "But—"

"I am here to uncover the details behind the quadrupeds' failure, not investigate some deeper conspiracy that may be at work," he said. "That is not my job. But this fault—the supposed sabotage that led to the quadrupeds' failure—*that* I have the authority to discuss and thus determine a course of action, should the failure be the responsibility of anyone here." He glanced up from lieutenant-general's logbook. "Miss Wade, you are the designing engineer. Explain to me what you know of the quadrupeds' malfunction. What caused the failure?"

She sucked in a deep breath. "There was an error in the design," she explained, "a faulty axle plate that when engaged by the quadruped's primary drive systems rendered the machine inoperable due to rotational disparity between the connecting gear trains, applying too much pressure to the tension springs and causing a fracture. Without the tension springs to regulate the erratic changes in power distribution during operation, the machine's disparate systems fall out of synchronicity within a matter of minutes, causing widespread failure to the interconnected systems."

"And how was this error introduced?"

Petra swallowed hard. "A miscalculation on my part, at the design level."

"A miscalculation placed there with malicious purpose," Julian spat. "Whatever fault existed in the quadruped was a result of intentional sabotage, not an error. She *deliberately* designed the machine to fail."

"Minister . . ." the magistrate warned. "I will not ask you again. Be *silent.*"

"The fault wasn't deliberate," she said, the lie slipping easily through her lips. "The quadruped is a complex piece of machinery, involving several different interconnecting systems. Had I been given more time to complete the schematics, I might have caught the error, but being pressed for time, I was unable to regulate the quality of the design. With only a week—"

"A week?" The magistrate blinked at her. "You designed this machine—this quadruped—in a single week?"

She nodded. "That was the deadline I was given."

"I see . . . So, rushed for time, you designed the machine within the week and turned the imperfect designs over to the Guild, who then began preparations for initial production."

"That's right."

"Then the error slipped past the notice of your engineering team and remained in the final design that was approved for prototype construction. This is the fault that caused the quadrupeds to malfunction in France. Correct?"

"Yes, but—"

"But you repaired it—the prototype," he said, reaching across the council bench for a sheaf of papers. He riffled through the pages. "You removed this faulty axle plate, the one causing the rotational disparity."

"I did, yes," she said with a frown. She glanced from the magistrate to Vice-Chancellor Lyndon and back. "When I discovered the error in the machine's design, I repaired the fault immediately. But how did you—"

"I have the report here, as signed by one of your fellow engineers and approved by Vice-Chancellor Lyndon," he said, waving a piece of paper in front of him. "But if you repaired the prototype, how then did this error manifest in the quadruped army that deployed in France?"

"Because the repair was a ruse," said Julian, his voice edged. "I daresay that much is obvious. Or else the quadrupeds would not have failed. Her attempted 'repair' was nothing but an effort to conceal the truth of her sabotage."

The magistrate turned toward Julian, regarding him with the full force of his cold, clinical stare. "So you were aware of her repair of the prototype?"

"I am aware of her *claim*," Julian said calmly, unruffled by the magistrate's words. "Though I would not call her sudden involvement in the prototype's development a 'repair.' If she made any changes to the prototype in the days before its completion, that is only further proof of her sabotage. Inevitably, her interference caused the machines built from the final design to fail."

"That could be," said the magistrate, conceding the point with a nod.

"No, that's not what happened," said Petra. "The quadrupeds failed because—"

"I have seen your quadruped prototype, Miss Wade," said the magistrate, his sharp voice bullying hers into silence. "Vice-Chancellor Lyndon was kind enough to grant me access to the workshop where it was built. While I reviewed your designs and examined the machine—I am a mechanical engineer myself, you see, a University graduate—I found no fault in the prototype's design, no issue of rotational disparity or mismatched gear systems; the defunct regulator had been removed, as outlined in your repair. By all accounts, the prototype works. No malfunction whatsoever." He folded his hands across the table in front of him and leaned forward. "And yet the quadrupeds at France still failed. If the prototype was repaired and the report filed, why would the quadruped army still fail?"

Petra swallowed hard. "Because Julian commissioned the quadruped army before the prototype was finished. He used the initial prototype design, the one approved by the engineering team, the design containing the flaw."

The magistrate shuffled through a few more pages of notes and conferred with one of the other men sitting nearby. "Vice-Chancellor Lyndon . . . you claim to have evidence to support this statement, do you not? Evidence to suggest that Minister Goss did indeed know of the repair to the quadruped, prior to the deployment of this early-commissioned army."

"I do, sir," said Lyndon, stepping forward. "I believe Minister Goss manufactured the quadruped army from an early draft of the quadruped design, and that he knew of the repair to the prototype prior to the deployment of that army. After he arrested Miss Wade for attempted sabotage, I shared with him the repair order she had filed, but he obviously chose to ignore the repair—or else the quadruped army would not have failed."

"None of this can be proven," said Julian. "I—"

"There are multiple testimonies to support this claim," said the magistrate. "I have testimony from Yancy Lyndon confirming the repair of the prototype, and here, a testimony from Rupert Larson, the designing engineer of the new Royal Forces warship. According to *his* written statement, he discovered the quadruped army several days before the completion of the prototype."

"Their testimonies prove nothing," said Julian. "Larson is an intimate associate of Miss Wade's and cannot be trusted to testify against her; I would not be surprised if he shared her anti-imperialist sentiments. As for the Lyndon boy, he was on the quadruped engineering team, often seen in deep conversation with the girl, as many of the other engineers will attest. For all we know, he might have helped her sabotage the machine, using his connections to his father to cover up their schemes."

"And what evidence do you have of such claims?" asked the magistrate. "As yet, you have failed to produce anything substantial against Miss Wade, neither to support your claims that she is an anti-imperialist or that she willfully sabotaged the quadruped project."

The magistrate leaned forward in his chair. "The facts are this, Minister: the quadruped army failed as a result of some measure of neglect—willful or not— and their failure resulted in the loss of British lives. I have reviewed enough evidence to suggest Miss Wade be absolved of any responsibility in regards to their failure. However, I cannot say the same for you."

"Then allow me to bring forth my own witnesses," said Julian. "They will testify to the truth, not these traitorous lies."

The magistrate seemed to consider it. "I believe you are allowed witnesses as a part of your defense, once an official investigation has begun," he said, sitting up in his chair. He folded his hands. "I may not have the legal authority to arrest you on these accusations of conspiracy, but I must consider what would motivate you to manufacture an entire army of war machines from an untested prototype—or why you would not repair those machines once learning of a fault in their design, a fault that would surely lead to their failure. There are too many questions still left unanswered, and more than enough evidence to implicate some deeper motive to your actions."

He reached for the gavel next to the scattered paperwork littering the council bench. "Therefore, I declare this preliminary hearing ended. As a result of our initial findings, Julian Goss, Minister to the Vice-Chancellor, is hereby placed into Royal Society custody for suspicion of negligence, an investigation to be held forthwith." The gavel rapped against the table like a thunderclap, and the magistrate gestured to a pair of Royal Forces soldiers to the side of the bench. "Take him somewhere secure while we conduct our preliminary investigations. We leave for London first thing tomorrow."

Julian stalked toward the council bench, brushing the two soldiers away. "I will not be treated this way, like a common criminal," he said, glaring at the magistrate. "I have given everything to the Guild, to the Empire. Everything I have done has been in the best interest of our future, for the good of science, for the good of the *world*. Only a fool would fail to see where my loyalties lie."

"That may be," said the magistrate. "But the *evidence* points to—"

"I should not be the one on trial here," Julian said, pointing an accusing finger at Petra. "That girl is an anti-imperialist traitor, a known saboteur and French informer, planted here to sow discord within the Guild. Already, she has swayed the vice-chancellor and her peers to her cause, falsifying evidence to discredit me and all I have done to advance this institution forward. She is our *enemy*, and if she is not dealt with to the full extent of the law, she will destroy everything we have worked for, everything we have built. Already, she destroyed the automaton; she sabotaged an entire army of war machines and caused the deaths of hundreds of British lives. Is that not evidence enough?"

A heavy silence followed his words, and the magistrate leaned forward in his chair. "I have every intention of bringing the person responsible for the deaths of those soldiers to justice," he said evenly. "But I follow evidence, Mr. Goss, not hearsay, and given the evidence as presented to me, I do not believe that Miss Wade is the one who is at fault for the quadrupeds' failure."

"Lies and deceit," he hissed. "She has fooled you all."

"No," Petra said, finally stepping forward, her hands clenched into fists at her sides. "I have shown them the truth. You've lost, Julian. It's over."

He scowled at her, a muscle twitching in his jaw.

The magistrate gestured again to the two Royal Forces soldiers, and the two men swept in and seized Julian by the arms.

"You are making a mistake, Magistrate," he said, standing tall and proud despite the soldiers' firm grip. "While you waste your time investigating me, France will recover from their losses at Amiens and Calais, and they will come for us, stronger than ever. I hope you are prepared when they do."

"Take him away."

The soldiers dragged him out of the council chambers, the doors shutting soundly behind them. Only then did Petra dare breathe a sigh of relief.

It was done.

"Now," said the magistrate, leaning back in his chair. "The Privy Council in London will soon expect a report of our findings, so I should like to review as much evidence as possible before we send word of our suspicions. While our official investigation pertains only to the technological failure of the quadrupeds, if we can convince the Privy Council that your suspicions of conspiracy have merit, that there is substantial enough evidence to support your claims, then we may be able to bring forward a full investigation into the matter. Should we find anything of consequence, Minister Goss will join us in London for our meeting with the Privy Council, where we will hold him until trial. If you could provide me with access to the minister's office, the names of any potential co-conspirators, close associates, or subordinates who may have reported directly to the minister in the last several months, and any other applicable evidence that may aid our investigation, we can then begin to build an argument to suggest that Minister Goss conspired in the failure of the quadrupeds at Amiens and Calais, and that his knowledge of the fault in the design could have prevented the deaths that resulted from that failure."

Vice-Chancellor Lyndon executed a deep bow. "The Guild is at your disposal, Magistrate."

"Very good. I should also advise you to recall any engineers who may still be afield, anyone who may have ties with the minister, or who might have information relevant to the investigation. We will need to question anyone who might know more of his affairs."

"Of course," said the vice-chancellor. "I will do so at once."

The magistrate rose from his chair behind the council bench. "Then we shall take our leave of you and begin our preliminary investigation of these matters. We have a lot to do before we return to London."

Petra stepped forward. "What about the war?"

"I beg your pardon?"

"It's just . . . If you can prove Julian was responsible for the deaths at Amiens and not the French, then surely the war cannot go on. It can be stopped, can't it?"

The magistrate pressed his lips into a grim frown. "If Minister Goss is indeed responsible for the deaths of those soldiers, then we will find what evidence we can of his involvement and bring him to justice, but I'm afraid that there is little we can do to stem the tides of war. Blood has been spilled, and whether by his hand or not, men are dead—on both sides of this conflict. All we can do now is deliver our findings to the Privy Council and hope to mitigate the damage."

"But surely the Privy Council can call for a cease-fire? They have the power to stop this war before it goes any further. They must do something."

"It's out of our hands, Petra," said Lyndon, laying a hand on her shoulder.

"Then we've lost," she said, her chest tight. She turned toward the vice-chancellor. "After everything, he still managed to start a war. We failed."

"No, Petra . . ." he said gently. "Julian will pay for what he has done. Eventually, the truth will come out and he *will* be brought to justice." He squeezed her shoulder. "We won today. You should be proud."

She swallowed hard and glanced around the council chambers, a sinking feeling deep in her chest. "Then why does it feel like it isn't over yet?"

A month later, Petra stood once again in the hallway outside the council chambers, a future ahead of her without Julian standing in her way. The day after the hearing, he had been hauled away to London by the Royal Society for suspicion of his crimes at Amiens, enough preliminary evidence found to suggest an ulterior motive behind the early manufacture of the quadrupeds. Whether or not there was evidence to prove he was guilty of a conspiracy to start a war . . . she had to believe they would find it, that the Royal Society would succeed where she had failed.

Eventually, Julian would pay for what he had done at Amiens. He would pay for all those lives lost, for the failure of the quadrupeds and the bombing of the battlefield. He would pay for everything he had done to secure his war.

It was only a matter of time.

And now, with Julian gone, she faced the very real prospect of a future without his threats, without the constant fear of retribution. For the first time in almost a year, she was free.

Free to pursue her dreams on her own terms.

"I wish I could stay," said Braith, standing next to her in front of the council room doors. "But the Royal Society wants me at the evidentiary hearing before the Privy Council tomorrow morning, and if I'm to make it back to London in time, I need to leave on the next ship."

He wore a new uniform now, the jacket crisply pressed and unmarred by the dark smears of blood and soot he had earned at Amiens. That uniform lay at the bottom of the Thames, forever trapped in the thick muck that lined the riverbed, but the scars of that battle still remained, deeper than his uniform, deeper than skin. The memory of it haunted the shadows in his eyes, a weariness that had not been there before.

But they had made it, the two of them.

Together.

And the thought of him leaving now left a deep ache in her chest. For months, he had been there for her, at her side. They had survived a battle together, had stood at the brink of all-out war together, and then they had come back from it, working together to stop Julian's conspiracy, knowing they would both die if they failed.

That kind of thing changed a person.

For Petra, it had changed everything.

"How long will you be stationed in London?" she asked.

"A few months, I think. For as long as they need me."

"Oh." She pressed her lips together and bowed her head, her hair falling across her face. She let out a long sigh. "Then I guess this is goodbye," she said hoarsely, her throat tight.

"Only for a little while," he said, taking a step closer. He reached forward and brushed her hair from her eyes. "I'll be back," he said. "As soon as I have leave to visit."

"You'll keep me updated, won't you?" she asked, her voice strained. "About the investigation? I want to know if anything changes."

"Of course I will." A gentle smile broke through the mask of melancholy that had plagued him since Amiens. "Just stay out of trouble while I'm gone, will you?"

She forced a smile to her lips. "No promises."

His somber gaze lingered on her face a moment longer as his smile slowly faded. "I should go," he said quietly, bowing his head. "I'm sure the council is waiting, and I shouldn't—"

Petra stepped forward and hugged him tight, tears stinging her eyes. She had no words, but she didn't need them. Some things didn't need saying.

Braith relaxed and sighed into her hair. "If you ever need anything, just let me know," he said quietly. "I'll only be a telegram away."

She withdrew, her chest tight. She wasn't ready to

see him go. Not yet. Not after everything they had been through. "Braith—"

"We'll see each other again, Petra," he said, brushing his thumb over her cheek.

"You promise?"

"I promise."

He pulled her into another hug and she clung tightly to his chest, remembering the last time he had held her like this, caught in the aftermath at Amiens, not knowing if they would live or die. She squeezed her eyes shut, her heart turning cold at the thought of him leaving. She didn't want to say goodbye, but there was nothing she could say to keep him here. He had his duties, and she had hers. That's how it would always be.

Finally, he pulled away. "I have to go," he said quietly, his voice strained.

"I know."

A brief smile touched his lips. "Goodbye, Petra."

"Goodbye, Braith," she whispered.

He dropped his hands to his sides and slowly stepped away, his jaw tight as he held her gaze one last time. And then suddenly he was gone, stealing away without another word—back to London and the life of a soldier, no longer bound to the Guild . . . or her.

The world seemed less somehow with him gone.

She let out a sigh and turned back toward the council room doors, a deep ache settling in her chest. There was something there, between them. Something that made the world seem worth living in, that made her feel alive again. What it was, she didn't know, but maybe . . . maybe when he came back, they could figure it out.

Right now, she had other things to do.

With a slow, steadying breath, she smothered whatever feelings she had for Braith deep in her chest and approached the council chambers once more, her dreams finally in her grasp. All her life, all she ever wanted was to be a Guild engineer, to be respected for who she was, for what she could do with machines. Today, that was going to become a reality.

Standing up a little straighter, she sucked in a deep breath, reached forward, and knocked.

Sudden footsteps neared, and the door swung inward, revealing the brightly lit council chamber beyond—the long curved table and attending council members, the Guild seal ticking rhythmically against the far wall, and—

"Hello, Petra."

That voice . . . so familiar, so real and warm compared to the hollow echo that she had listened to across the telephone, striking her with the warmth of old memories—long nights spent in the Guild offices, stolen moments between fitting machine parts together, the touch of his lips and the feel of her fingers in his air, the warmth of his arms around her and the smell of metal on his skin.

She stopped, her heart suddenly failing to beat.

There he was, standing in the doorway—his copper

eyes and dark hair, the curve of his crooked smile, the angle of his jaw . . .

"Emmerich?"

She swallowed against the tightness in her throat and haltingly stepped forward, scarcely believing he was here, after all this time. His hair was shorter than she remembered it, that day they parted at the city harbor, not knowing if they would see each other again, but the way he looked at her now . . . there was no disguising the glowing intensity in his eyes, that fervid zeal.

He smiled and suddenly his arms were around her, and hers around him, as if nothing had changed, as if he had never left, as if they hadn't spent the last year apart. It had been so long since she last saw his face, since she last stood in his arms, and it felt now as if she had been drowning all that time, scarcely breathing since he left her standing on the beach that fateful day. A weight fell from her shoulders—a weight she hadn't realized she was carrying—and she shuddered in his arms, his steady heartbeat thrumming against her cheek.

"Oh, God . . . it is you."

He laughed, and she could almost believe nothing had changed.

And yet . . .

Everything had changed.

She pulled back and gazed into those familiar copper eyes. The sight of him transported her to a different time, a different life, when nothing else mattered but the touch of his hand, the feel of his lips on hers . . . But this wasn't that life anymore.

He'd left that life behind.

And so had she.

"Emmerich . . . what are you doing here?" she asked. "I thought you were still in Paris."

"I was until about a week ago," he said. "I came as soon as I could, but after what happened at Amiens, it was near impossible getting passage out of France." A smile broke across his face again, and he took her hands into his, the warmth of his fingers spreading deep into her bones. "But I'm here now. Petra, I'm *here*."

The sound of his voice wrapped tightly around her heart, threatening to never let go, and she bit her lip, studying his familiar face, every freckle, every dimple, remembering how real it had been, loving him—the touch of his lips against hers, the feel of his breath on her skin, the way she lost herself in his arms, the rest of the world falling into oblivion.

But that was a lifetime ago.

And now that he was here again . . . How could they pick up the pieces of a life that no longer existed, a life they both left behind? Now, when she had finally begun to heal?

"I have something for you," he said suddenly, retrieving a small unsealed envelope from his pocket.

"What is it?" she asked, taking the parcel from his hands. There was a single piece of folded paper inside.

"You remember the last time we spoke, on the telephone? When I contacted you from Taverny?"

Petra swallowed hard and nodded, her chest suddenly tight as she slipped the paper free.

"It was her," he said, those words lighting up a part of Petra's heart that she hadn't realized was there. "I found her . . . your mother's sister. She was there the day you were born. She claimed you as her own to protect your mother's reputation, never telling anyone that the young girl Adelaide Chroniker took with her back to Chroniker City was actually Adelaide's daughter." He gestured then to the paper in her hands. "She kept that secret for eighteen years."

She glanced down at the paper in her hands, her fingers shaking as she slowly unfolded the paper, carefully smoothing out the creases as she realized what this was.

There, written in her mother's looping handwriting, was her name, her *real* name, the name her mother had given her at birth:

Petra Sofia Chroniker, born April 19th, 1864,
to mother Adelaide Francine Chroniker, aged twenty,
and father (undisclosed),
in the commune of Taverny, France.

The paper trembled in Petra's hands, and a tear splashed onto the page.

"She knows about you now," Emmerich went on. "She knows that you're alive, that you survived the fire—after believing for so long that you died with your mother. When I told her about you, that you were an engineer with the skill to match Adelaide Chroniker herself, she laughed, and it was . . ." He smiled then, a dreamy look in his eye. "It was what I remember of your mother's laugh, so full of life. So unrestrained. She wasn't surprised. She said engineering was in your blood, as it was your mother's."

Petra touched the familiar handwriting, as if she could reach through time and watch her mother's hand write the words across the page eighteen years ago.

"Do you realize what this means?" he asked. "We have proof now—proof of who you are, of your heritage, your legacy. If you want, you can take her place now. You can take her name."

Petra glanced up and met Emmerich's eyes, blazing with that familiar molten fire she had gazed into a thousand times before, achingly raw. She swallowed, her mouth suddenly dry as she considered what he was saying.

"Is this enough to prove it?" she asked. "Would anyone believe me?"

"It's enough for me. And for Lyndon."

"You showed him?"

Emmerich nodded. "He will support you, whatever you choose." He stepped forward and took her hand, his touch warming her through to the bone. "And so will I."

She glanced at the council room doors. To take her mother's name, to claim herself a Chroniker . . .

Was that what she wanted?

"It's your choice, Petra. And you certainly don't have to make it now. If you would rather—"

"No," she said, swallowing against the lump in her throat. "It's time."

He hesitated. "Are you sure? Are you ready?"

"They need to know, Emmerich . . ." she said, her voice quavering. "They need to know my mother isn't gone, that the things she believed in aren't gone, not while her daughter still lives and breathes, not while the Chroniker name is mine to carry. They need to remember her, to remember her vision, a world of scientific prosperity—not one of war." She swallowed thickly, staring at her mother's name on the birth certificate, written just below hers. "If I can remind them of that . . . of her . . . then maybe I can be a daughter she would be proud of."

Emmerich squeezed her hand. "Then let's go make her proud."

Vice-Chancellor Lyndon sat at the center of the council bench, glancing up as they entered the council chambers. "Are we ready to proceed?"

Emmerich turned toward Petra, and she nodded, handing him the envelope with the copy of her birth certificate inside. "We are," he said, leaving her side to approach the council bench. "Though there is to be a change of formal identification."

"Indeed?"

Petra stood in the center of the room, her chin held high. She watched, hardly able to breathe, as Emmerich passed the envelope to the vice-chancellor. No turning back now.

Lyndon opened the envelope and stopped. "This is your wish?" he asked.

She sucked in a deep breath and nodded. "It is."

"Very well." The vice-chancellor stood and cleared his throat, addressing the present councilors. "Today, after a formal review of her work with the Guild, it is with great pleasure I present to you our newest member." He paused for breath, lifting the copy of her birth certificate for all to see. "With written confirmation of her true identity—verified by Lady Isobel Chroniker Fontaine, the recently rediscovered holder of the Chroniker estate—I now introduce to you the only daughter of the late Lady Adelaide Chroniker, heir to the Chroniker name and rightful beneficiary of all the honors and titles deserving of her station: esteemed engineer, Miss Petra Sofia Chroniker."

Petra couldn't help but laugh, her heart full to bursting.

"Welcome to the Guild, Miss Chroniker."

ACKNOWLEDGMENTS

Every book has its challenges, and this one ran the gamut. It took me nearly five years to write this novel, from conception to finished manuscript, with many drafts in between, and if not for a lot of different people, this series might have died before the story ever got a chance to see itself on the printed page. First, a big thank you to Kelly O'Connor for taking the book on with Harper Voyager in the first place and forcing me to continue the story I began in *The Brass Giant*. If not for my publishing contract, this story might have never been more than a half-finished draft on my hard drive.

Second, massive thanks to R. J. Blain, who helped me revitalize my love of this story by pushing me past my ambivalence and giving me the character I needed to do it. Braith owes his entire existence to her incessant wheedling, and this book would not exist as it does if not for her help.

Additional thanks to my earliest readers, BFFs Jaime and Rachel, for helping me stay sane during the writing and editing of this book, and to Gabe, for helping me polish the final draft (even if not all of his suggestions made it into the finished book—sorry, Gabe!).

Of course, I must thank my editor, Rebecca Lucash, for helping me iron out all those fuzzy plot details I managed to overlook in my own revisions, and for convincing me to stick to my guns in my vision for the story and its characters. Throughout the writing and editing process, I doubted myself a lot, both my writing ability and the actual story I was trying to tell, but in the end, Rebecca helped me shape this into a book that I am immensely proud of.

And one final thank you to my husband, Aaron, for ignoring the heaps of laundry and dishes and the ever-growing collection of clutter that manifested over the several long months of writing and editing this book, for taking over toddler-watching duties when I needed to grab a few hours at the library to meet my deadlines, and for being the most supportive partner I could possibly ask for. You're the best, sweetheart.

ABOUT THE AUTHOR

BROOKE JOHNSON is a stay-at-home mom and tea-loving writer. As the jack-of-all-trades bard of the family, she journeys through life with her husband, daughter, and dog. She currently resides in Northwest Arkansas but hopes to one day live somewhere more mountainous. You can find her on Twitter @brookenomicon.

brooke-johnson.com

Discover great authors, exclusive offers, and more at hc.com.

ABOUT THE AUTHOR

BROOKE JOHNSON is a stay-at-home mom and text-loving writer. As the self-proclaimed head of the family, she focuses much of her life with her husband, daughter, and dog. She currently resides in Northwest Arkansas, but hopes to one day live somewhere more mountainous. You can find her on Twitter @brooksiejohnson.

brookiejohnson.com

Discover great authors, exclusive offers, and more at hc.com